PUP DETECT

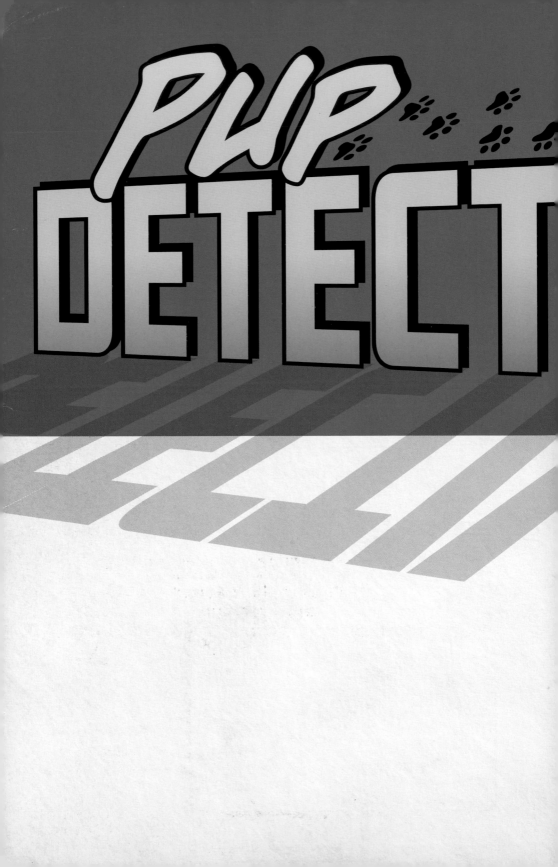

IVES

THE TIGER'S EYE

Written by **FELIX GUMPAW**
Illustrated by **WALMIR ARCHANJO**
at GLASS HOUSE GRAPHICS

 LITTLE SIMON
NEW YORK   LONDON   TORONTO   SYDNEY   NEW DELHI

LITTLE SIMON
AN IMPRINT OF SIMON & SCHUSTER CHILDREN'S PUBLISHING DIVISION
1230 AVENUE OF THE AMERICAS, NEW YORK, NEW YORK 10020
FIRST LITTLE SIMON EDITION FEBRUARY 2021
COPYRIGHT © 2021 BY SIMON & SCHUSTER, INC.
ALL RIGHTS RESERVED, INCLUDING THE RIGHT OF REPRODUCTION IN WHOLE OR IN PART IN ANY FORM. LITTLE SIMON IS A REGISTERED TRADEMARK OF SIMON & SCHUSTER, INC., AND ASSOCIATED COLOPHON IS A TRADEMARK OF SIMON & SCHUSTER, INC. FOR INFORMATION ABOUT SPECIAL DISCOUNTS FOR BULK PURCHASES, PLEASE CONTACT SIMON & SCHUSTER SPECIAL SALES AT 1-866-506-1949 OR BUSINESS@SIMONANDSCHUSTER.COM. ART AND COLOR BY WALMIR ARCHANJO, LELO ALVES, JOÃO MÁRIO & JOÃO ZOD • COLORS BY WALMIR ARCHANJO & JOÃO ZOD • LETTERING BY MARCOS MASSAO INOUE • ART SERVICES BY GLASS HOUSE GRAPHICS • THE SIMON & SCHUSTER SPEAKERS BUREAU CAN BRING AUTHORS TO YOUR LIVE EVENT. FOR MORE INFORMATION OR TO BOOK AN EVENT CONTACT THE SIMON & SCHUSTER SPEAKERS BUREAU AT 1-866-248-3049 OR VISIT OUR WEBSITE AT WWW.SIMONSPEAKERS.COM.
DESIGNED BY NICHOLAS SCIACCA
MANUFACTURED IN CHINA 1120 SCP
10 9 8 7 6 5 4 3 2 1
LIBRARY OF CONGRESS CATALOGING-IN-PUBLICATION DATA
NAMES: GUMPAW, FELIX, AUTHOR. I GLASS HOUSE GRAPHICS, ILLUSTRATOR.
TITLE: THE TIGER'S EYE / BY FELIX GUMPAW ; ILLUSTRATED BY GLASS HOUSE GRAPHICS.
DESCRIPTION: FIRST LITTLE SIMON EDITION. I NEW YORK : LITTLE SIMON, 2021. I SERIES: PUP DETECTIVES ; BOOK 2 I AUDIENCE: AGES 5-9 I AUDIENCE: GRADES 2-3 I SUMMARY: "RIDER WOOFSON AND THE PI PACK ARE CALLED BACK TO DUTY BY PRINCIPAL BARKLEY WHEN A VALUABLE STATUE THAT WAS ON DISPLAY AT PAWSTON ELEMENTARY GOES MISSING"— PROVIDED BY PUBLISHER. IDENTIFIERS: LCCN 2020024874 (PRINT) I LCCN 2020024875 (EBOOK) I ISBN 9781534474970 (PAPERBACK) I ISBN 9781534474987 (HARDCOVER) I ISBN 9781534474994 (EBOOK). SUBJECTS: LCSH: GRAPHIC NOVELS. I CYAC: GRAPHIC NOVELS. I MYSTERY AND DETECTIVE STORIES. I DOGS–FICTION. CLASSIFICATION: LCC PZ7.7.G858 TI 2021 (PRINT) I LCC PZ7.7.G858 (EBOOK) I DDC 741.5/973–DC23. LC RECORD AVAILABLE AT HTTPS://LCCN.LOC.GOV/2020024874. LC EBOOK RECORD AVAILABLE AT HTTPS://LCCN.LOC.GOV/2020024875.

CONTENTS

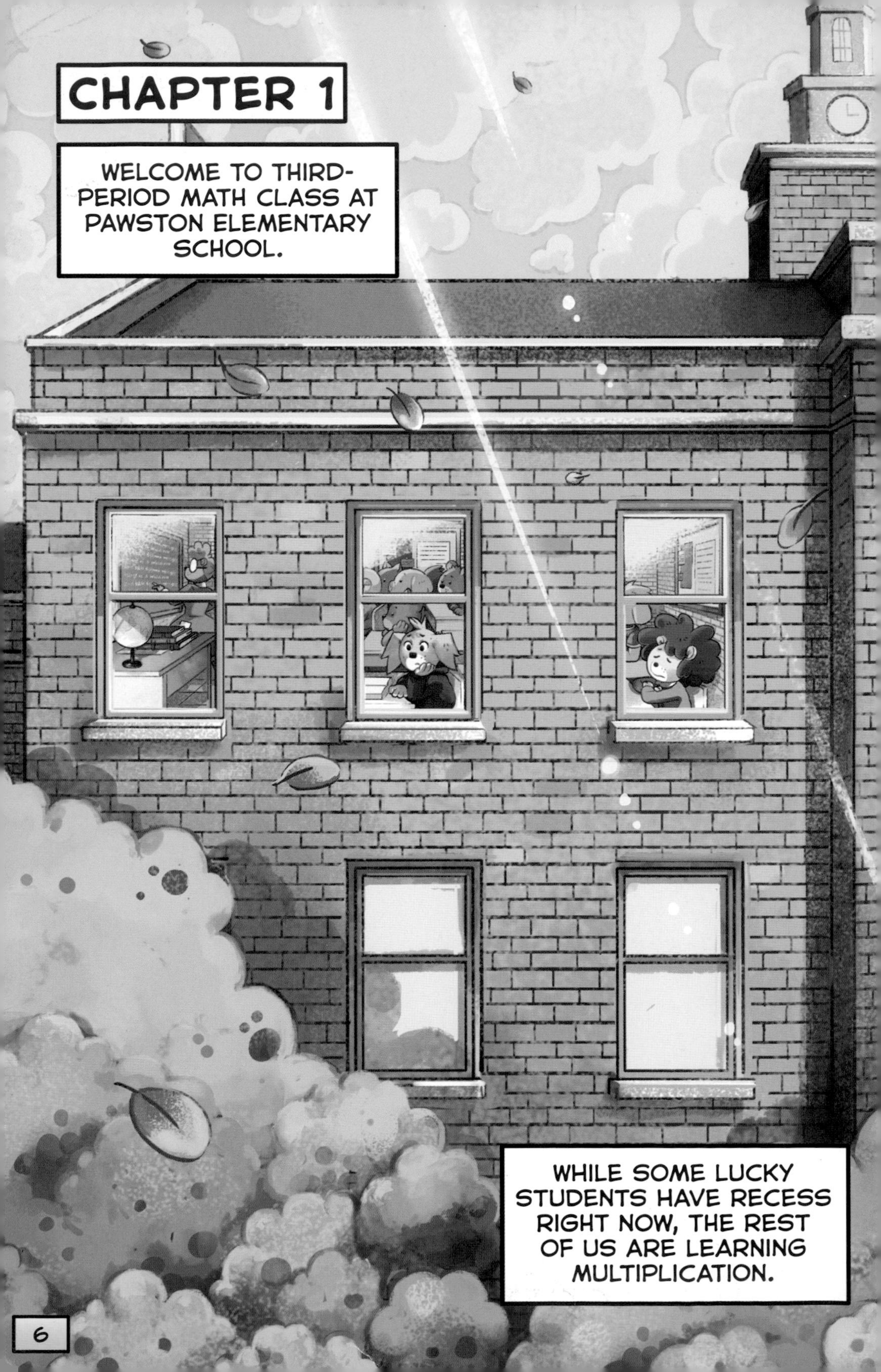
CHAPTER 1
WELCOME TO THIRD-PERIOD MATH CLASS AT PAWSTON ELEMENTARY SCHOOL.
WHILE SOME LUCKY STUDENTS HAVE RECESS RIGHT NOW, THE REST OF US ARE LEARNING MULTIPLICATION.

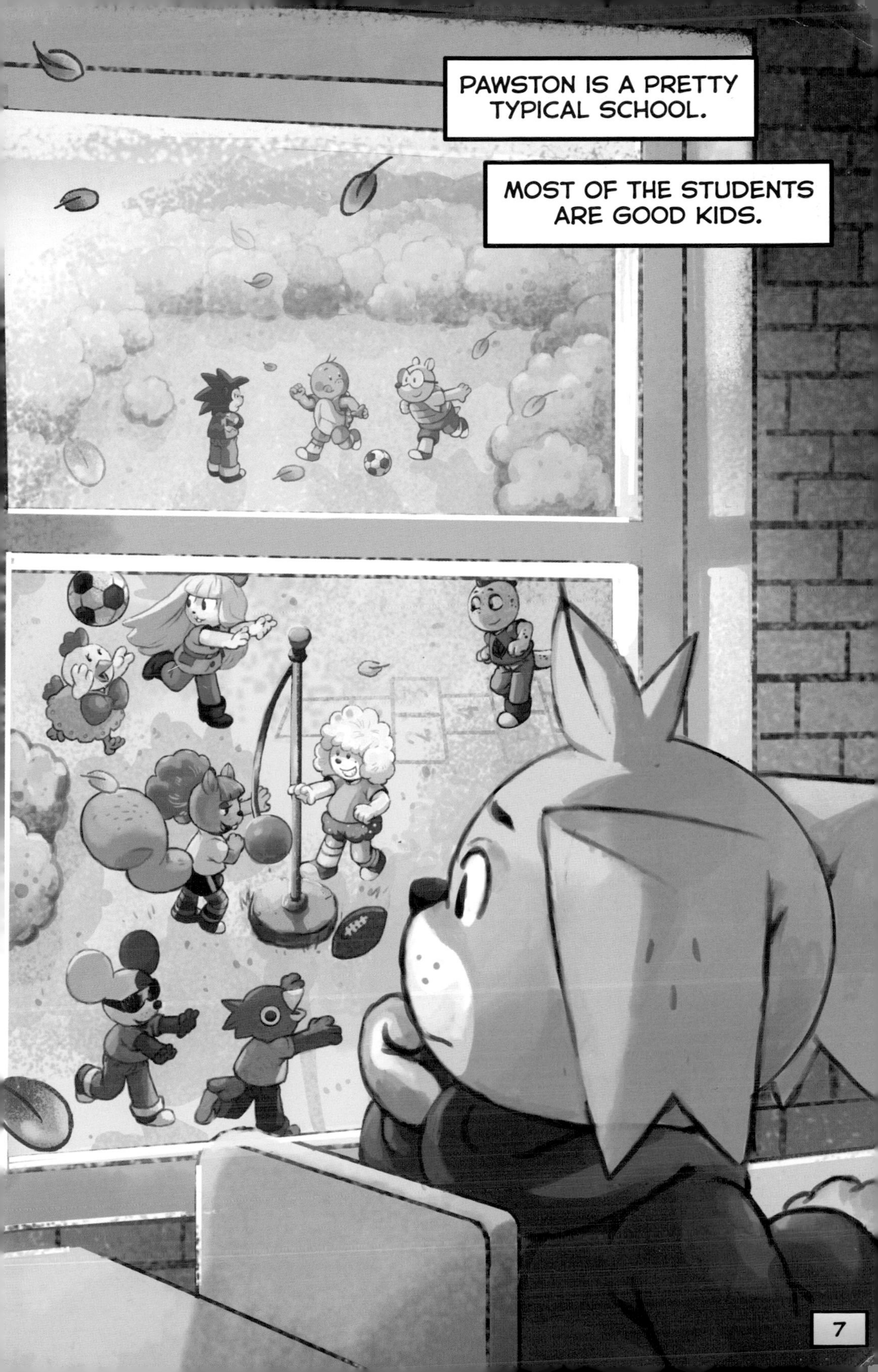
PAWSTON IS A PRETTY TYPICAL SCHOOL.
MOST OF THE STUDENTS ARE GOOD KIDS.

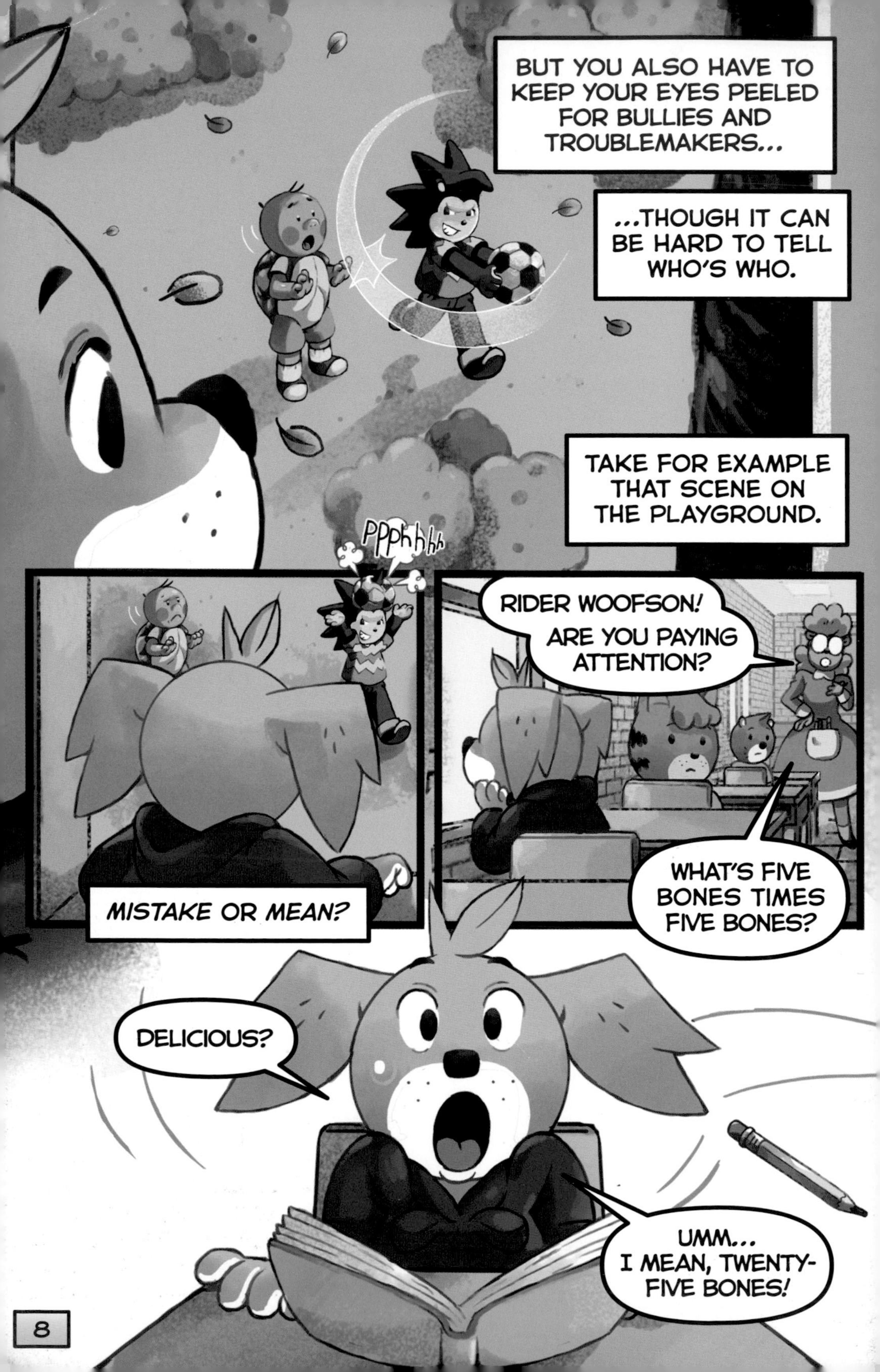
BUT YOU ALSO HAVE TO KEEP YOUR EYES PEELED FOR BULLIES AND TROUBLEMAKERS...
...THOUGH IT CAN BE HARD TO TELL WHO'S WHO.
TAKE FOR EXAMPLE THAT SCENE ON THE PLAYGROUND.
PPPhhhh
MISTAKE OR MEAN?
RIDER WOOFSON!
ARE YOU PAYING ATTENTION?
WHAT'S FIVE BONES TIMES FIVE BONES?
DELICIOUS?
UMM... I MEAN, TWENTY-FIVE BONES!

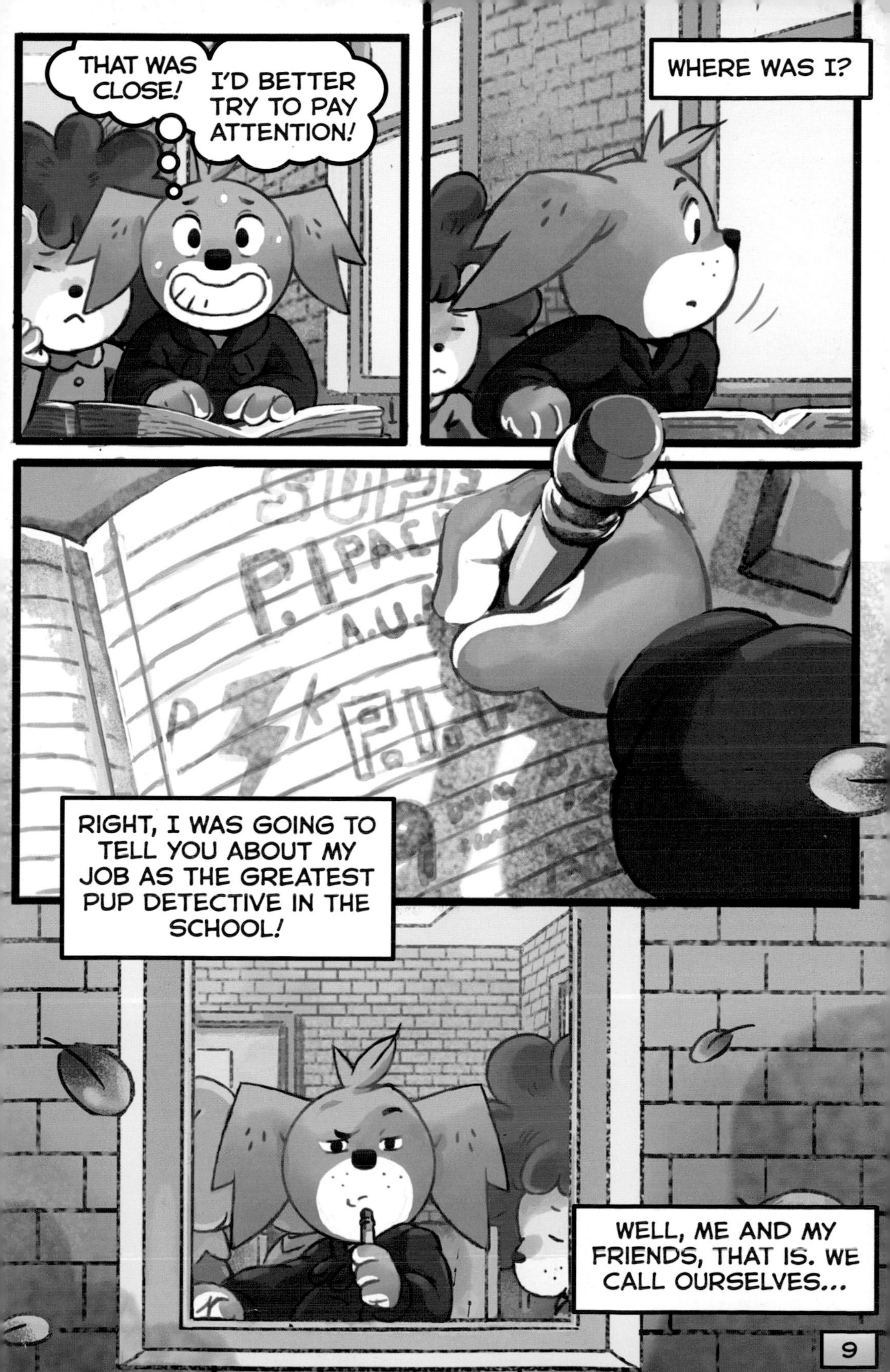
THAT WAS CLOSE!
I'D BETTER TRY TO PAY ATTENTION!
WHERE WAS I?
RIGHT, I WAS GOING TO TELL YOU ABOUT MY JOB AS THE GREATEST PUP DETECTIVE IN THE SCHOOL!
WELL, ME AND MY FRIENDS, THAT IS. WE CALL OURSELVES...

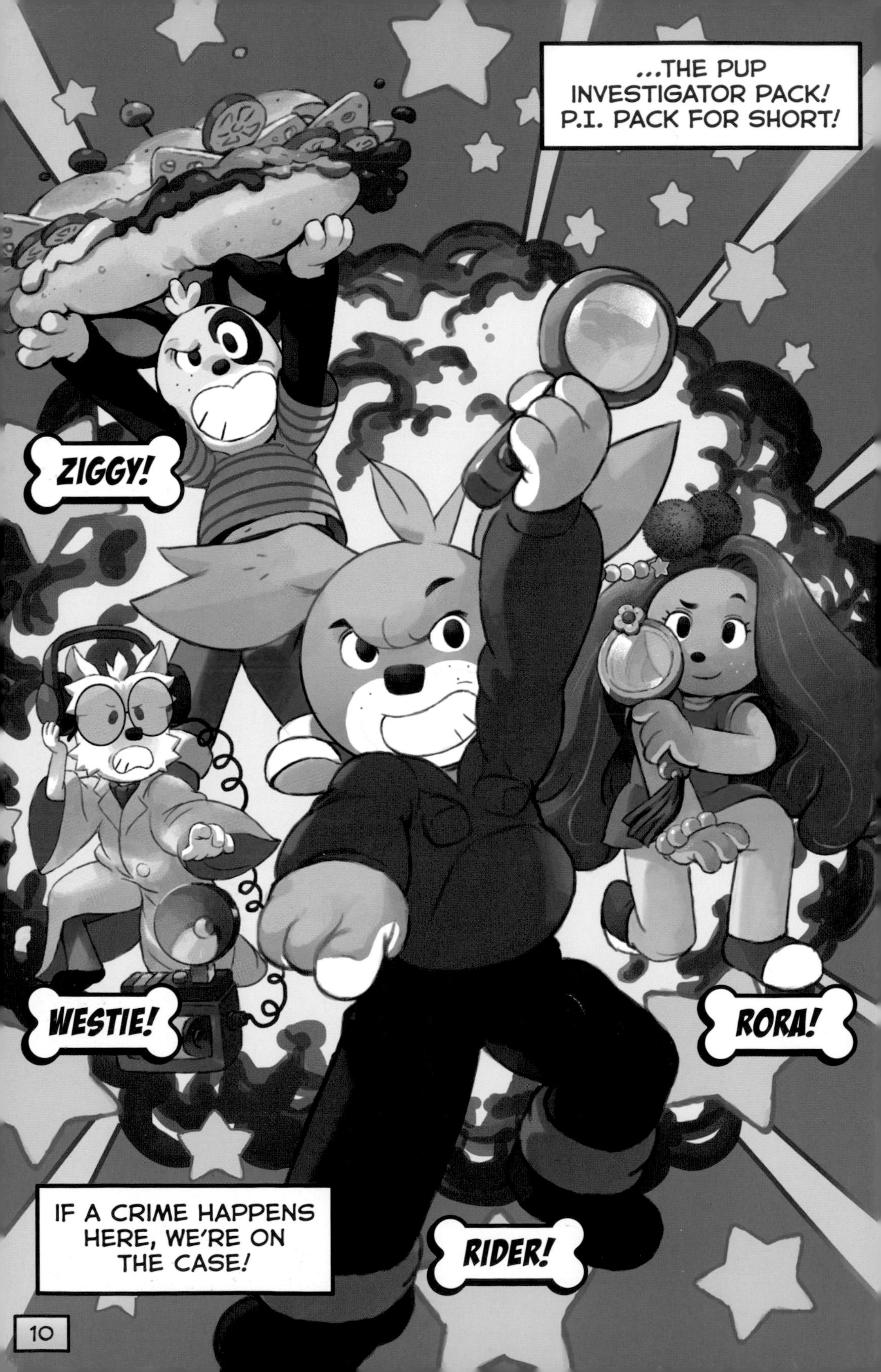
...THE PUP INVESTIGATOR PACK! P.I. PACK FOR SHORT!
ZIGGY!
WESTIE!
RORA!
IF A CRIME HAPPENS HERE, WE'RE ON THE CASE!
RIDER!

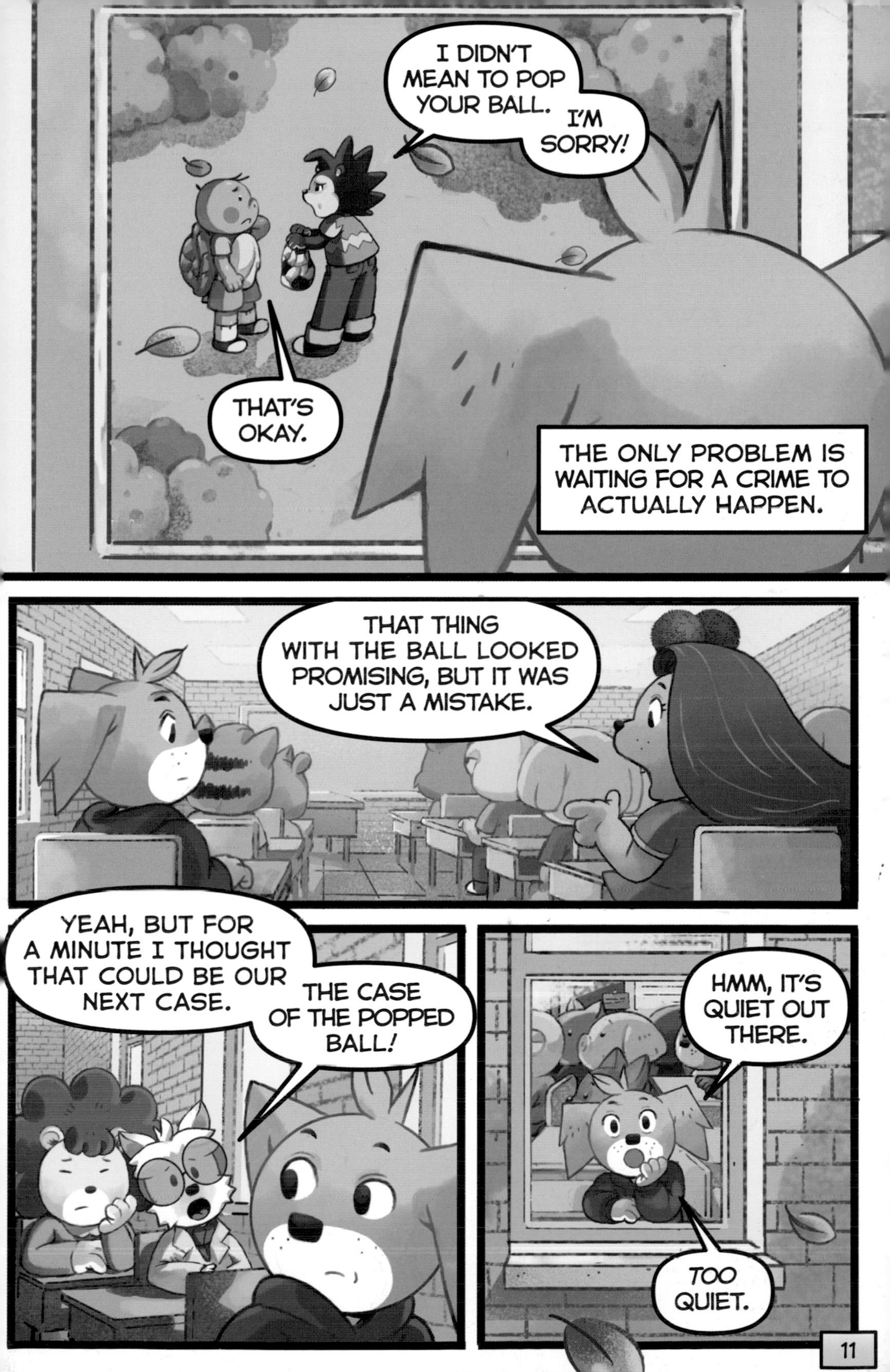
I DIDN'T MEAN TO POP YOUR BALL.
I'M SORRY!
THAT'S OKAY.
THE ONLY PROBLEM IS WAITING FOR A CRIME TO ACTUALLY HAPPEN.
THAT THING WITH THE BALL LOOKED PROMISING, BUT IT WAS JUST A MISTAKE.
YEAH, BUT FOR A MINUTE I THOUGHT THAT COULD BE OUR NEXT CASE.
THE CASE OF THE POPPED BALL!
HMM, IT'S QUIET OUT THERE.
TOO QUIET.

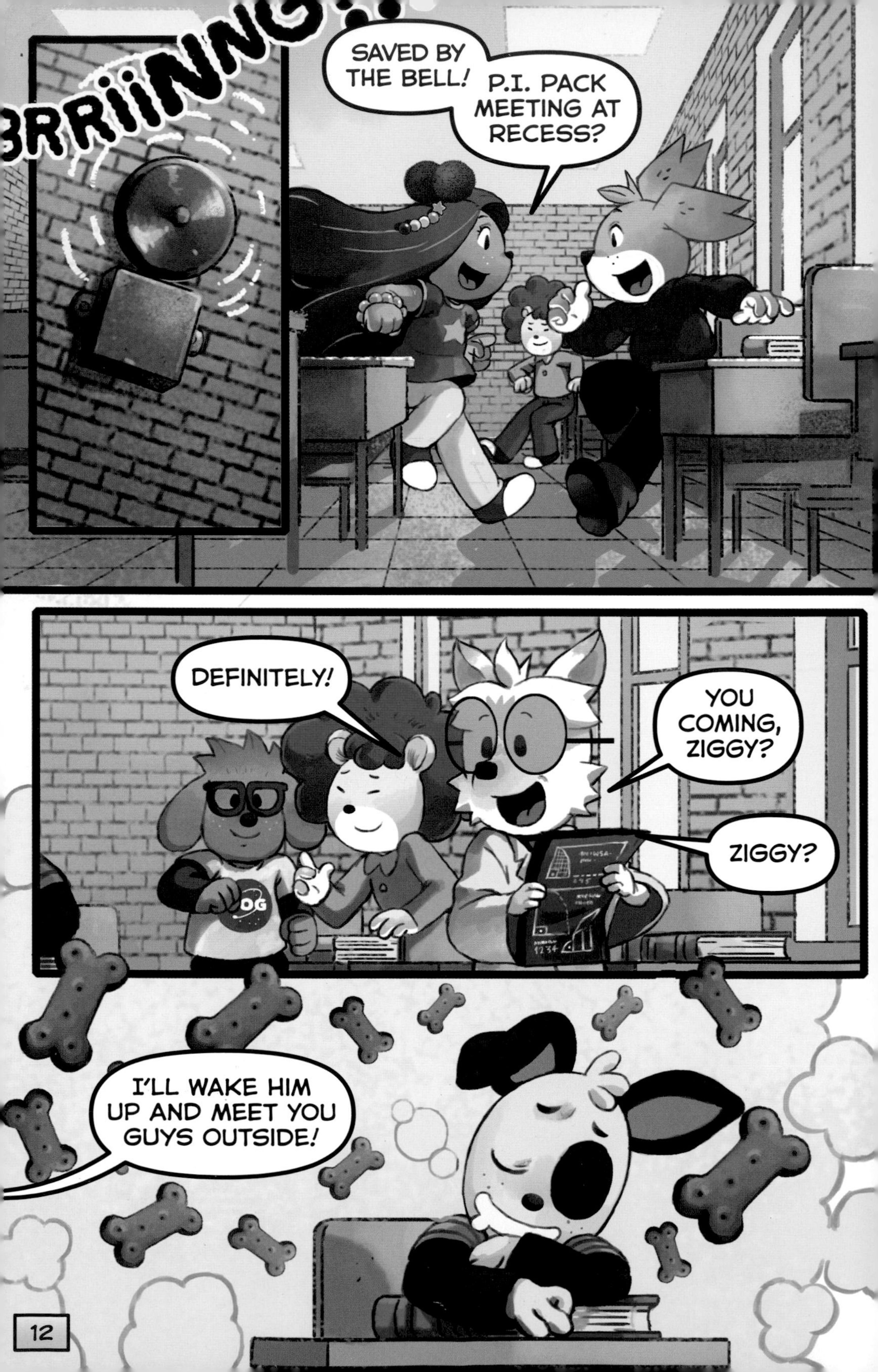
BRRIIINNG...
SAVED BY THE BELL!
P.I. PACK MEETING AT RECESS?
DEFINITELY!
YOU COMING, ZIGGY?
ZIGGY?
I'LL WAKE HIM UP AND MEET YOU GUYS OUTSIDE!

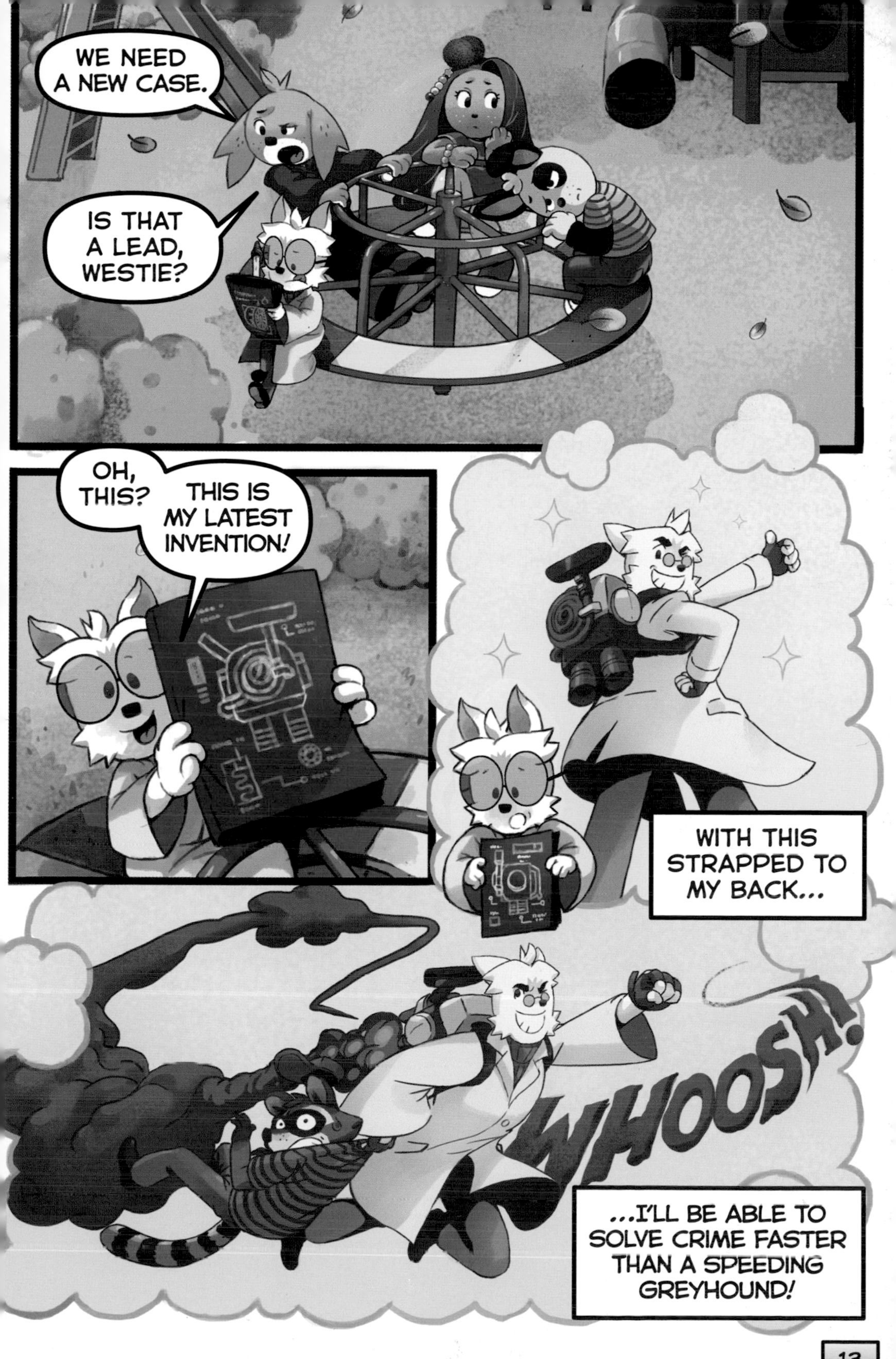
WE NEED A NEW CASE.
IS THAT A LEAD, WESTIE?
OH, THIS?
THIS IS MY LATEST INVENTION!
WITH THIS STRAPPED TO MY BACK...
WHOOSH!
...I'LL BE ABLE TO SOLVE CRIME FASTER THAN A SPEEDING GREYHOUND!

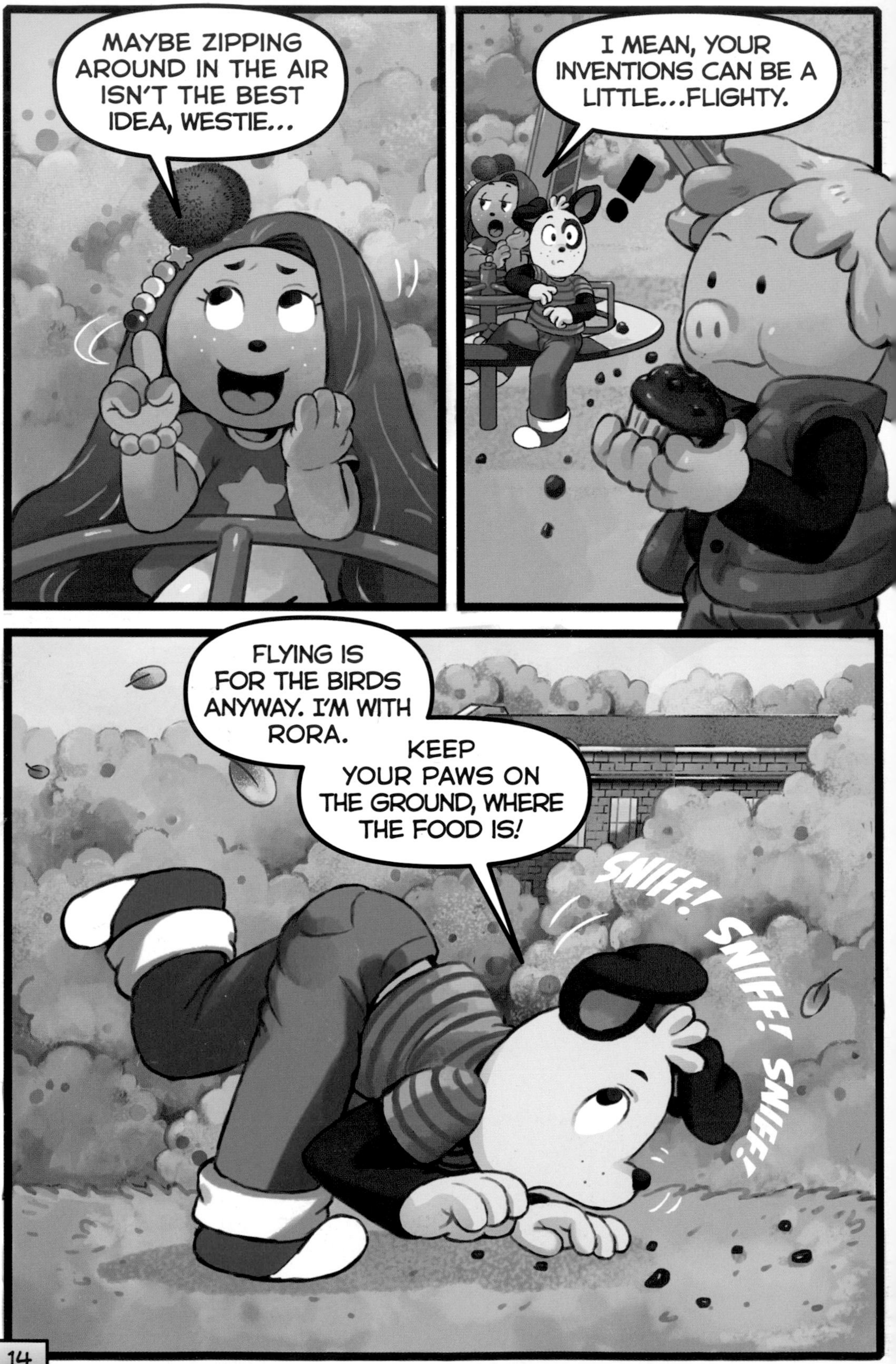
MAYBE ZIPPING AROUND IN THE AIR ISN'T THE BEST IDEA, WESTIE...
I MEAN, YOUR INVENTIONS CAN BE A LITTLE...FLIGHTY.
!
FLYING IS FOR THE BIRDS ANYWAY. I'M WITH RORA.
KEEP YOUR PAWS ON THE GROUND, WHERE THE FOOD IS!
SNIFF! SNIFF! SNIFF! SNIFF!

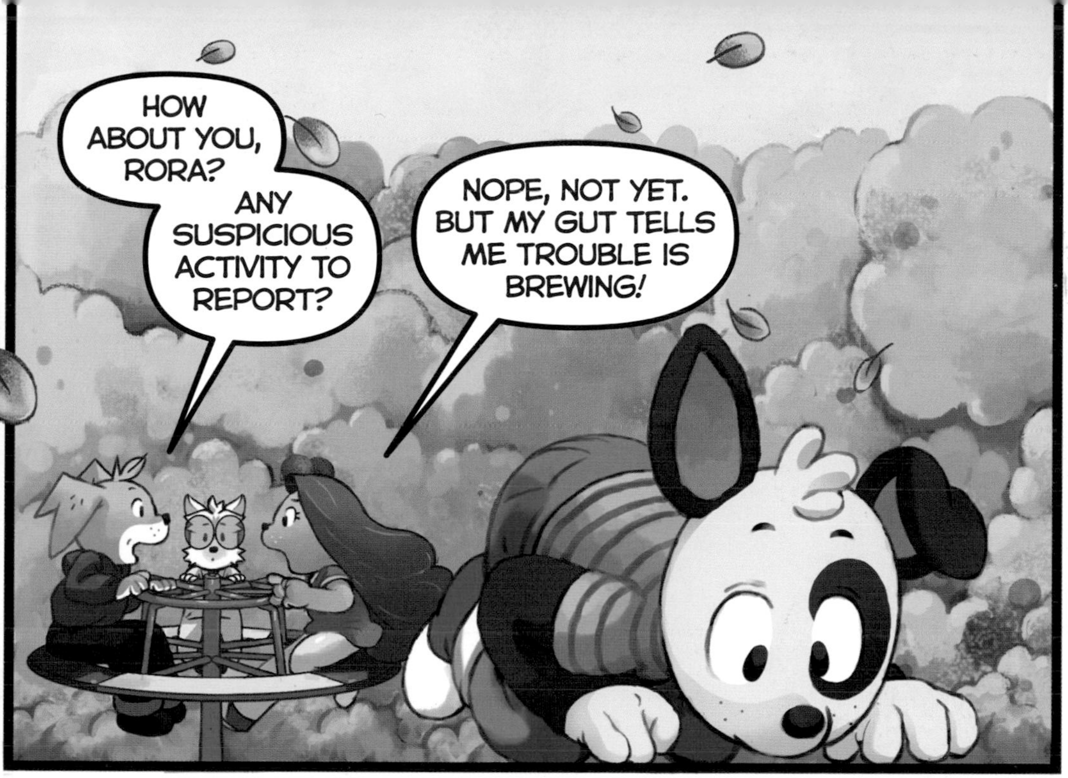
HOW ABOUT YOU, RORA?
ANY SUSPICIOUS ACTIVITY TO REPORT?
NOPE, NOT YET. BUT MY GUT TELLS ME TROUBLE IS BREWING!

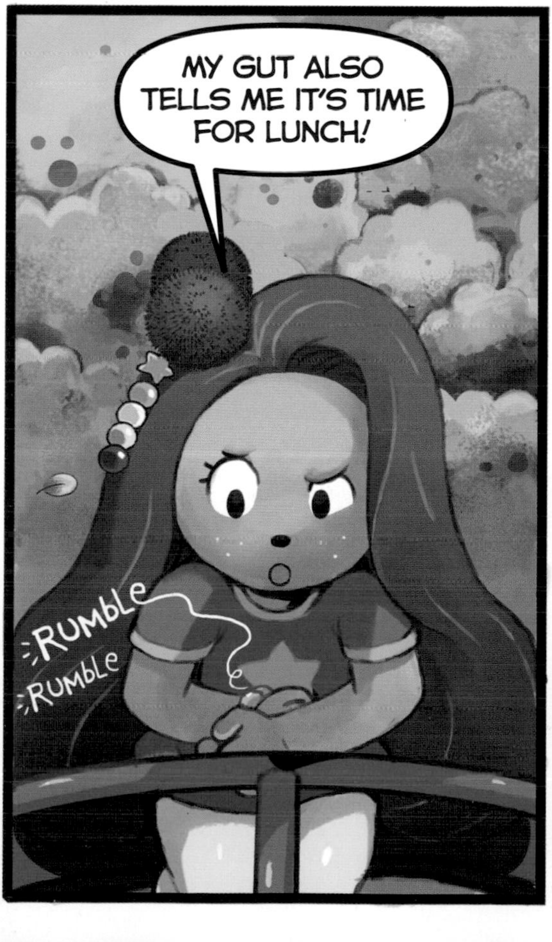
MY GUT ALSO TELLS ME IT'S TIME FOR LUNCH!
RUMBLE
RUMBLE

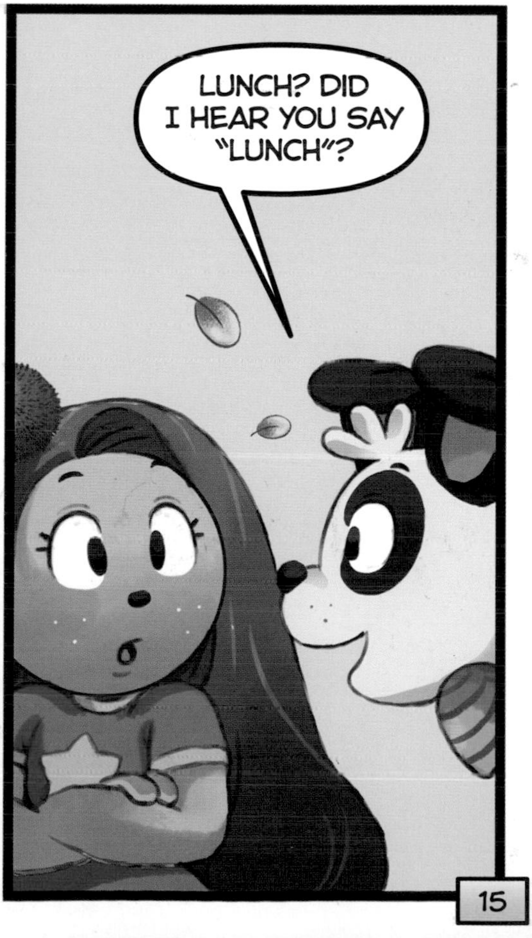
LUNCH? DID I HEAR YOU SAY "LUNCH"?

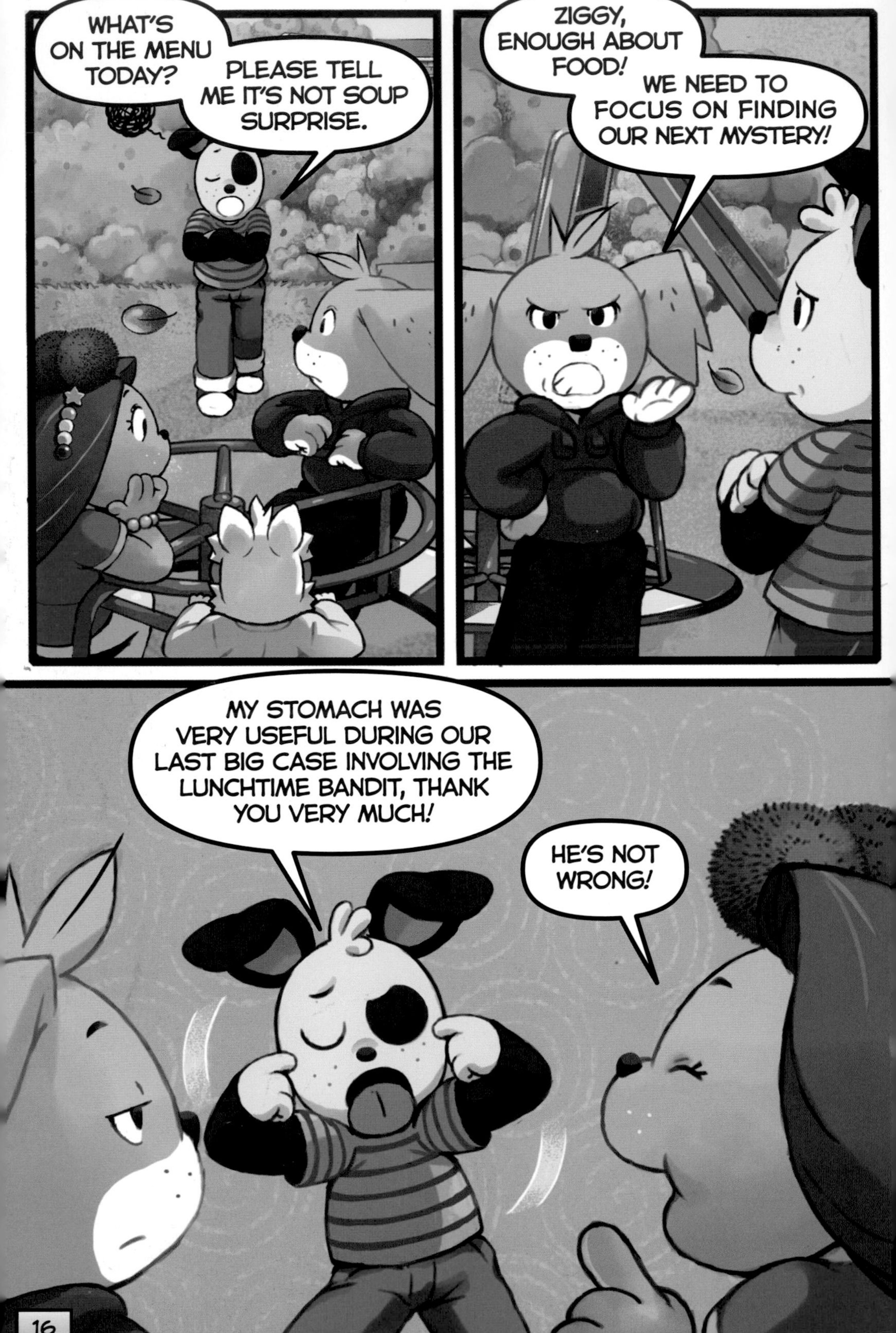
WHAT'S ON THE MENU TODAY?
PLEASE TELL ME IT'S NOT SOUP SURPRISE.
ZIGGY, ENOUGH ABOUT FOOD!
WE NEED TO FOCUS ON FINDING OUR NEXT MYSTERY!
MY STOMACH WAS VERY USEFUL DURING OUR LAST BIG CASE INVOLVING THE LUNCHTIME BANDIT, THANK YOU VERY MUCH!
HE'S NOT WRONG!

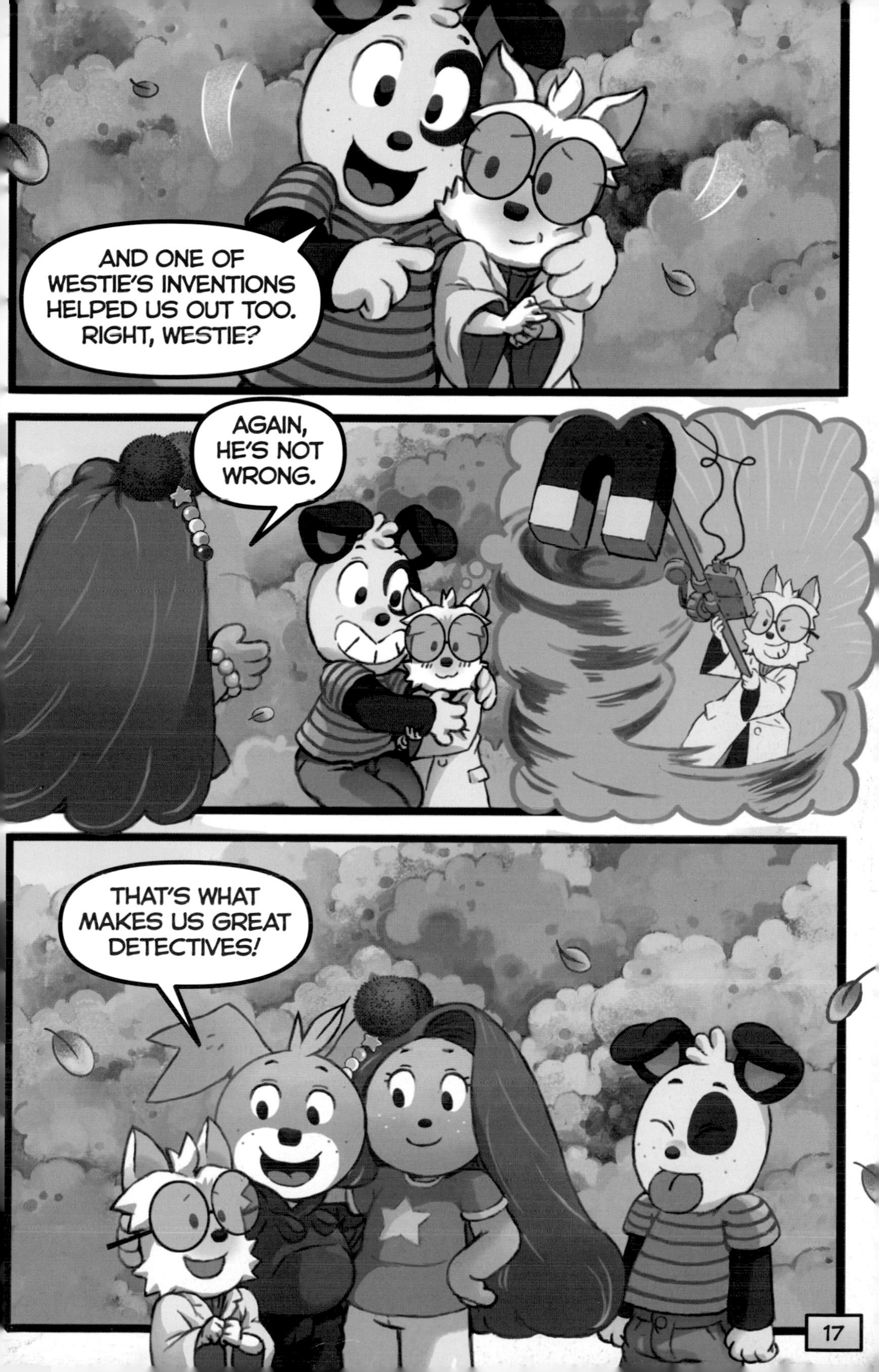
AND ONE OF WESTIE'S INVENTIONS HELPED US OUT TOO. RIGHT, WESTIE?
AGAIN, HE'S NOT WRONG.
THAT'S WHAT MAKES US GREAT DETECTIVES!

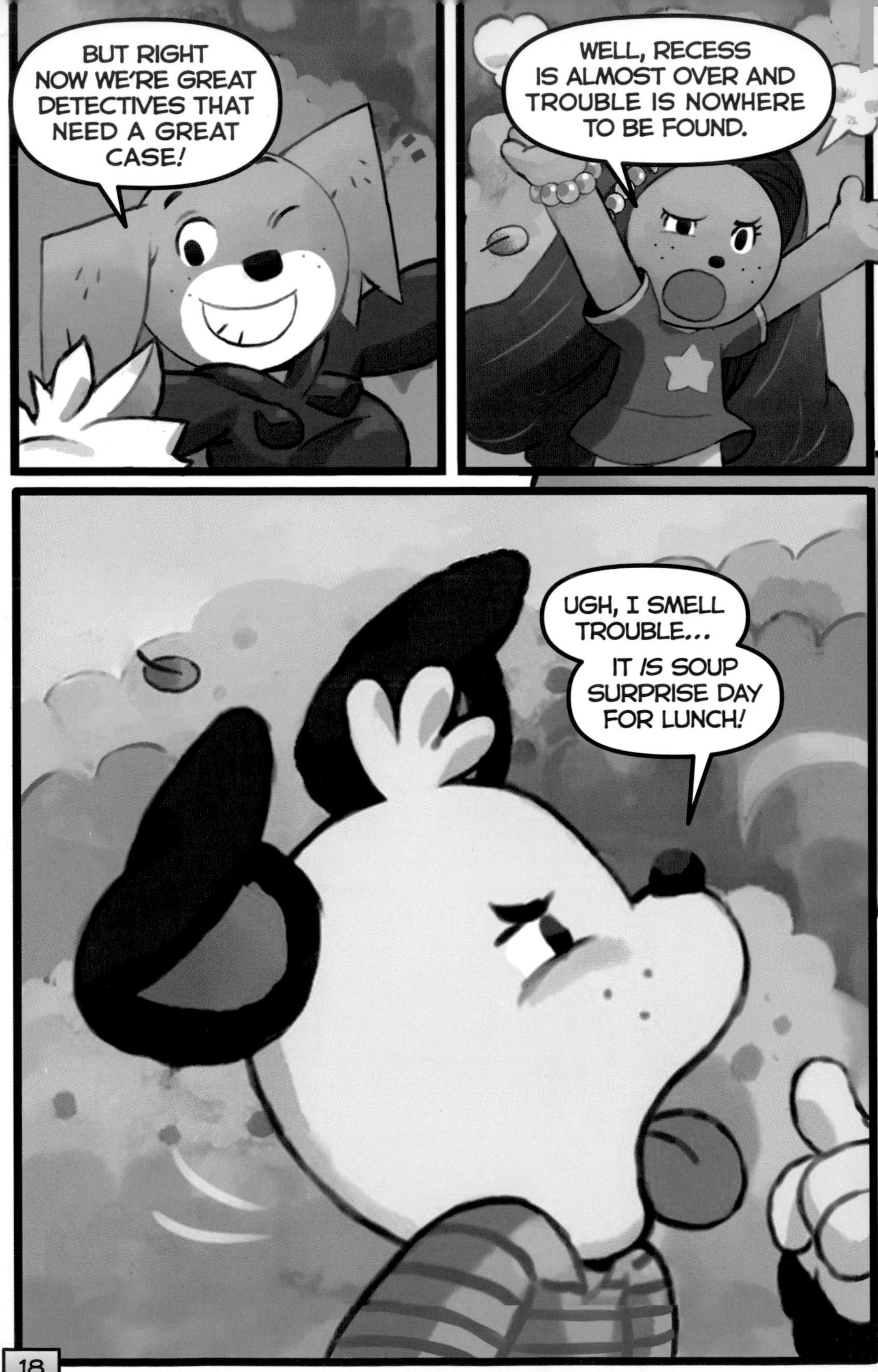
BUT RIGHT NOW WE'RE GREAT DETECTIVES THAT NEED A GREAT CASE!
WELL, RECESS IS ALMOST OVER AND TROUBLE IS NOWHERE TO BE FOUND.
UGH, I SMELL TROUBLE...
IT IS SOUP SURPRISE DAY FOR LUNCH!

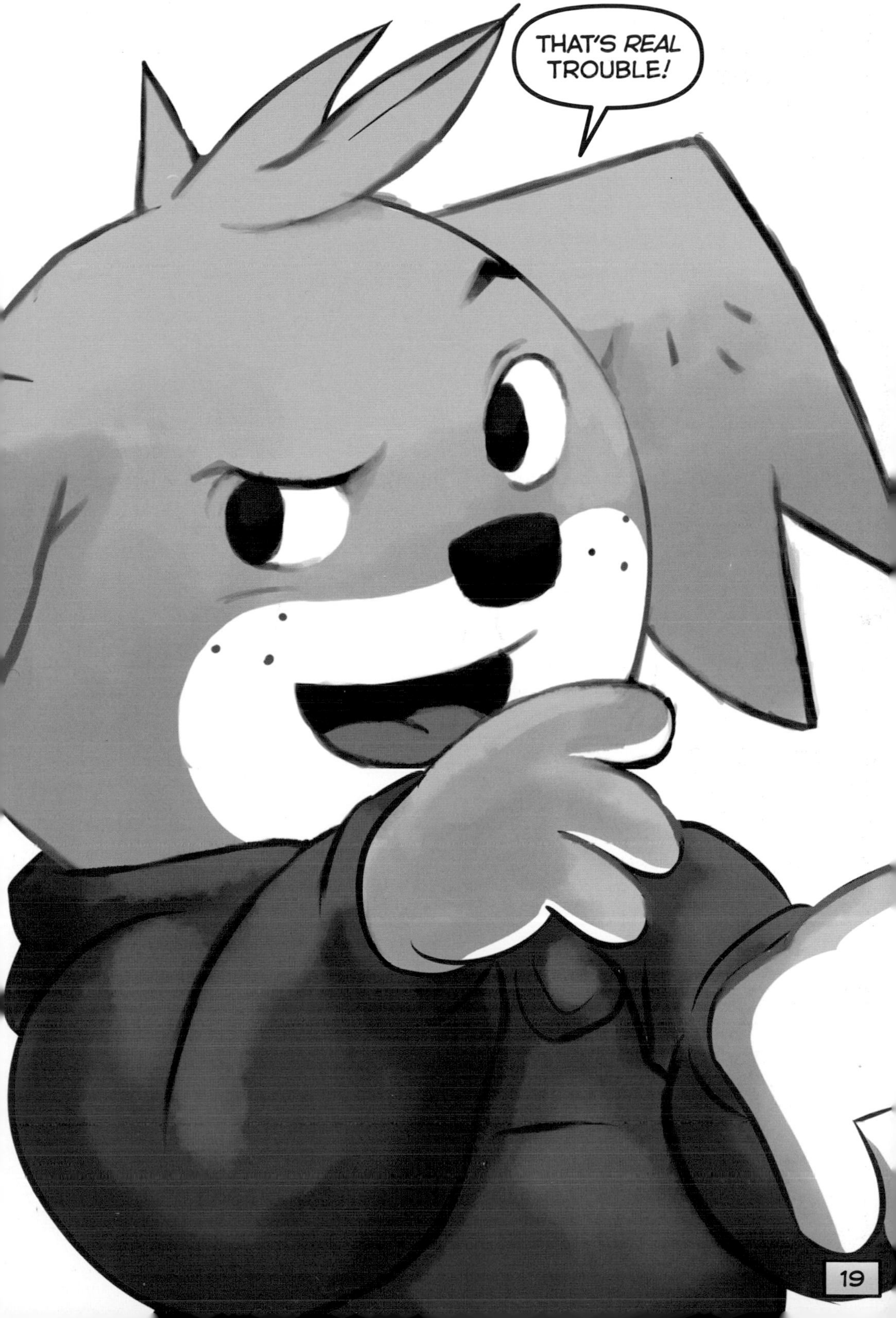
THAT'S *REAL* TROUBLE!

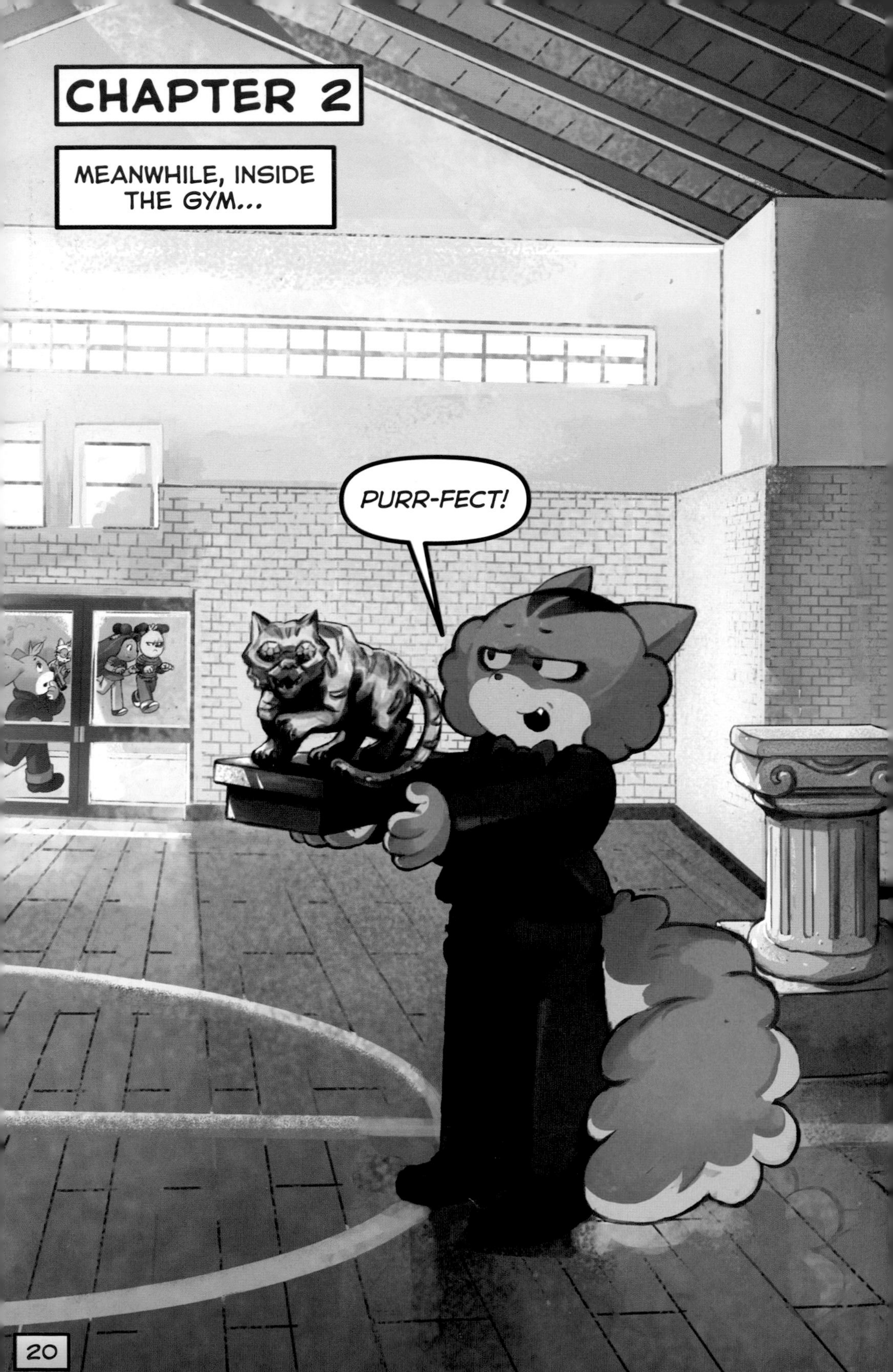
CHAPTER 2
MEANWHILE, INSIDE THE GYM...
PURR-FECT!

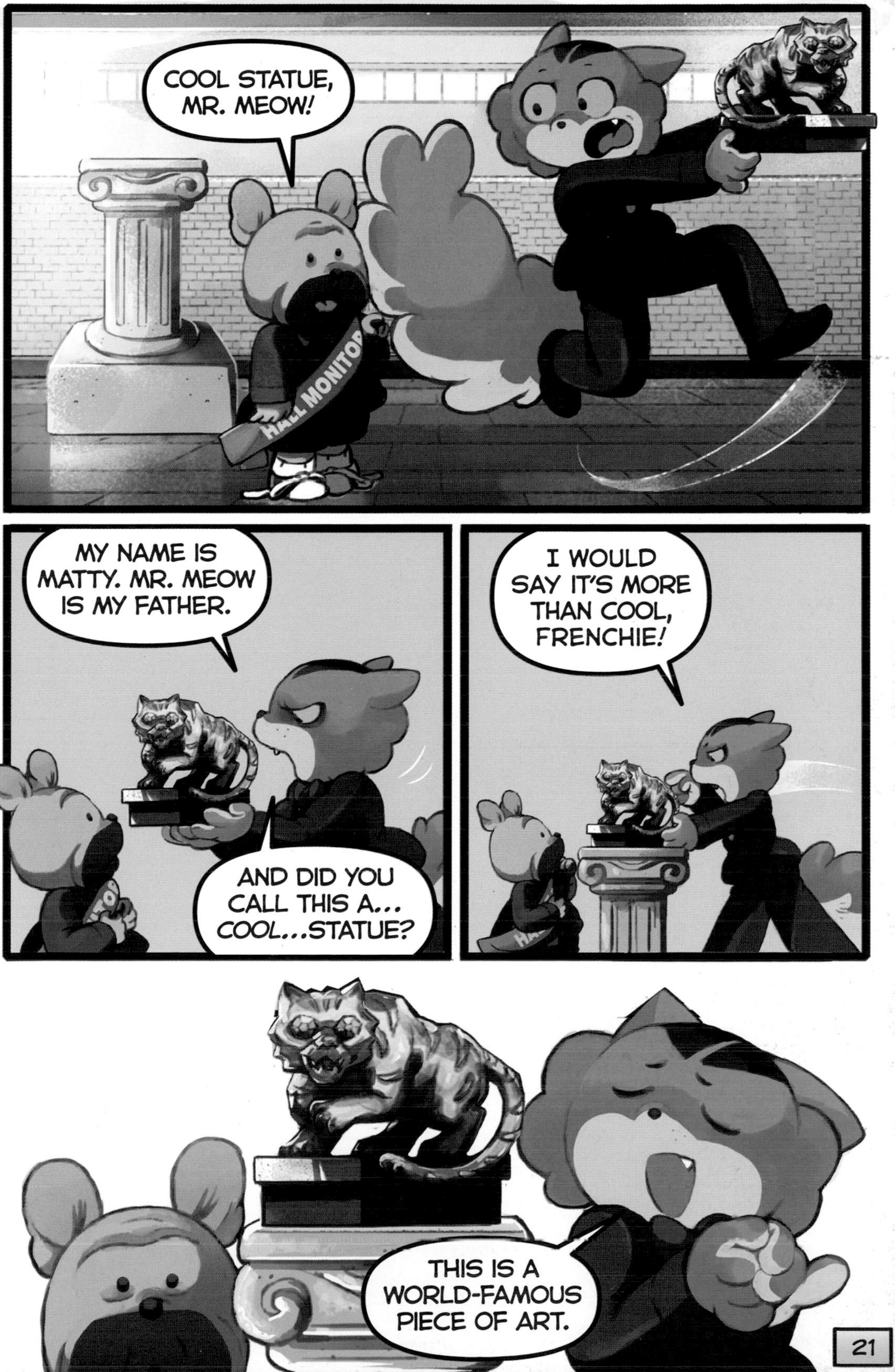
COOL STATUE, MR. MEOW!
HALL MONITOR
MY NAME IS MATTY. MR. MEOW IS MY FATHER.
AND DID YOU CALL THIS A... COOL...STATUE?
I WOULD SAY IT'S MORE THAN COOL, FRENCHIE!
THIS IS A WORLD-FAMOUS PIECE OF ART.

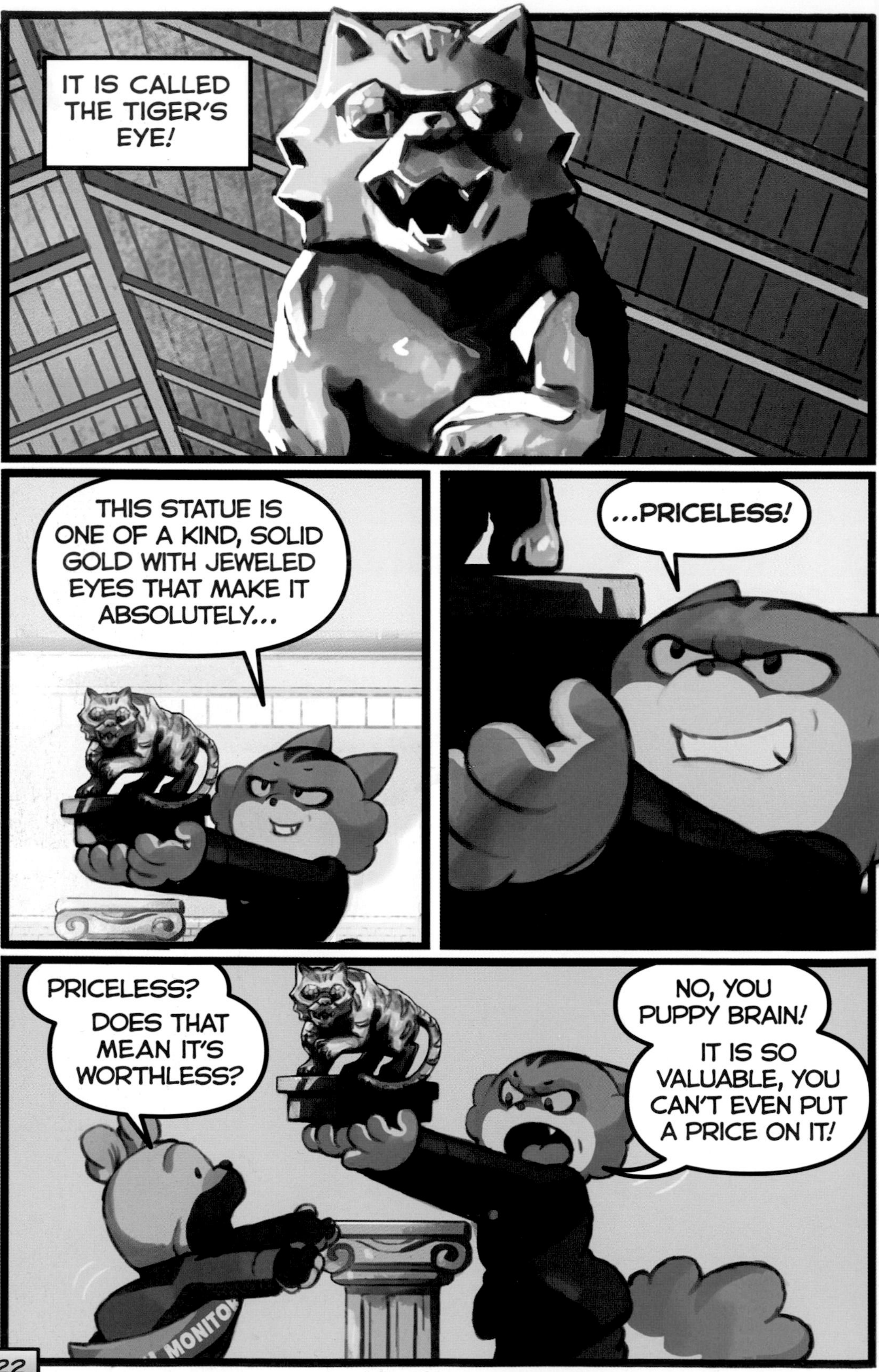
IT IS CALLED THE TIGER'S EYE!
THIS STATUE IS ONE OF A KIND, SOLID GOLD WITH JEWELED EYES THAT MAKE IT ABSOLUTELY...
...PRICELESS!
PRICELESS?
DOES THAT MEAN IT'S WORTHLESS?
NO, YOU PUPPY BRAIN!
IT IS SO VALUABLE, YOU CAN'T EVEN PUT A PRICE ON IT!
MONITOR

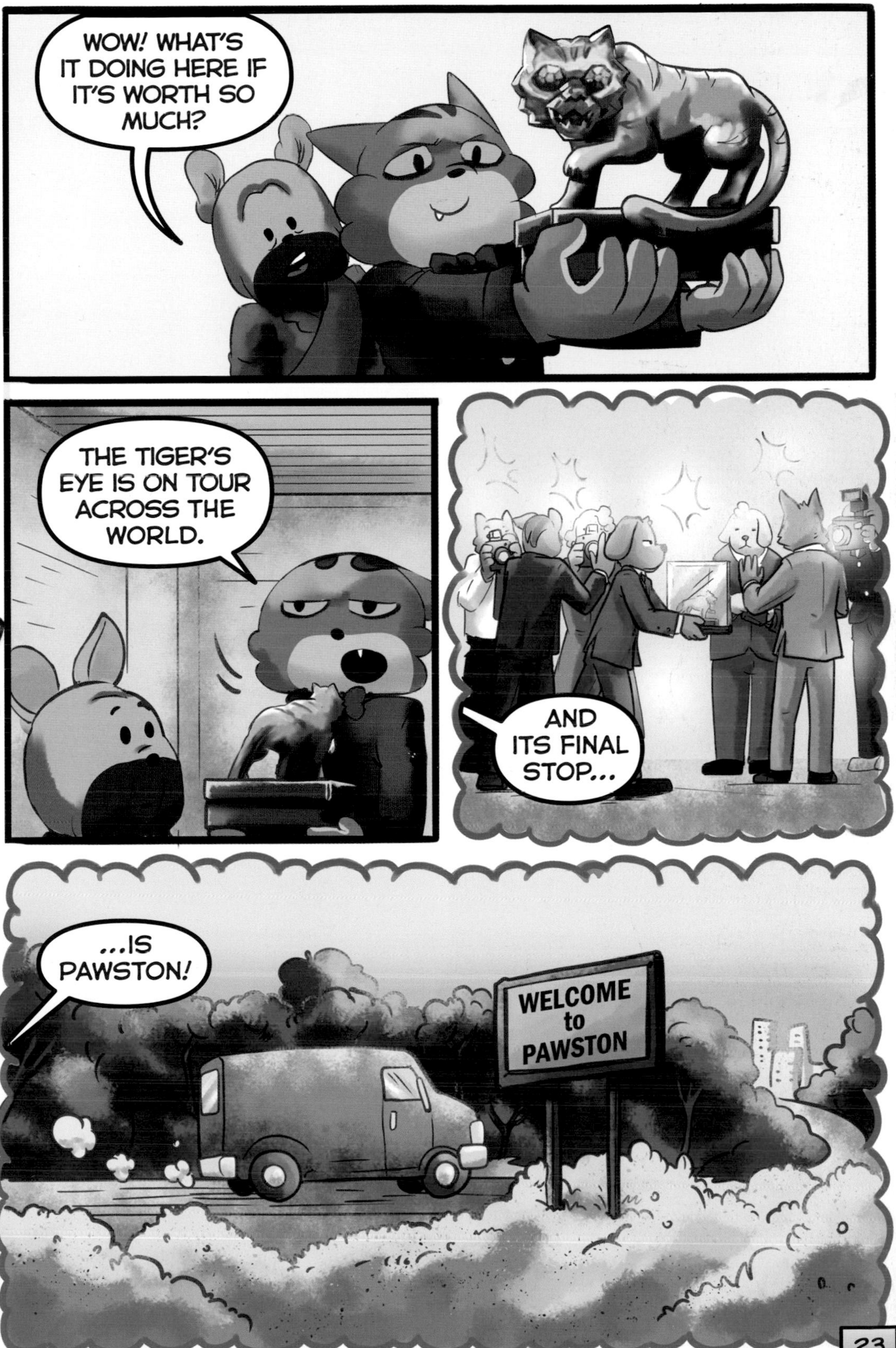
WOW! WHAT'S IT DOING HERE IF IT'S WORTH SO MUCH?
THE TIGER'S EYE IS ON TOUR ACROSS THE WORLD.
AND ITS FINAL STOP...
...IS PAWSTON!
WELCOME to PAWSTON

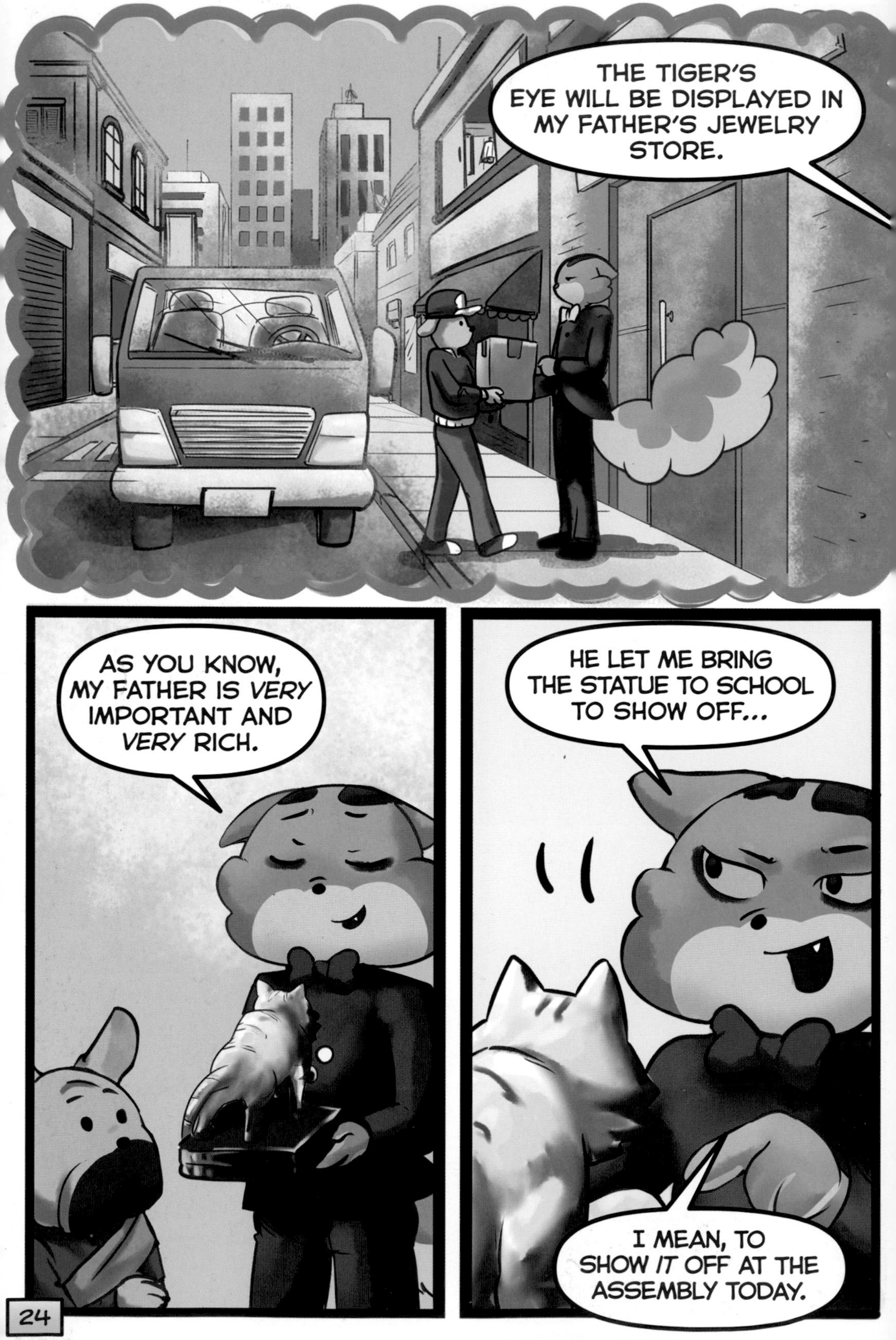
THE TIGER'S EYE WILL BE DISPLAYED IN MY FATHER'S JEWELRY STORE.
AS YOU KNOW, MY FATHER IS *VERY* IMPORTANT AND *VERY* RICH.
HE LET ME BRING THE STATUE TO SCHOOL TO SHOW OFF...
I MEAN, TO SHOW *IT* OFF AT THE ASSEMBLY TODAY.

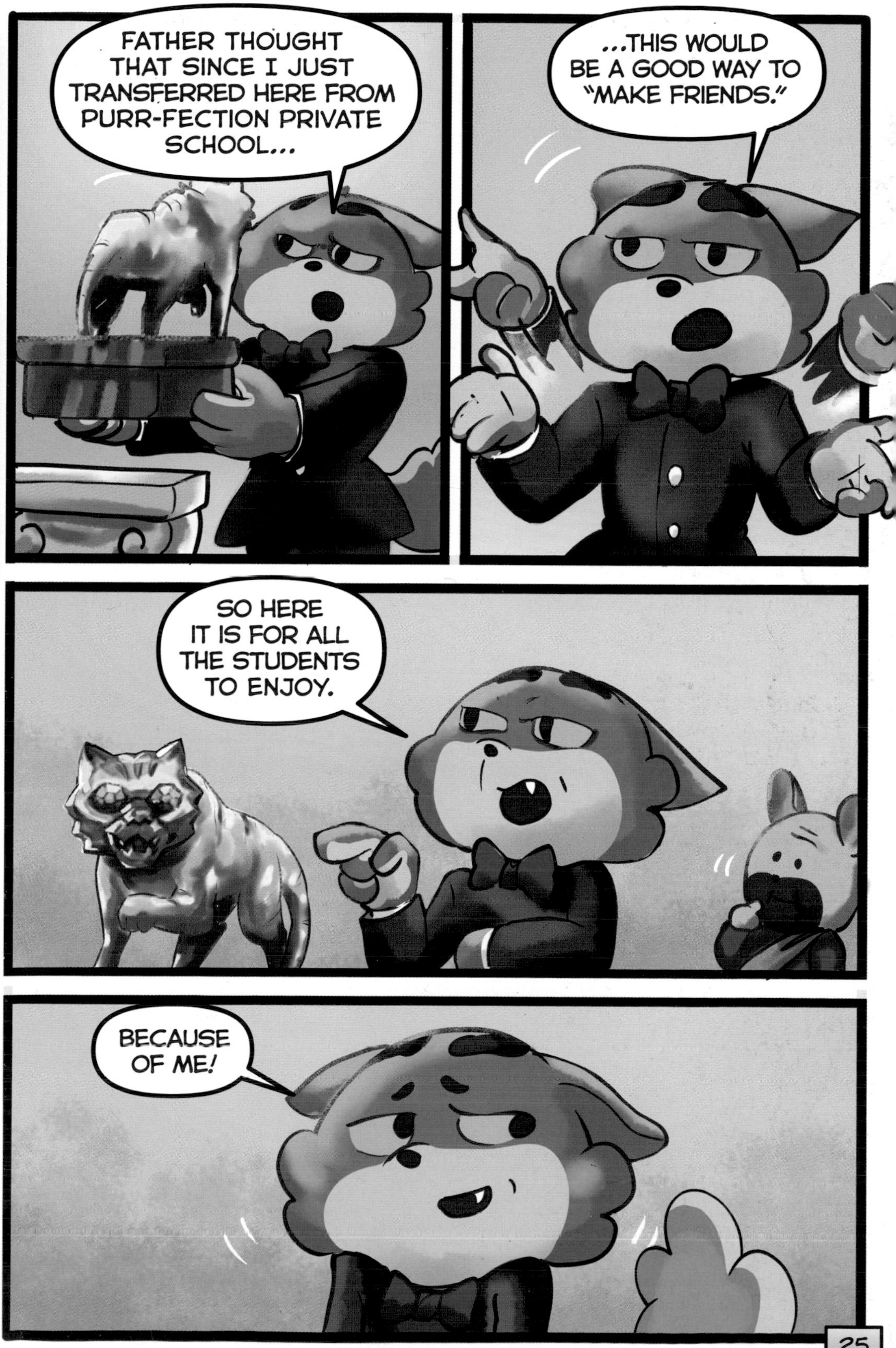
FATHER THOUGHT THAT SINCE I JUST TRANSFERRED HERE FROM PURR-FECTION PRIVATE SCHOOL...
...THIS WOULD BE A GOOD WAY TO "MAKE FRIENDS."
SO HERE IT IS FOR ALL THE STUDENTS TO ENJOY.
BECAUSE OF ME!

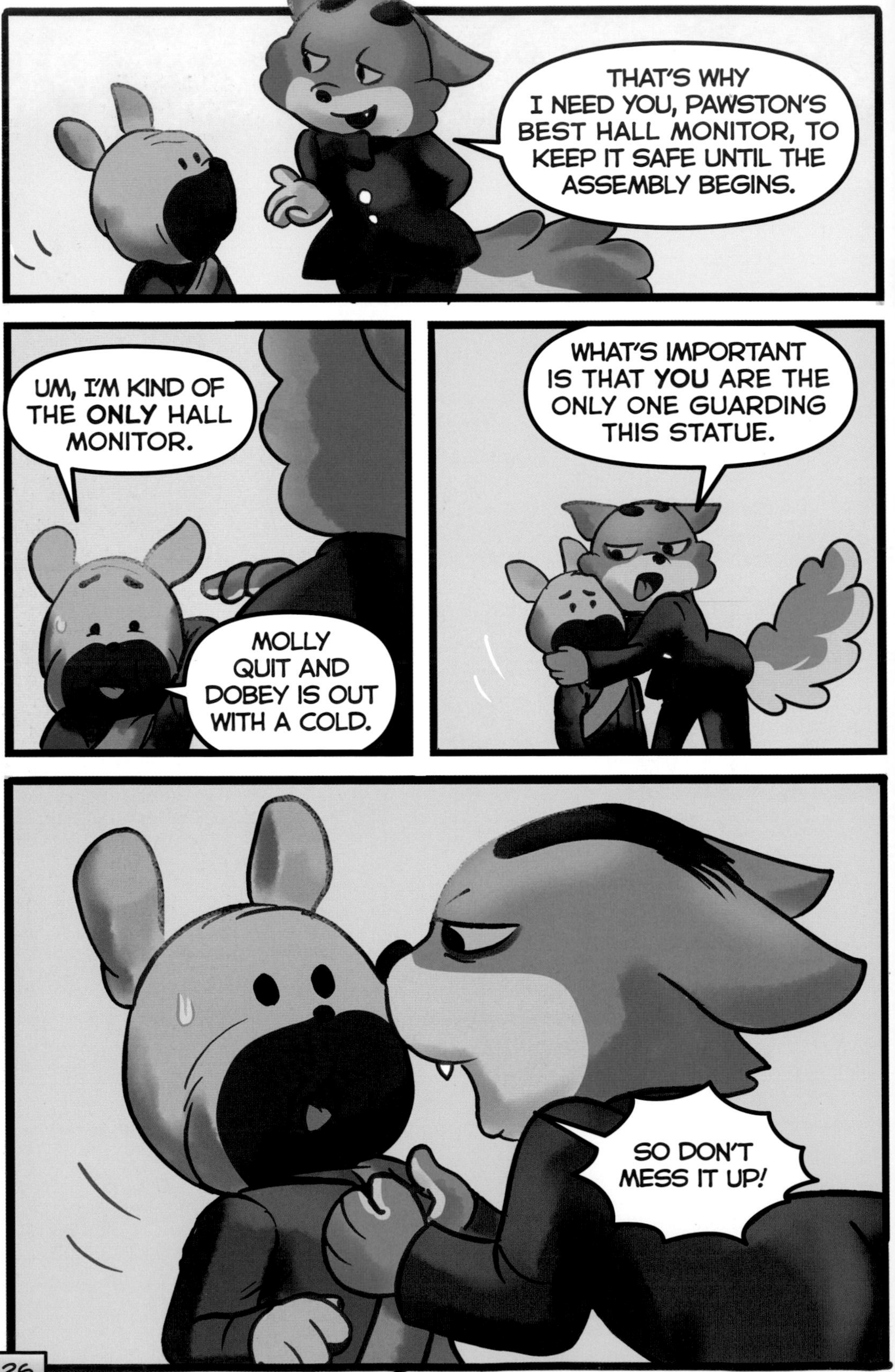
THAT'S WHY I NEED YOU, PAWSTON'S BEST HALL MONITOR, TO KEEP IT SAFE UNTIL THE ASSEMBLY BEGINS.
UM, I'M KIND OF THE **ONLY** HALL MONITOR.
MOLLY QUIT AND DOBEY IS OUT WITH A COLD.
WHAT'S IMPORTANT IS THAT **YOU** ARE THE ONLY ONE GUARDING THIS STATUE.
SO DON'T MESS IT UP!

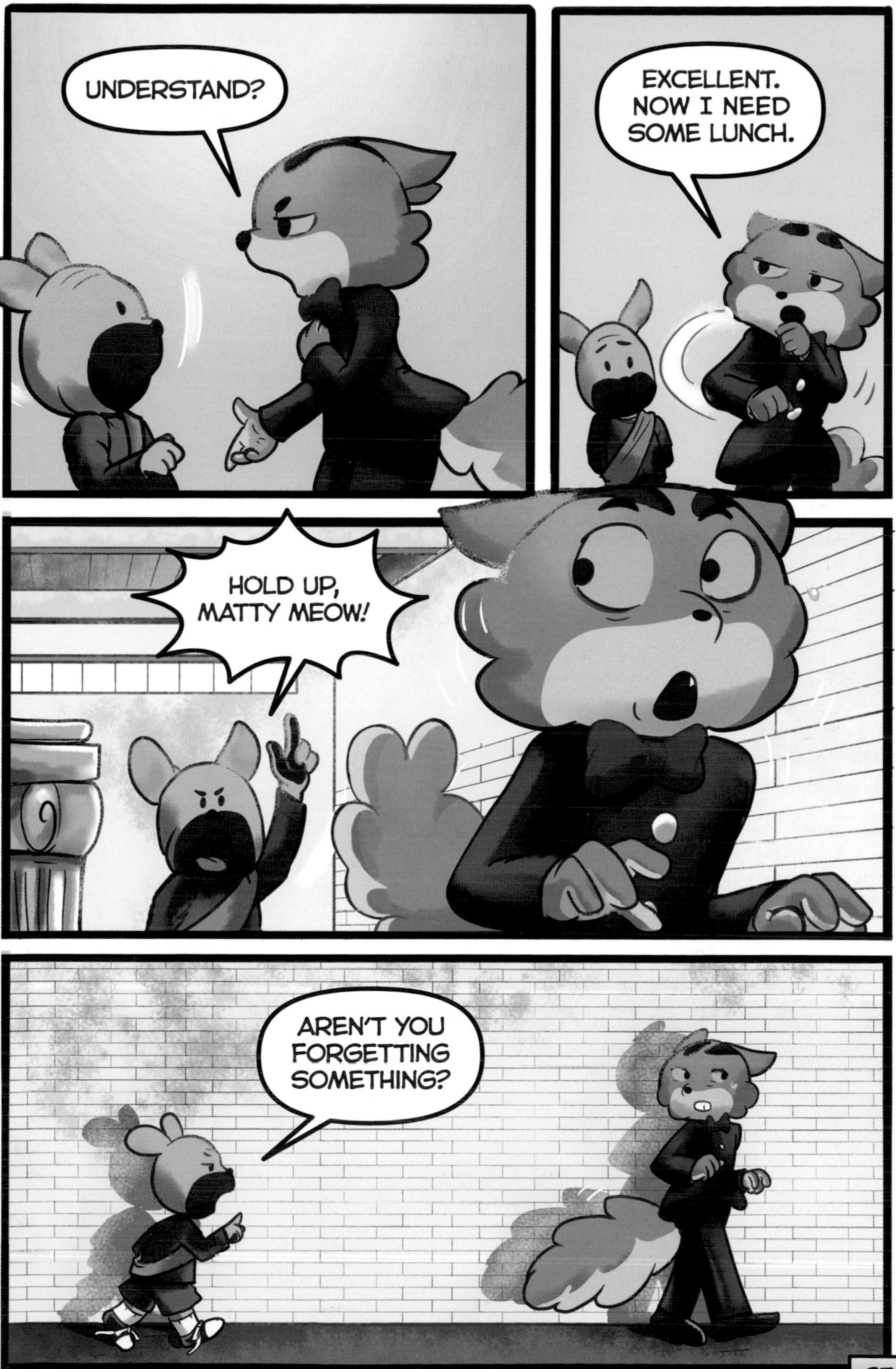
UNDERSTAND?
EXCELLENT. NOW I NEED SOME LUNCH.
HOLD UP, MATTY MEOW!
AREN'T YOU FORGETTING SOMETHING?

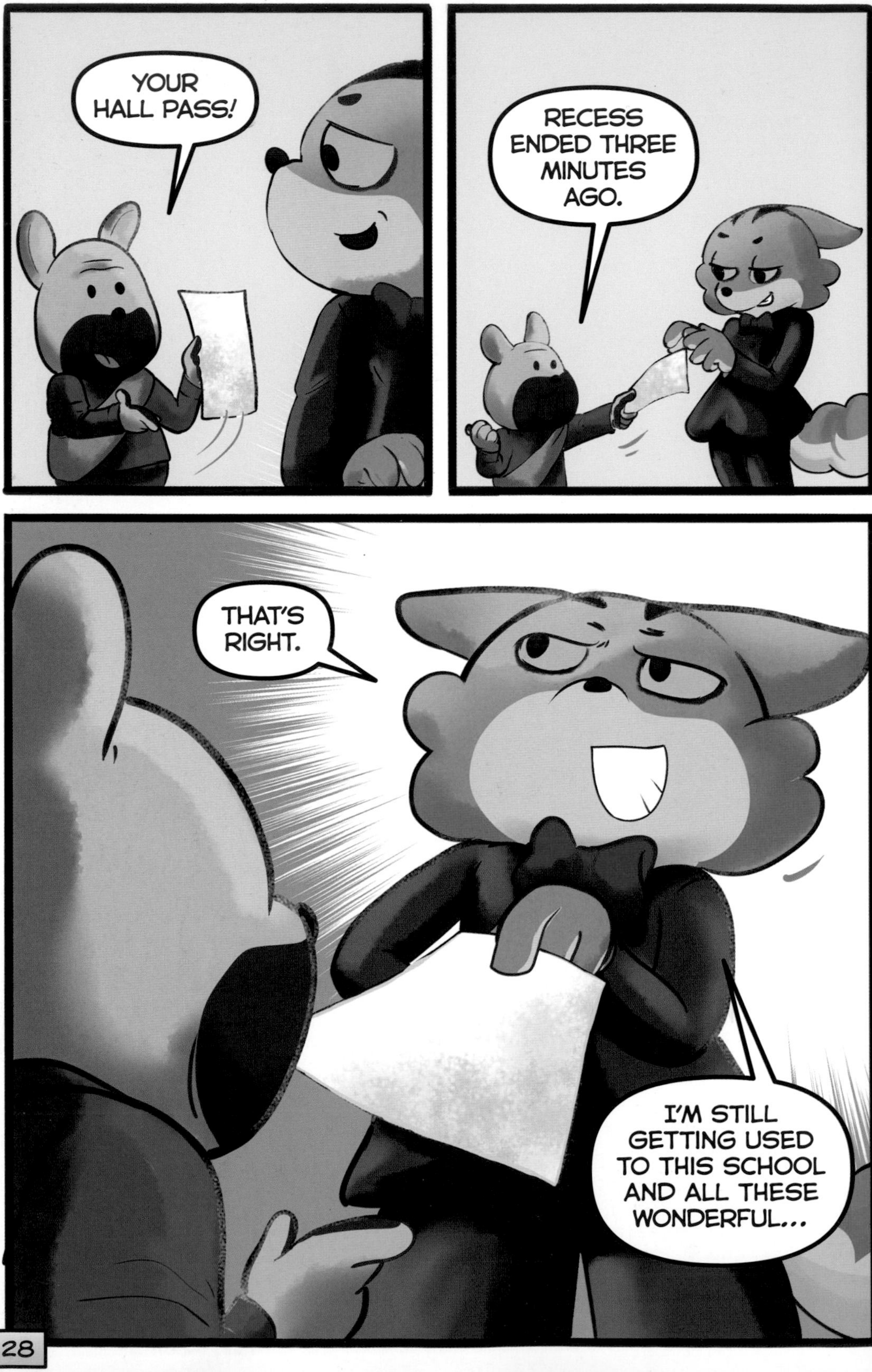
YOUR HALL PASS!
RECESS ENDED THREE MINUTES AGO.
THAT'S RIGHT.
I'M STILL GETTING USED TO THIS SCHOOL AND ALL THESE WONDERFUL...

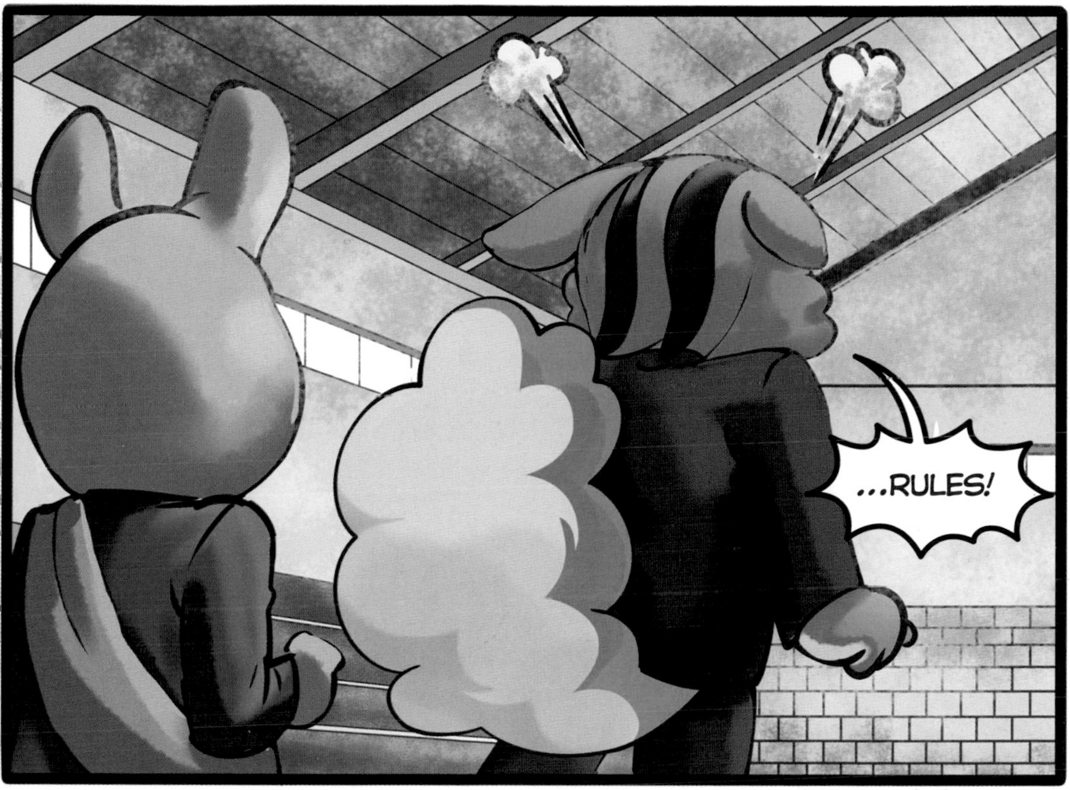
...RULES!

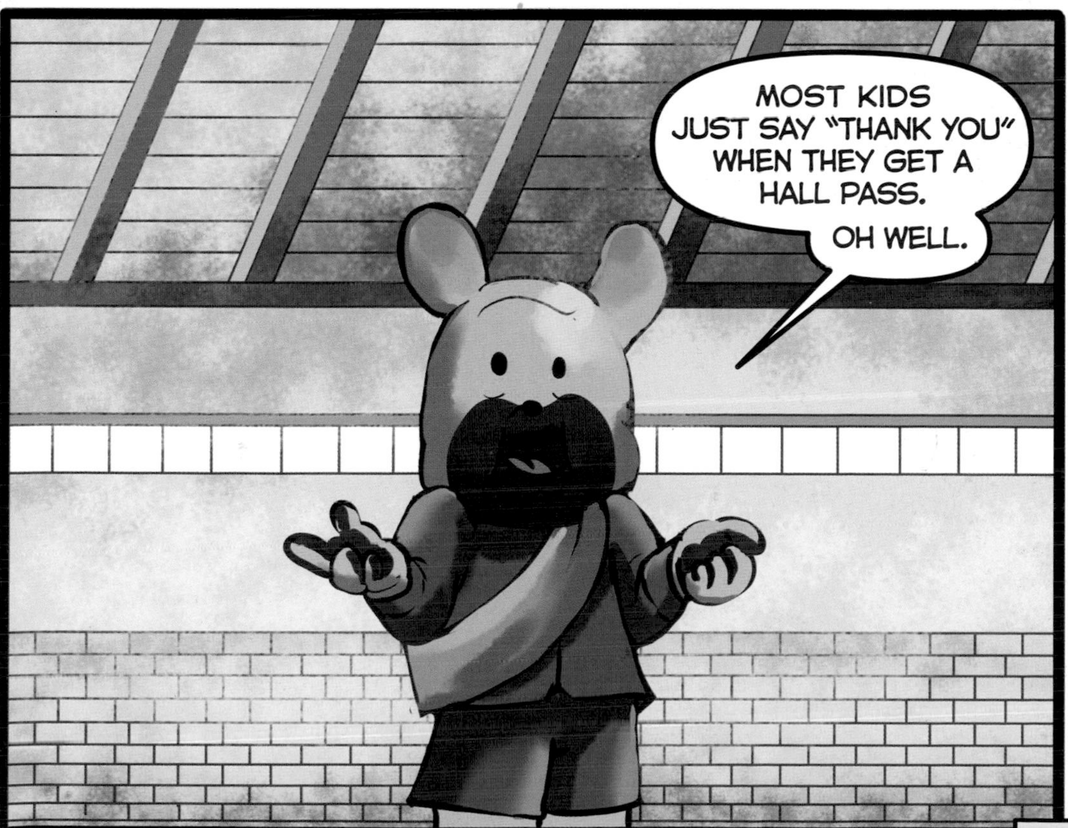
MOST KIDS JUST SAY "THANK YOU" WHEN THEY GET A HALL PASS.
OH WELL.

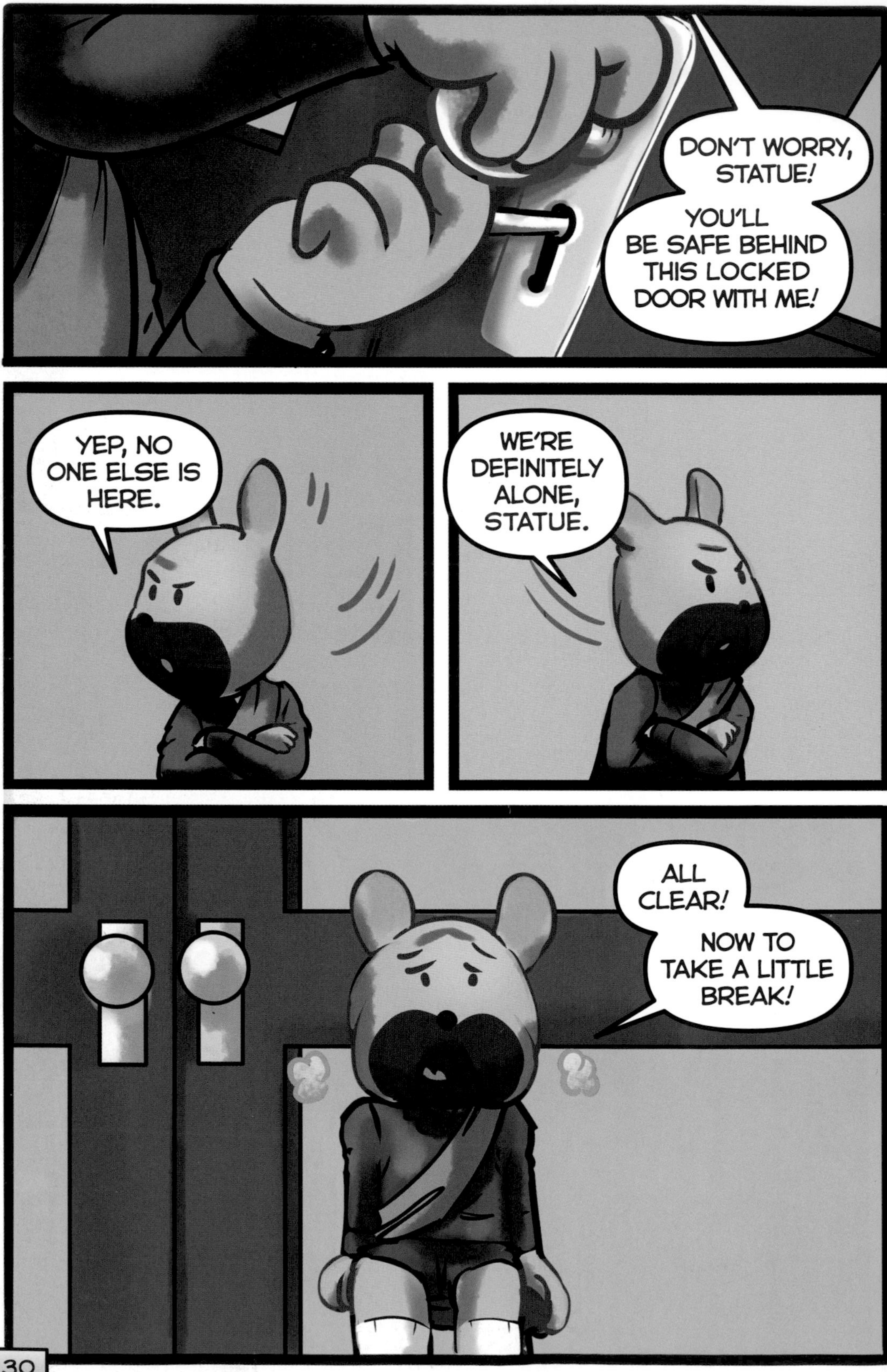
DON'T WORRY, STATUE!
YOU'LL BE SAFE BEHIND THIS LOCKED DOOR WITH ME!
YEP, NO ONE ELSE IS HERE.
WE'RE DEFINITELY ALONE, STATUE.
ALL CLEAR!
NOW TO TAKE A LITTLE BREAK!

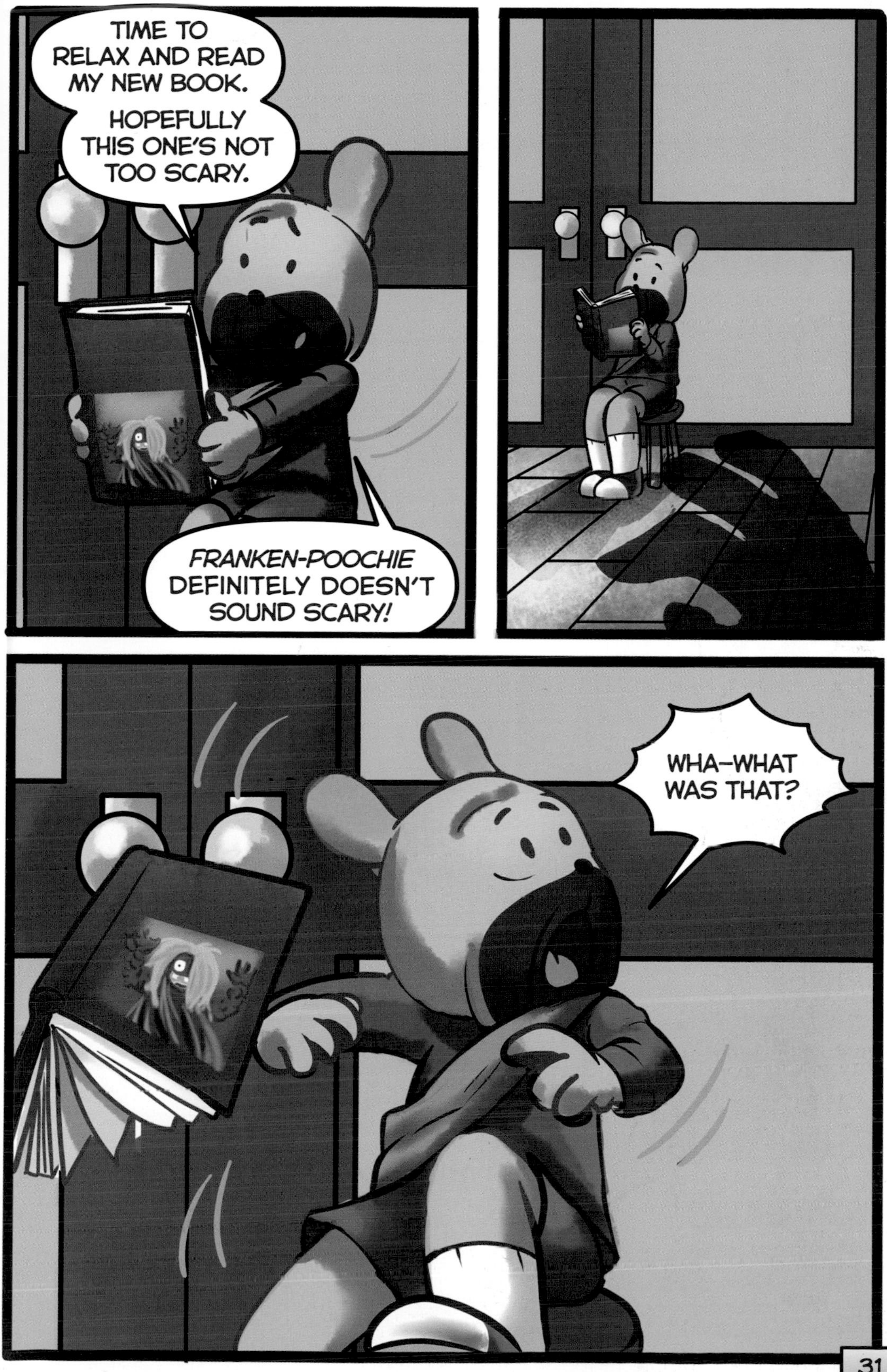
TIME TO RELAX AND READ MY NEW BOOK.
HOPEFULLY THIS ONE'S NOT TOO SCARY.
FRANKEN-POOCHIE DEFINITELY DOESN'T SOUND SCARY!
WHA-WHAT WAS THAT?

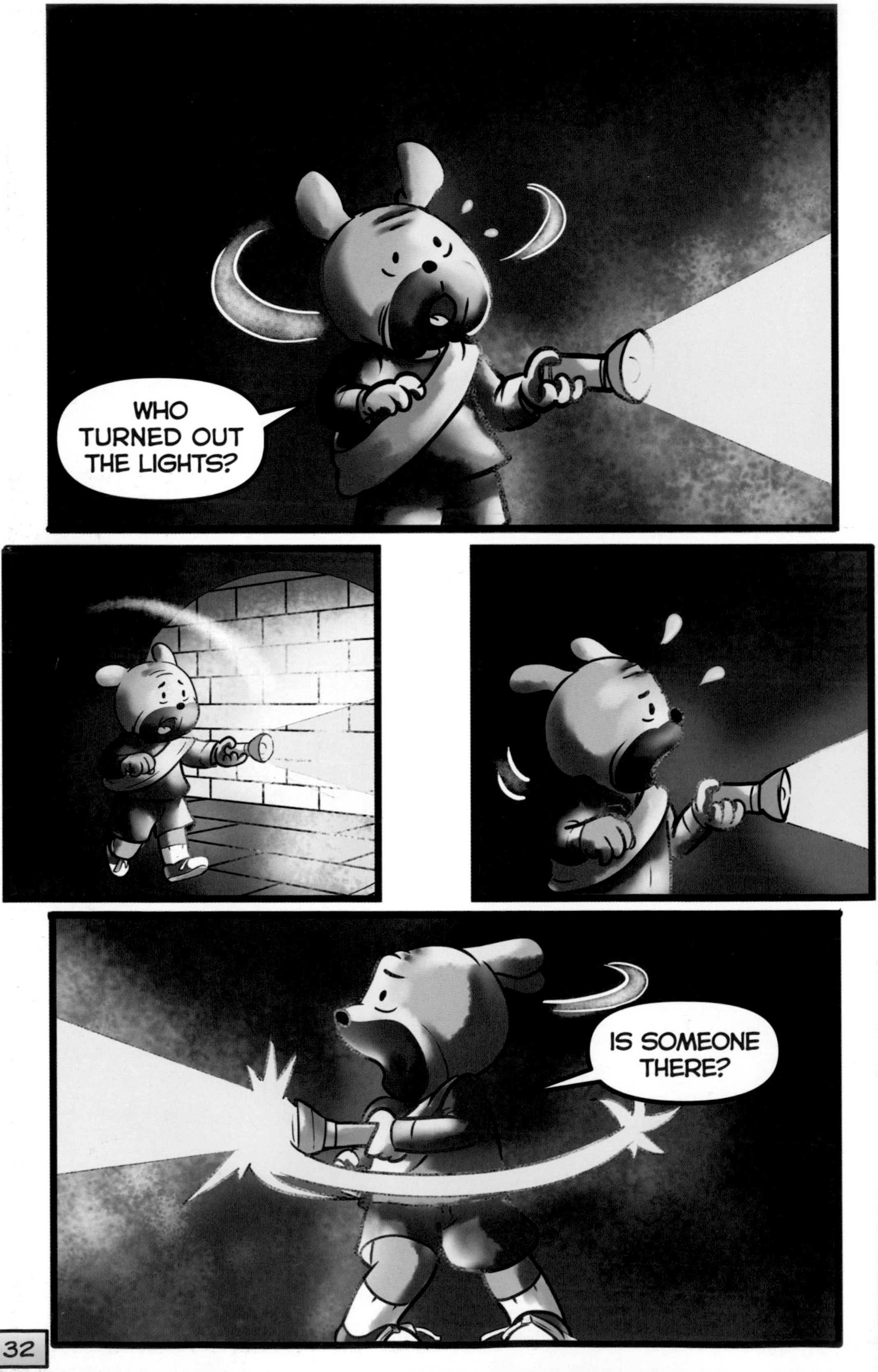
WHO TURNED OUT THE LIGHTS?
IS SOMEONE THERE?

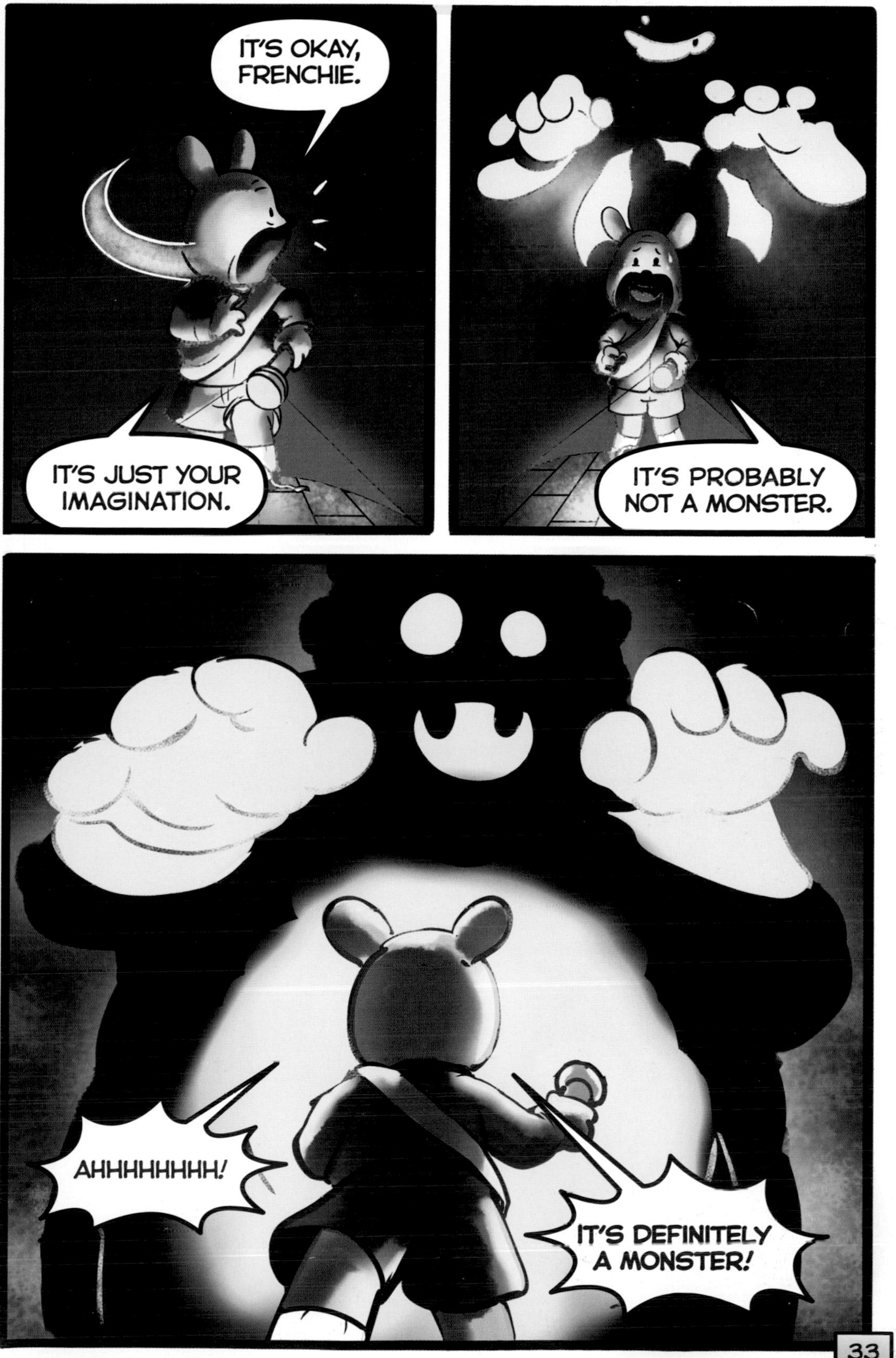
IT'S OKAY, FRENCHIE.
IT'S JUST YOUR IMAGINATION.
IT'S PROBABLY NOT A MONSTER.
AHHHHHHHH!
IT'S DEFINITELY A MONSTER!

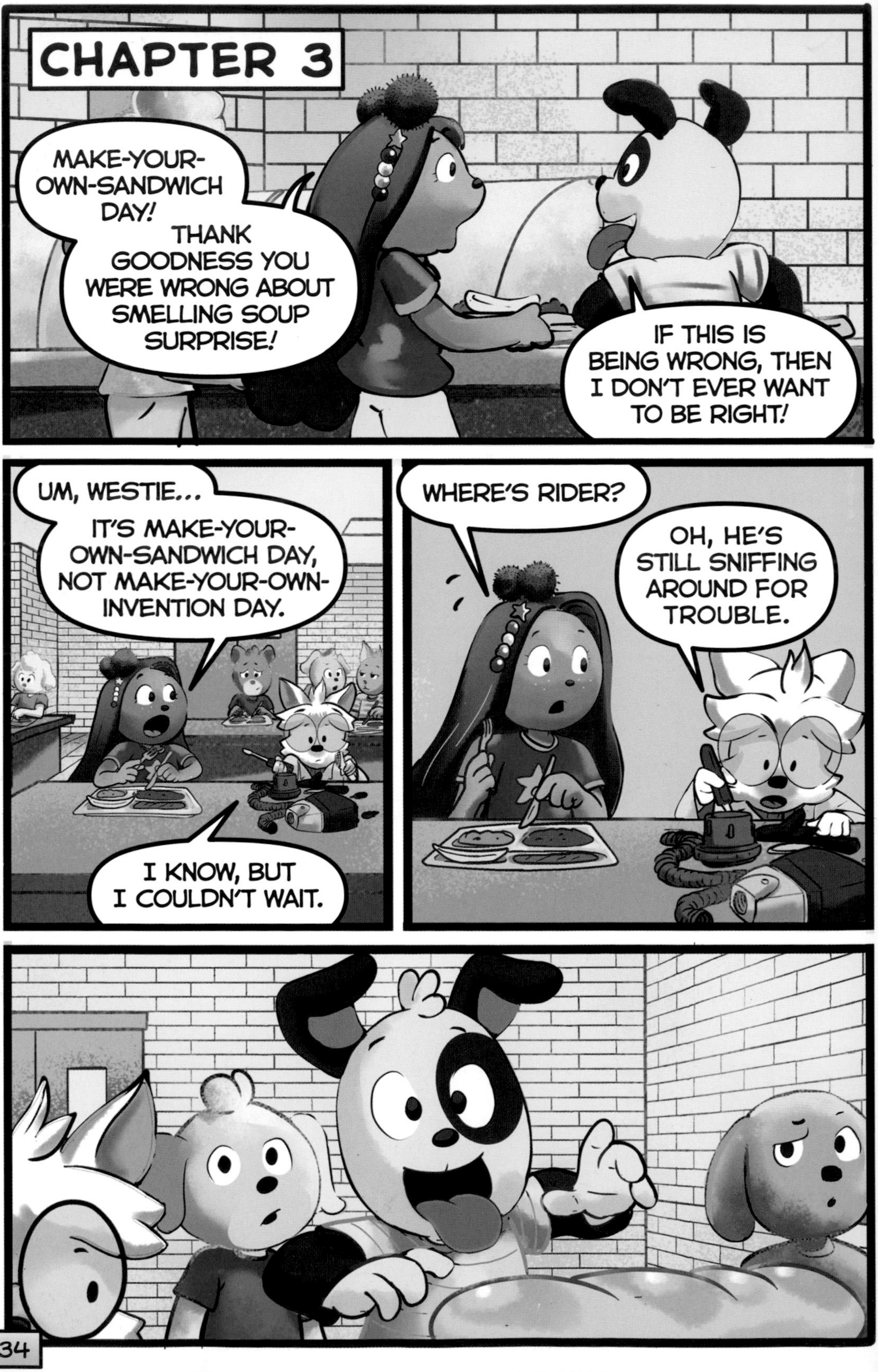
CHAPTER 3
MAKE-YOUR-OWN-SANDWICH DAY!
THANK GOODNESS YOU WERE WRONG ABOUT SMELLING SOUP SURPRISE!
IF THIS IS BEING WRONG, THEN I DON'T EVER WANT TO BE RIGHT!
UM, WESTIE...
IT'S MAKE-YOUR-OWN-SANDWICH DAY, NOT MAKE-YOUR-OWN-INVENTION DAY.
I KNOW, BUT I COULDN'T WAIT.
WHERE'S RIDER?
OH, HE'S STILL SNIFFING AROUND FOR TROUBLE.

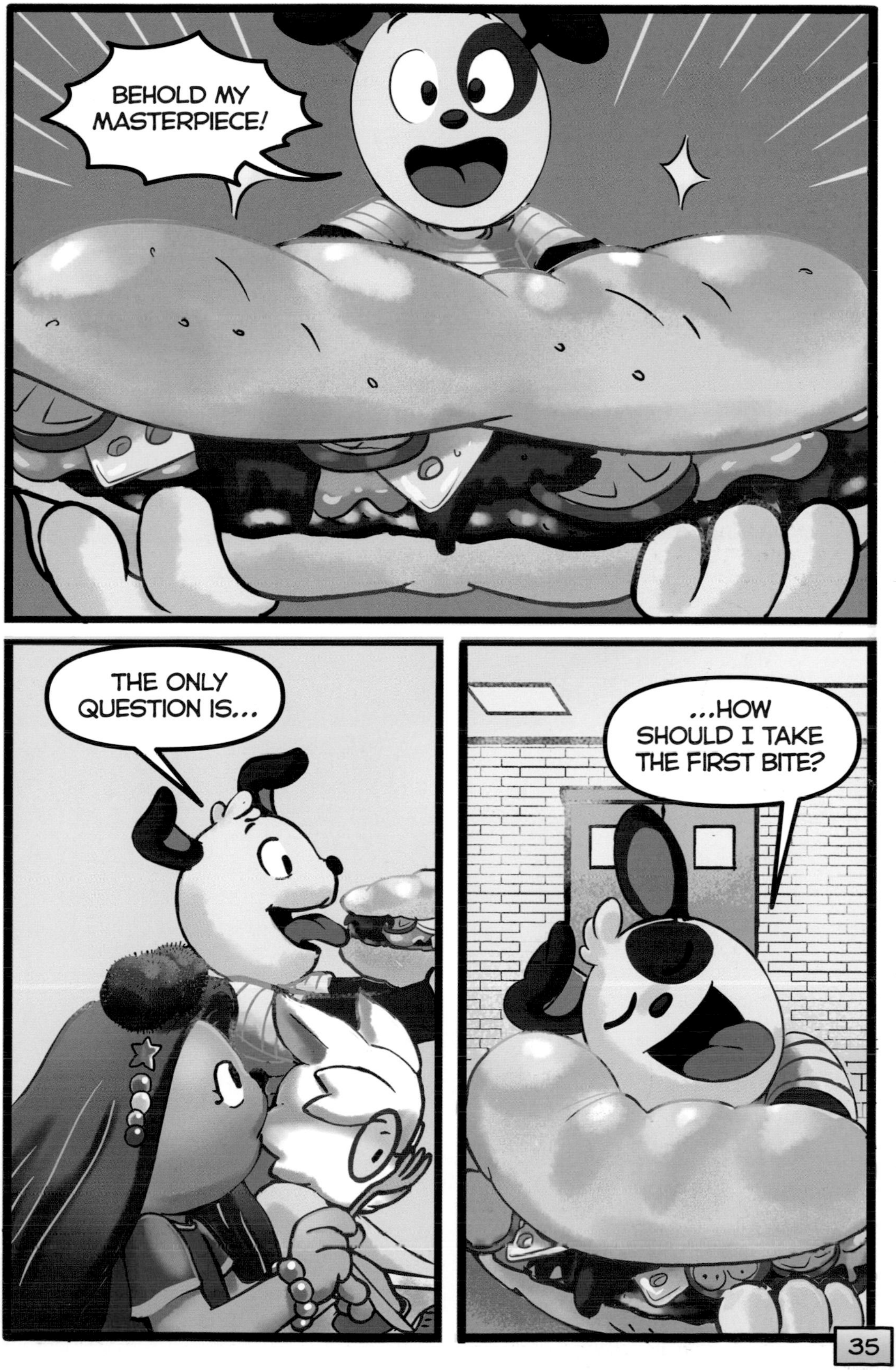
BEHOLD MY MASTERPIECE!
THE ONLY QUESTION IS...
...HOW SHOULD I TAKE THE FIRST BITE?

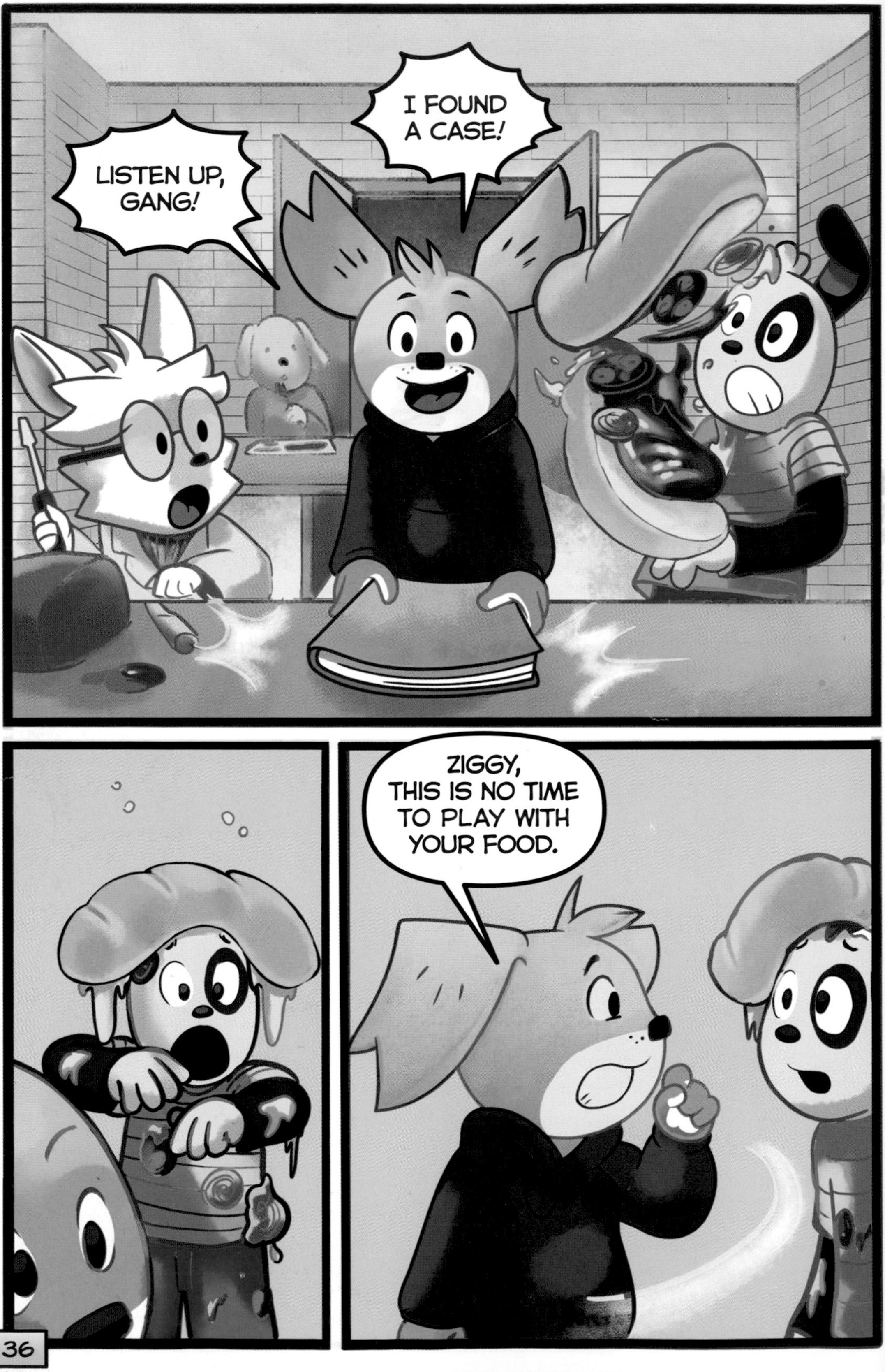
LISTEN UP, GANG!
I FOUND A CASE!
ZIGGY, THIS IS NO TIME TO PLAY WITH YOUR FOOD.

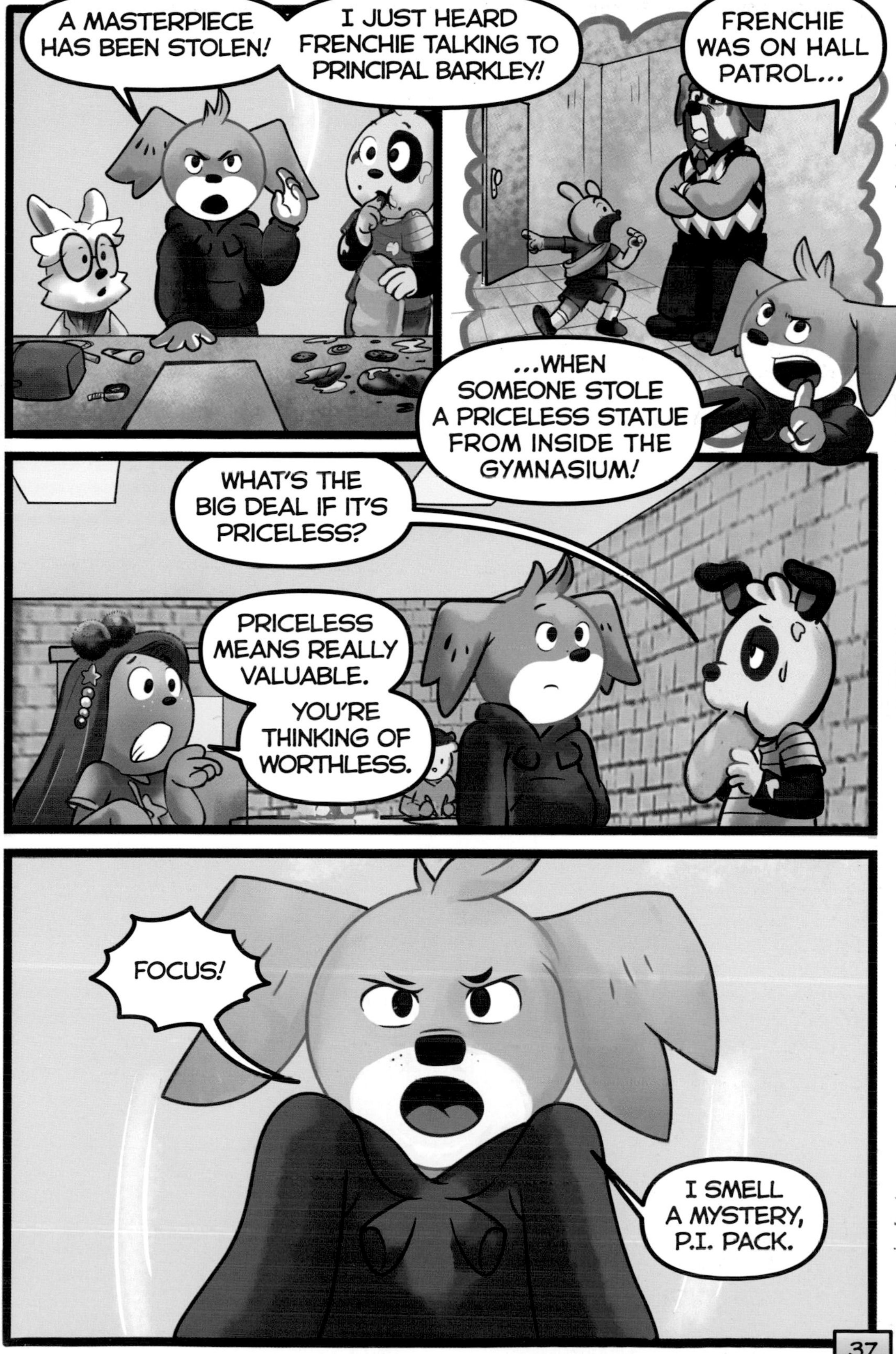
A MASTERPIECE HAS BEEN STOLEN!
I JUST HEARD FRENCHIE TALKING TO PRINCIPAL BARKLEY!
FRENCHIE WAS ON HALL PATROL...
...WHEN SOMEONE STOLE A PRICELESS STATUE FROM INSIDE THE GYMNASIUM!
WHAT'S THE BIG DEAL IF IT'S PRICELESS?
PRICELESS MEANS REALLY VALUABLE.
YOU'RE THINKING OF WORTHLESS.
FOCUS!
I SMELL A MYSTERY, P.I. PACK.

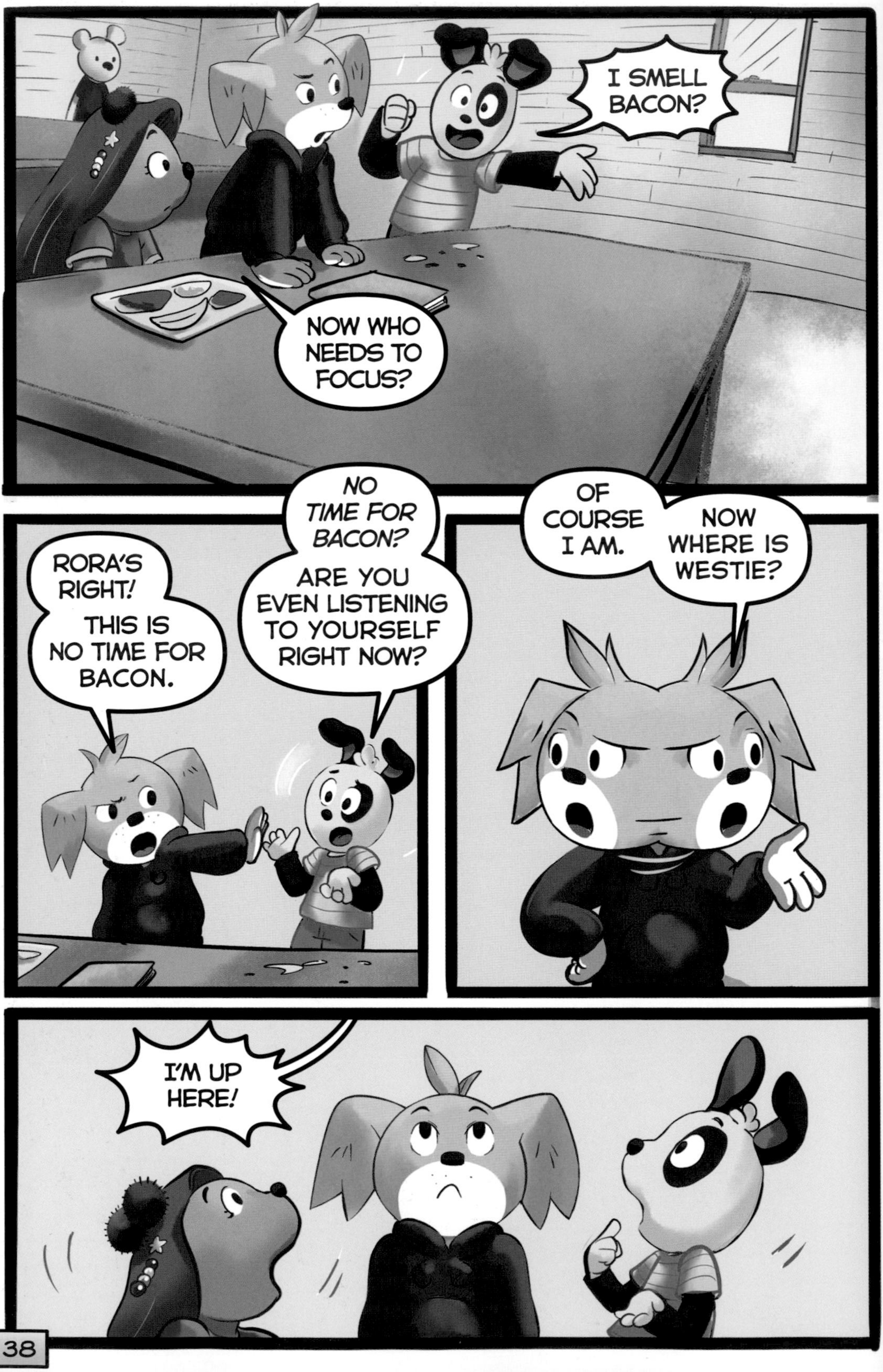
I SMELL BACON?
NOW WHO NEEDS TO FOCUS?
RORA'S RIGHT!
THIS IS NO TIME FOR BACON.
NO *TIME FOR BACON?*
ARE YOU EVEN LISTENING TO YOURSELF RIGHT NOW?
OF COURSE I AM.
NOW WHERE IS WESTIE?
I'M UP HERE!

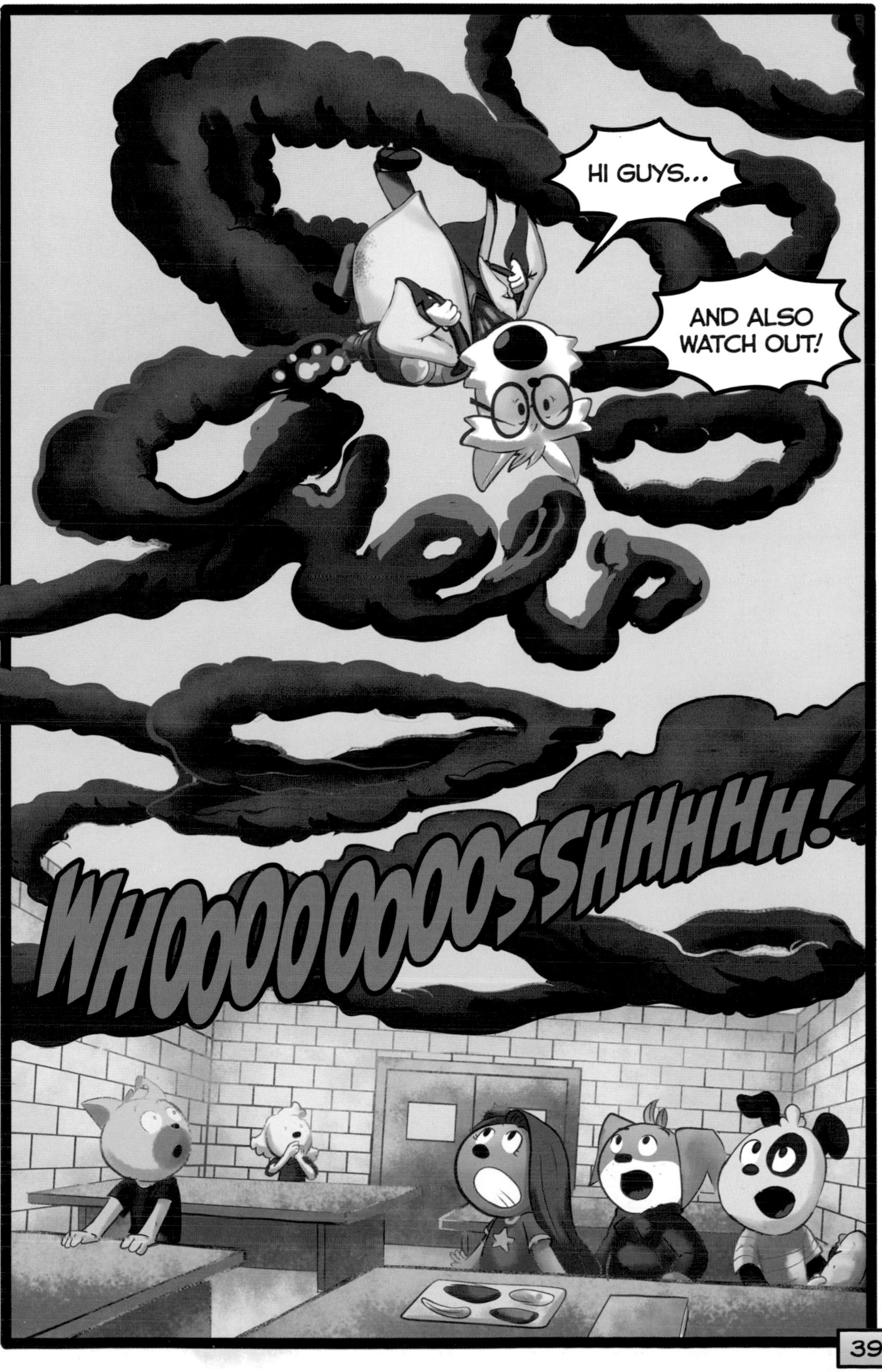
HI GUYS...
AND ALSO WATCH OUT!
WHOOOOOOOOSHHHHHH!

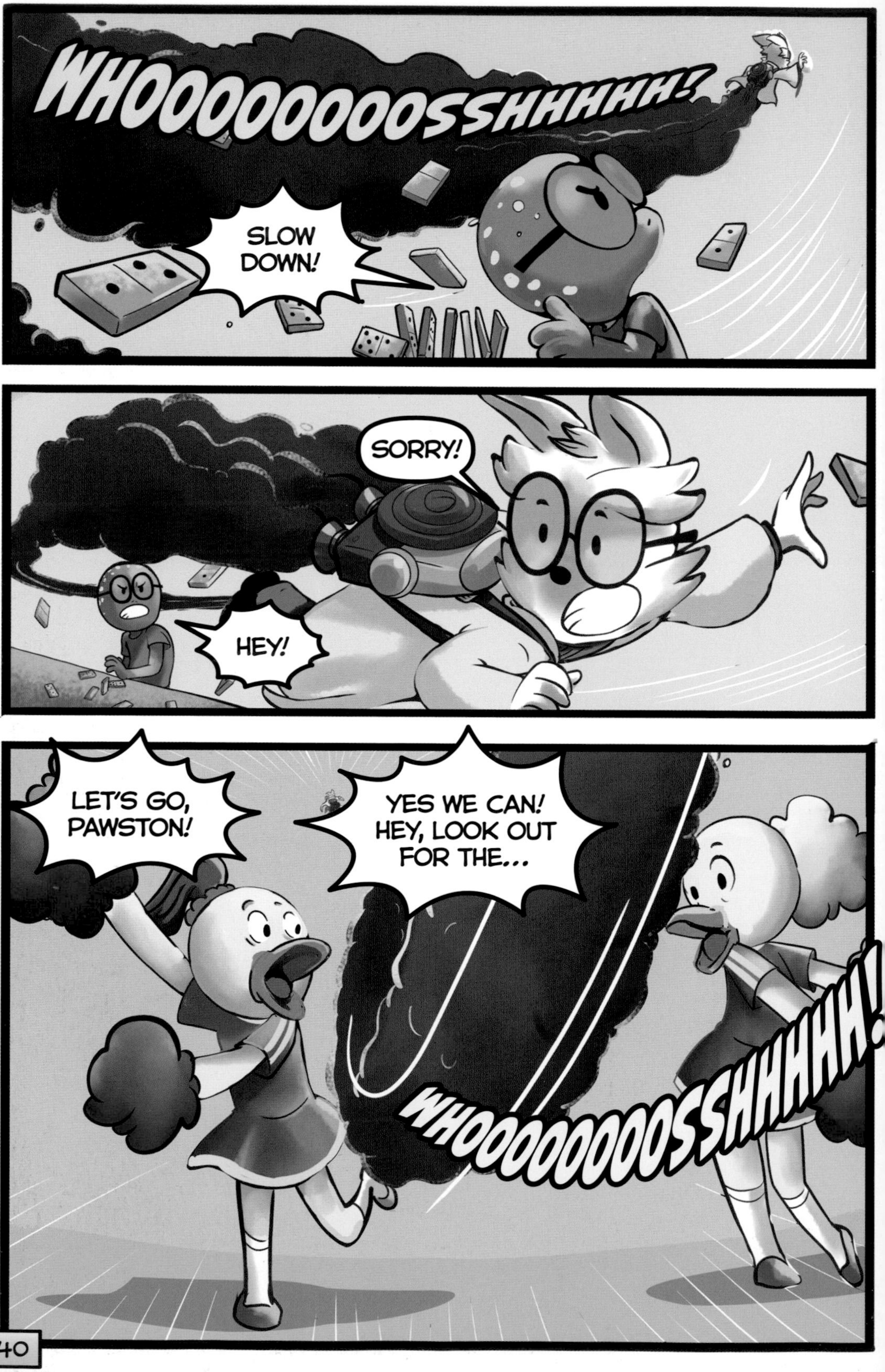
WHOOOOOOOOOSSHHHHH!
SLOW DOWN!
SORRY!
HEY!
LET'S GO, PAWSTON!
YES WE CAN! HEY, LOOK OUT FOR THE...
WHOOOOOOOOOSSHHHHH!

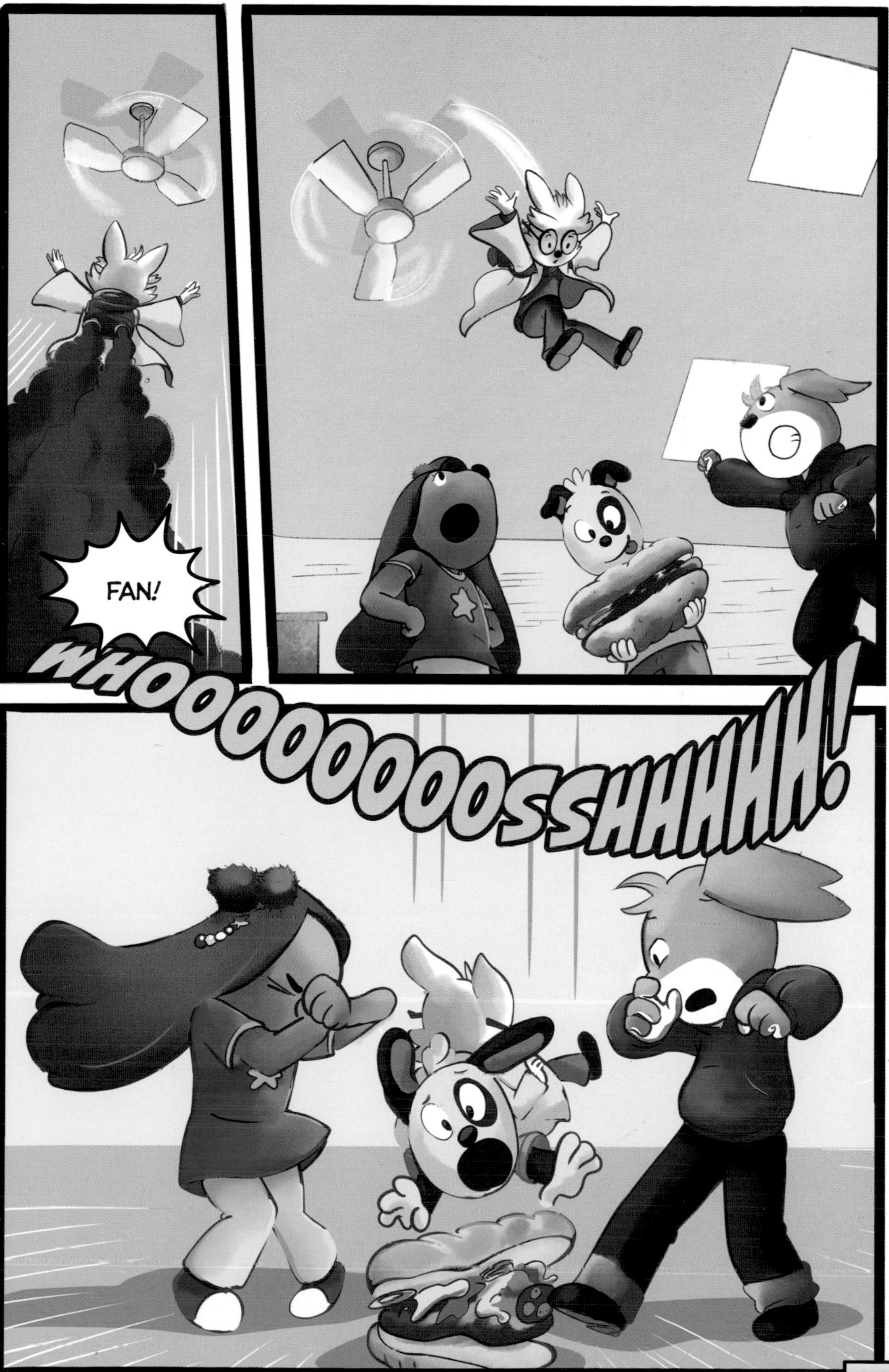
FAN!
WHOOOOOOOOOOSSHHHHHH!

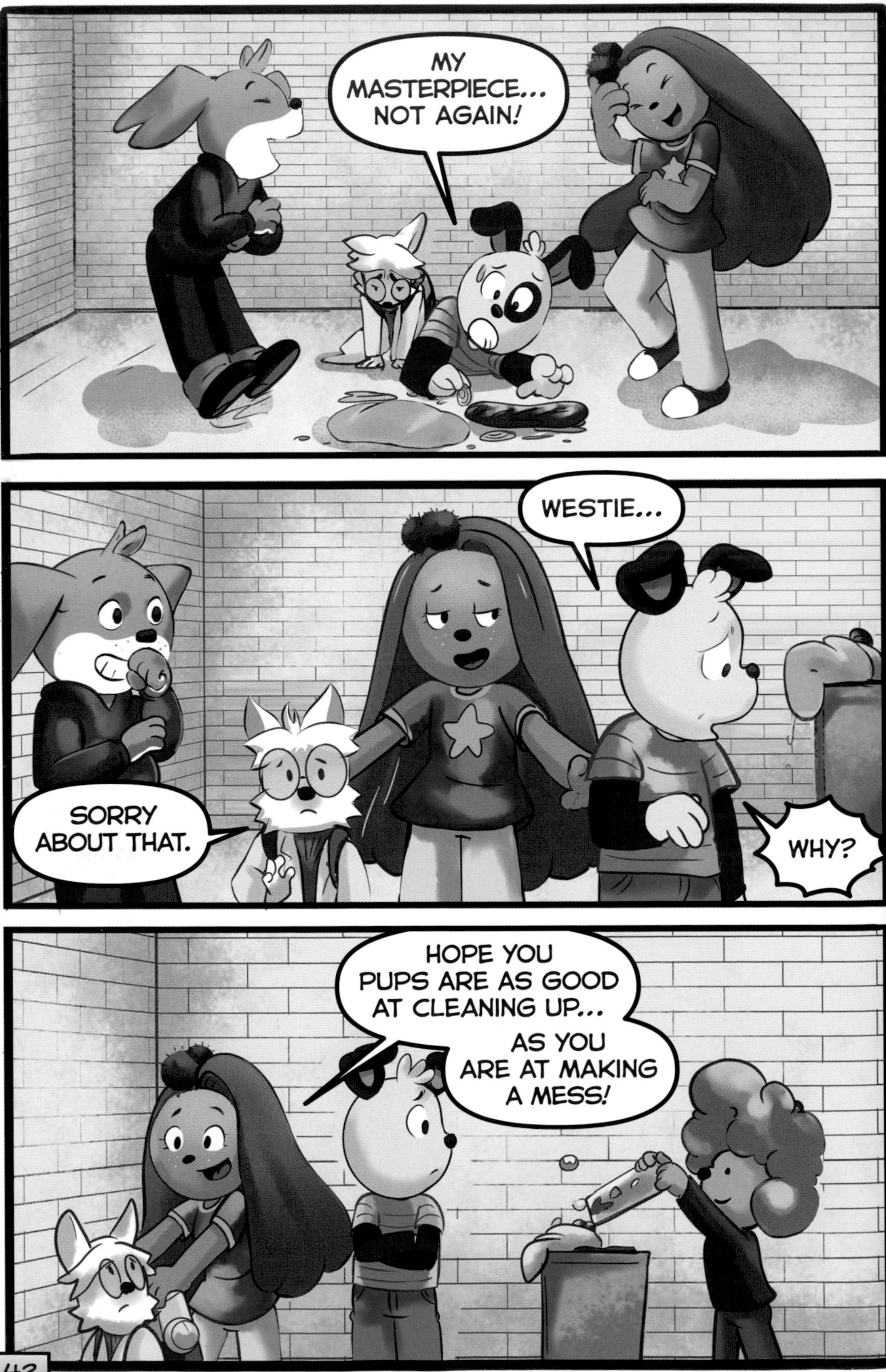
MY MASTERPIECE... NOT AGAIN!
WESTIE...
SORRY ABOUT THAT.
WHY?
HOPE YOU PUPS ARE AS GOOD AT CLEANING UP...
AS YOU ARE AT MAKING A MESS!

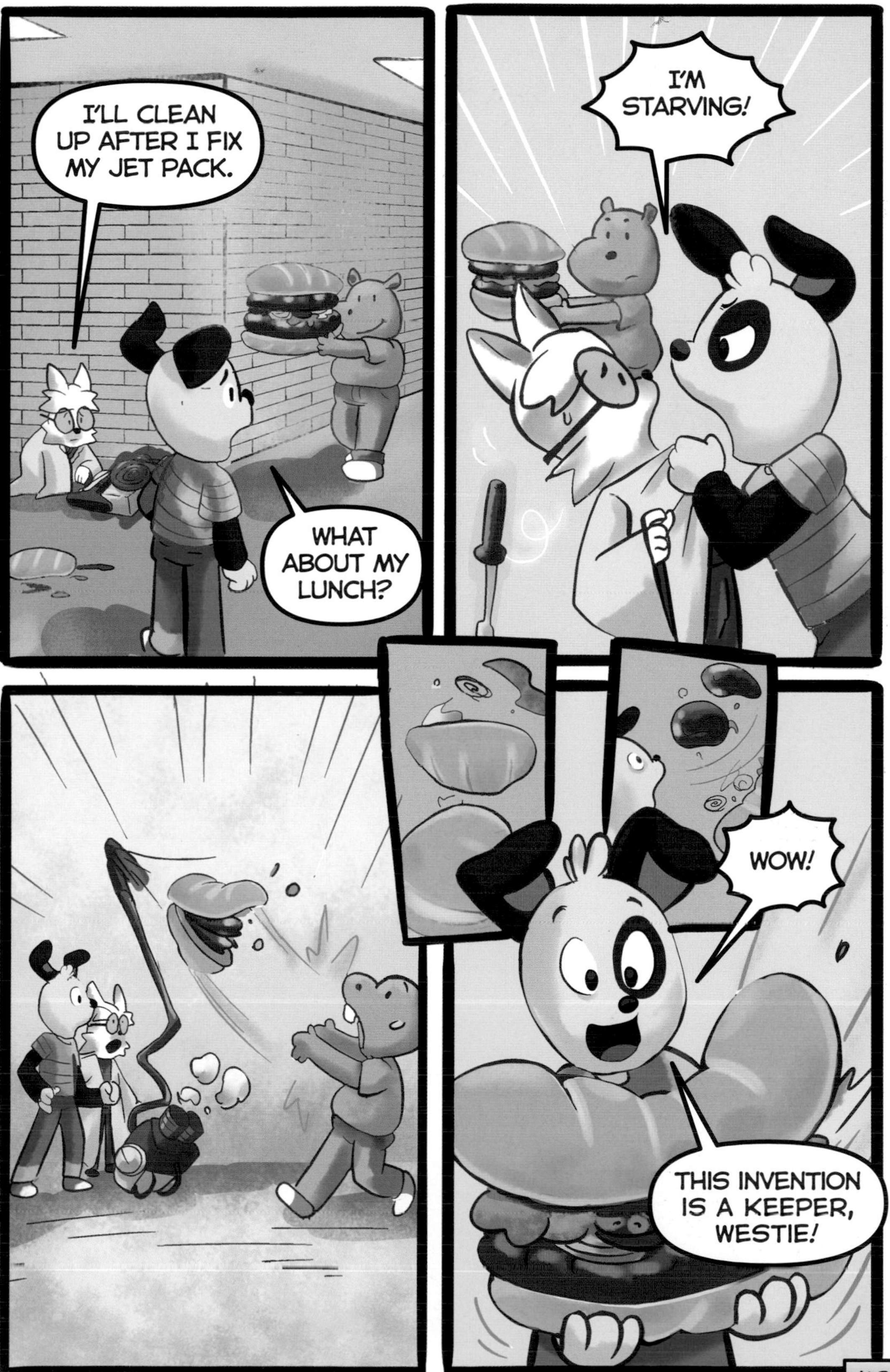
I'LL CLEAN UP AFTER I FIX MY JET PACK.
WHAT ABOUT MY LUNCH?
I'M STARVING!
WOW!
THIS INVENTION IS A KEEPER, WESTIE!

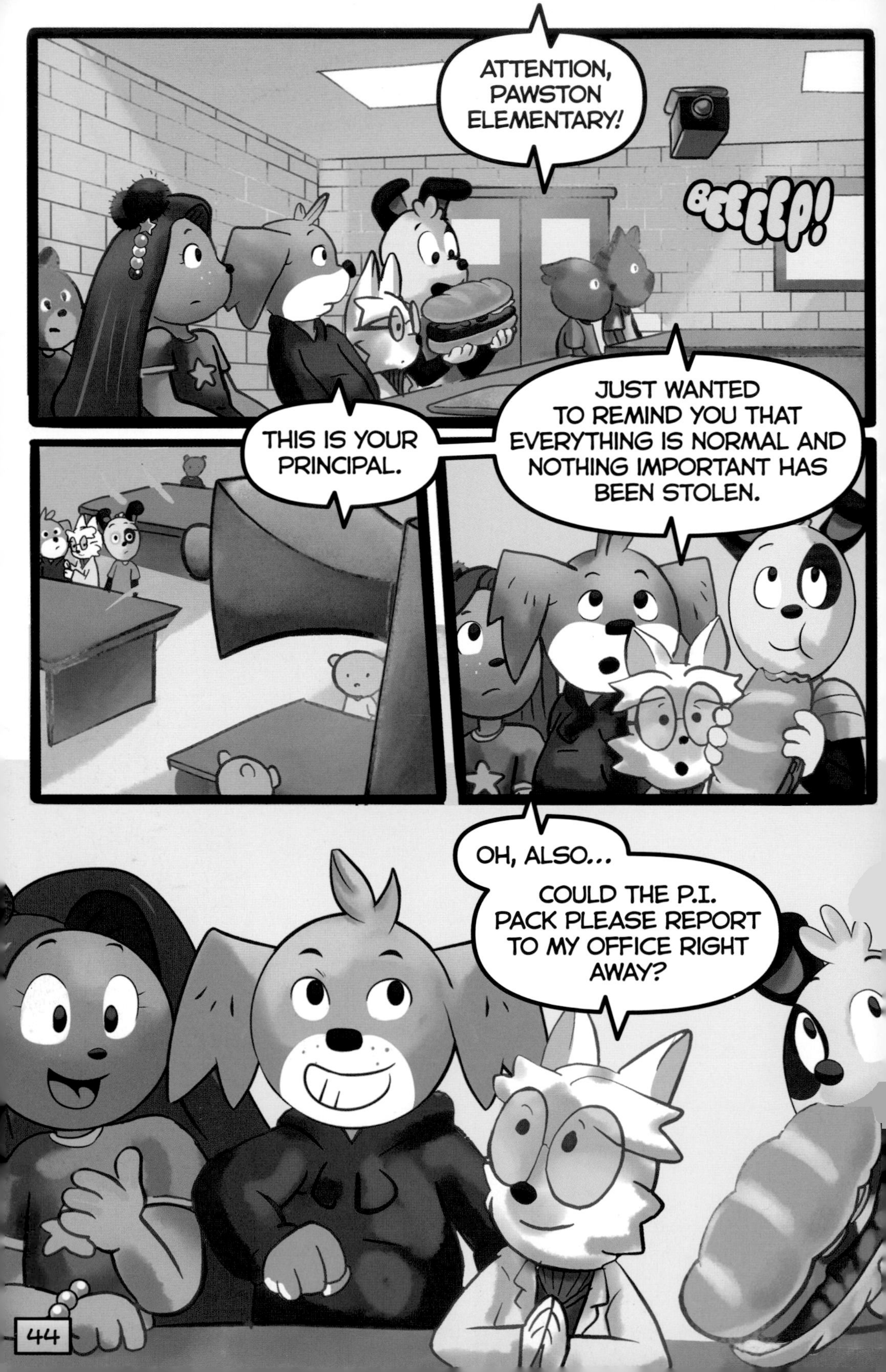
ATTENTION, PAWSTON ELEMENTARY!
BEEEEP!
THIS IS YOUR PRINCIPAL.
JUST WANTED TO REMIND YOU THAT EVERYTHING IS NORMAL AND NOTHING IMPORTANT HAS BEEN STOLEN.
OH, ALSO...
COULD THE P.I. PACK PLEASE REPORT TO MY OFFICE RIGHT AWAY?

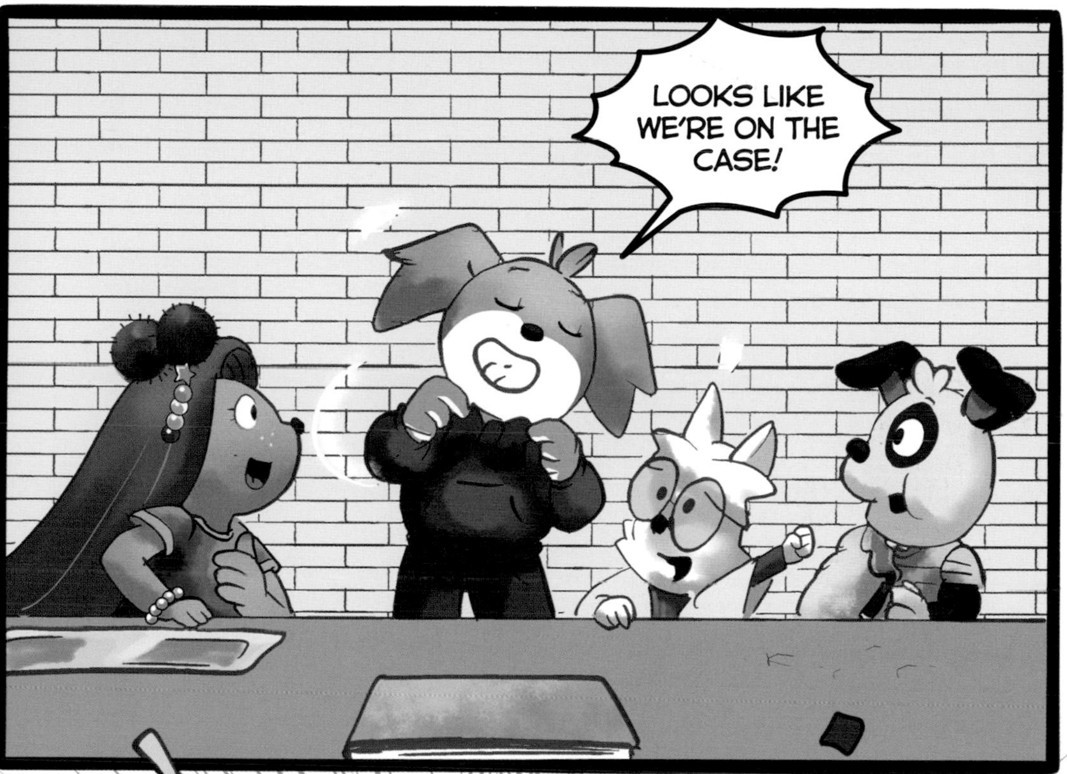
LOOKS LIKE
WE'RE ON THE
CASE!

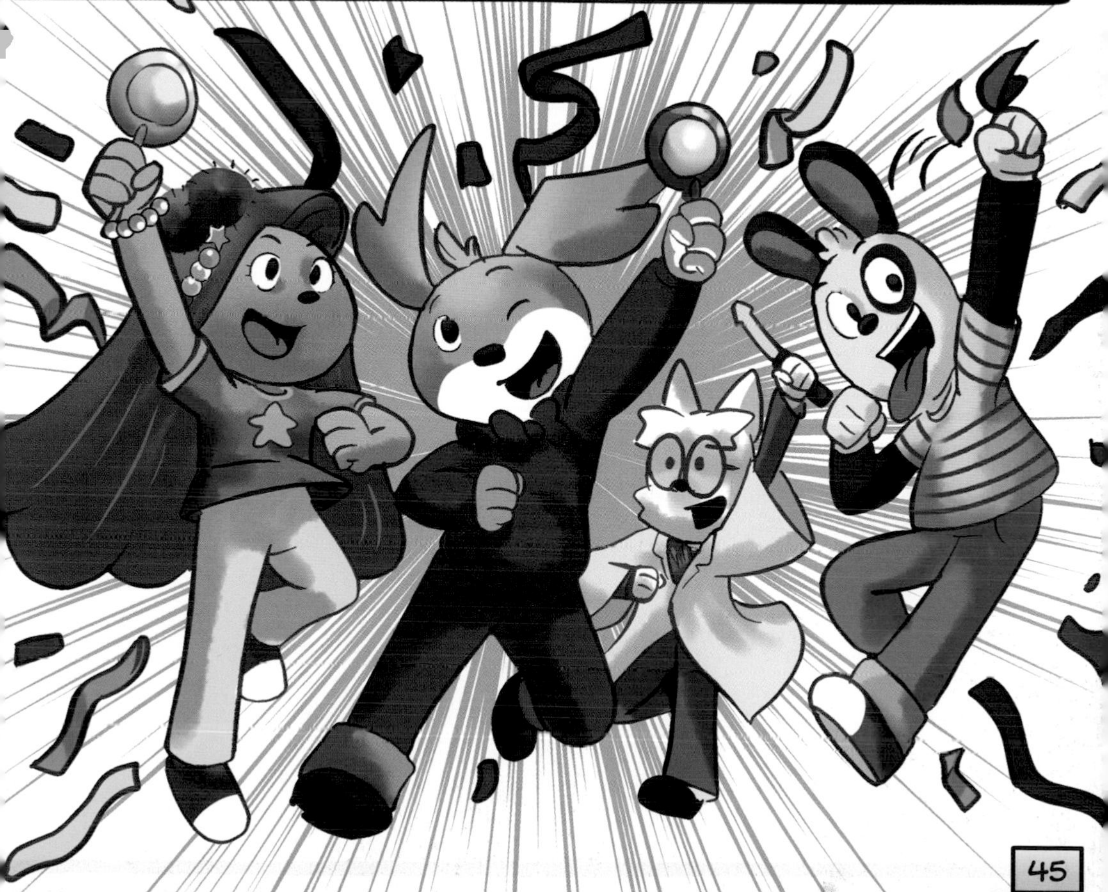

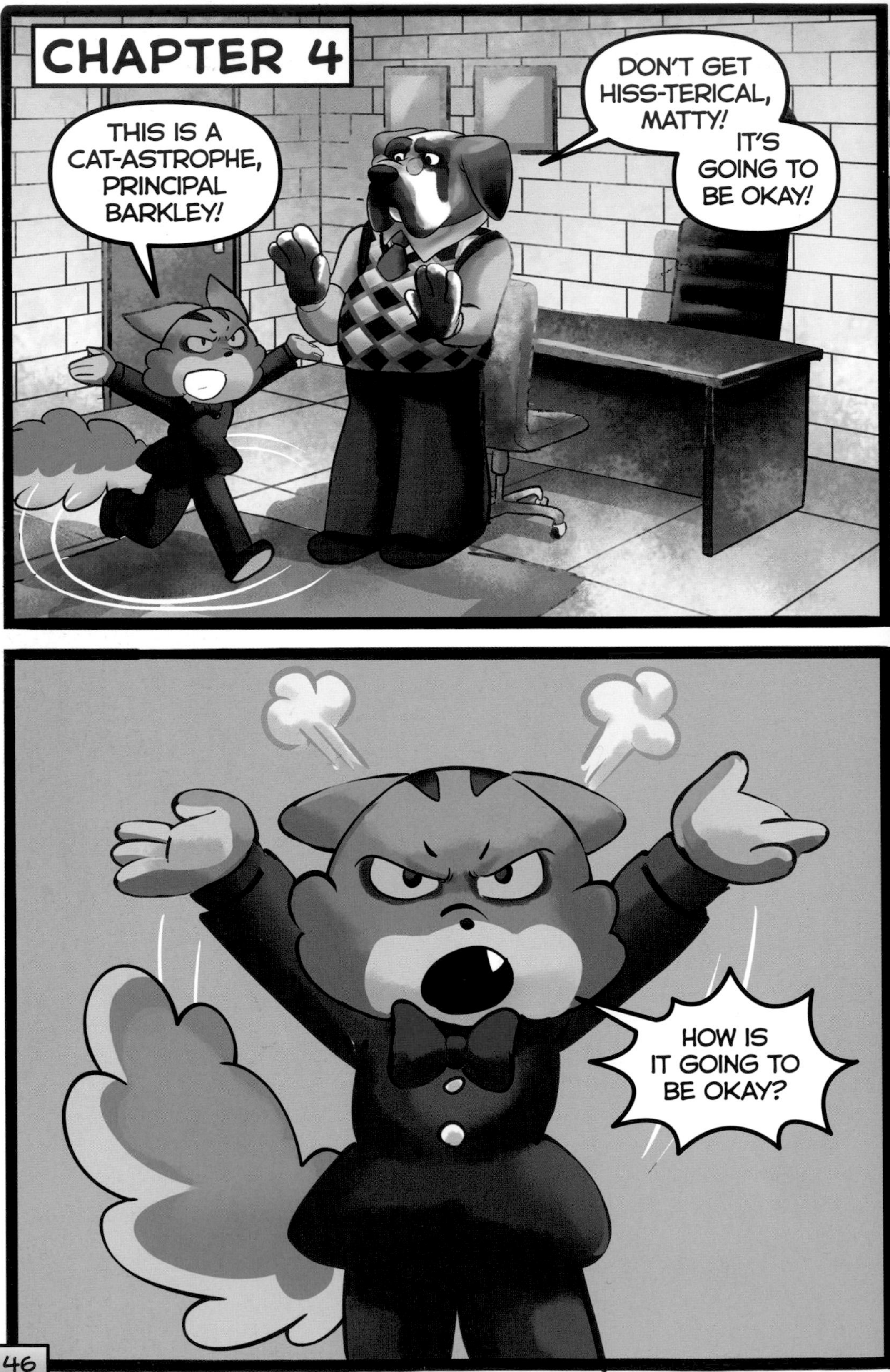
CHAPTER 4
THIS IS A CAT-ASTROPHE, PRINCIPAL BARKLEY!
DON'T GET HISS-TERICAL, MATTY!
IT'S GOING TO BE OKAY!
HOW IS IT GOING TO BE OKAY?

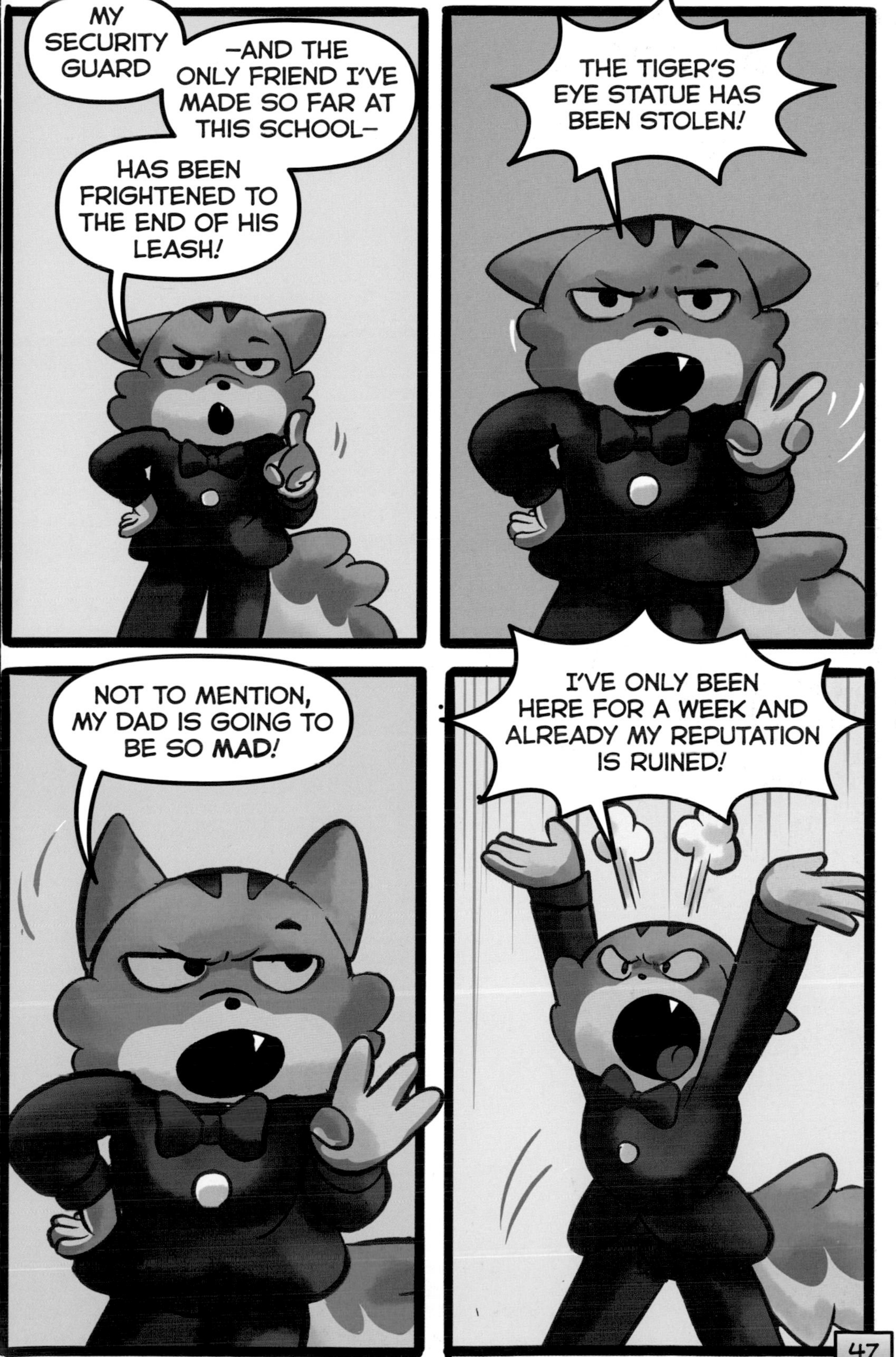
MY SECURITY GUARD
-AND THE ONLY FRIEND I'VE MADE SO FAR AT THIS SCHOOL-
HAS BEEN FRIGHTENED TO THE END OF HIS LEASH!
THE TIGER'S EYE STATUE HAS BEEN STOLEN!
NOT TO MENTION, MY DAD IS GOING TO BE SO MAD!
I'VE ONLY BEEN HERE FOR A WEEK AND ALREADY MY REPUTATION IS RUINED!

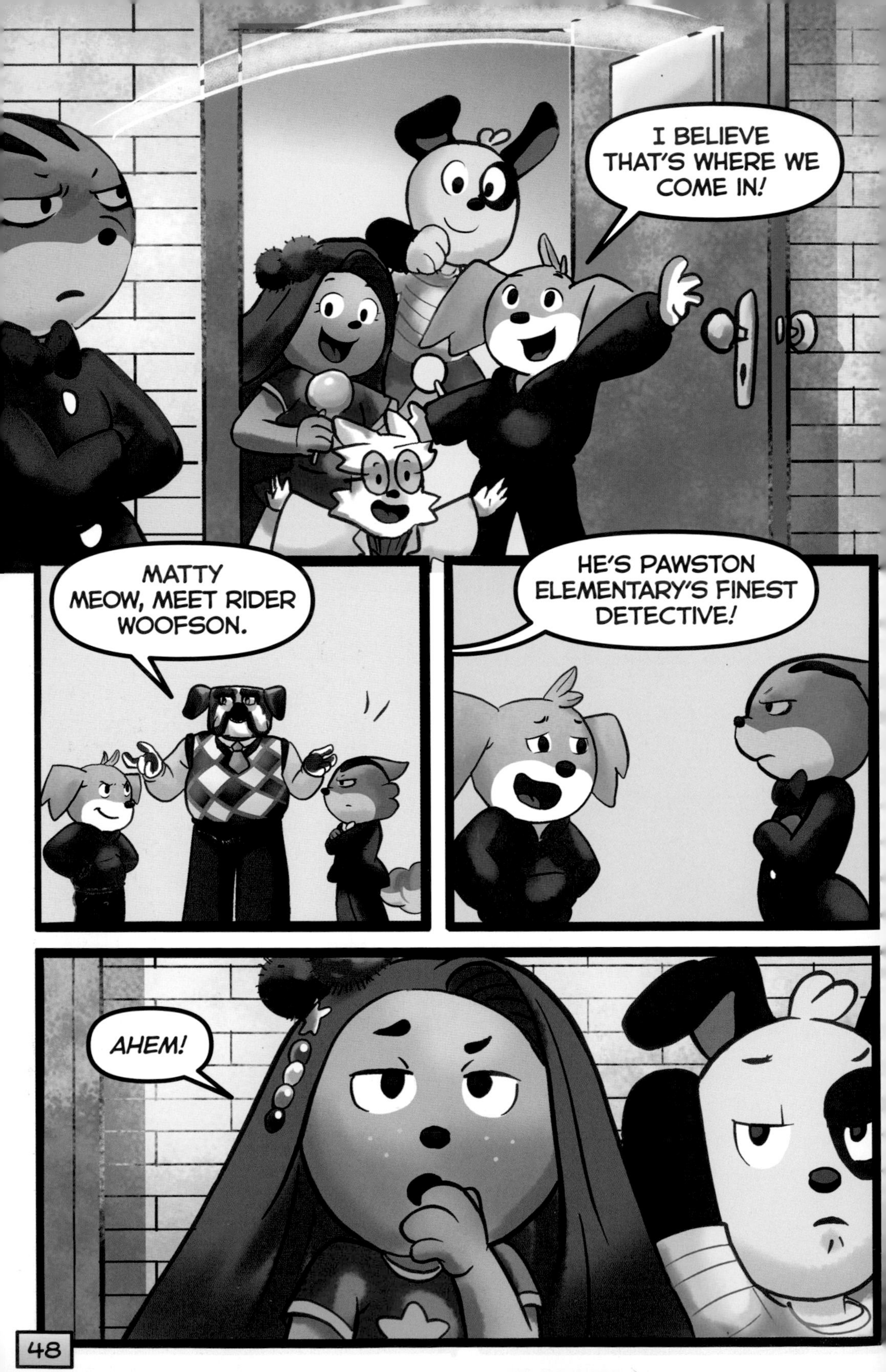
I BELIEVE THAT'S WHERE WE COME IN!
MATTY MEOW, MEET RIDER WOOFSON.
HE'S PAWSTON ELEMENTARY'S FINEST DETECTIVE!
AHEM!

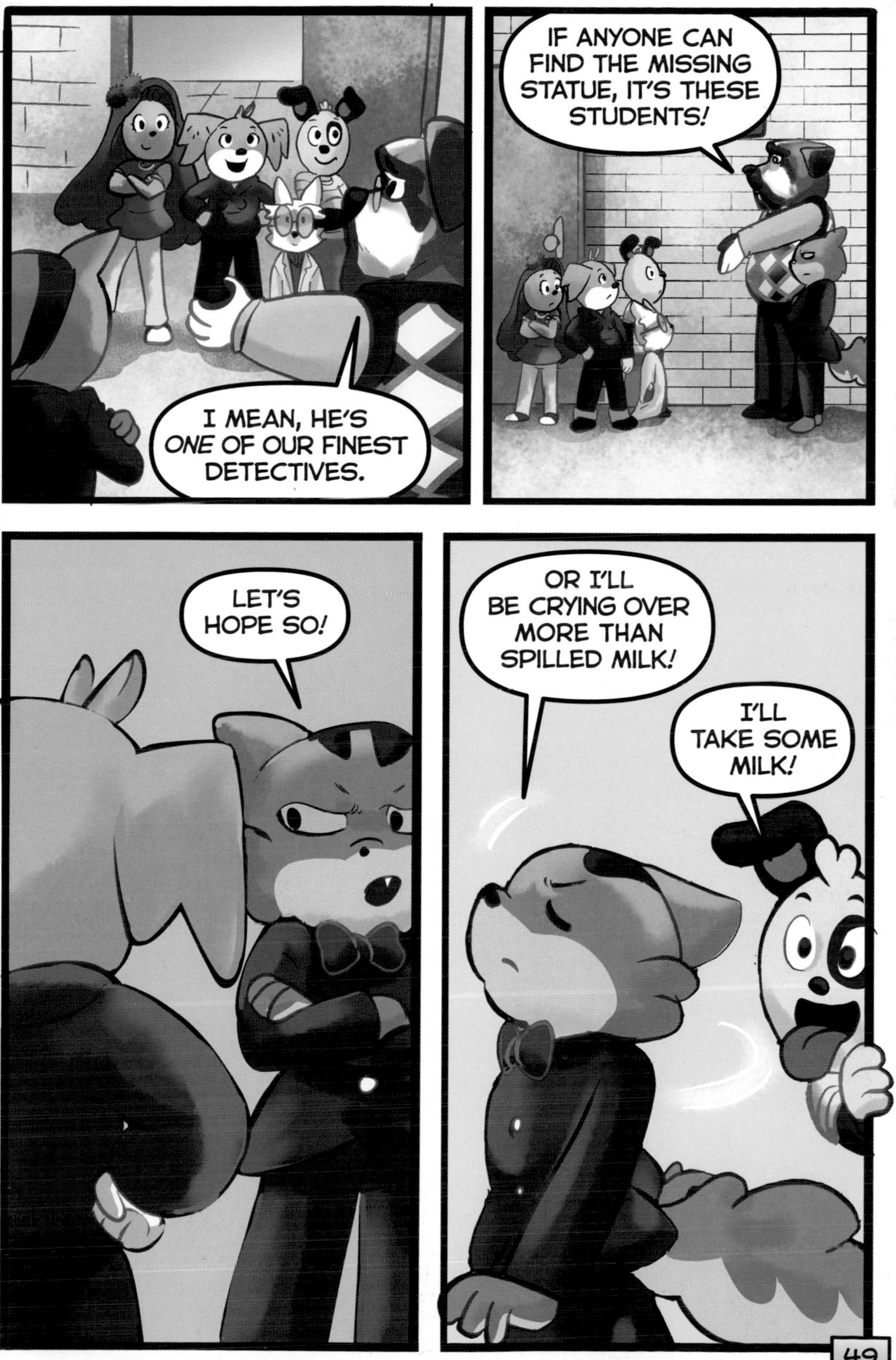
I MEAN, HE'S *ONE* OF OUR FINEST DETECTIVES.
IF ANYONE CAN FIND THE MISSING STATUE, IT'S THESE STUDENTS!
LET'S HOPE SO!
OR I'LL BE CRYING OVER MORE THAN SPILLED MILK!
I'LL TAKE SOME MILK!

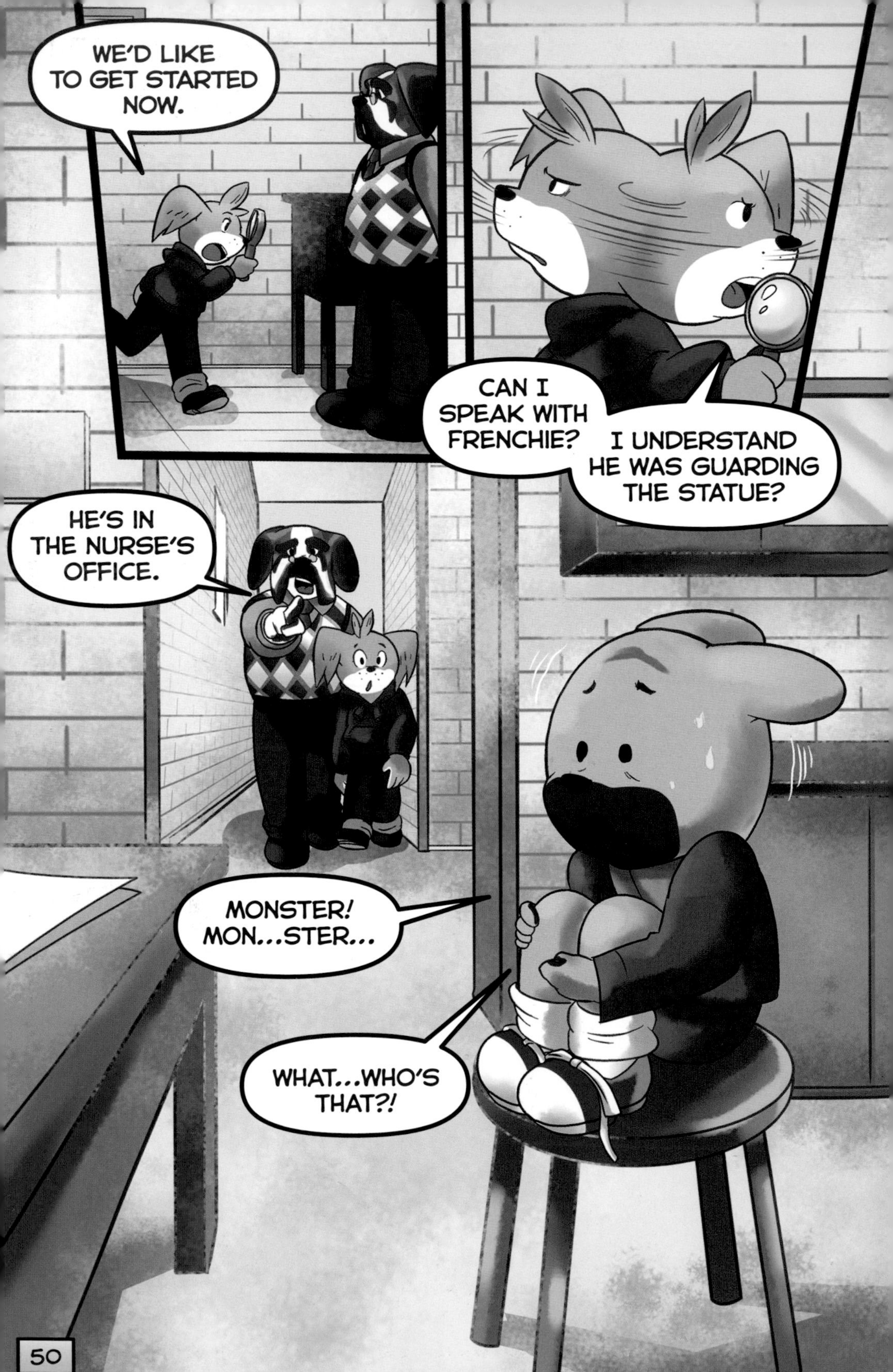
WE'D LIKE TO GET STARTED NOW.
CAN I SPEAK WITH FRENCHIE?
I UNDERSTAND HE WAS GUARDING THE STATUE?
HE'S IN THE NURSE'S OFFICE.
MONSTER! MON...STER...
WHAT...WHO'S THAT?!

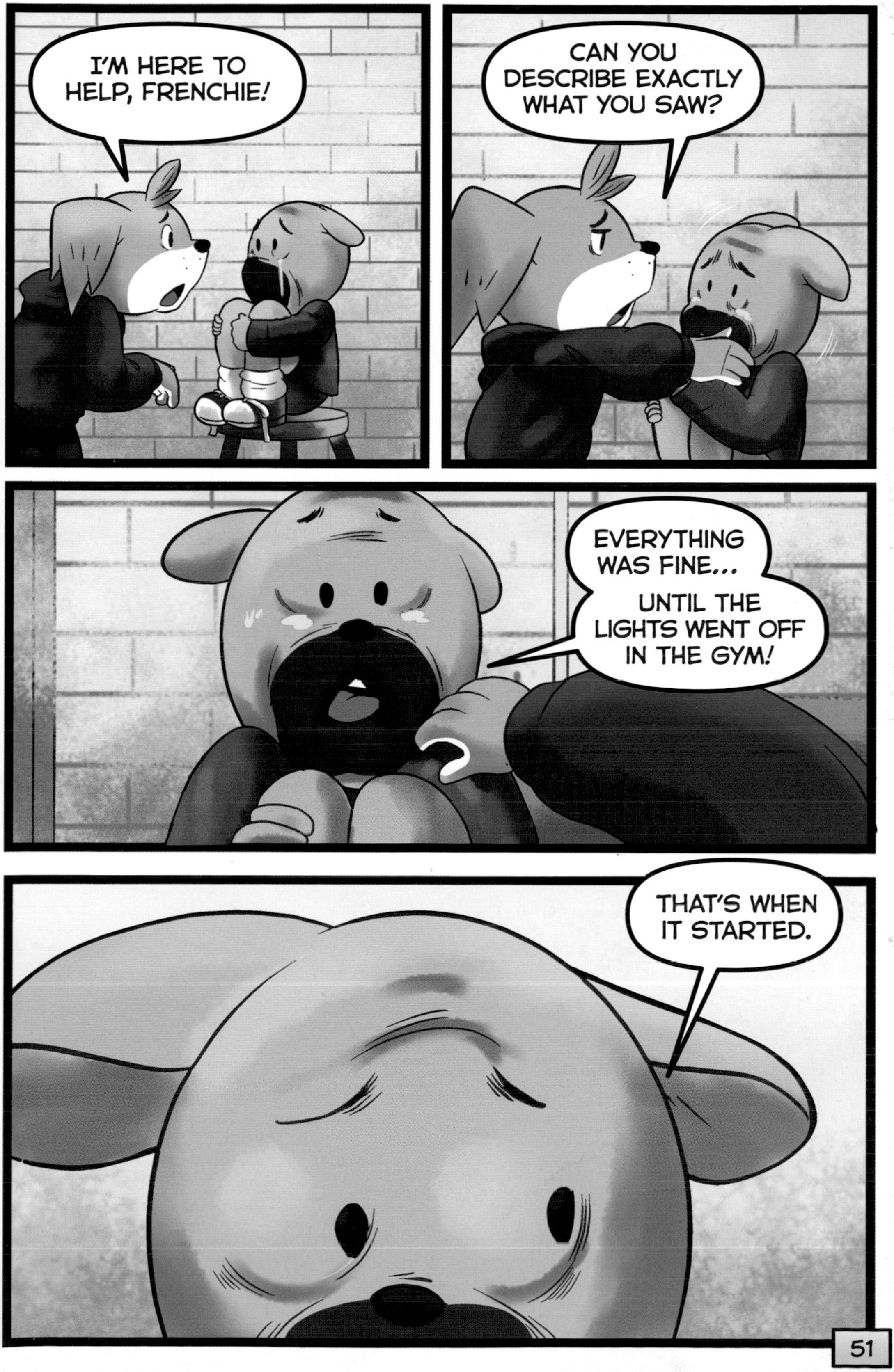
I'M HERE TO HELP, FRENCHIE!
CAN YOU DESCRIBE EXACTLY WHAT YOU SAW?
EVERYTHING WAS FINE...
UNTIL THE LIGHTS WENT OFF IN THE GYM!
THAT'S WHEN IT STARTED.

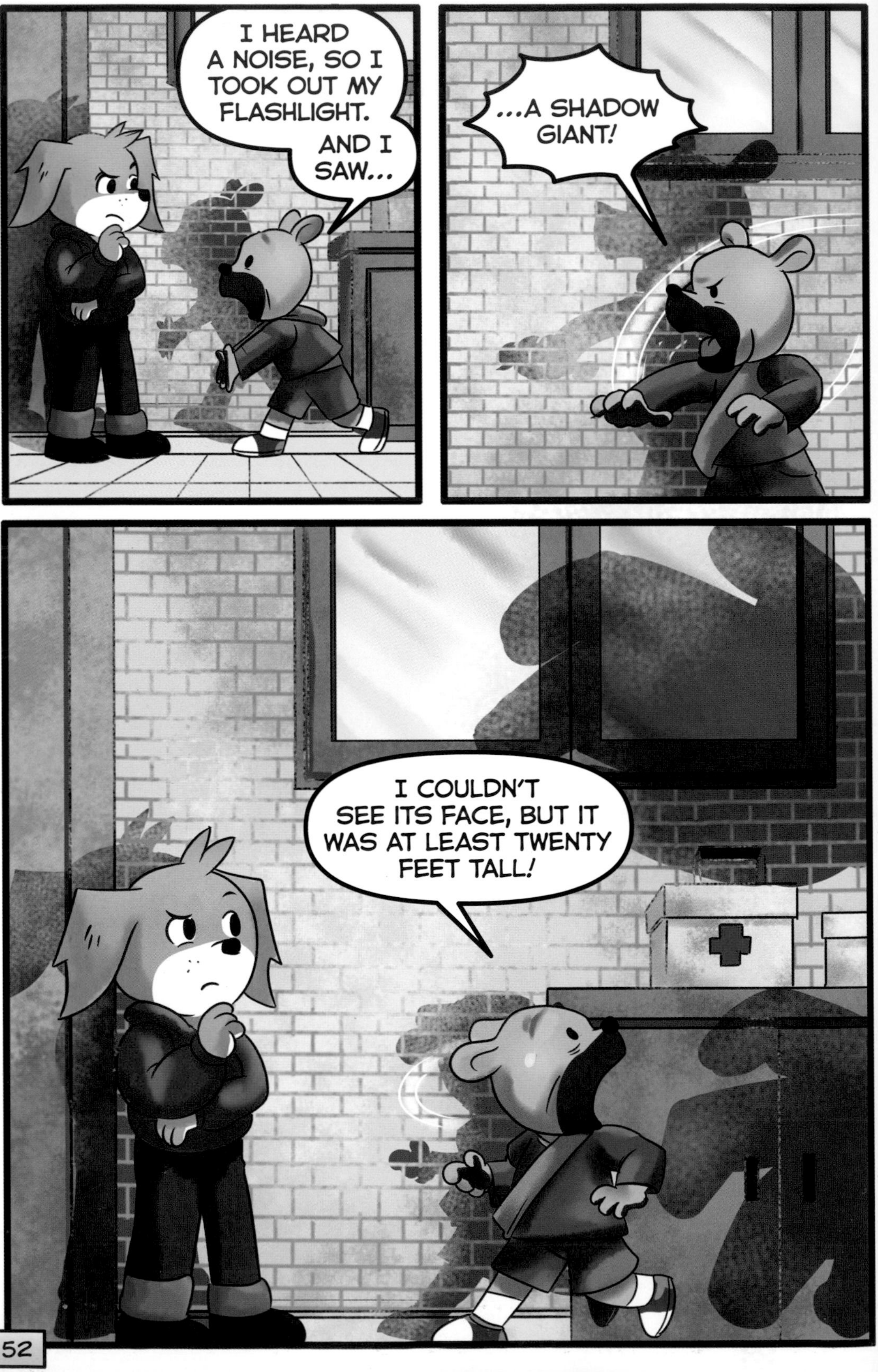
I HEARD A NOISE, SO I TOOK OUT MY FLASHLIGHT.
AND I SAW...
...A SHADOW GIANT!
I COULDN'T SEE ITS FACE, BUT IT WAS AT LEAST TWENTY FEET TALL!

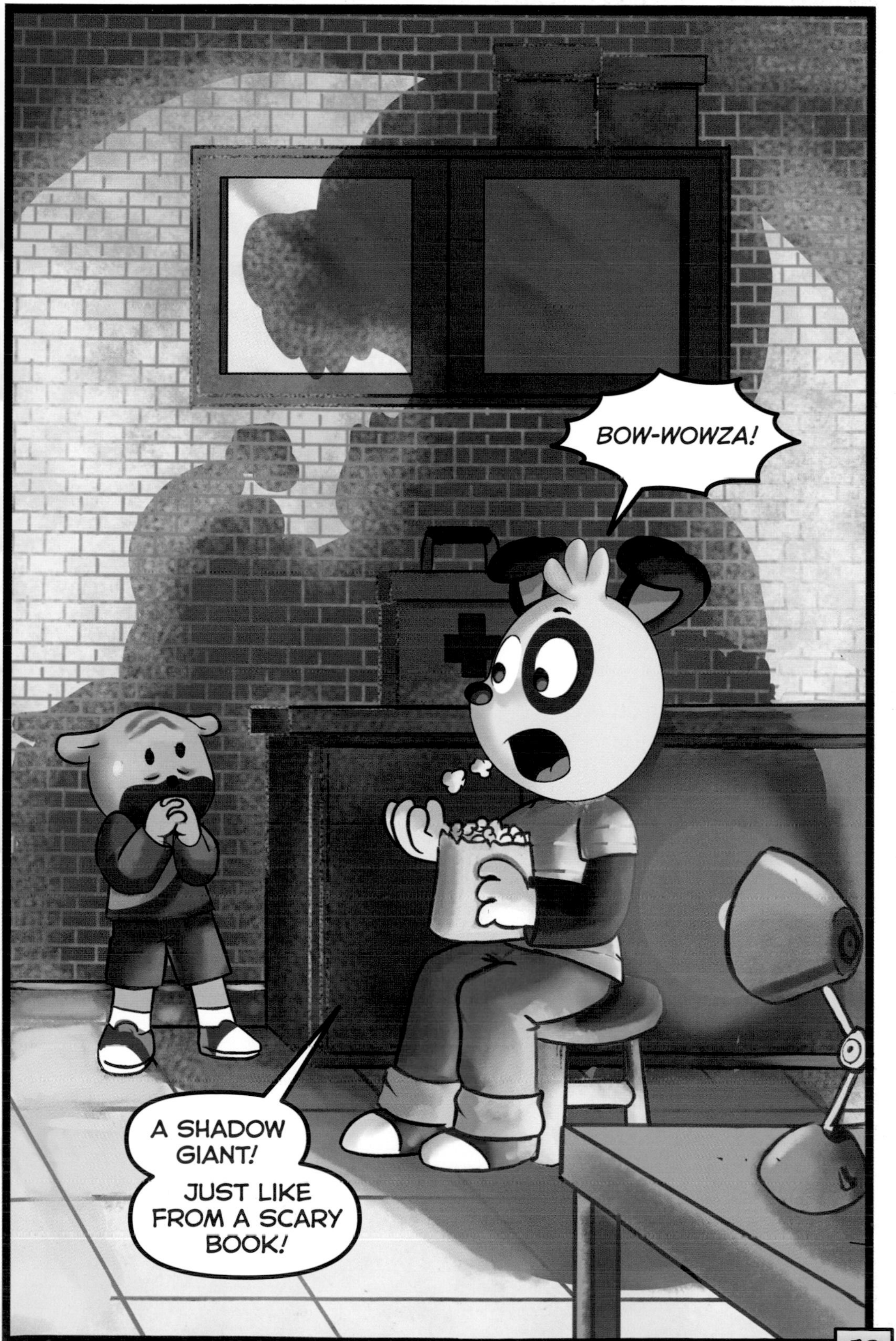
BOW-WOWZA!
A SHADOW GIANT! JUST LIKE FROM A SCARY BOOK!

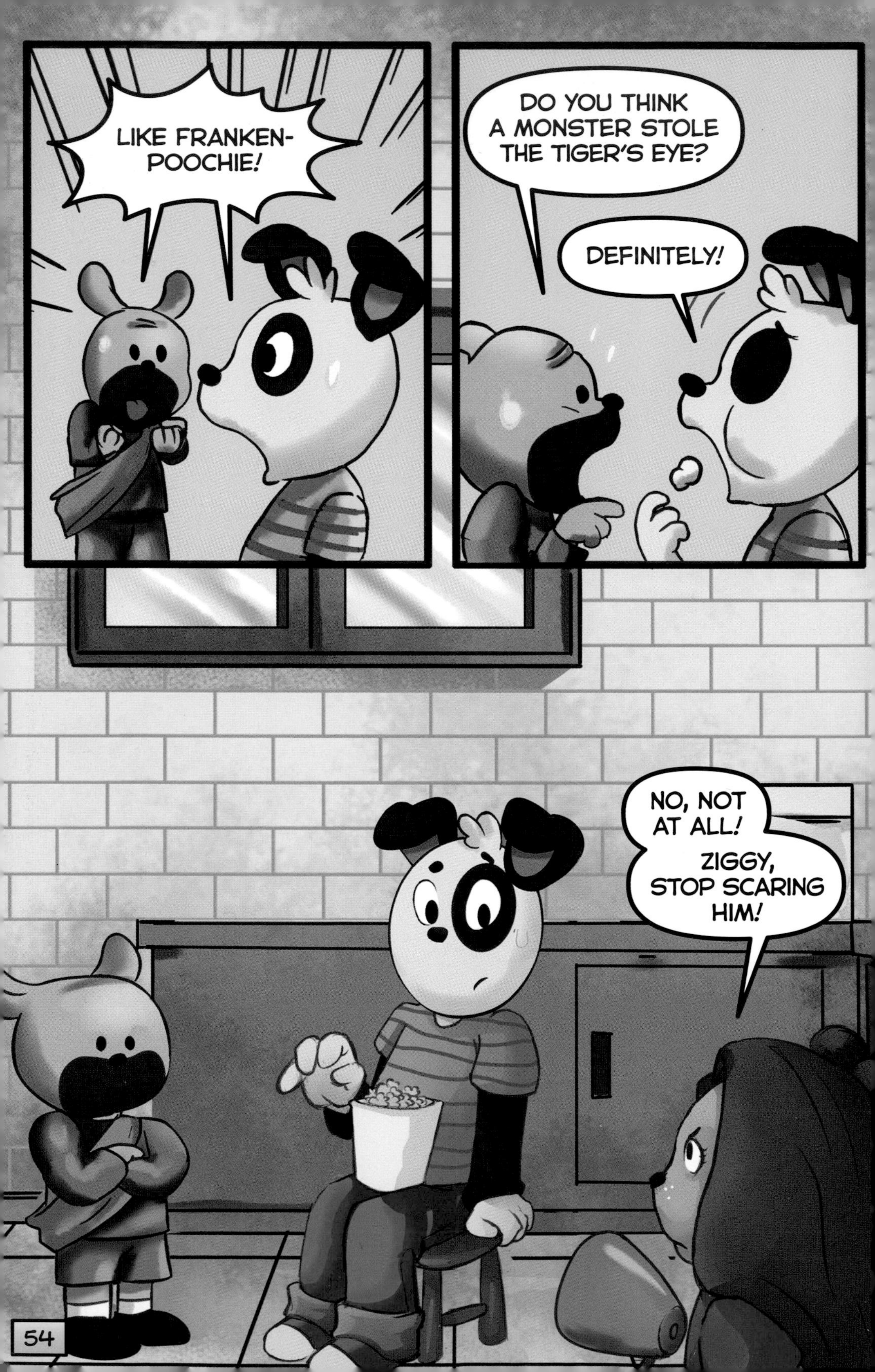
LIKE FRANKEN-POOCHIE!
DO YOU THINK A MONSTER STOLE THE TIGER'S EYE?
DEFINITELY!
NO, NOT AT ALL!
ZIGGY, STOP SCARING HIM!

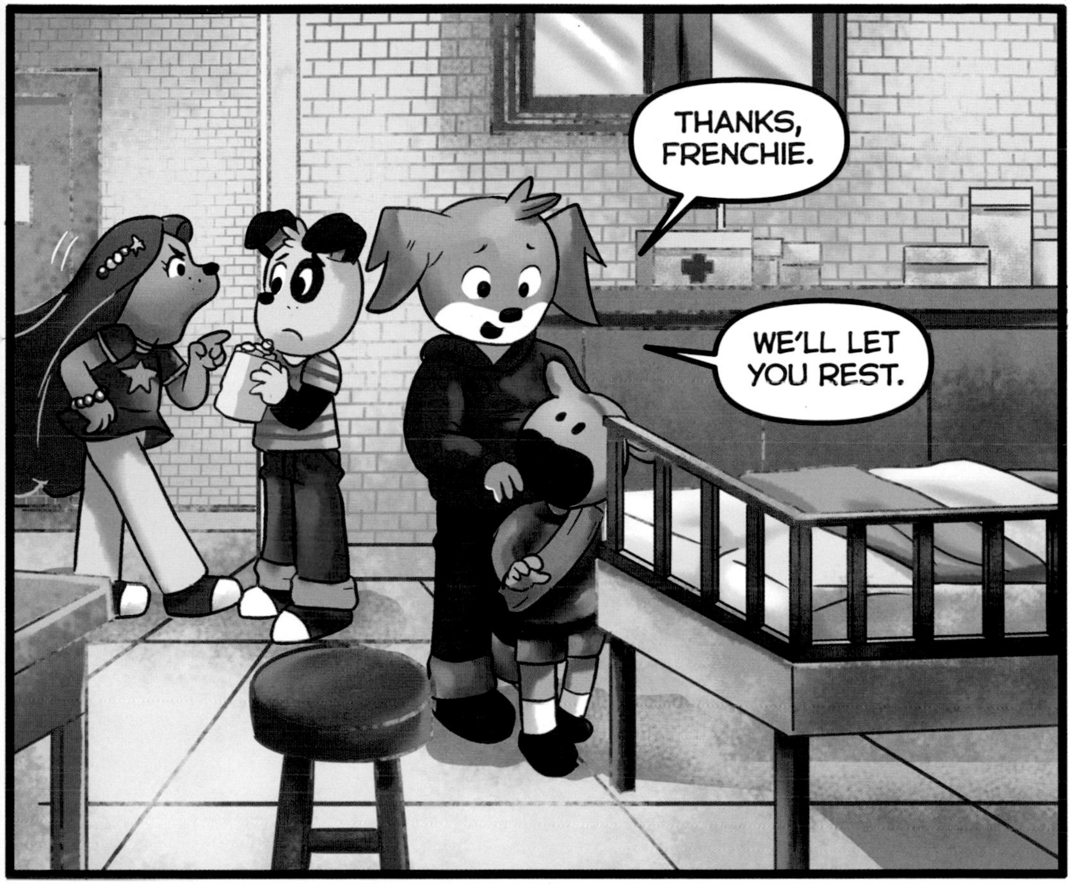
THANKS, FRENCHIE.
WE'LL LET YOU REST.

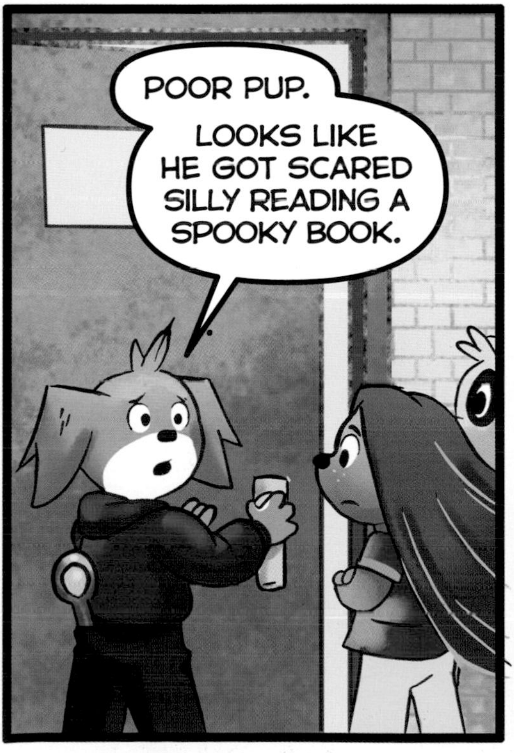
POOR PUP.
LOOKS LIKE HE GOT SCARED SILLY READING A SPOOKY BOOK.

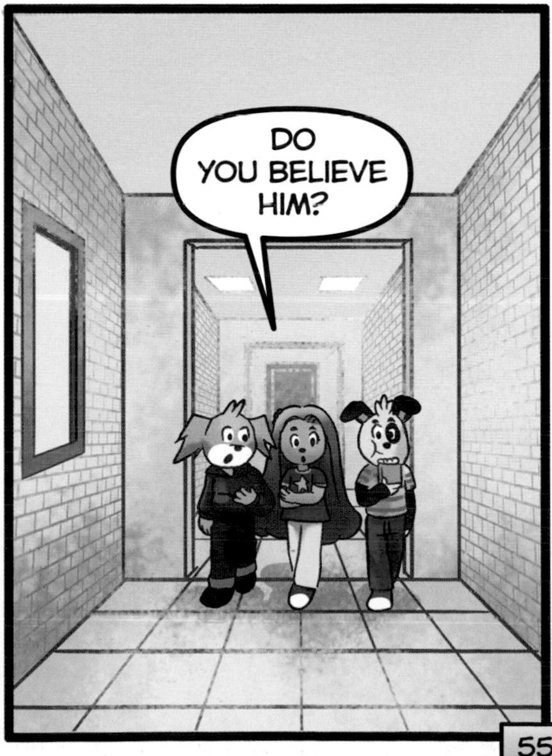
DO YOU BELIEVE HIM?

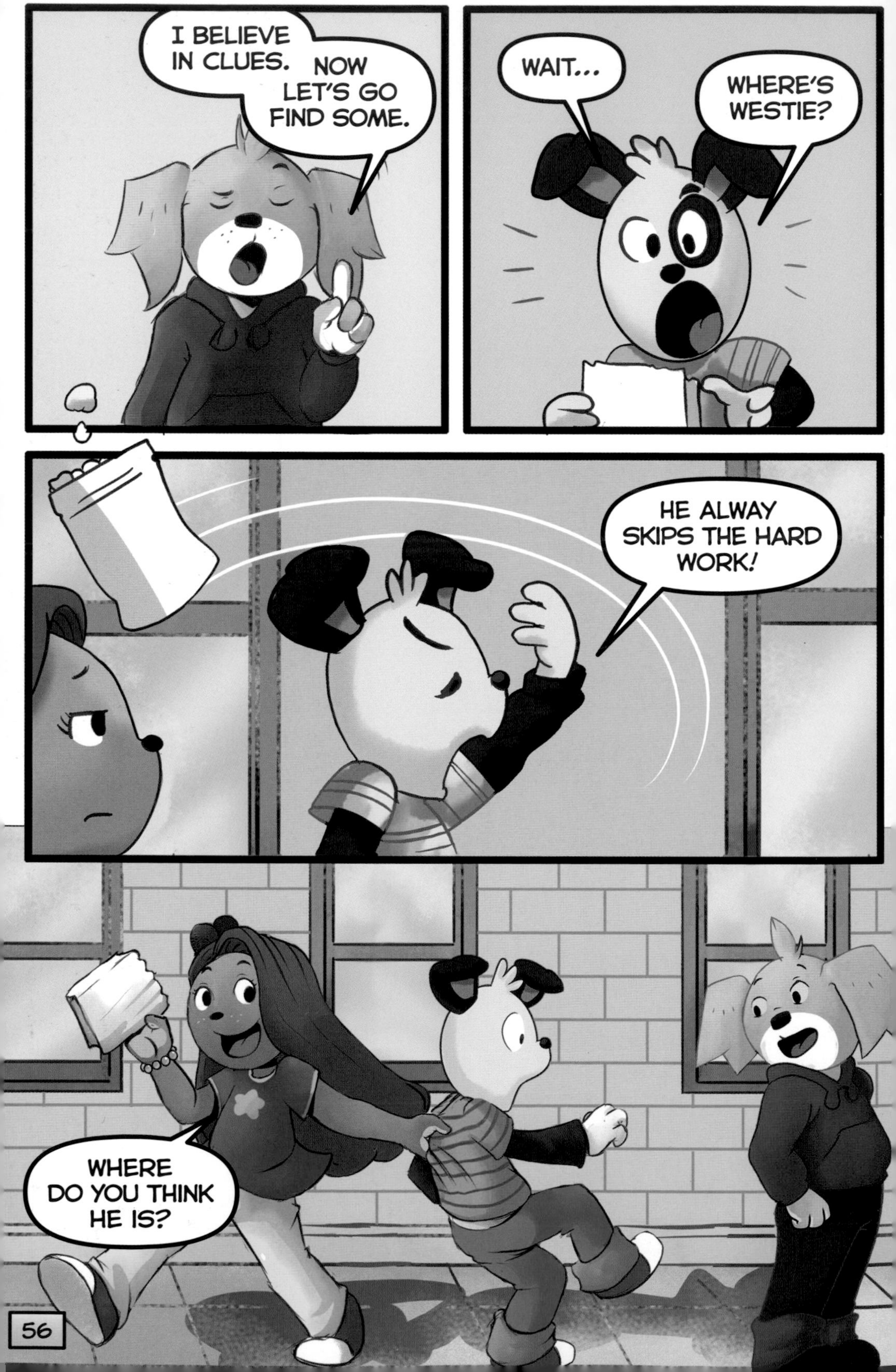

I BELIEVE IN CLUES.
NOW LET'S GO FIND SOME.
WAIT...
WHERE'S WESTIE?
HE ALWAY SKIPS THE HARD WORK!
WHERE DO YOU THINK HE IS?

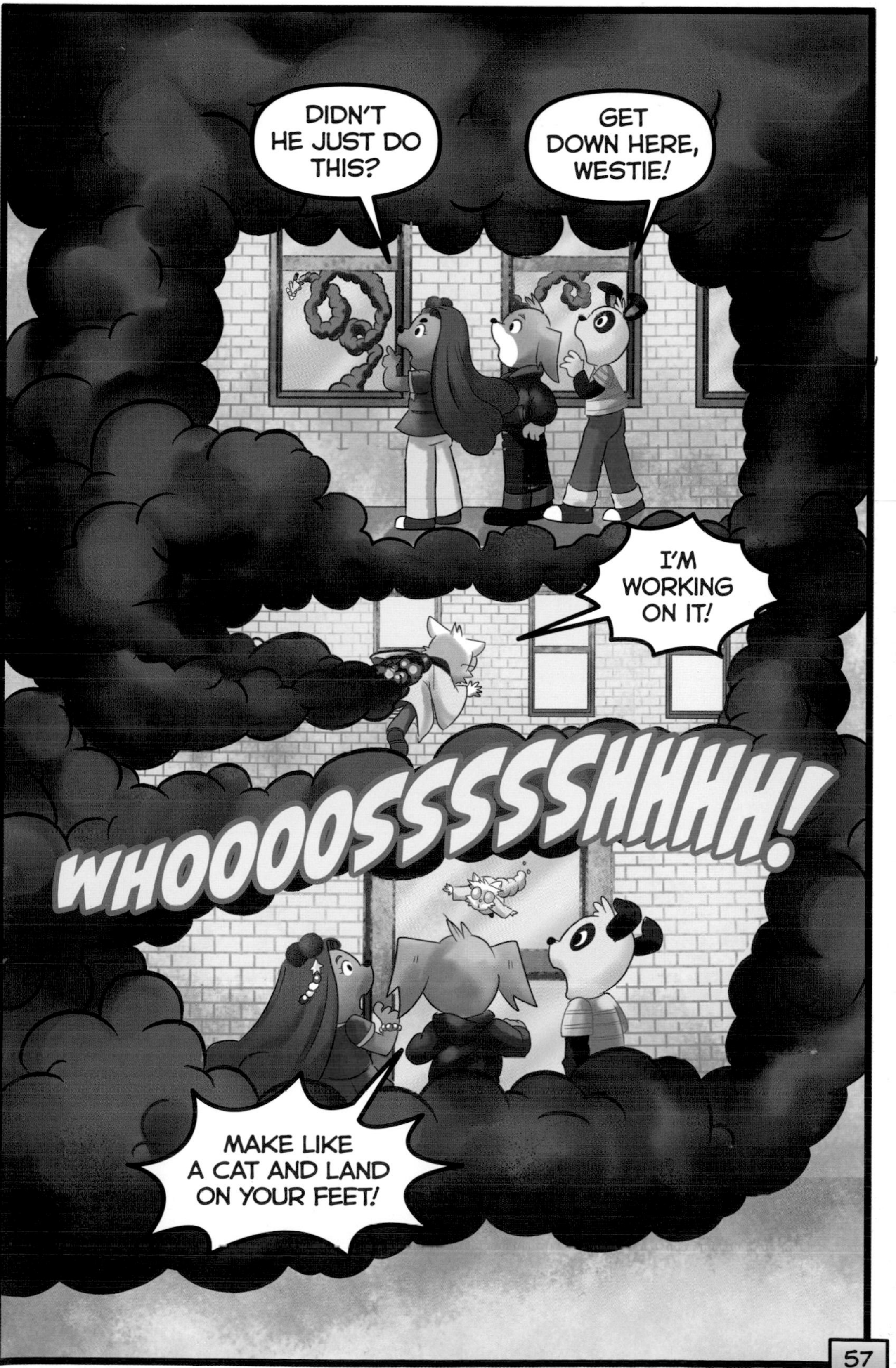
DIDN'T HE JUST DO THIS?
GET DOWN HERE, WESTIE!
I'M WORKING ON IT!
WHOOOOOSSSSSHHHHH!
MAKE LIKE A CAT AND LAND ON YOUR FEET!

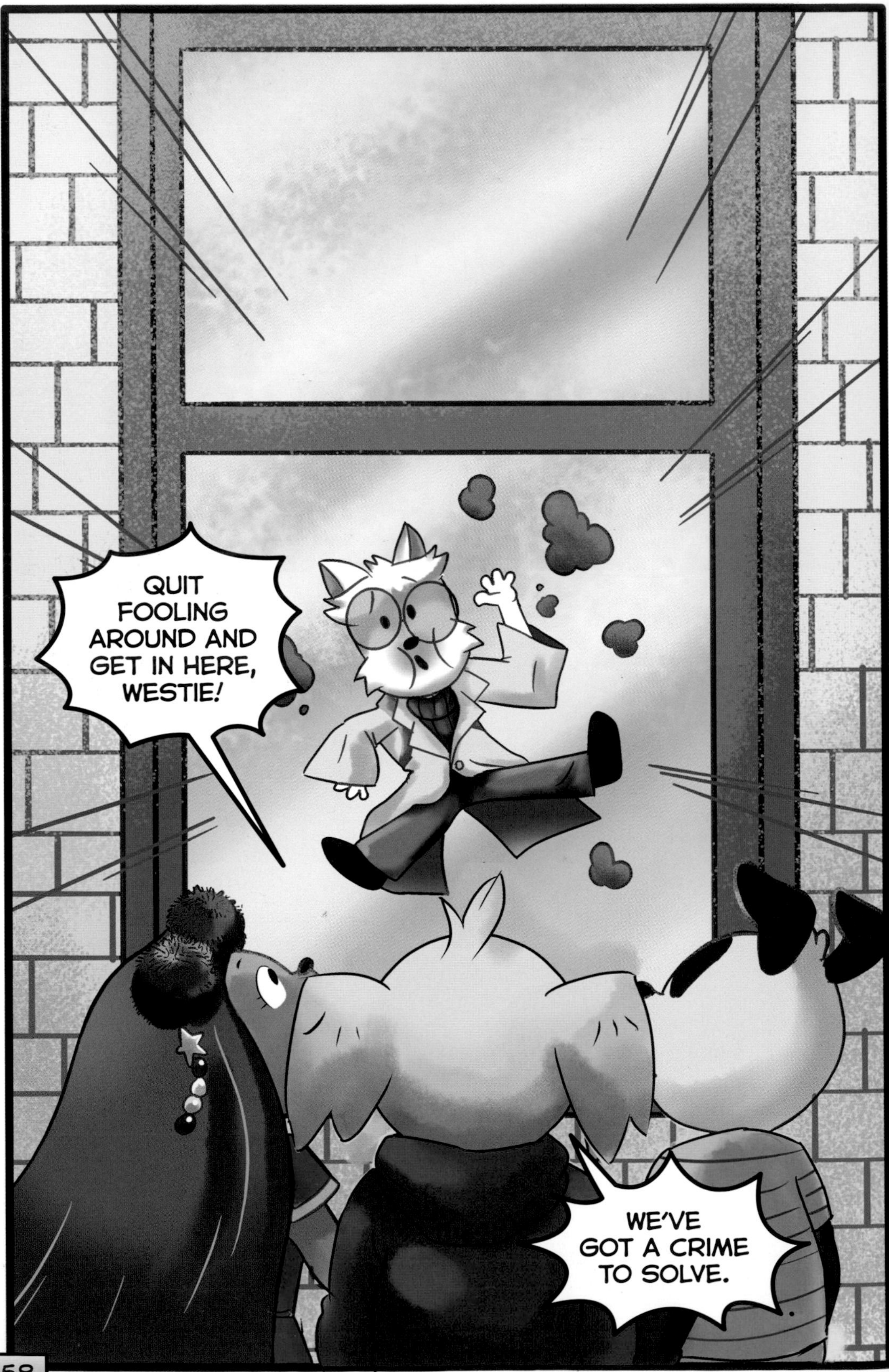
QUIT FOOLING AROUND AND GET IN HERE, WESTIE!
WE'VE GOT A CRIME TO SOLVE.

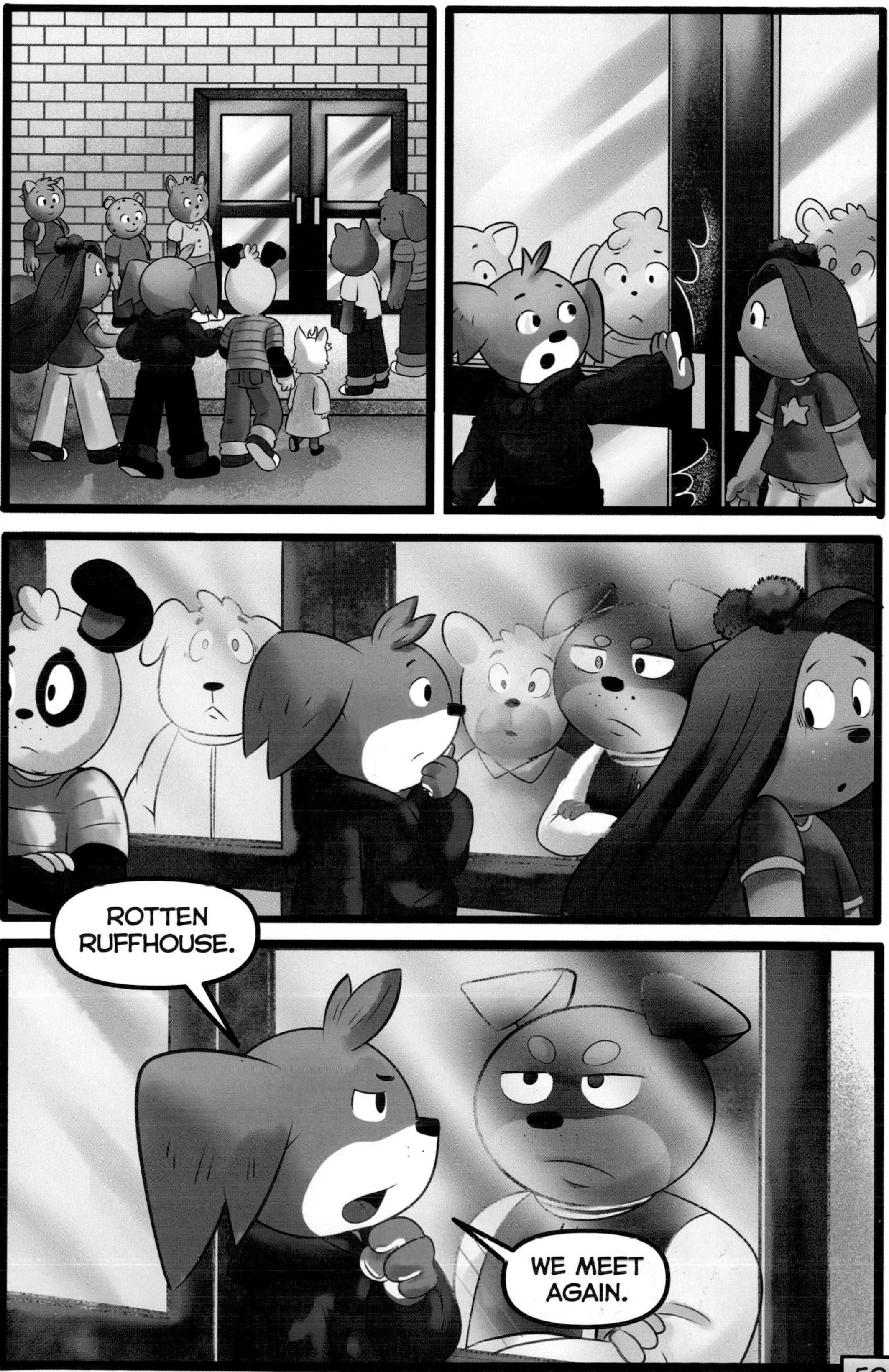
ROTTEN RUFFHOUSE.
WE MEET AGAIN.

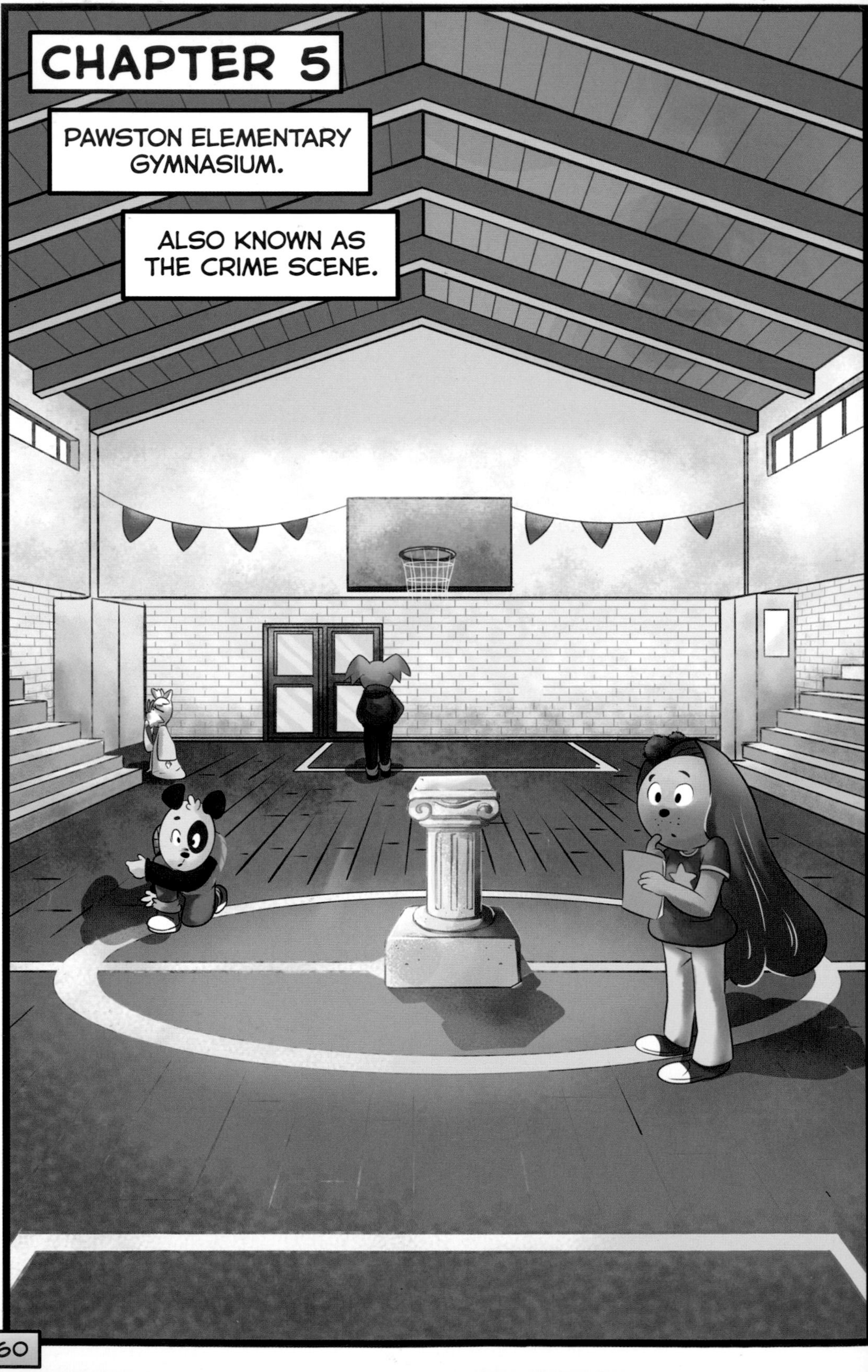
CHAPTER 5
PAWSTON ELEMENTARY GYMNASIUM.
ALSO KNOWN AS THE CRIME SCENE.

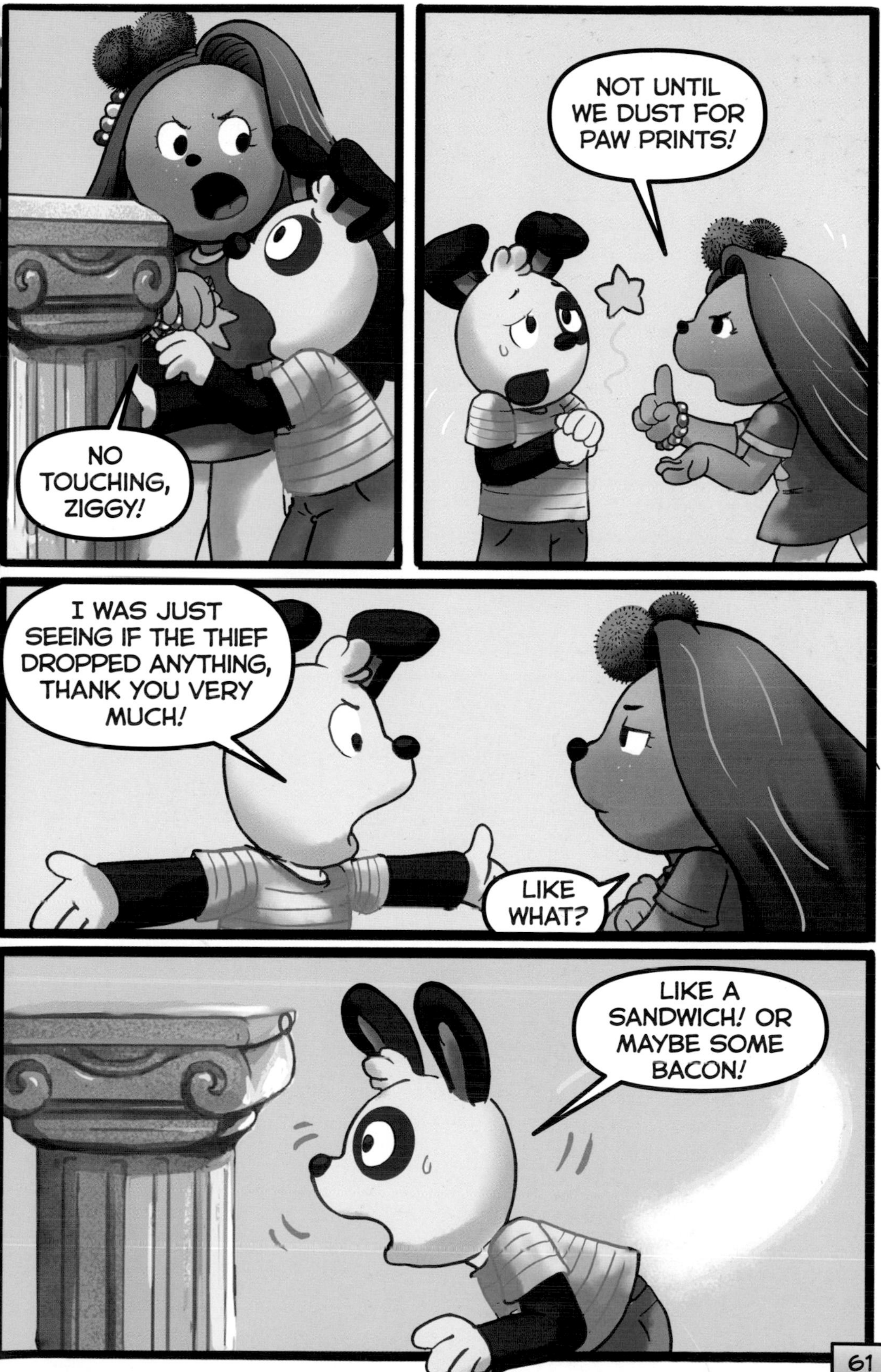
NO TOUCHING, ZIGGY!
NOT UNTIL WE DUST FOR PAW PRINTS!
I WAS JUST SEEING IF THE THIEF DROPPED ANYTHING, THANK YOU VERY MUCH!
LIKE WHAT?
LIKE A SANDWICH! OR MAYBE SOME BACON!

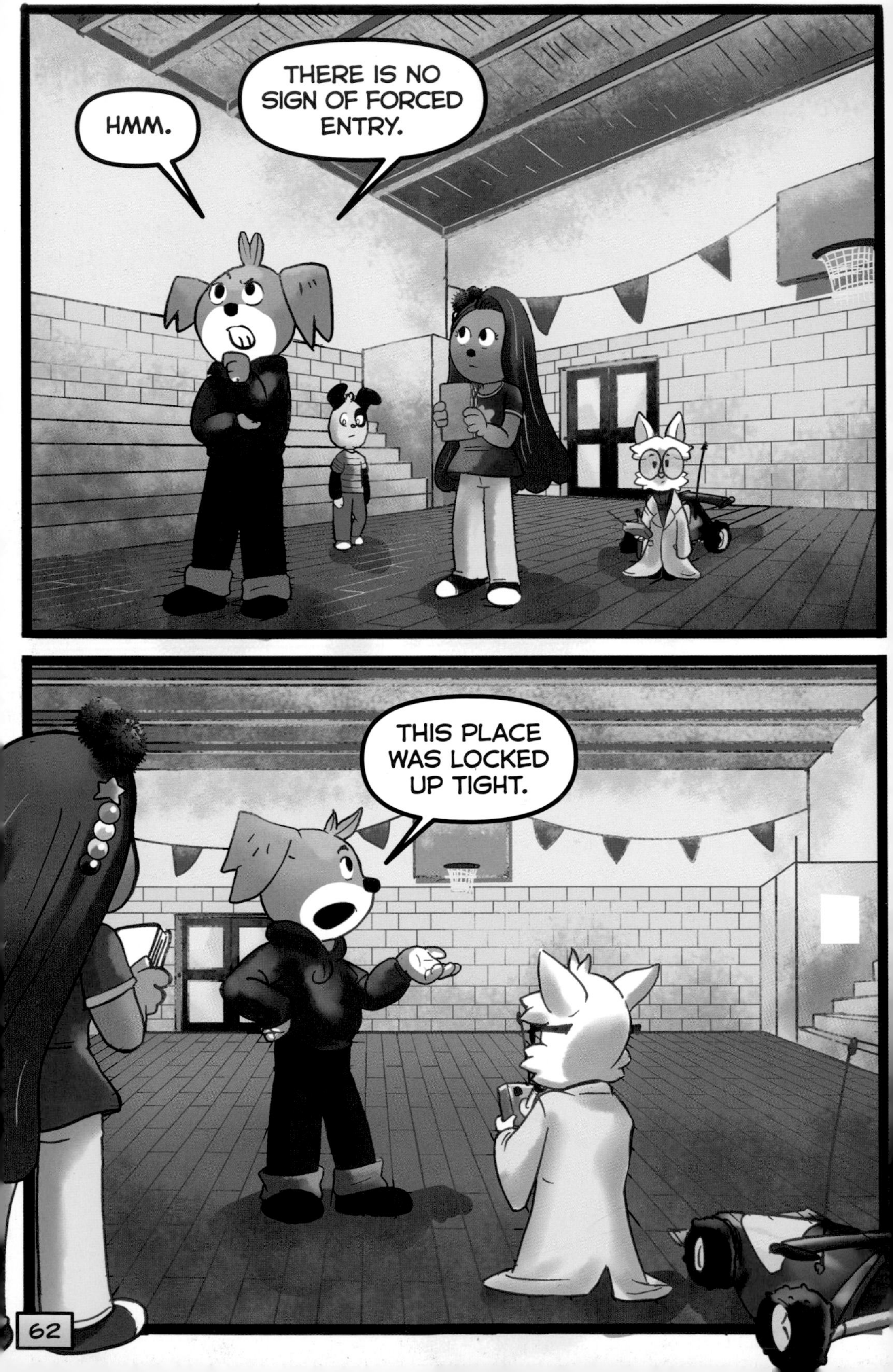
HMM.
THERE IS NO SIGN OF FORCED ENTRY.
THIS PLACE WAS LOCKED UP TIGHT.

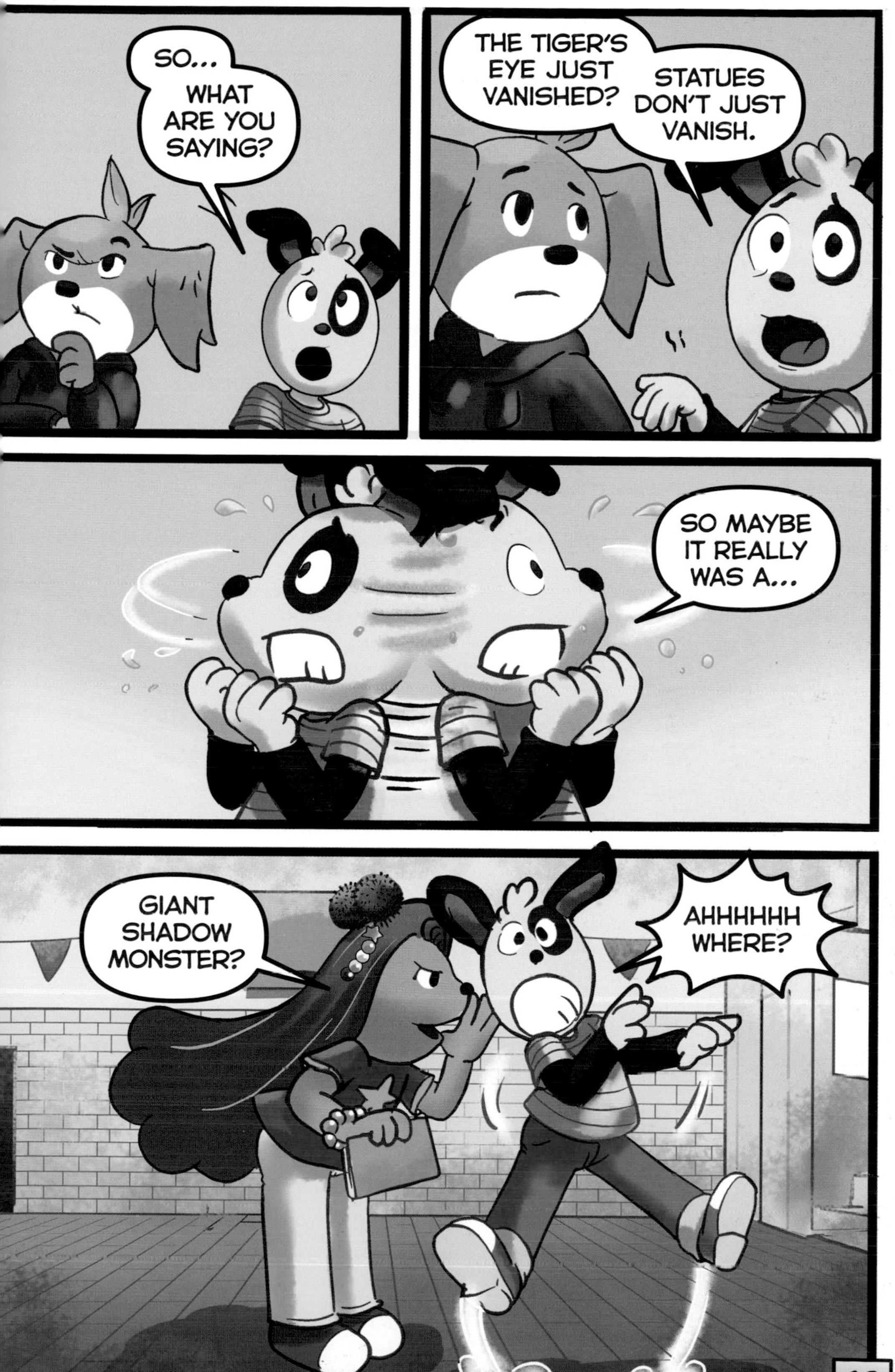
SO... WHAT ARE YOU SAYING?
THE TIGER'S EYE JUST VANISHED?
STATUES DON'T JUST VANISH.
SO MAYBE IT REALLY WAS A...
GIANT SHADOW MONSTER?
AHHHHHH WHERE?

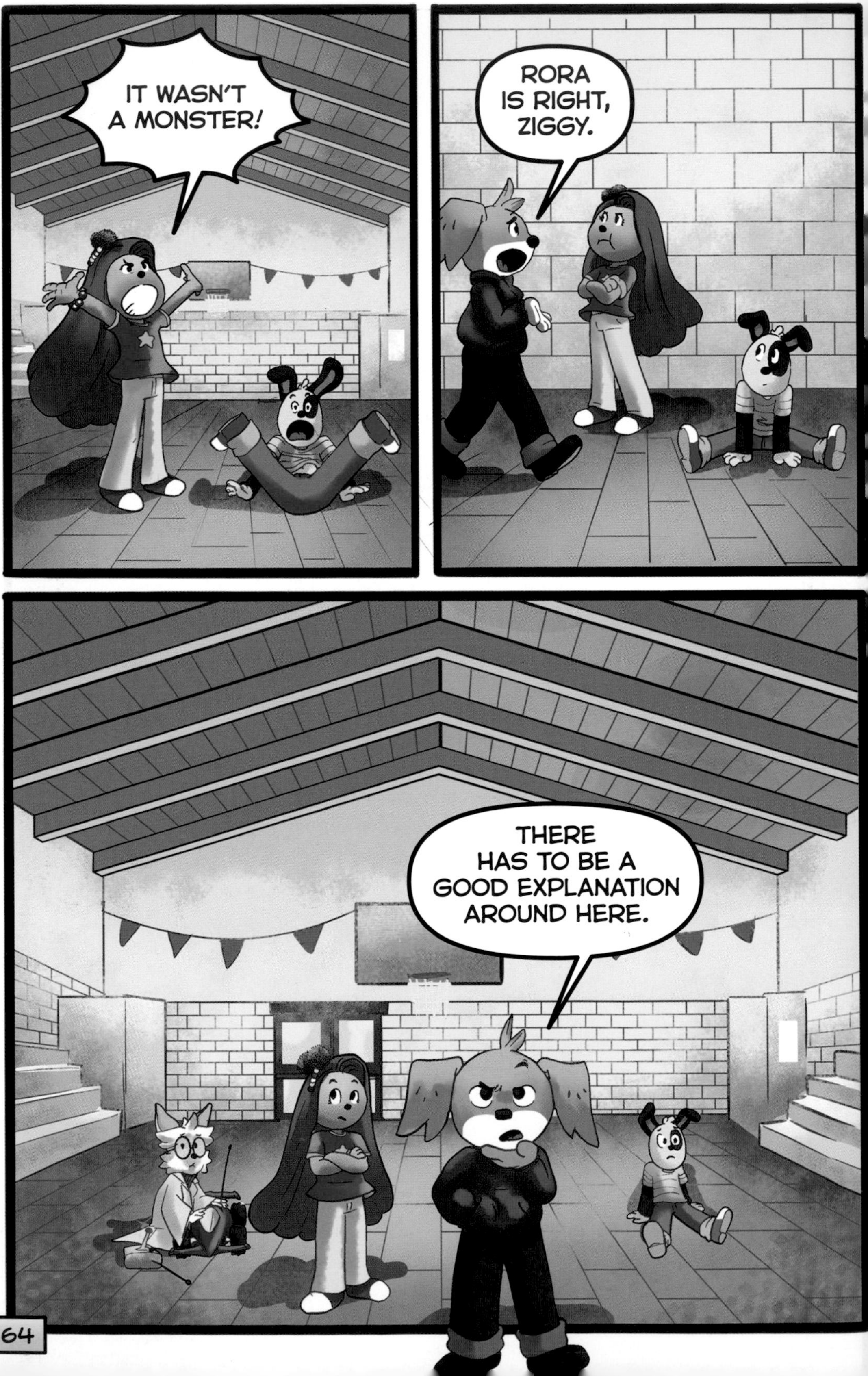
IT WASN'T A MONSTER!
RORA IS RIGHT, ZIGGY.
THERE HAS TO BE A GOOD EXPLANATION AROUND HERE.

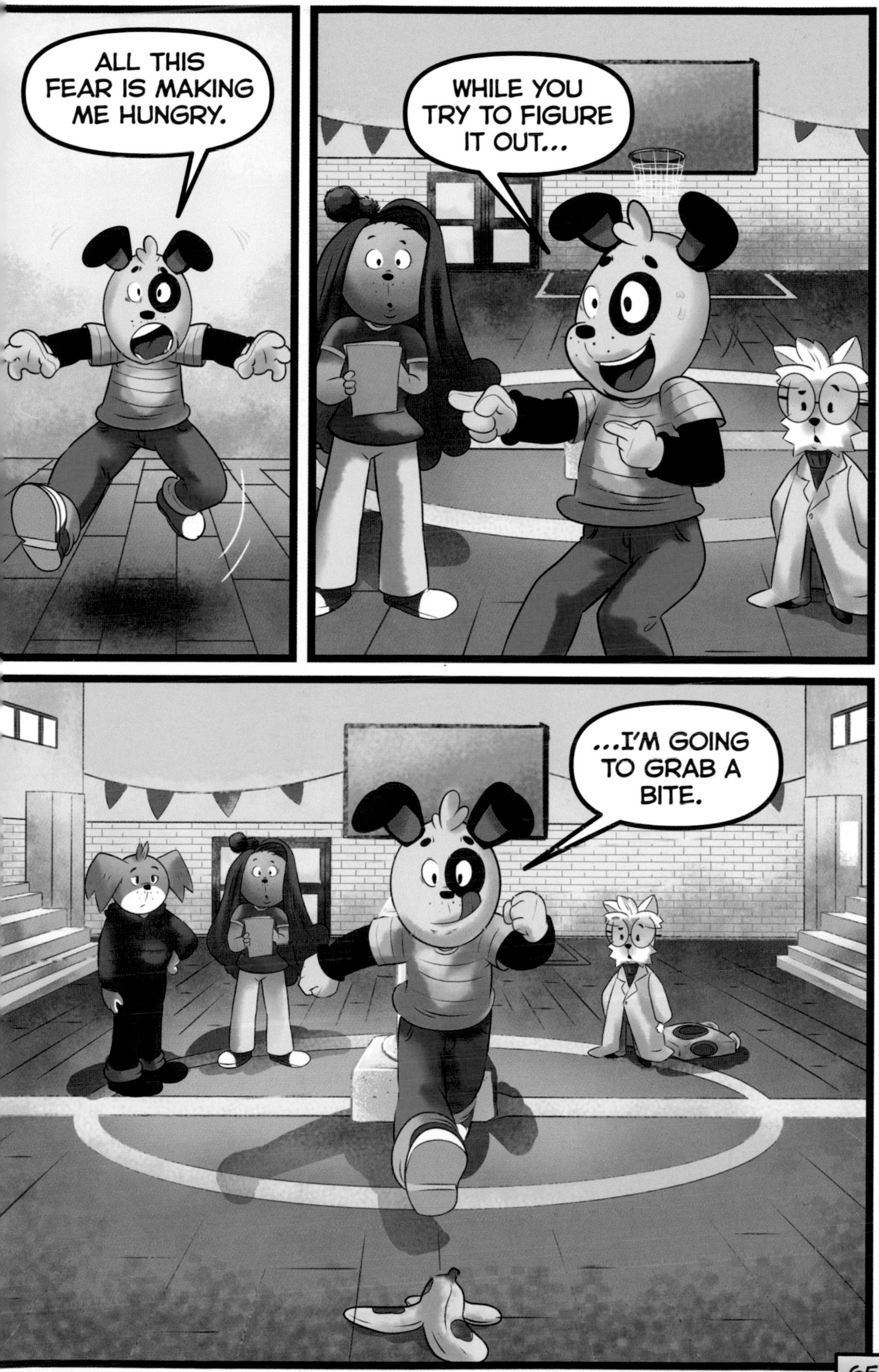
ALL THIS FEAR IS MAKING ME HUNGRY.
WHILE YOU TRY TO FIGURE IT OUT...
...I'M GOING TO GRAB A BITE.

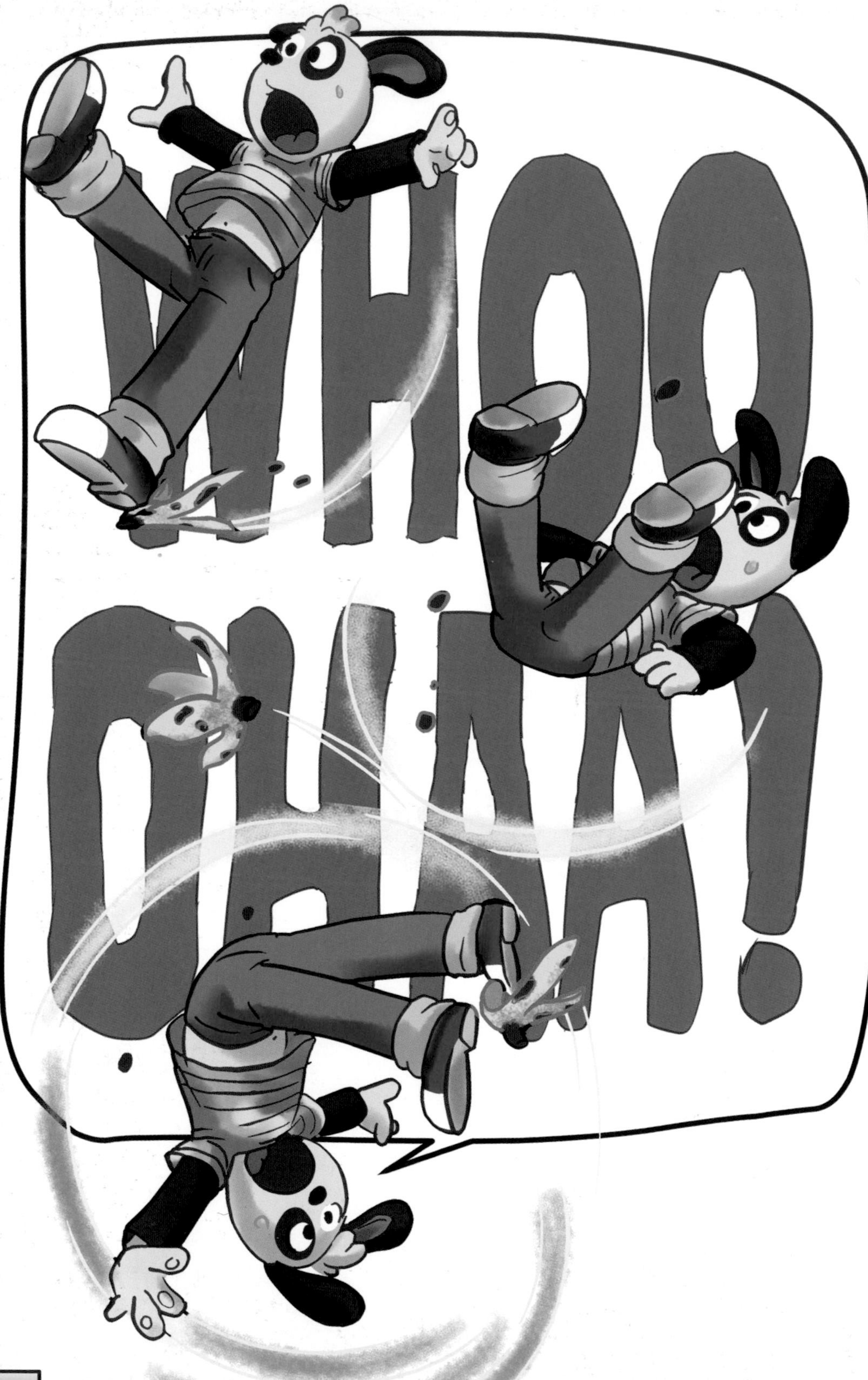
WHOO OAAA!

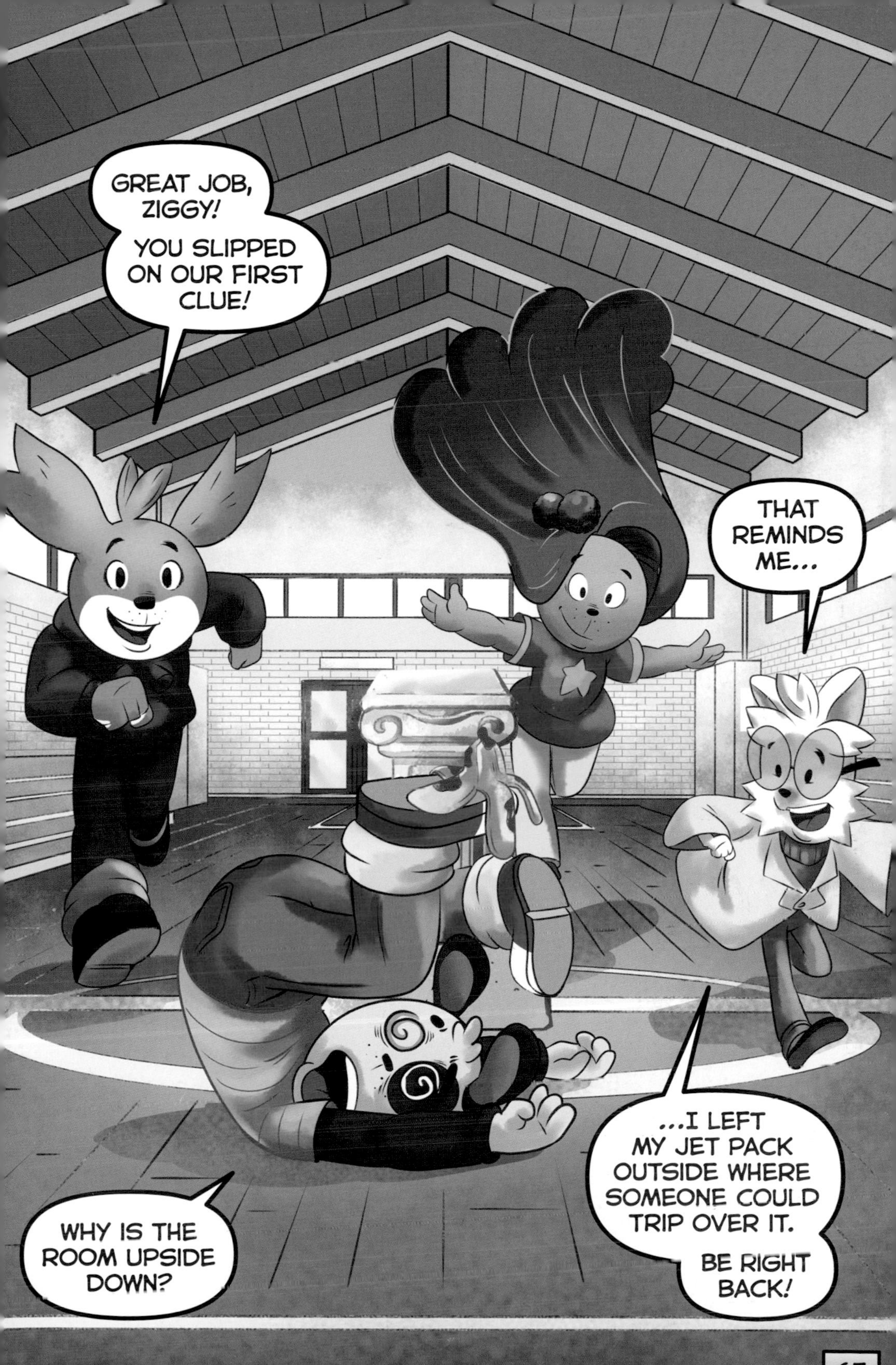
GREAT JOB, ZIGGY!
YOU SLIPPED ON OUR FIRST CLUE!
THAT REMINDS ME...
...I LEFT MY JET PACK OUTSIDE WHERE SOMEONE COULD TRIP OVER IT.
BE RIGHT BACK!
WHY IS THE ROOM UPSIDE DOWN?

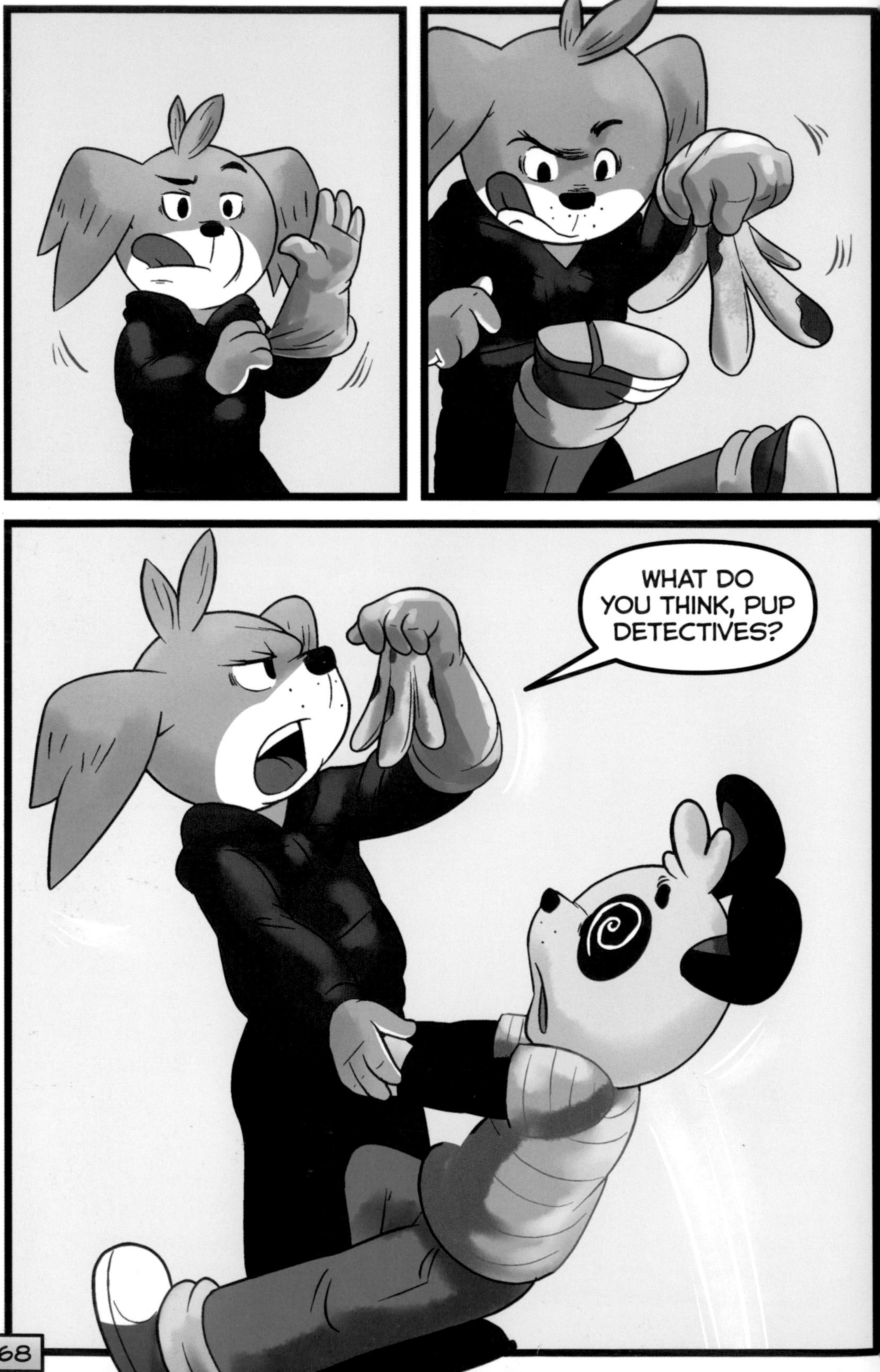
WHAT DO YOU THINK, PUP DETECTIVES?

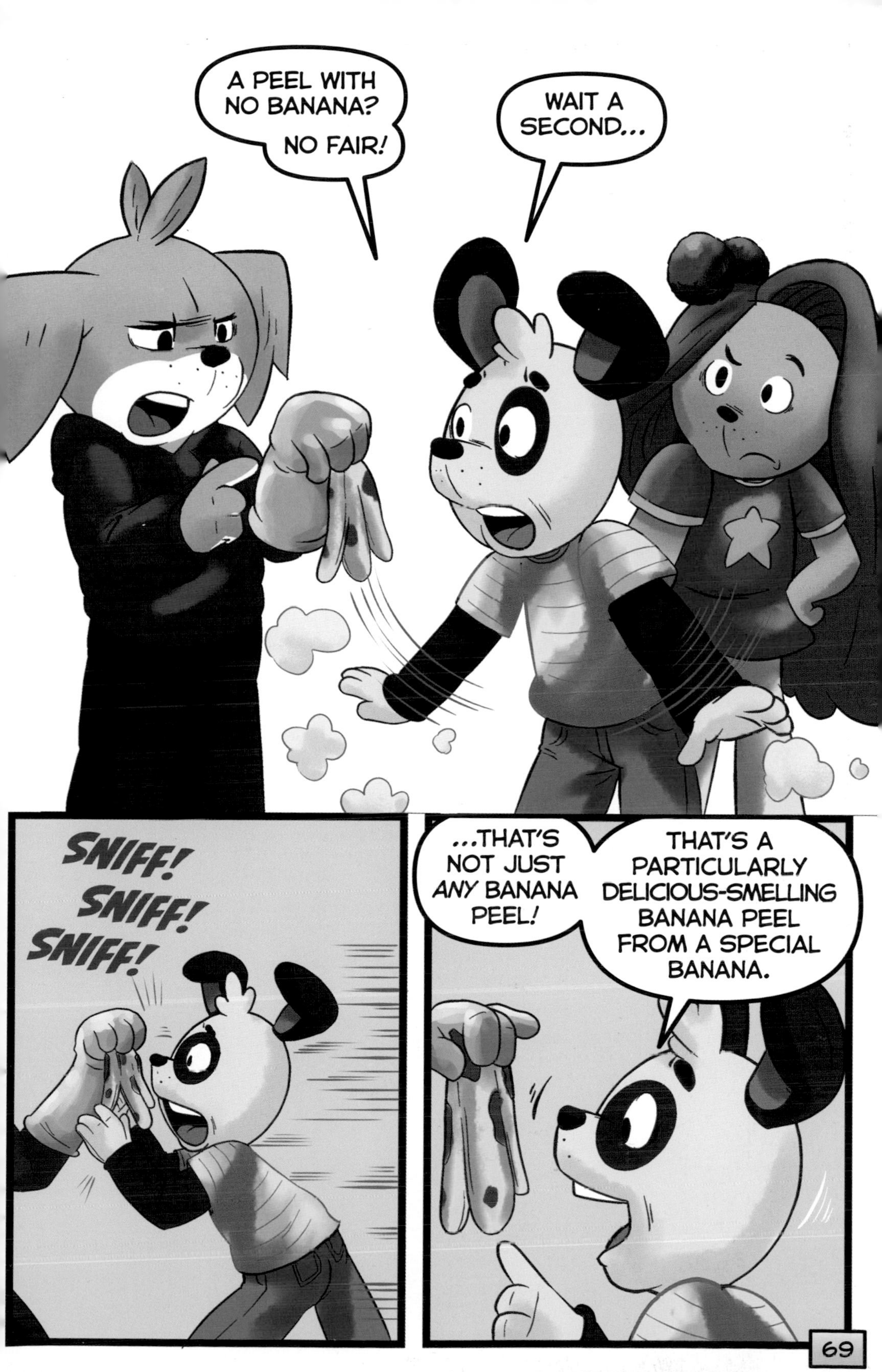
A PEEL WITH NO BANANA?
NO FAIR!
WAIT A SECOND...
SNIFF!
SNIFF!
SNIFF!
...THAT'S NOT JUST *ANY* BANANA PEEL!
THAT'S A PARTICULARLY DELICIOUS-SMELLING BANANA PEEL FROM A SPECIAL BANANA.

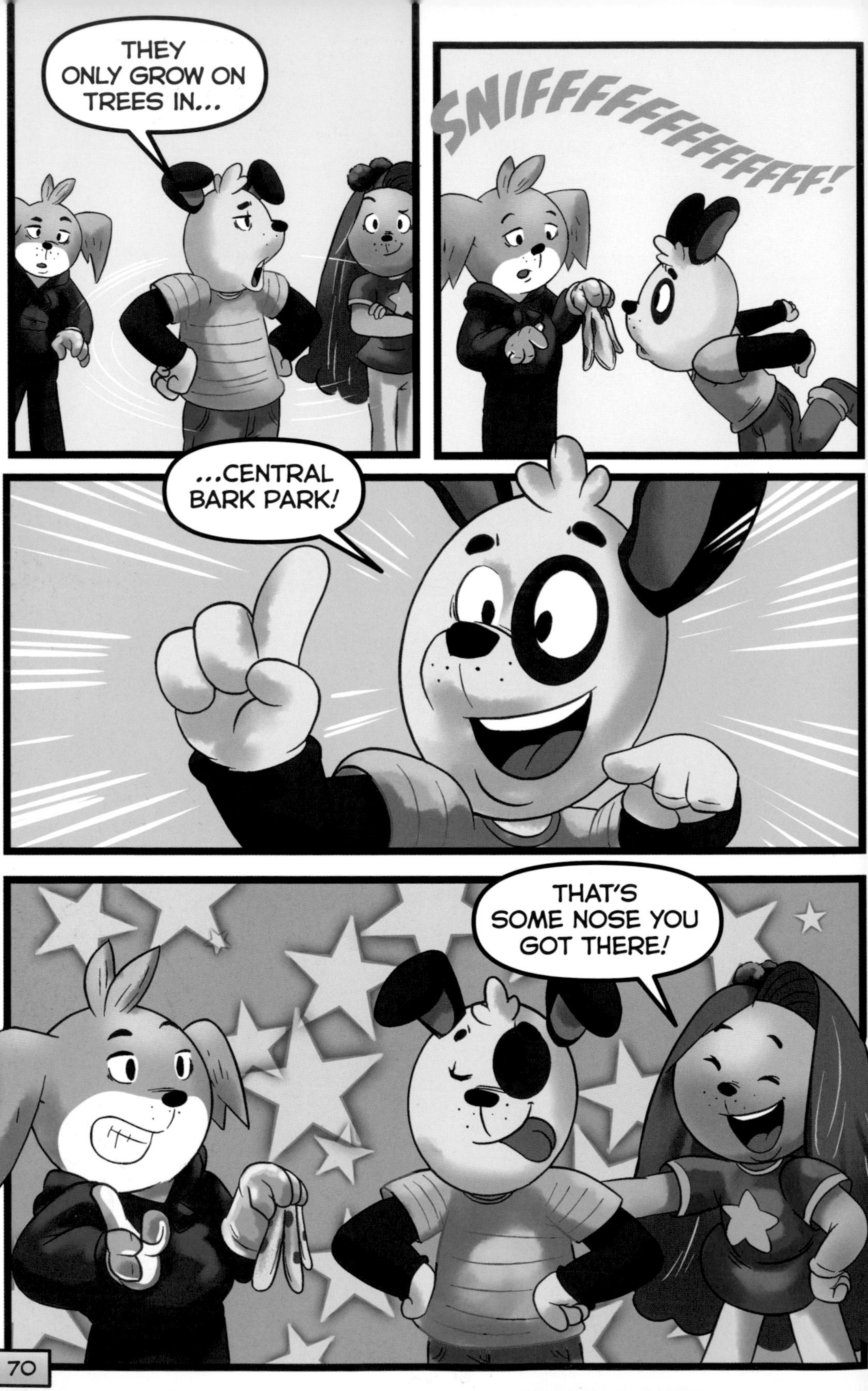
THEY ONLY GROW ON TREES IN...
SNIFFFFFFFFFFFFFF!
...CENTRAL BARK PARK!
THAT'S SOME NOSE YOU GOT THERE!

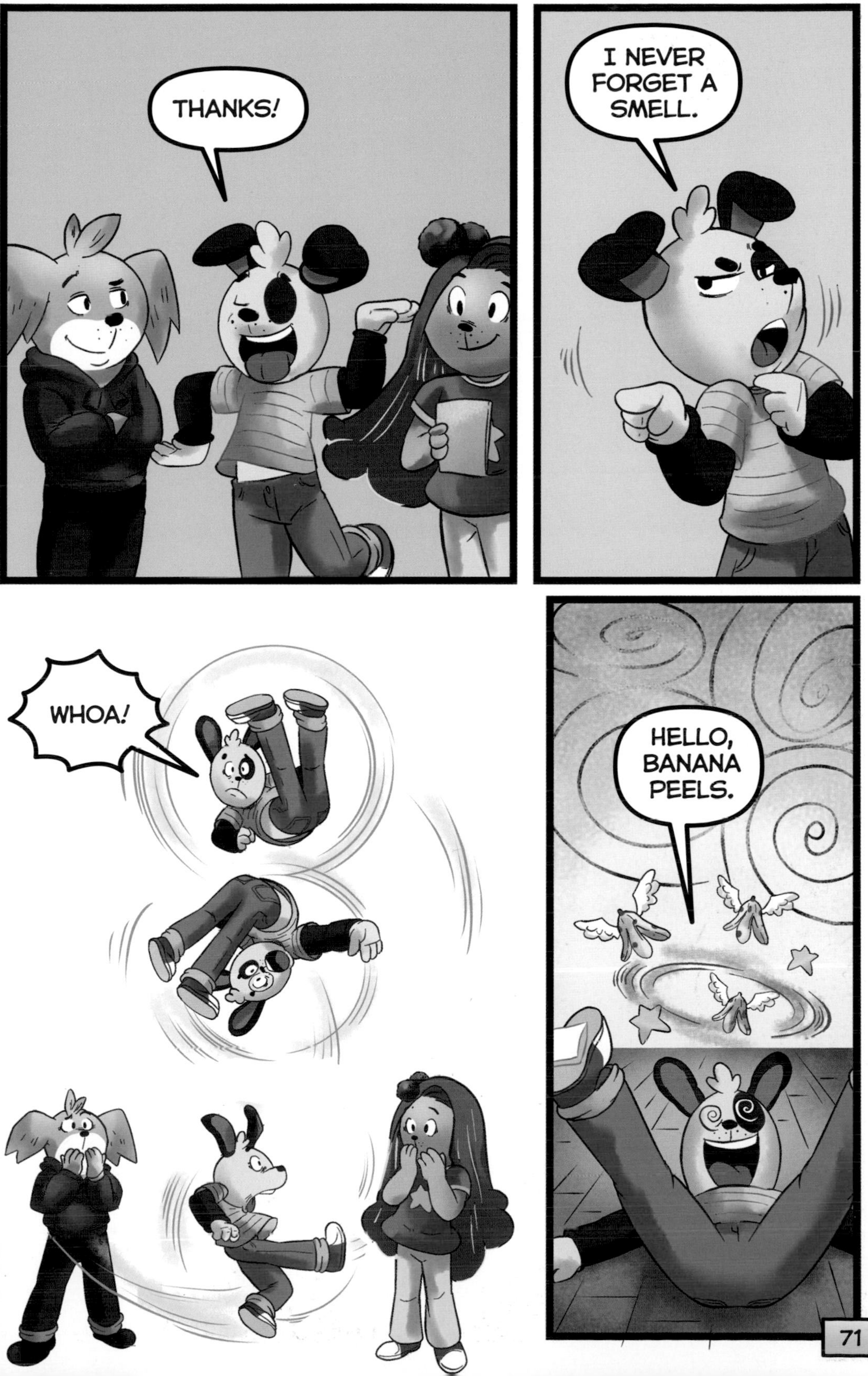
THANKS!
I NEVER FORGET A SMELL.
WHOA!
HELLO, BANANA PEELS.

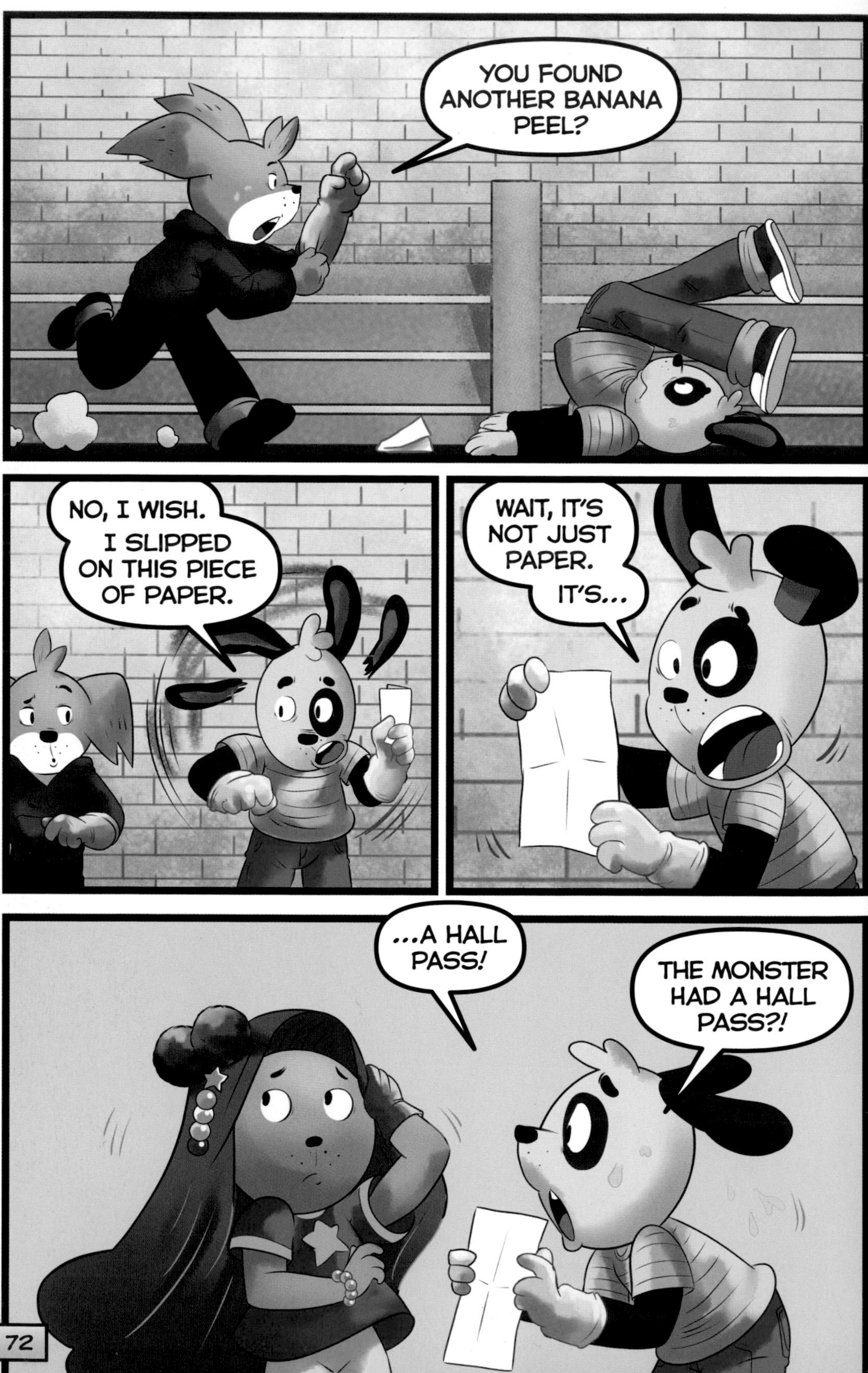
YOU FOUND ANOTHER BANANA PEEL?
NO, I WISH.
I SLIPPED ON THIS PIECE OF PAPER.
WAIT, IT'S NOT JUST PAPER.
IT'S...
...A HALL PASS!
THE MONSTER HAD A HALL PASS?!

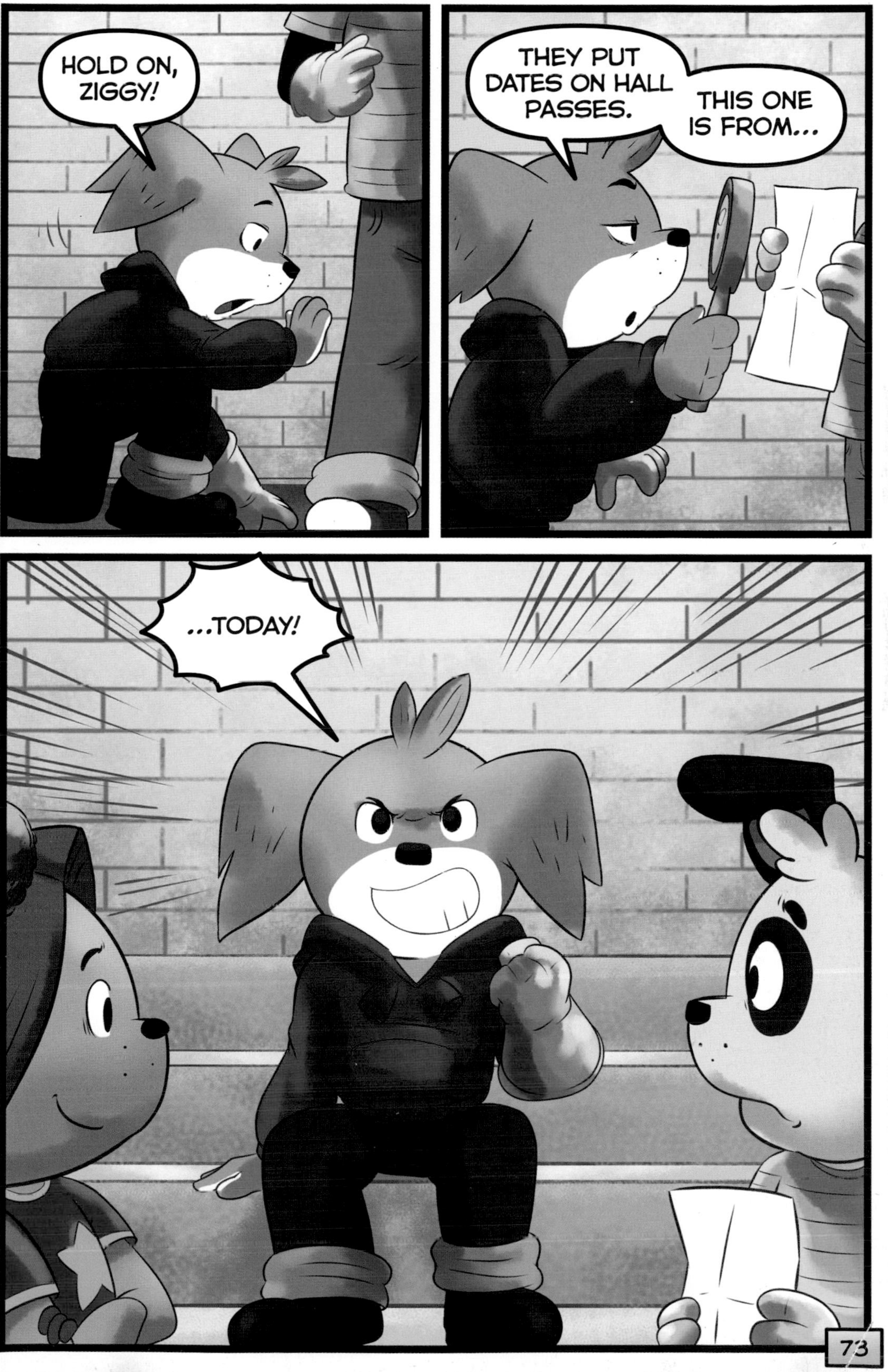
HOLD ON, ZIGGY!
THEY PUT DATES ON HALL PASSES.
THIS ONE IS FROM...
...TODAY!

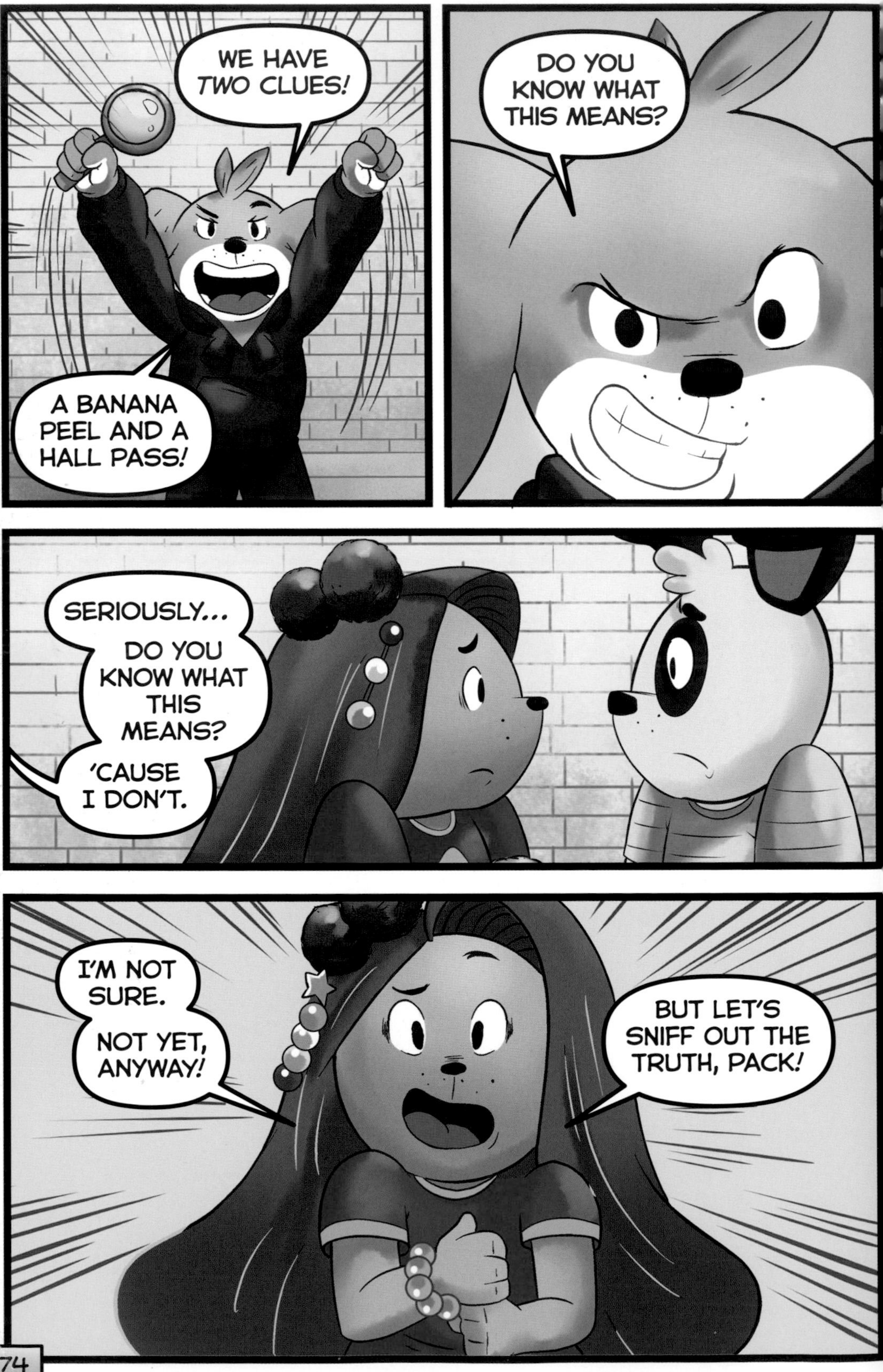
WE HAVE TWO CLUES!
A BANANA PEEL AND A HALL PASS!
DO YOU KNOW WHAT THIS MEANS?
SERIOUSLY...
DO YOU KNOW WHAT THIS MEANS?
'CAUSE I DON'T.
I'M NOT SURE.
NOT YET, ANYWAY!
BUT LET'S SNIFF OUT THE TRUTH, PACK!

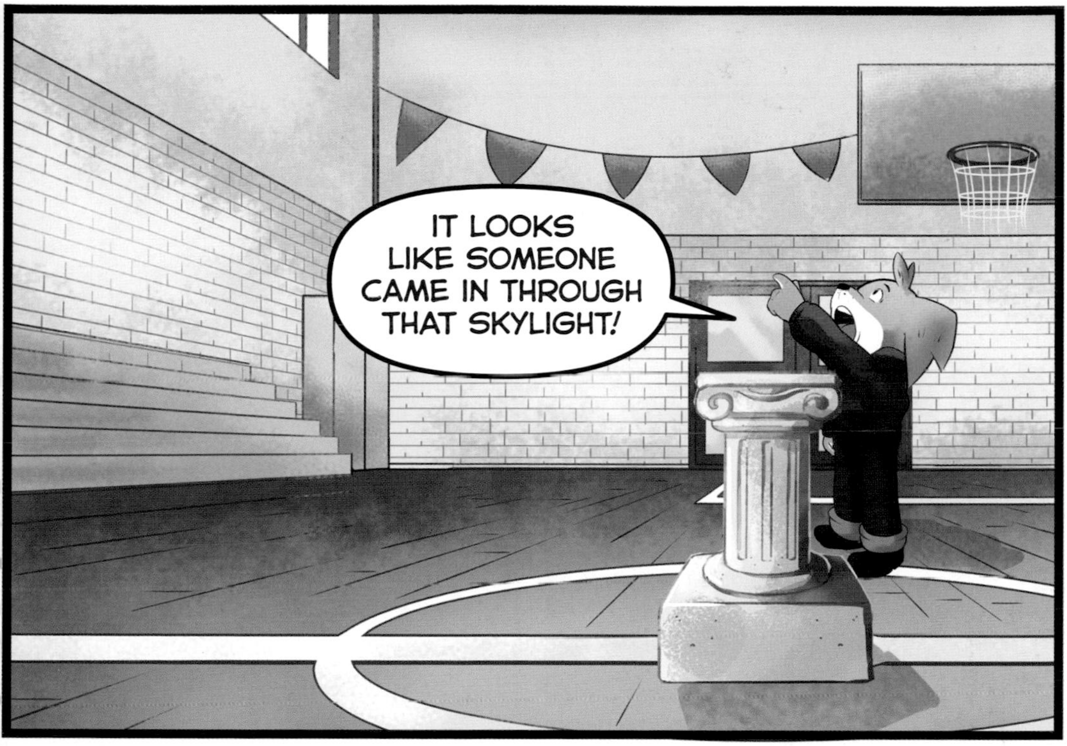
IT LOOKS LIKE SOMEONE CAME IN THROUGH THAT SKYLIGHT!

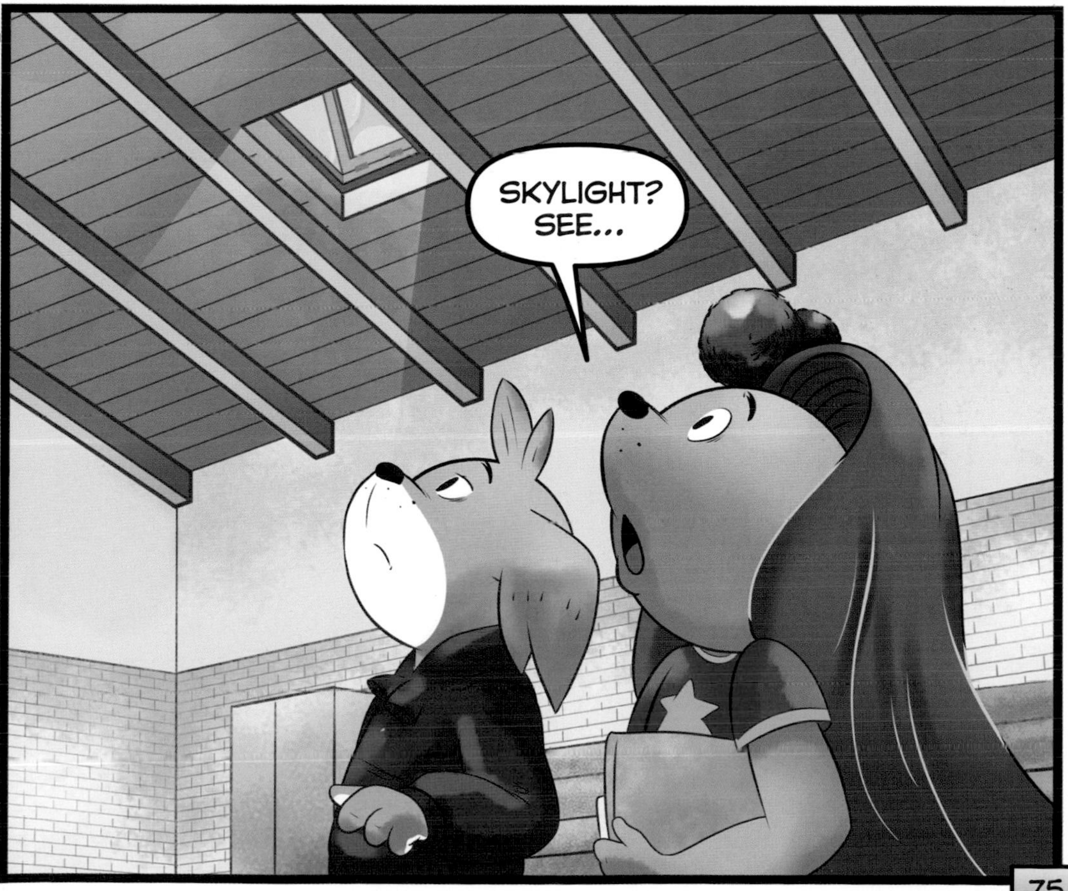
SKYLIGHT? SEE...

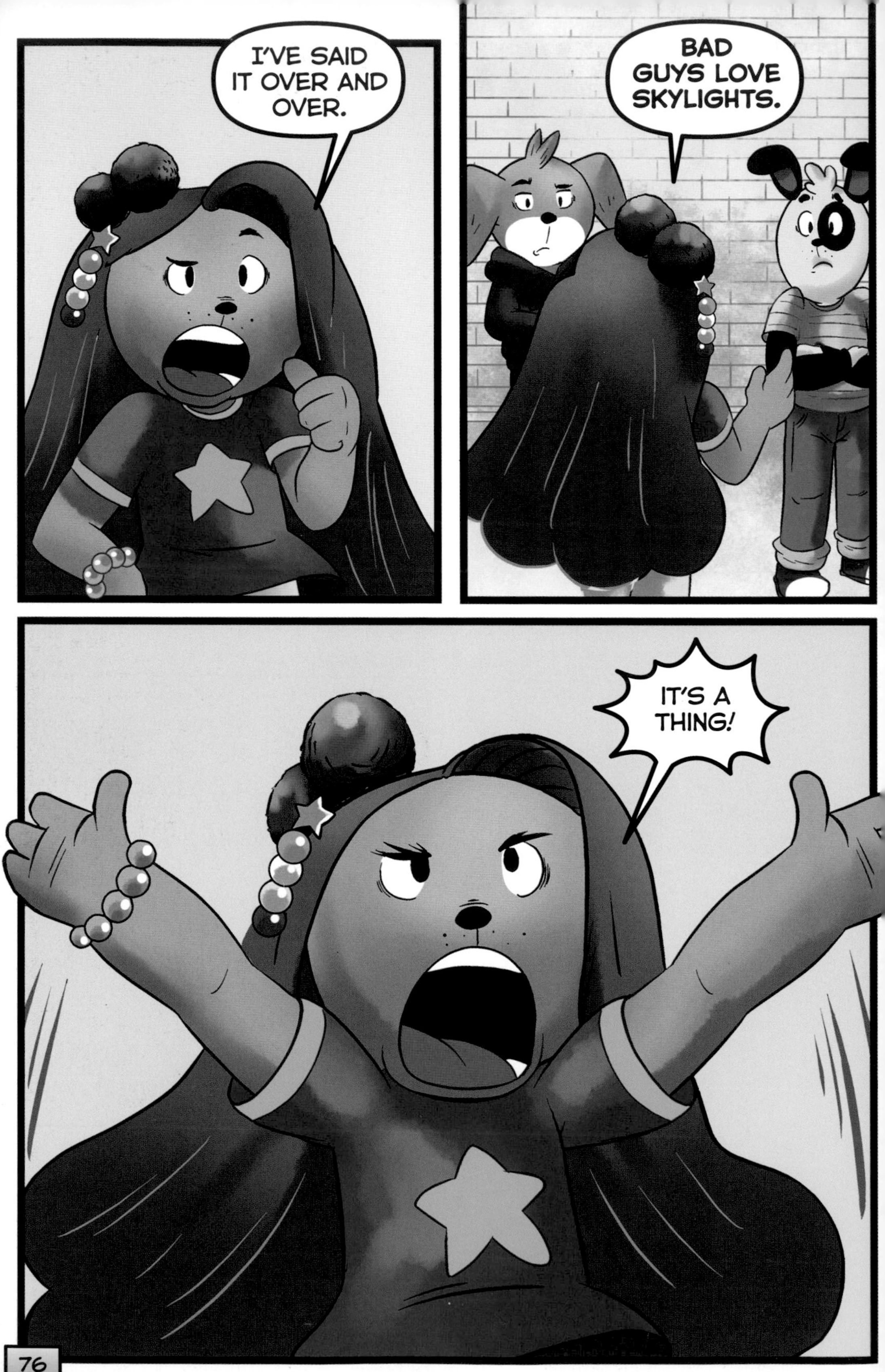
I'VE SAID IT OVER AND OVER.
BAD GUYS LOVE SKYLIGHTS.
IT'S A THING!

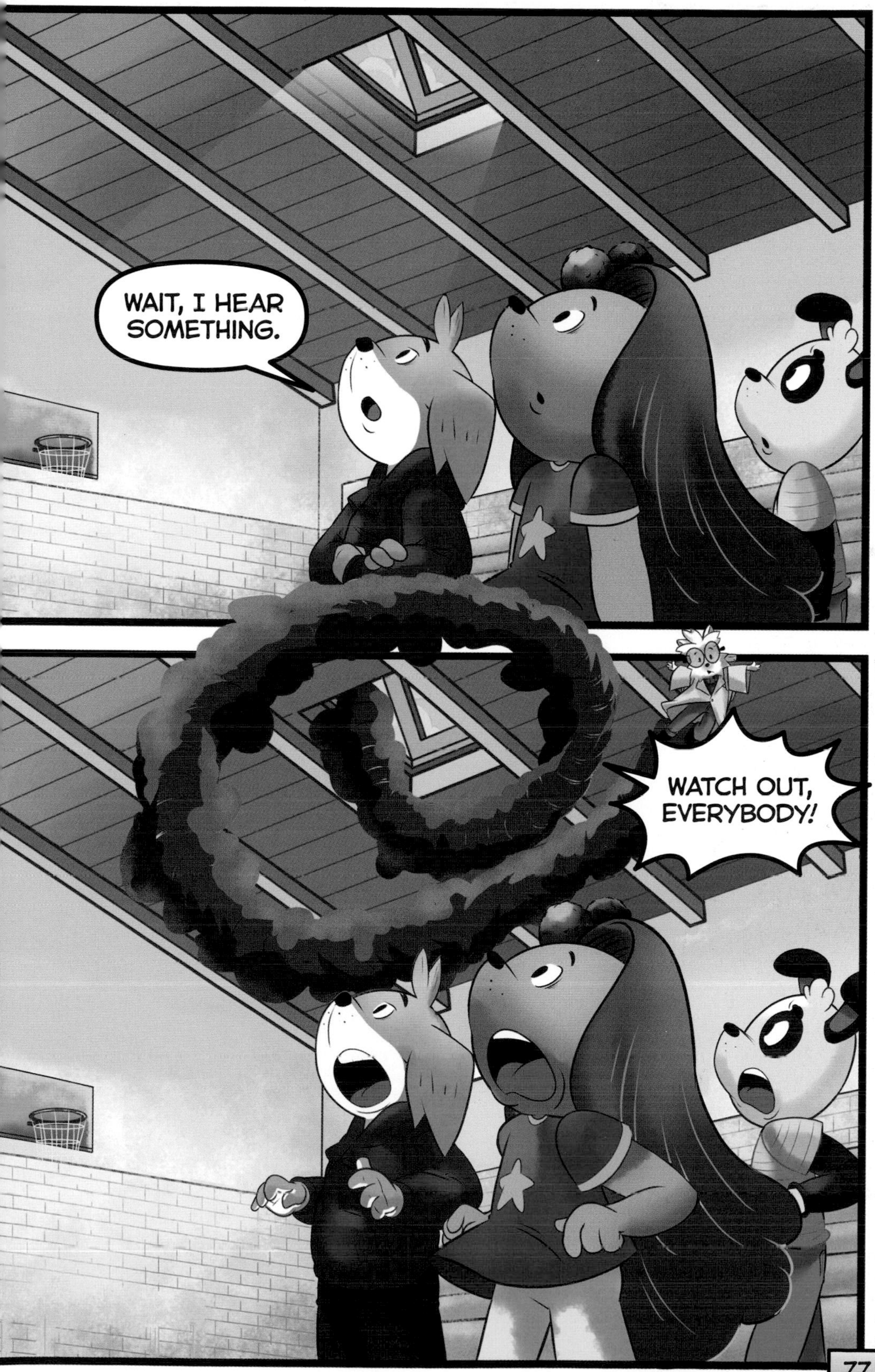
WAIT, I HEAR SOMETHING.
WATCH OUT, EVERYBODY!

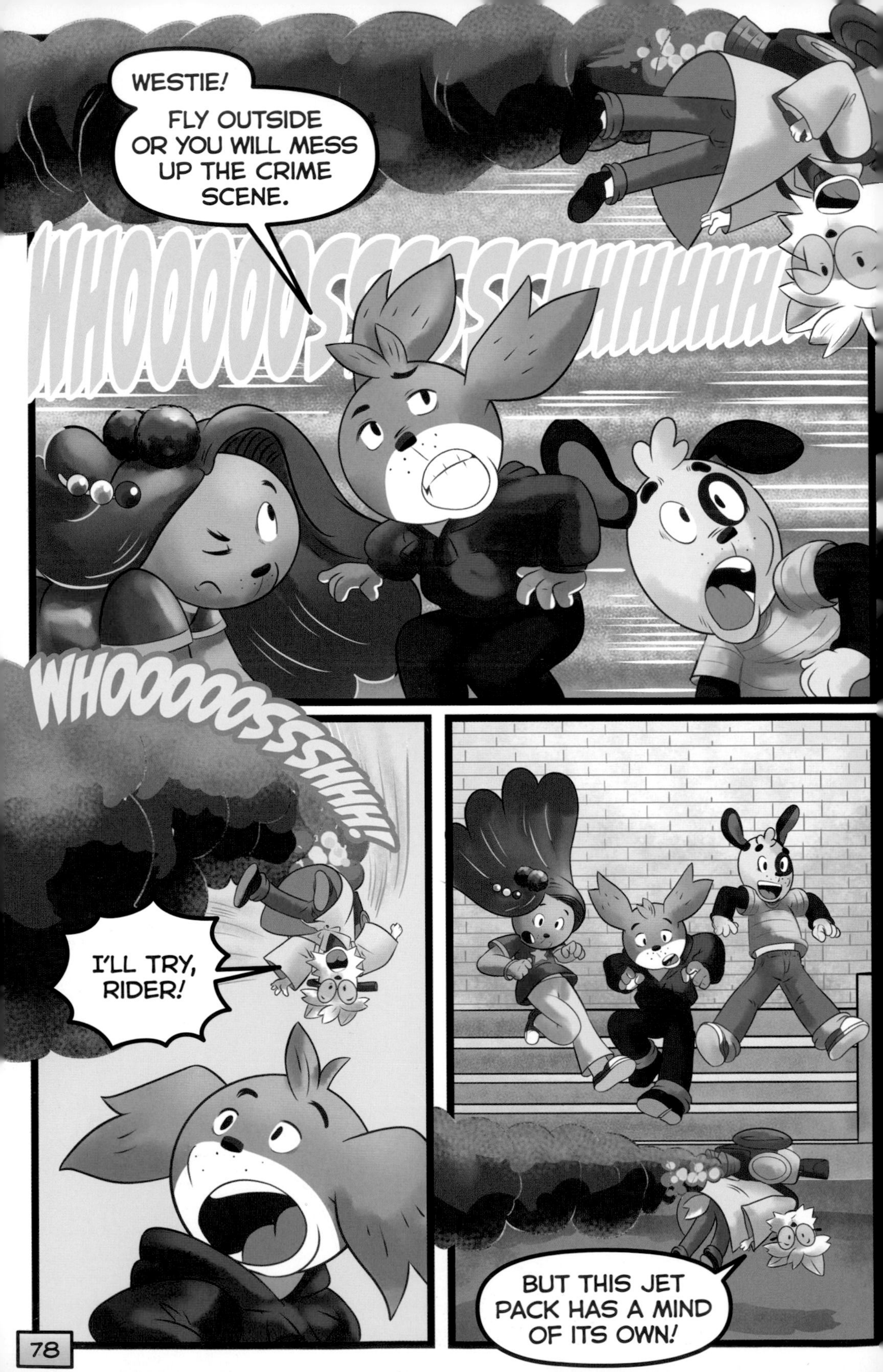
WESTIE!
FLY OUTSIDE OR YOU WILL MESS UP THE CRIME SCENE.
WHOOOOOOSSSSSHHHHHHH
WHOOOOOSSSSHHH!
I'LL TRY, RIDER!
BUT THIS JET PACK HAS A MIND OF ITS OWN!

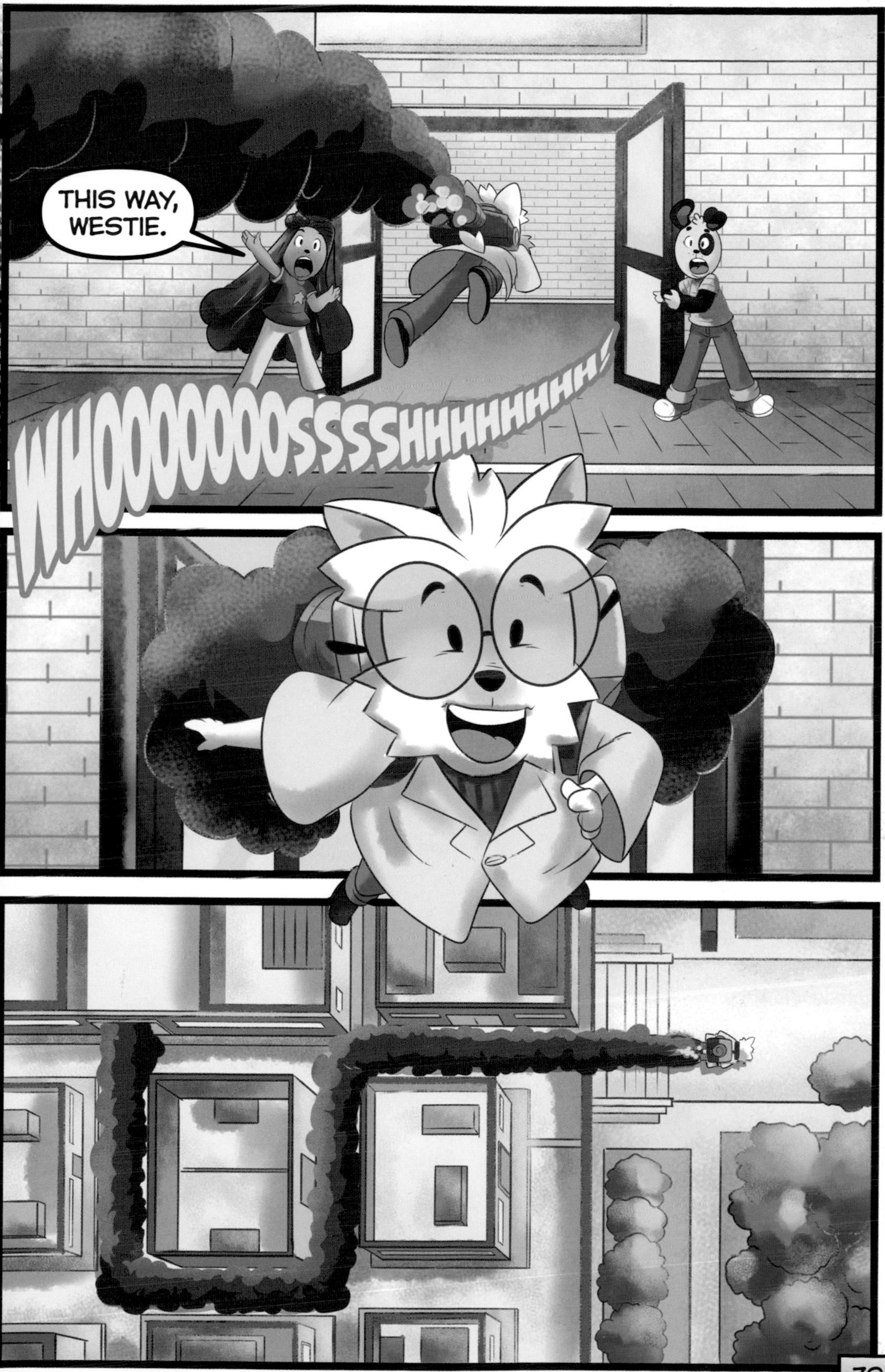

THIS WAY, WESTIE.
WHOOOOOOOSSSHHHHHHHH!

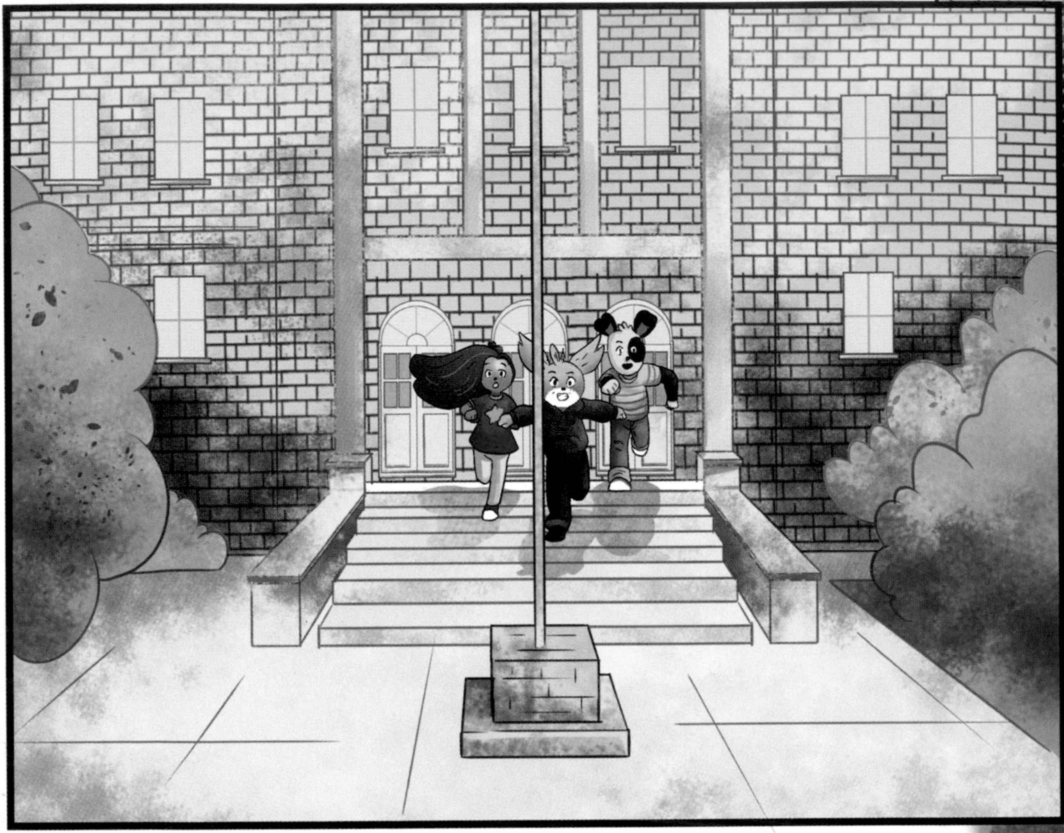

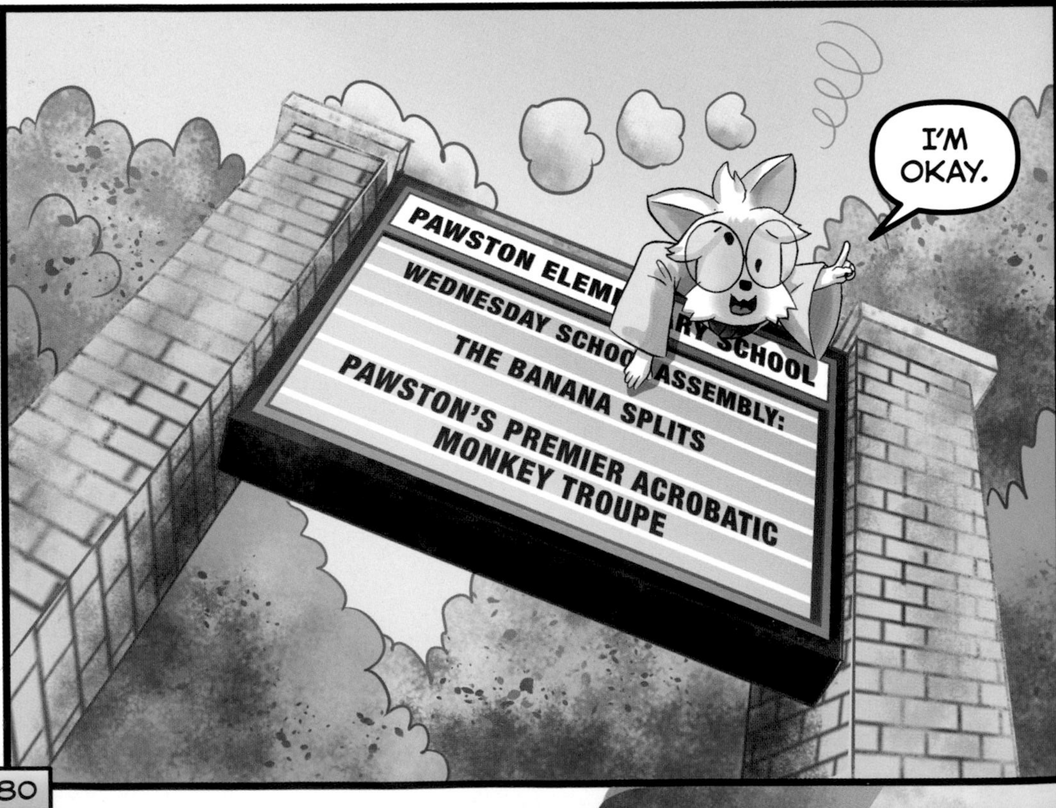
PAWSTON ELEM
ARY SCHOOL
WEDNESDAY SCHOO
ASSEMBLY:
THE BANANA SPLITS
PAWSTON'S PREMIER ACROBATIC
MONKEY TROUPE
I'M OKAY.

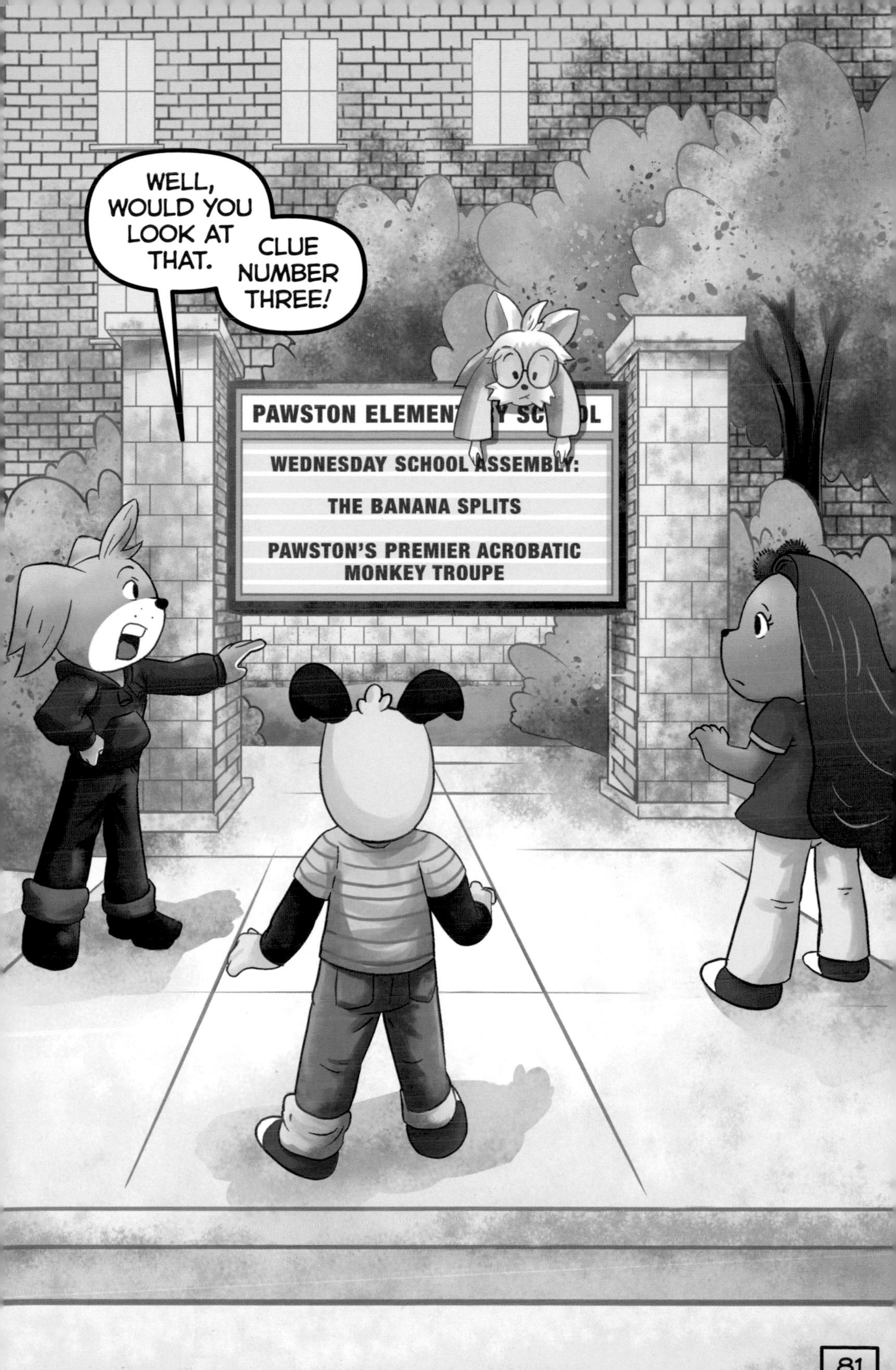

WELL, WOULD YOU LOOK AT THAT.
CLUE NUMBER THREE!
PAWSTON ELEMENT SC OL
WEDNESDAY SCHOOL ASSEMBLY:
THE BANANA SPLITS
PAWSTON'S PREMIER ACROBATIC MONKEY TROUPE

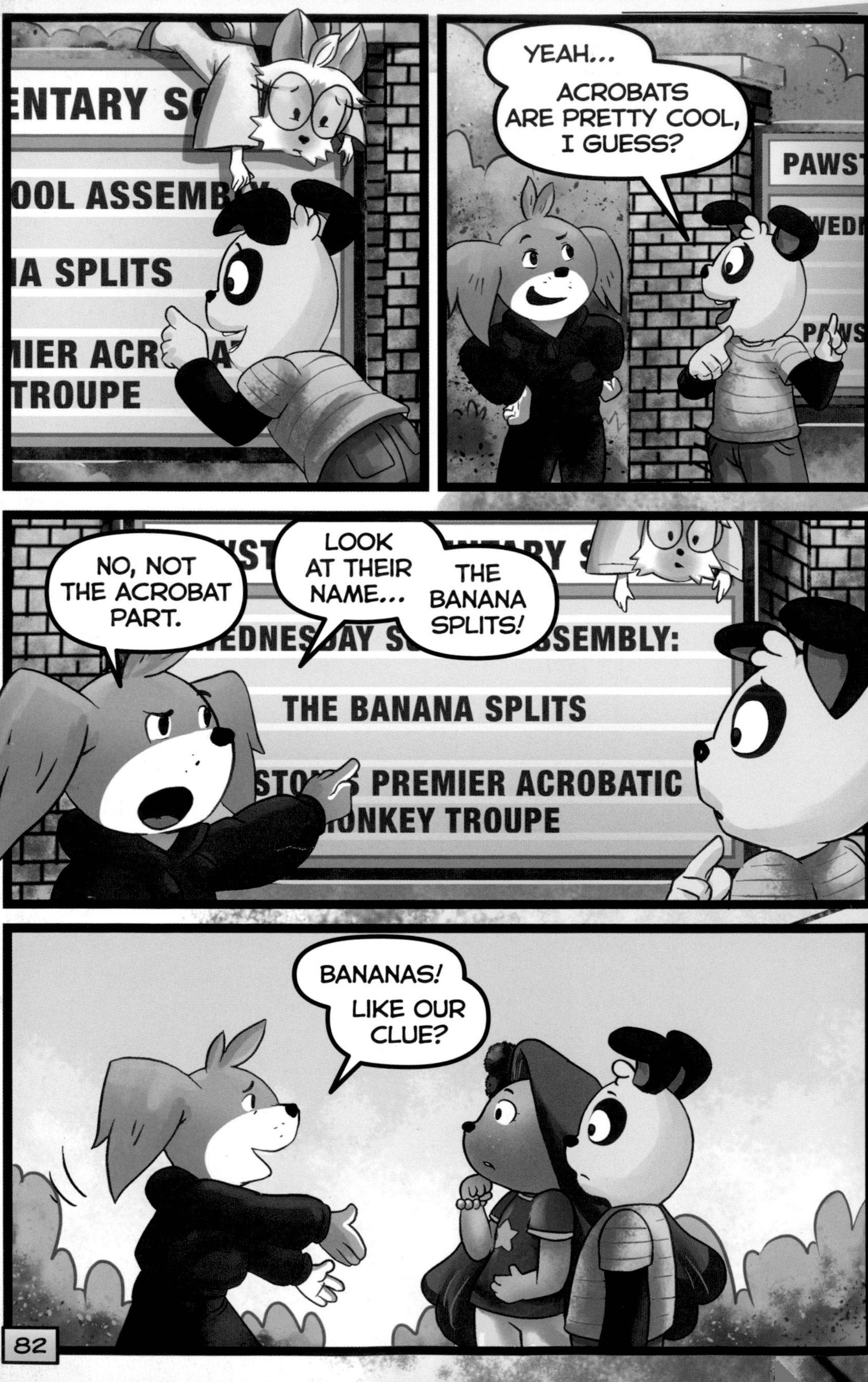
YEAH...
ACROBATS ARE PRETTY COOL, I GUESS?
NO, NOT THE ACROBAT PART.
LOOK AT THEIR NAME...
THE BANANA SPLITS!
THE BANANA SPLITS
PREMIER ACROBATIC
BANANAS!
LIKE OUR CLUE?

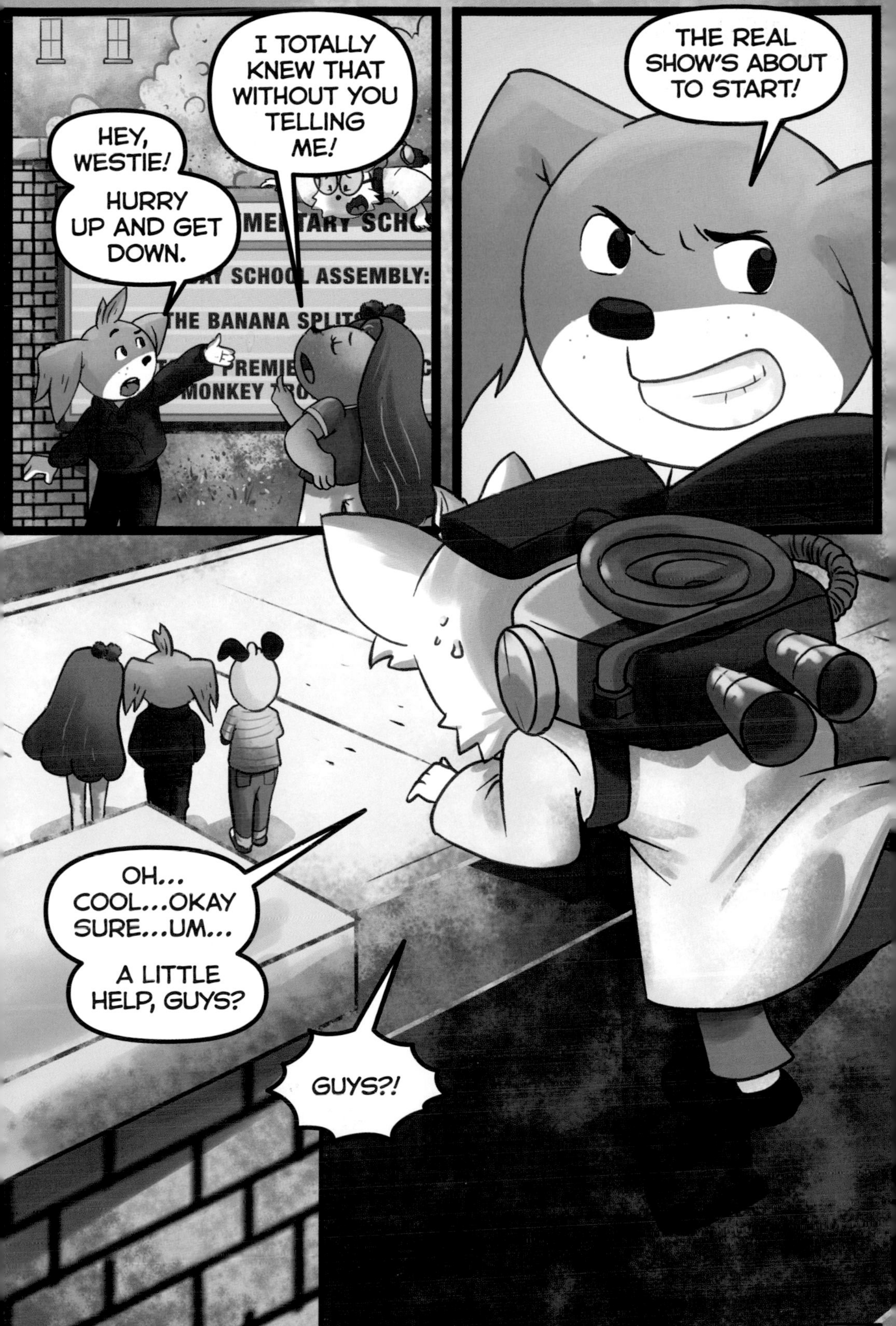
I TOTALLY KNEW THAT WITHOUT YOU TELLING ME!
HEY, WESTIE!
HURRY UP AND GET DOWN.
THE BANANA SPLITS
MONKEY
SCHOOL ASSEMBLY:
THE REAL SHOW'S ABOUT TO START!
OH... COOL...OKAY SURE...UM...
A LITTLE HELP, GUYS?
GUYS?!

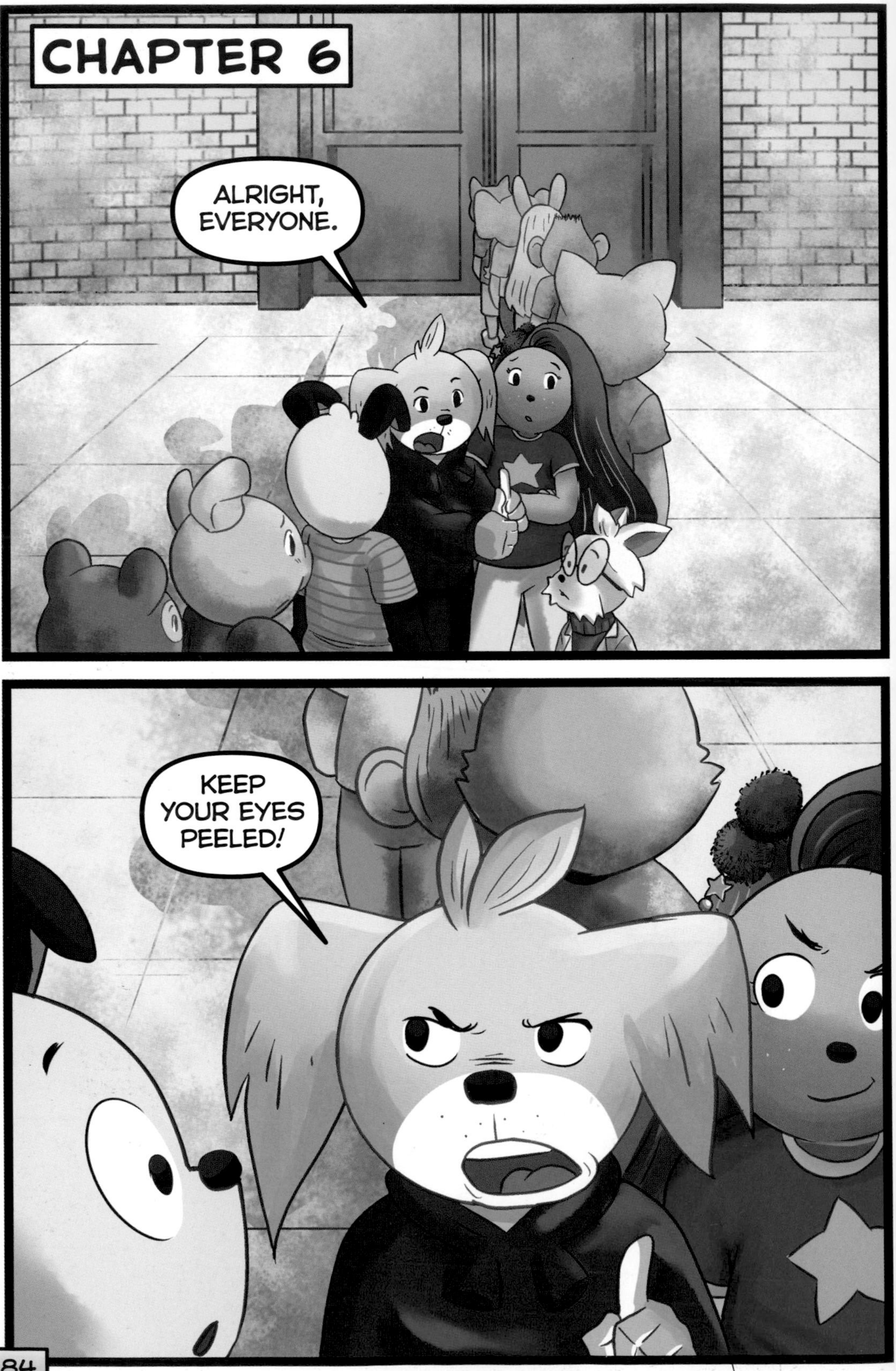
CHAPTER 6
ALRIGHT, EVERYONE.
KEEP YOUR EYES PEELED!

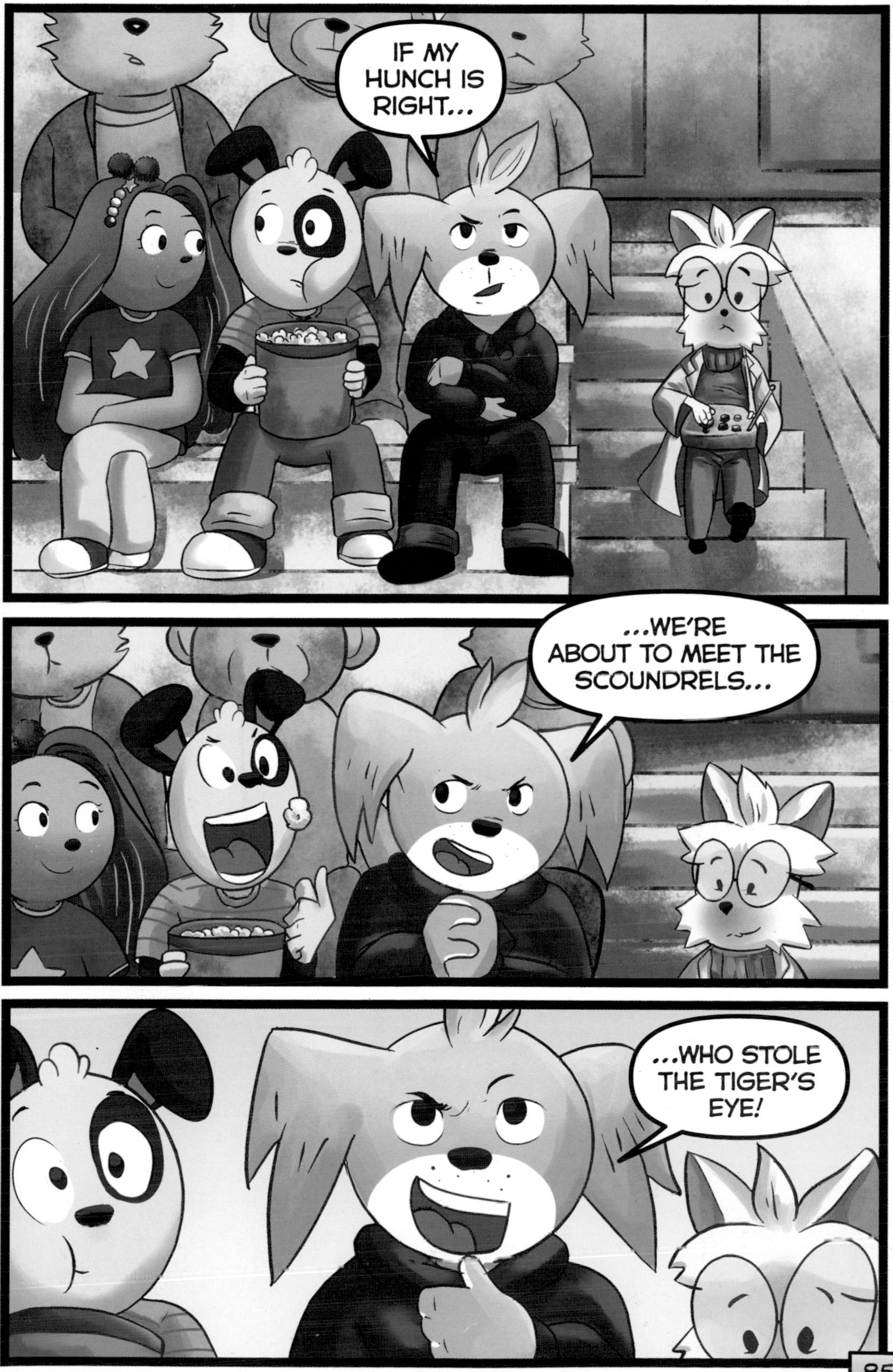
IF MY HUNCH IS RIGHT...
...WE'RE ABOUT TO MEET THE SCOUNDRELS...
...WHO STOLE THE TIGER'S EYE!

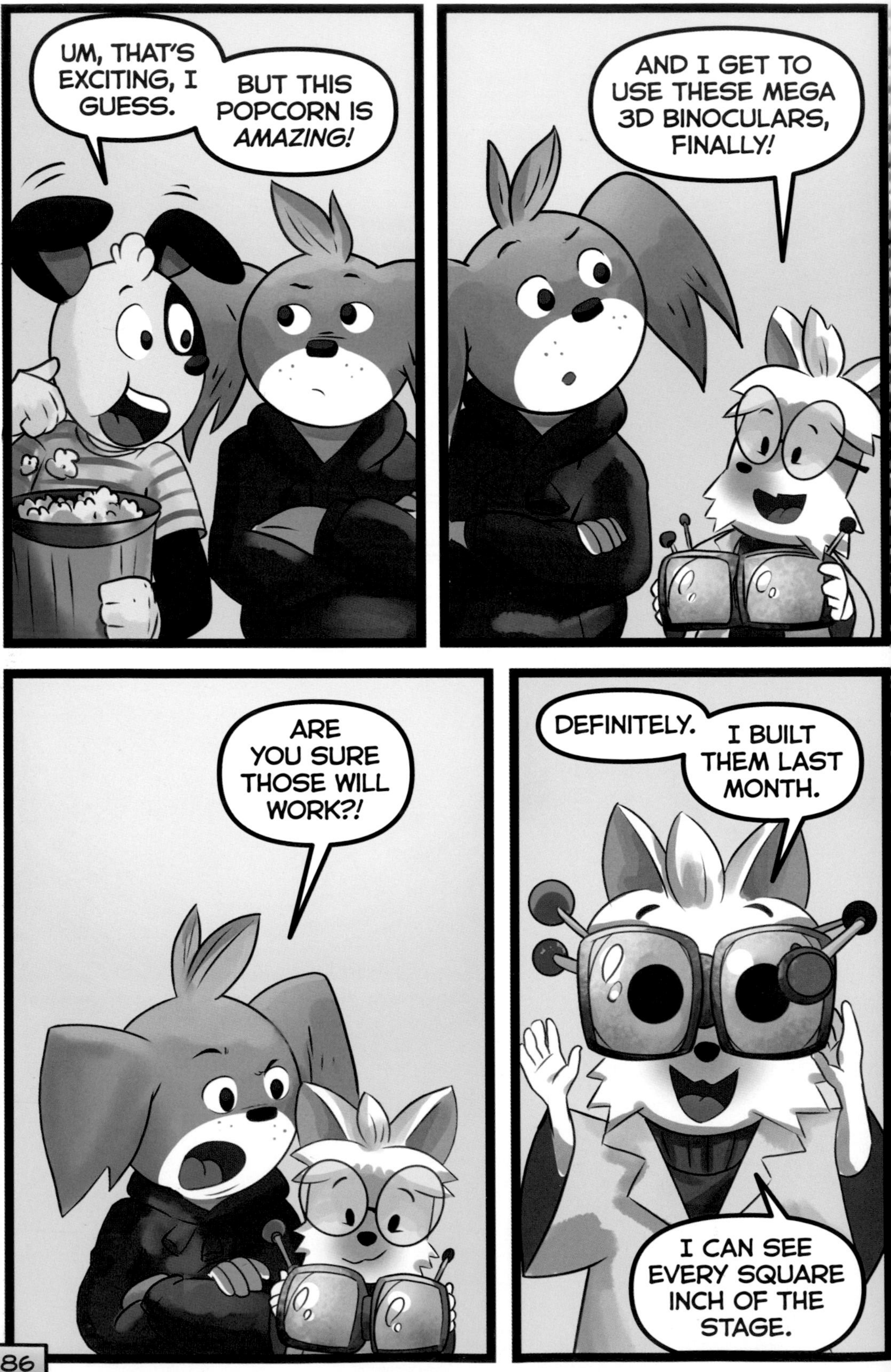
UM, THAT'S EXCITING, I GUESS.
BUT THIS POPCORN IS *AMAZING!*
AND I GET TO USE THESE MEGA 3D BINOCULARS, FINALLY!
ARE YOU SURE THOSE WILL WORK?!
DEFINITELY.
I BUILT THEM LAST MONTH.
I CAN SEE EVERY SQUARE INCH OF THE STAGE.

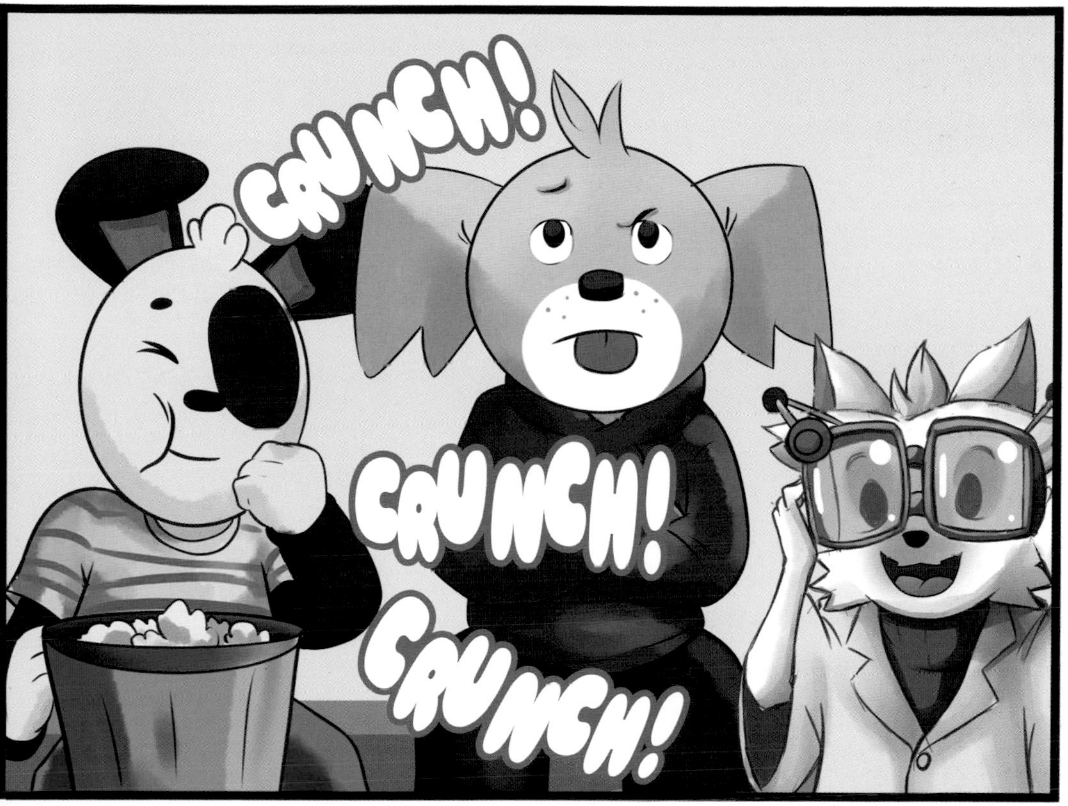
CRUNCH!
CRUNCH!
CRUNCH!

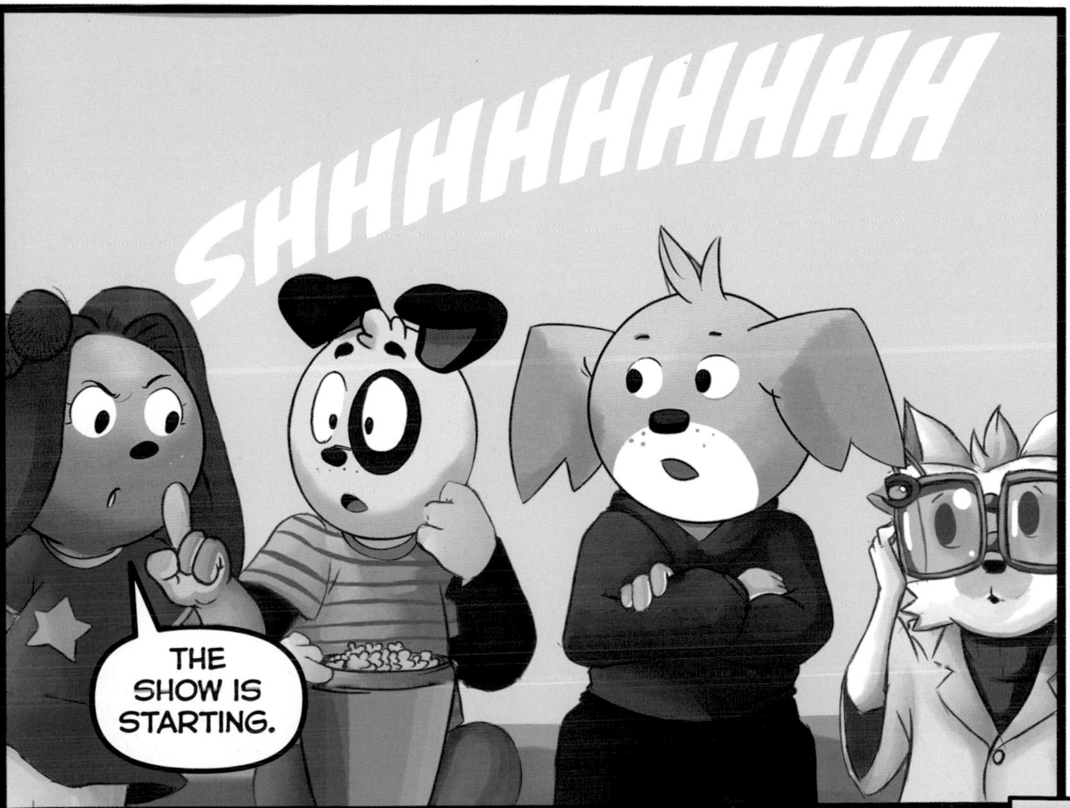
SHHHHHHHHHH
THE SHOW IS STARTING.

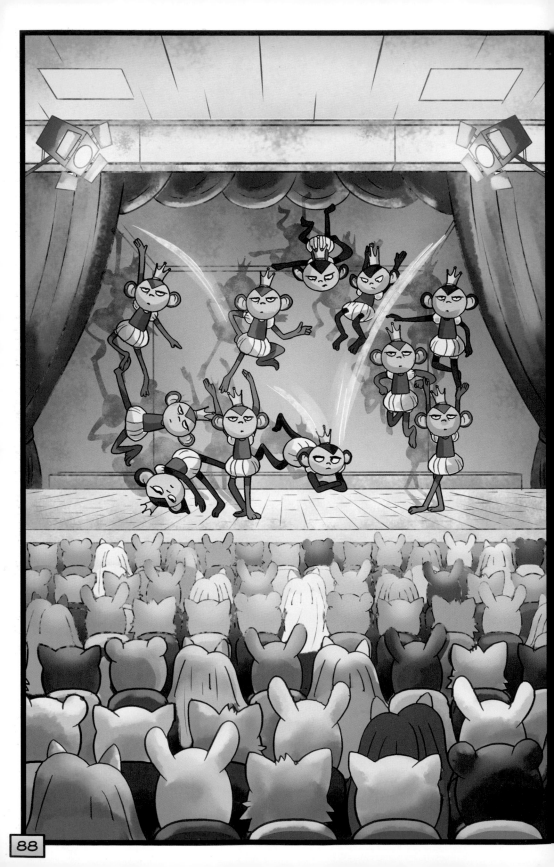

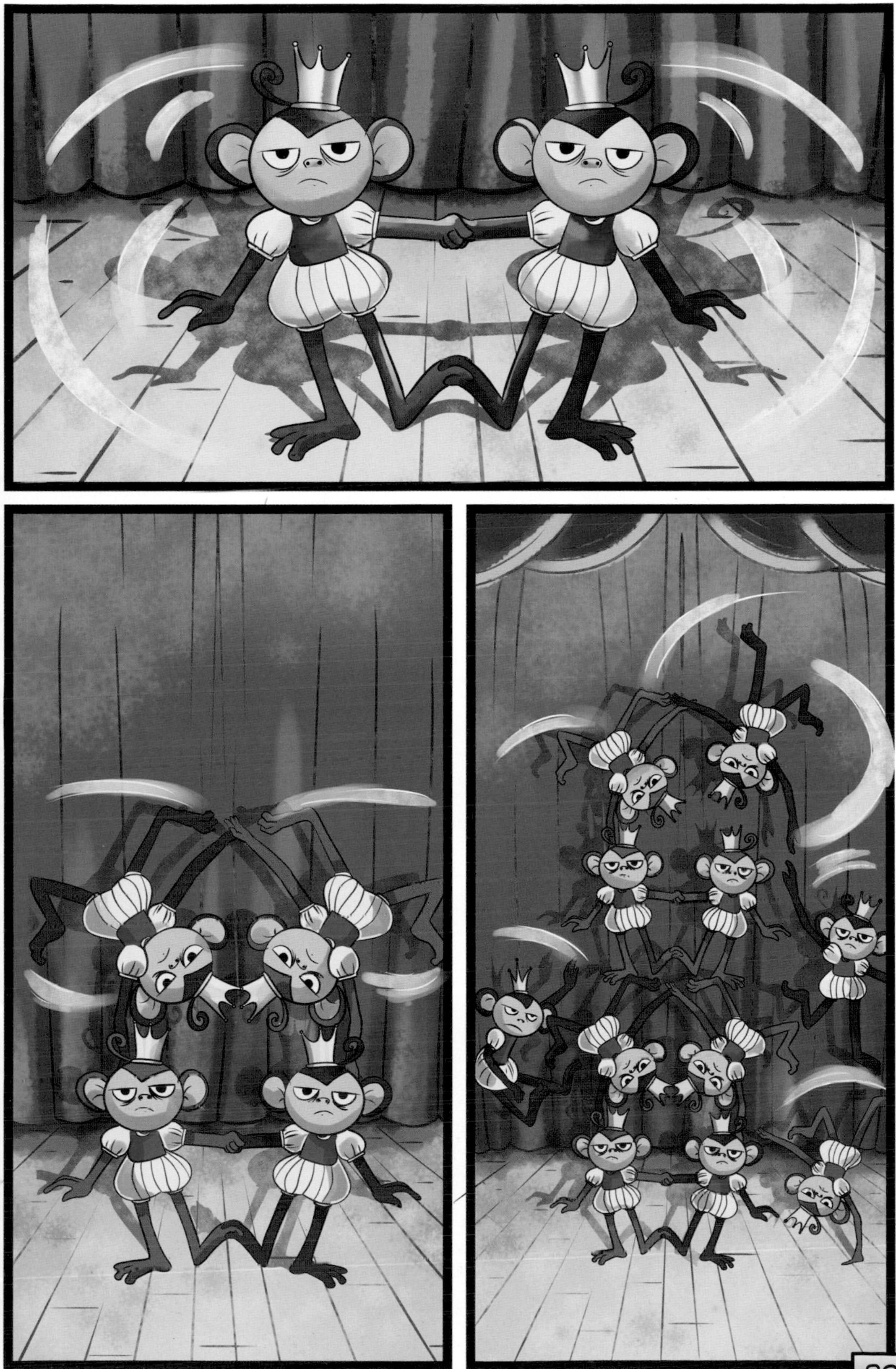

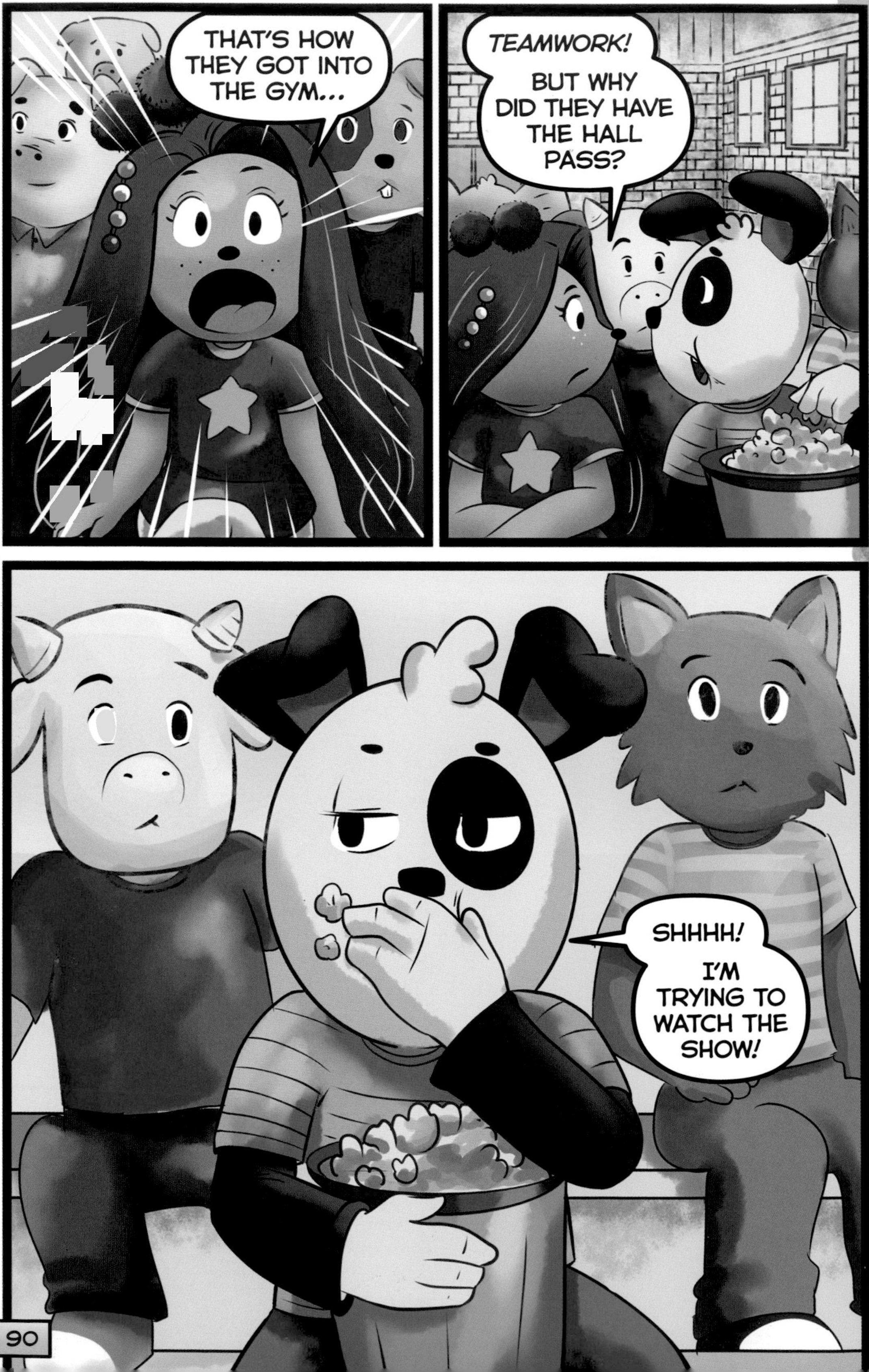
THAT'S HOW THEY GOT INTO THE GYM...
TEAMWORK!
BUT WHY DID THEY HAVE THE HALL PASS?
SHHHH!
I'M TRYING TO WATCH THE SHOW!

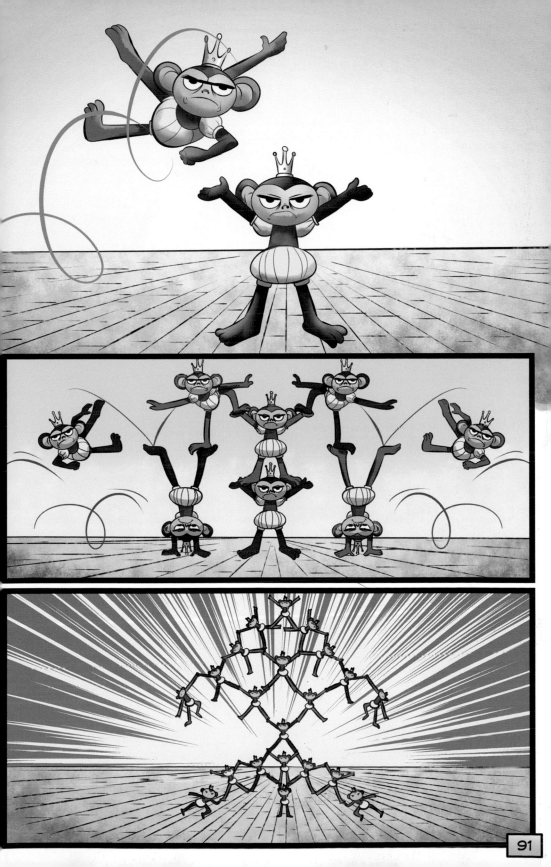

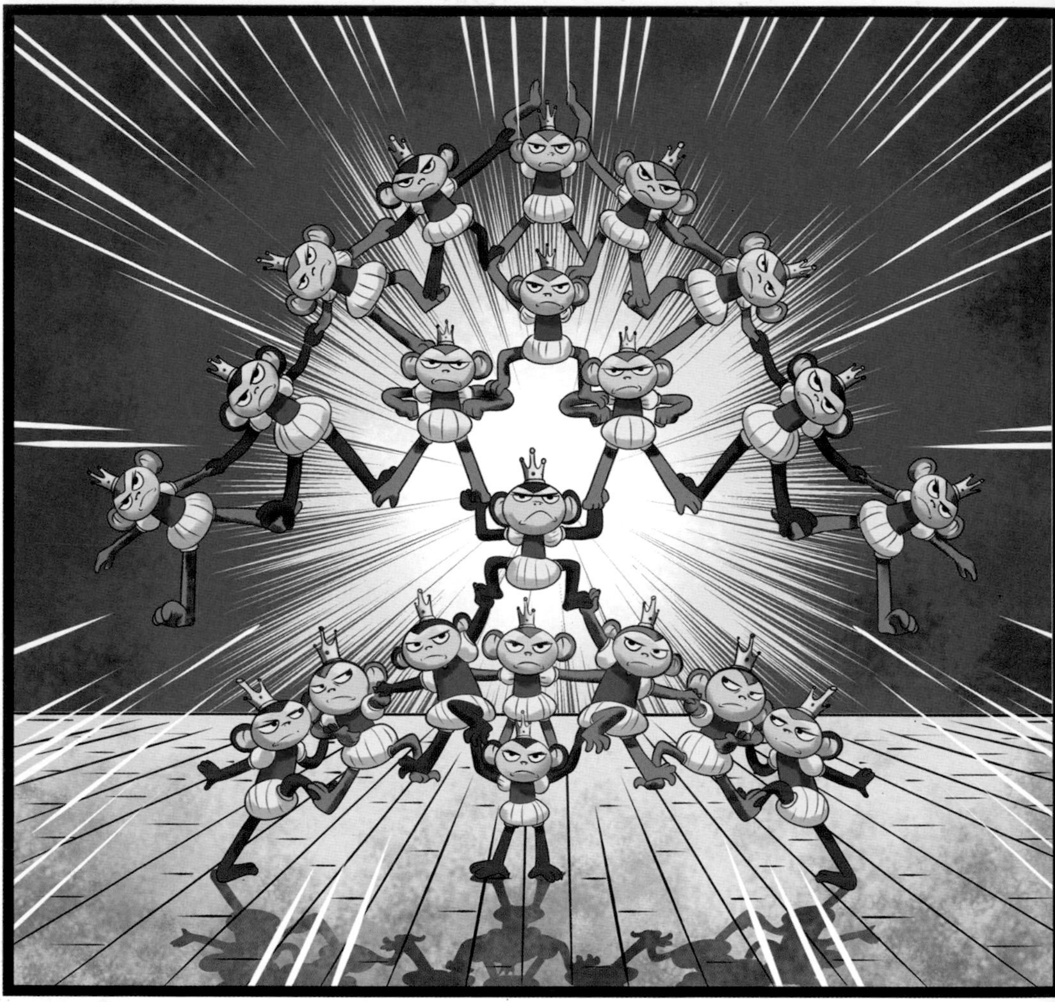

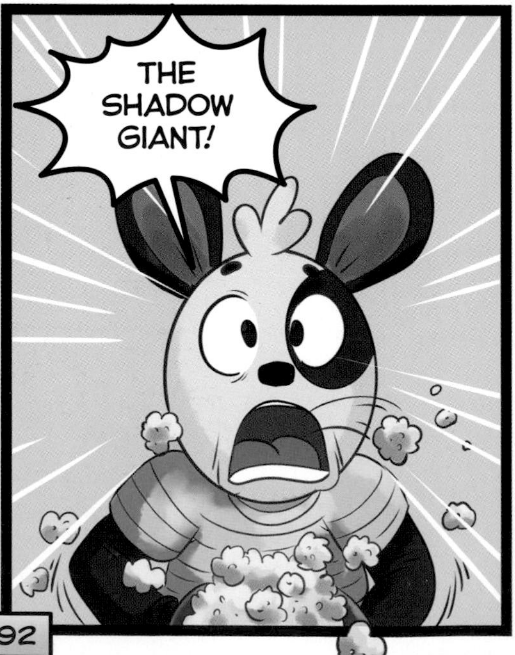
THE SHADOW GIANT!

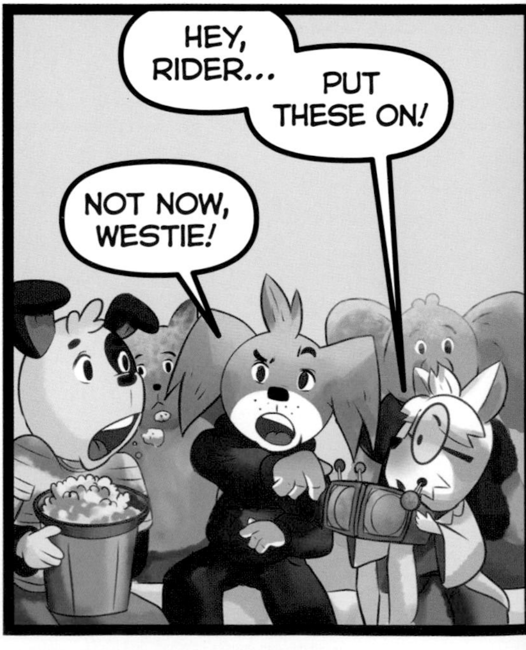
HEY, RIDER...
PUT THESE ON!
NOT NOW, WESTIE!

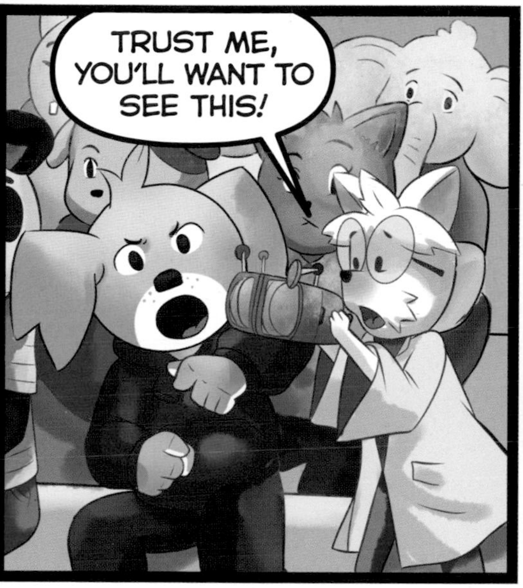
TRUST ME, YOU'LL WANT TO SEE THIS!

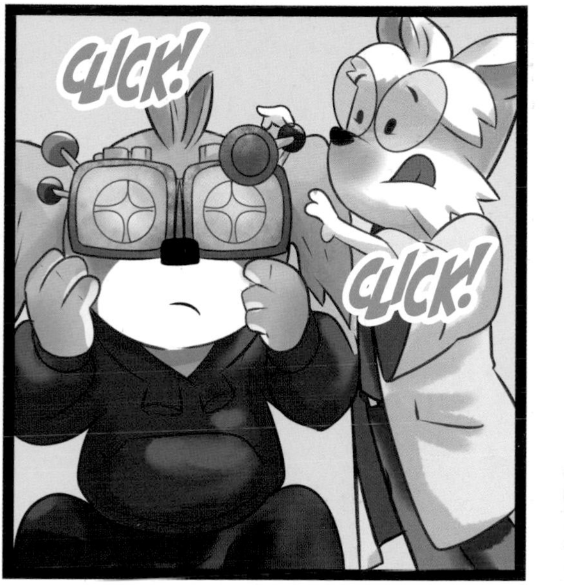
CLICK!
CLICK!

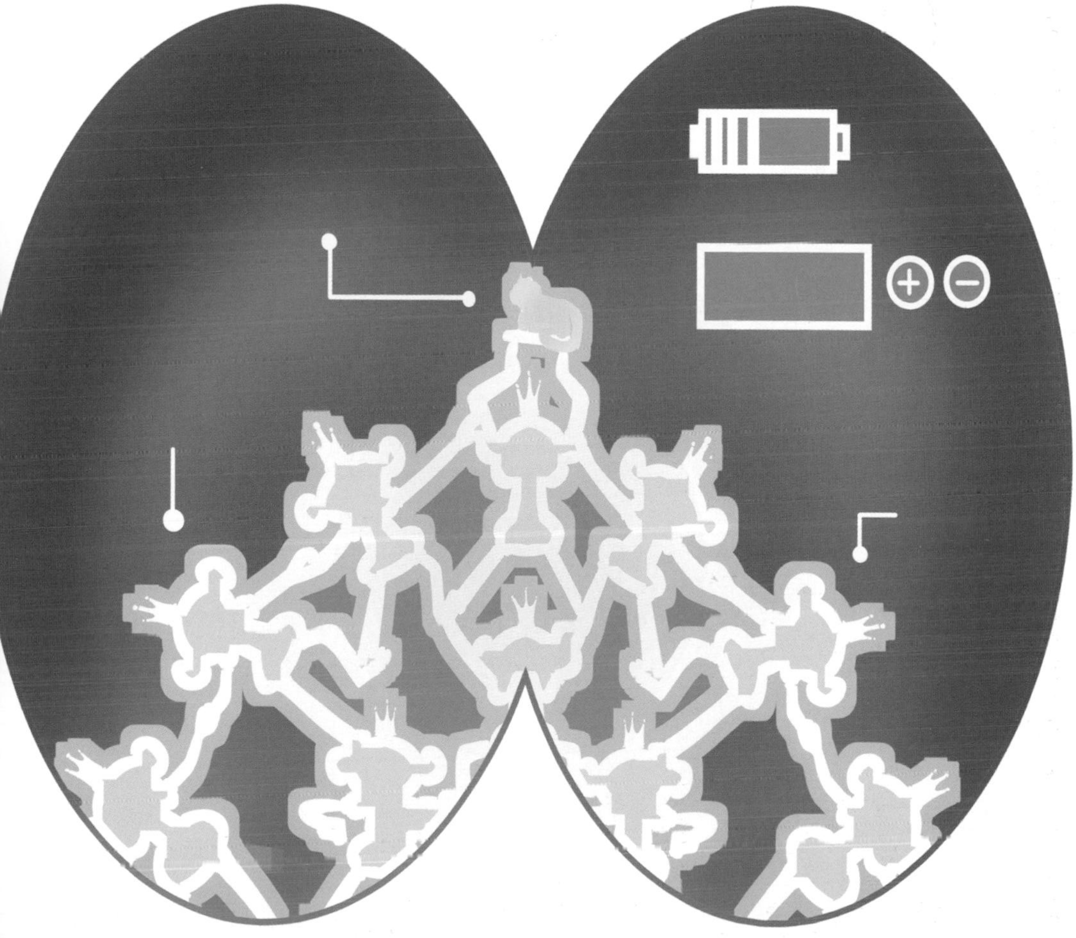

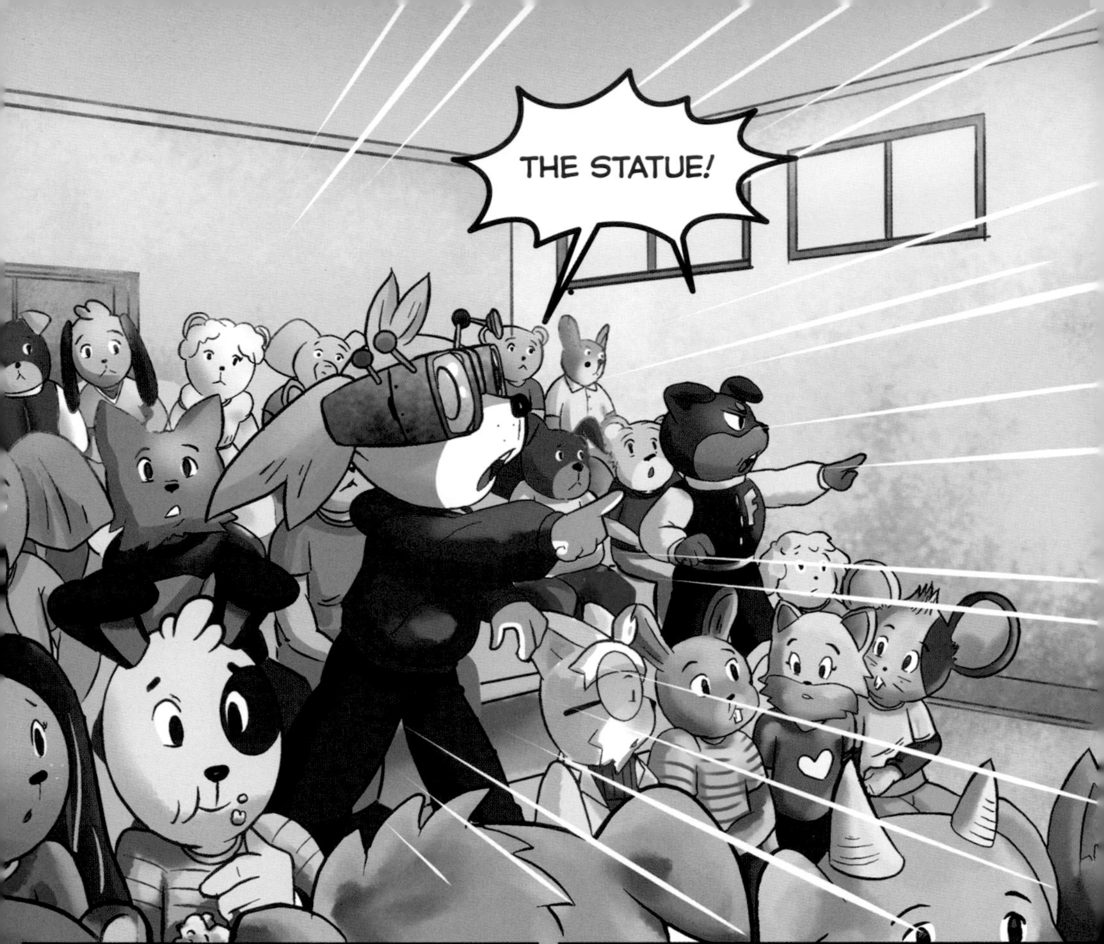
THE STATUE!

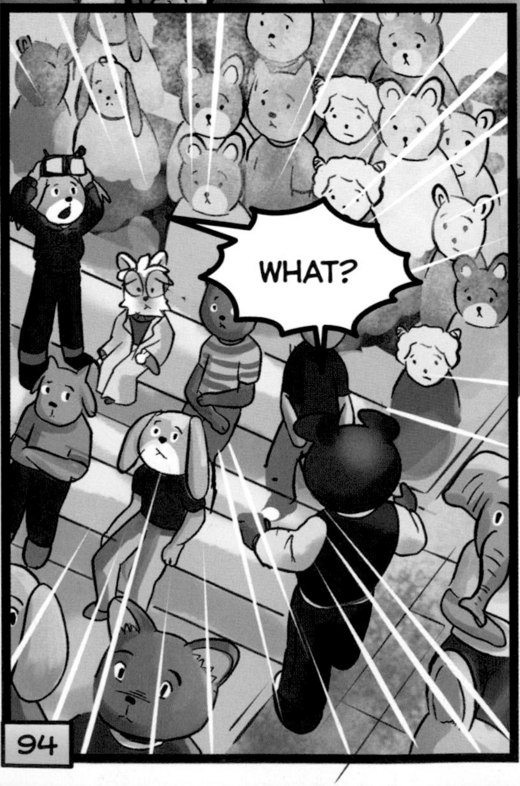
WHAT?

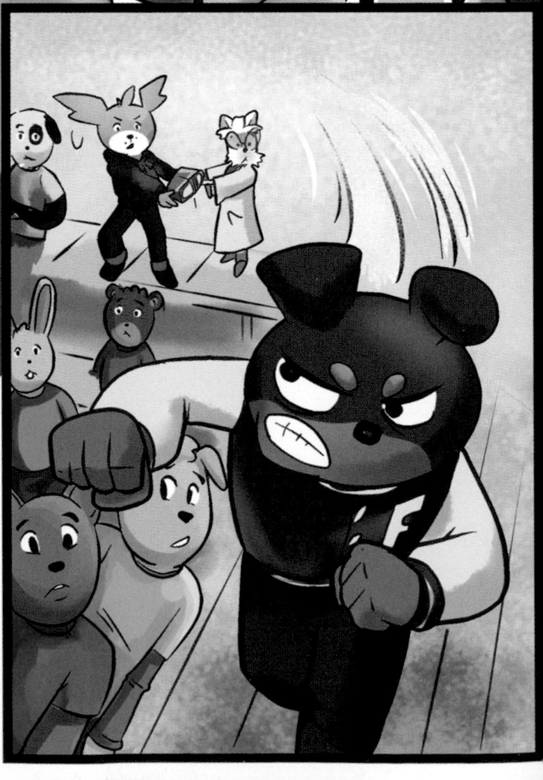

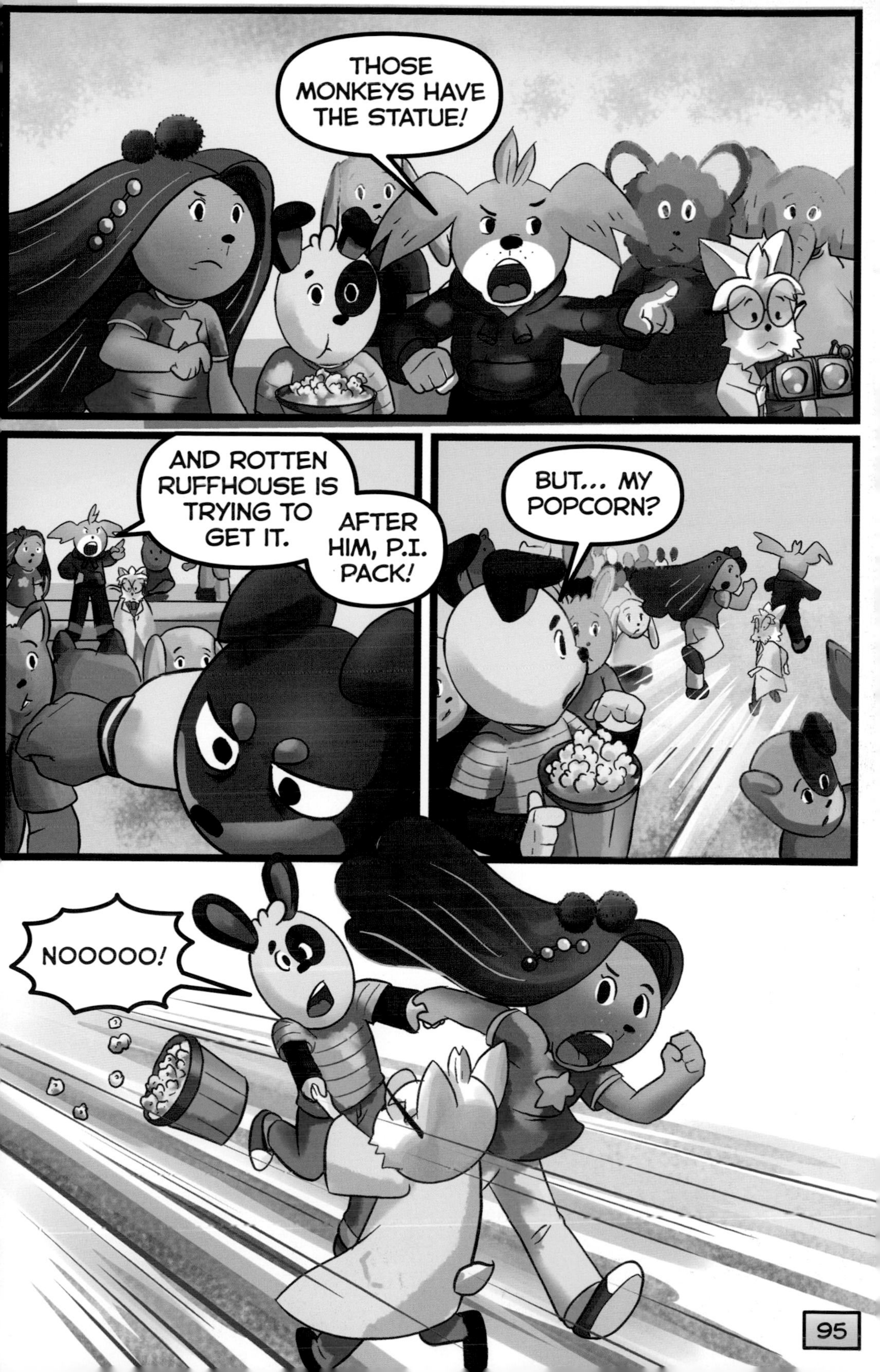
THOSE MONKEYS HAVE THE STATUE!
AND ROTTEN RUFFHOUSE IS TRYING TO GET IT.
AFTER HIM, P.I. PACK!
BUT... MY POPCORN?
NOOOOO!

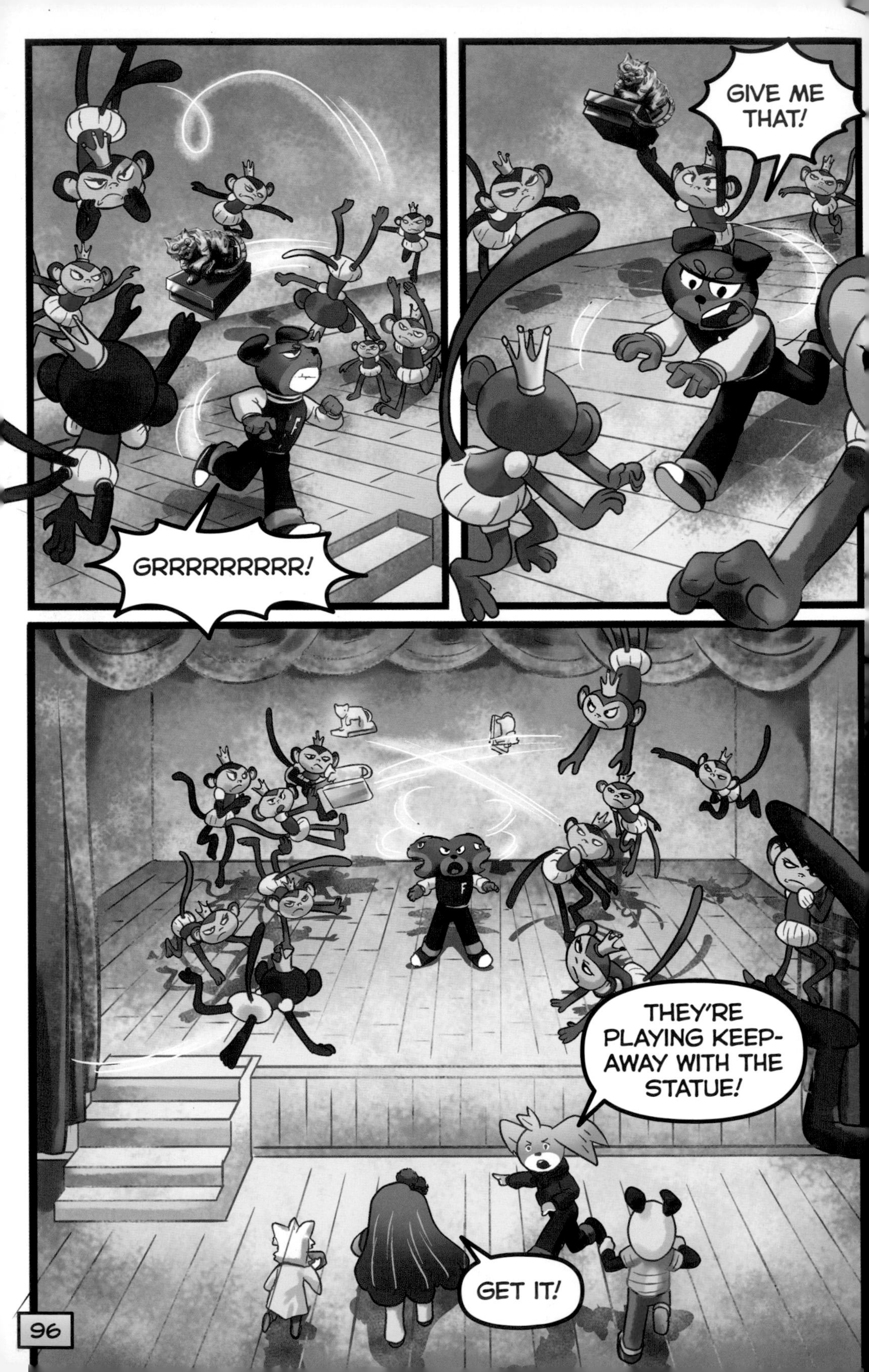
GRRRRRRRRR!
GIVE ME THAT!
THEY'RE PLAYING KEEP-AWAY WITH THE STATUE!
GET IT!

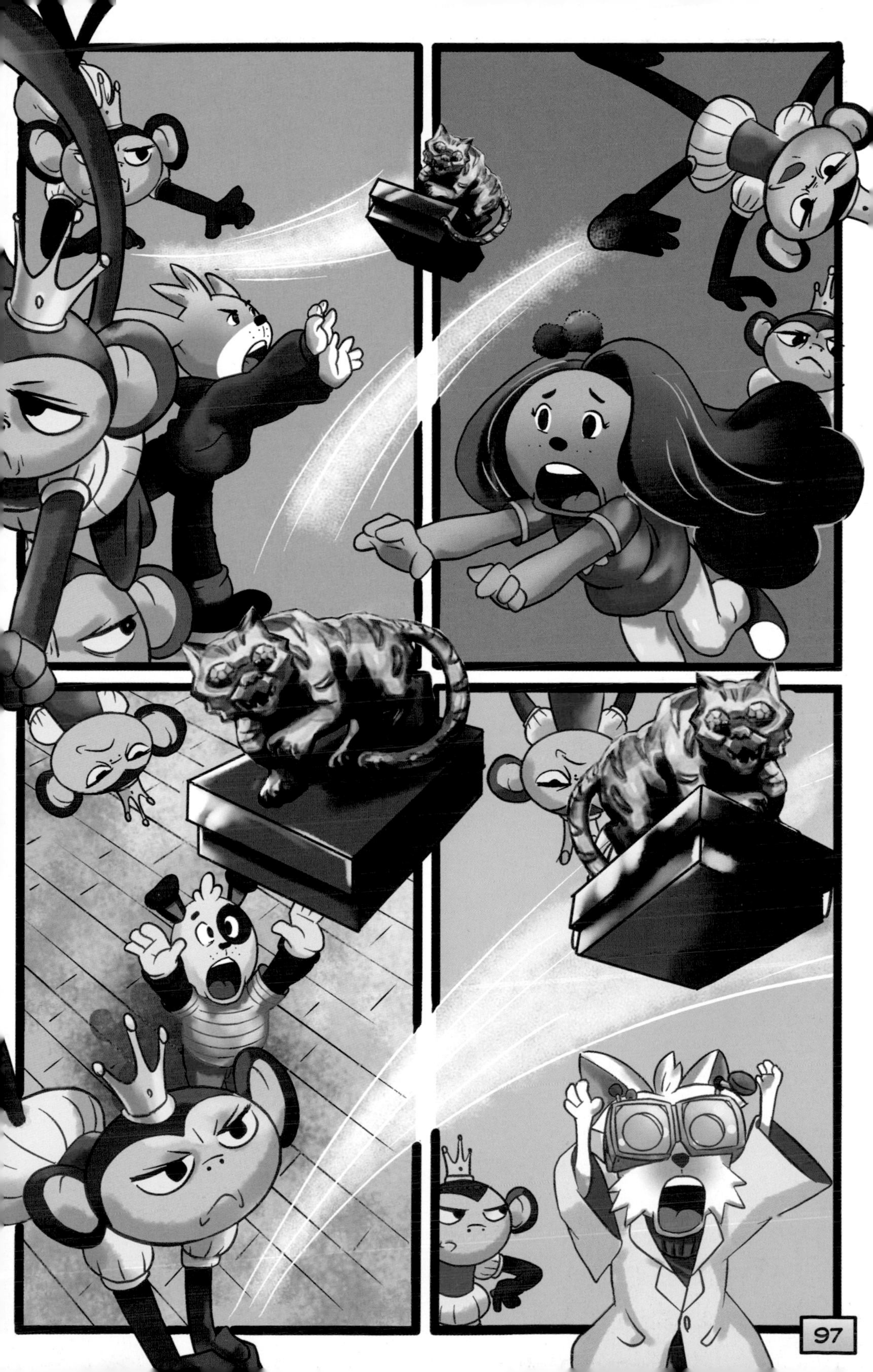

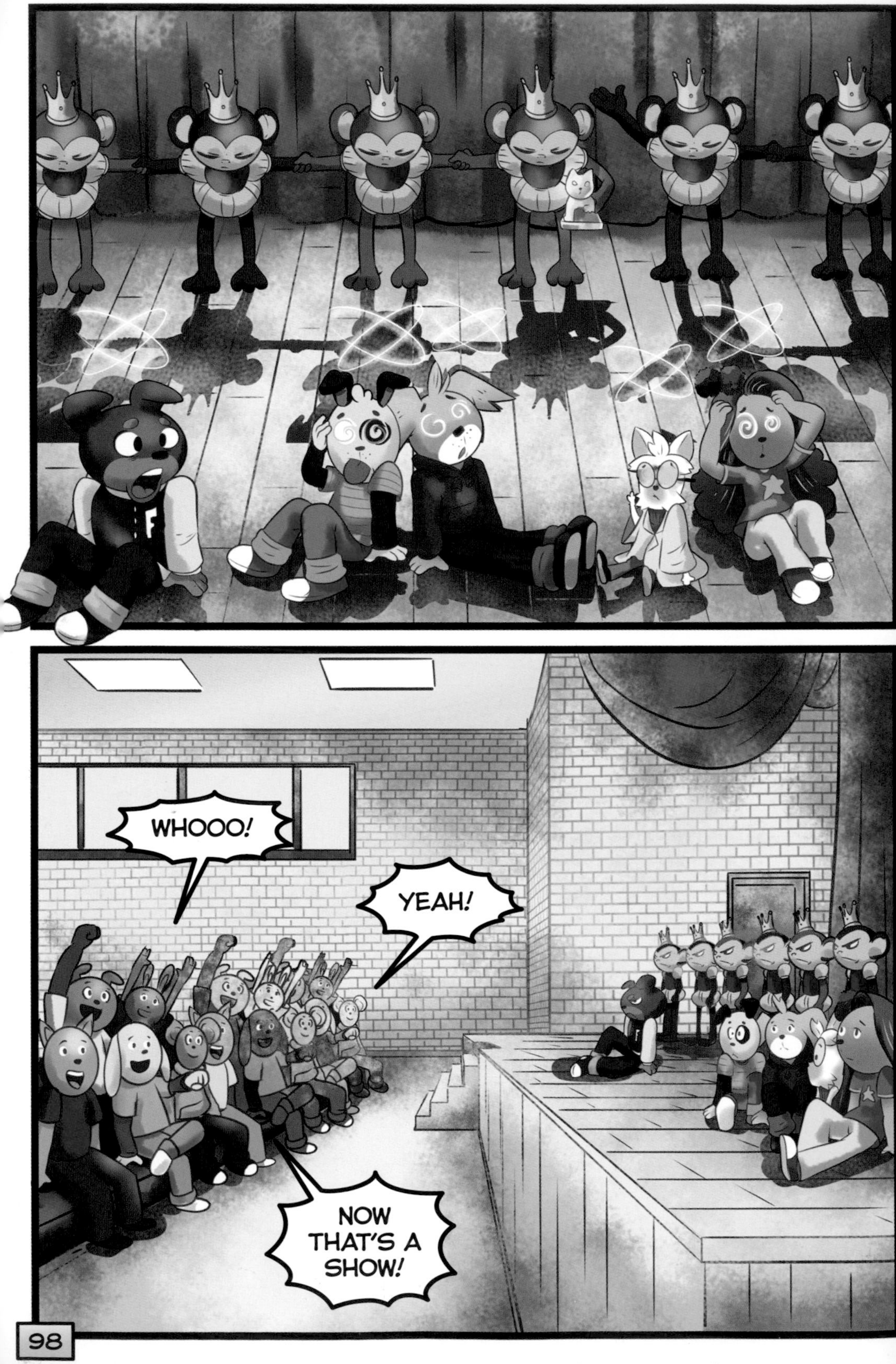
WHOOO!
YEAH!
NOW THAT'S A SHOW!

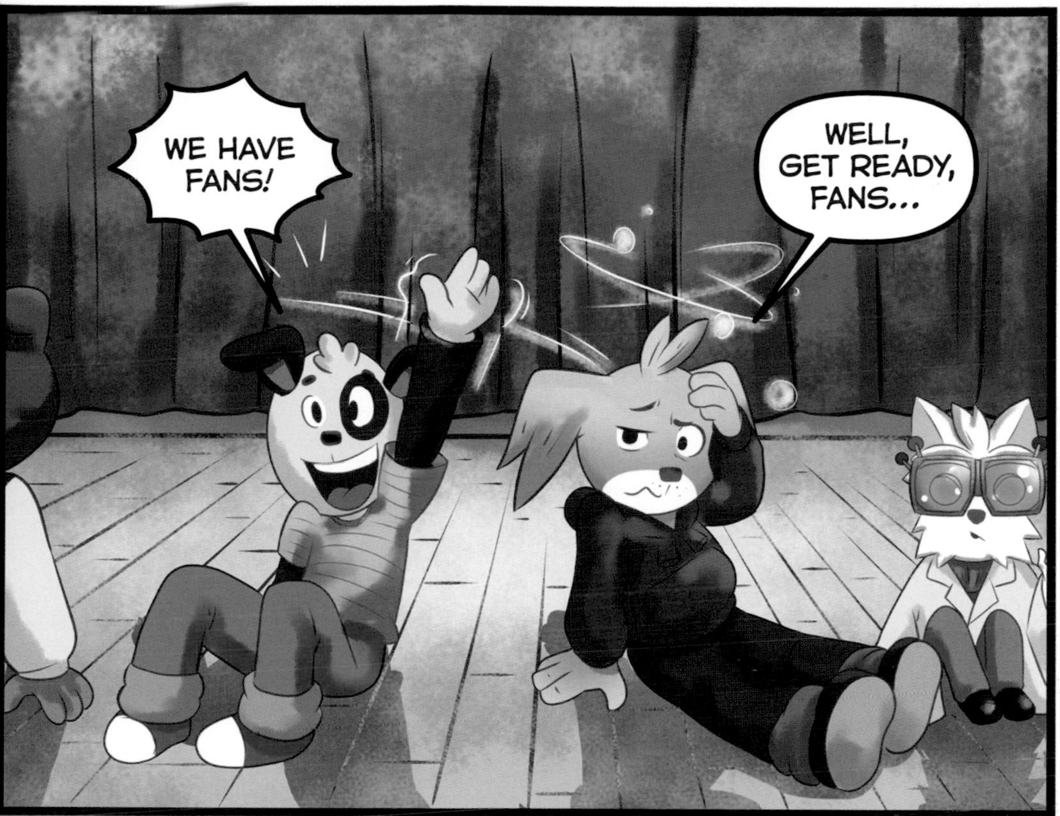
WE HAVE FANS!
WELL, GET READY, FANS...

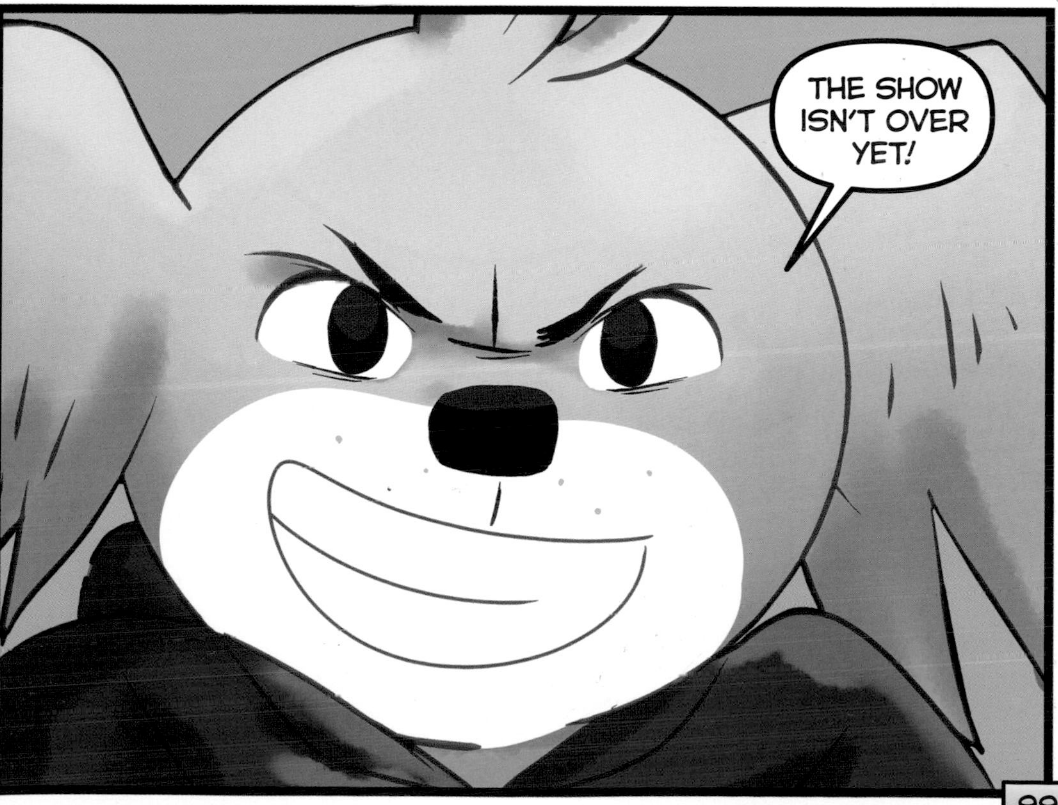
THE SHOW ISN'T OVER YET!

CHAPTER 7

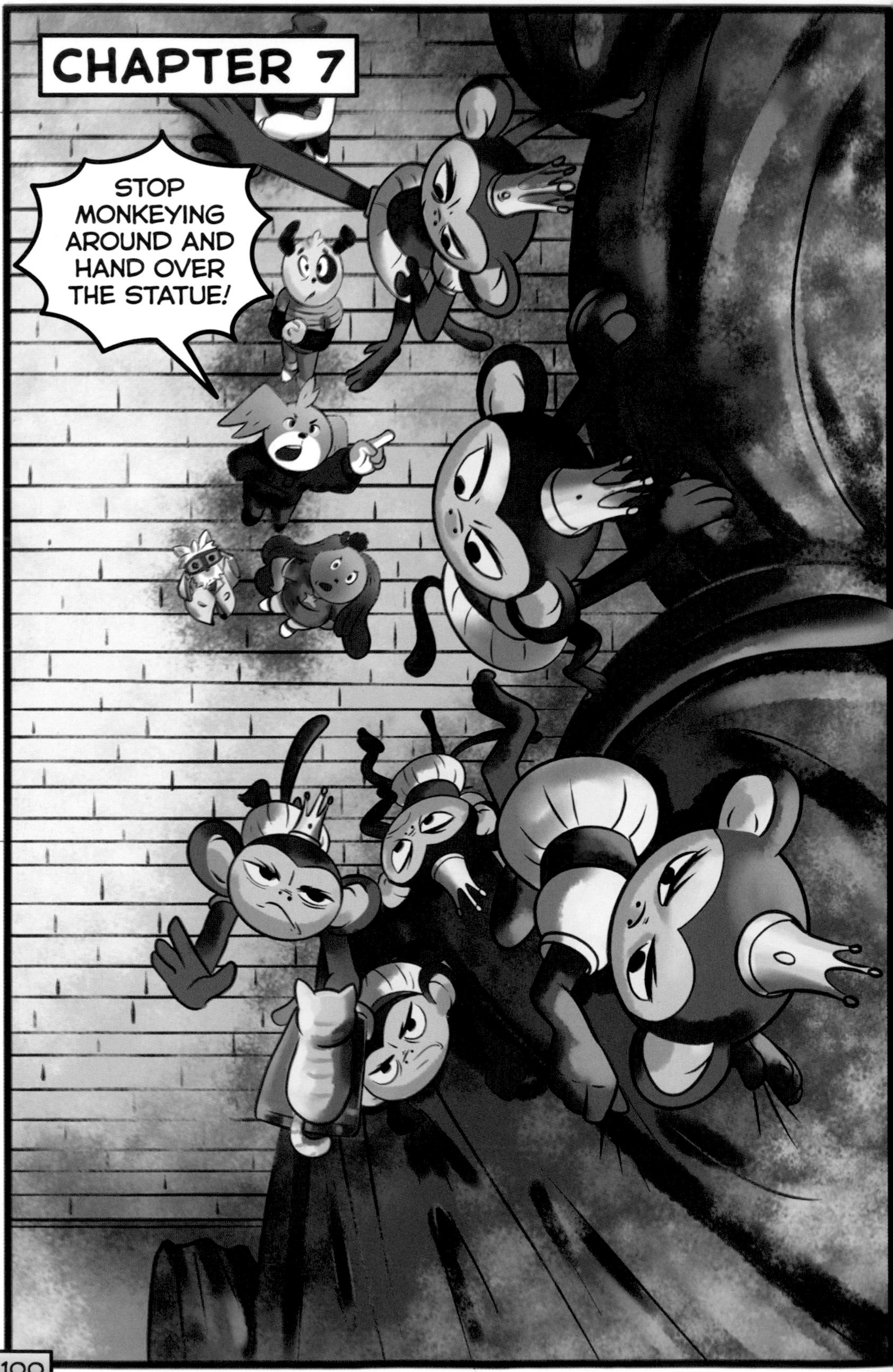
STOP MONKEYING AROUND AND HAND OVER THE STATUE!

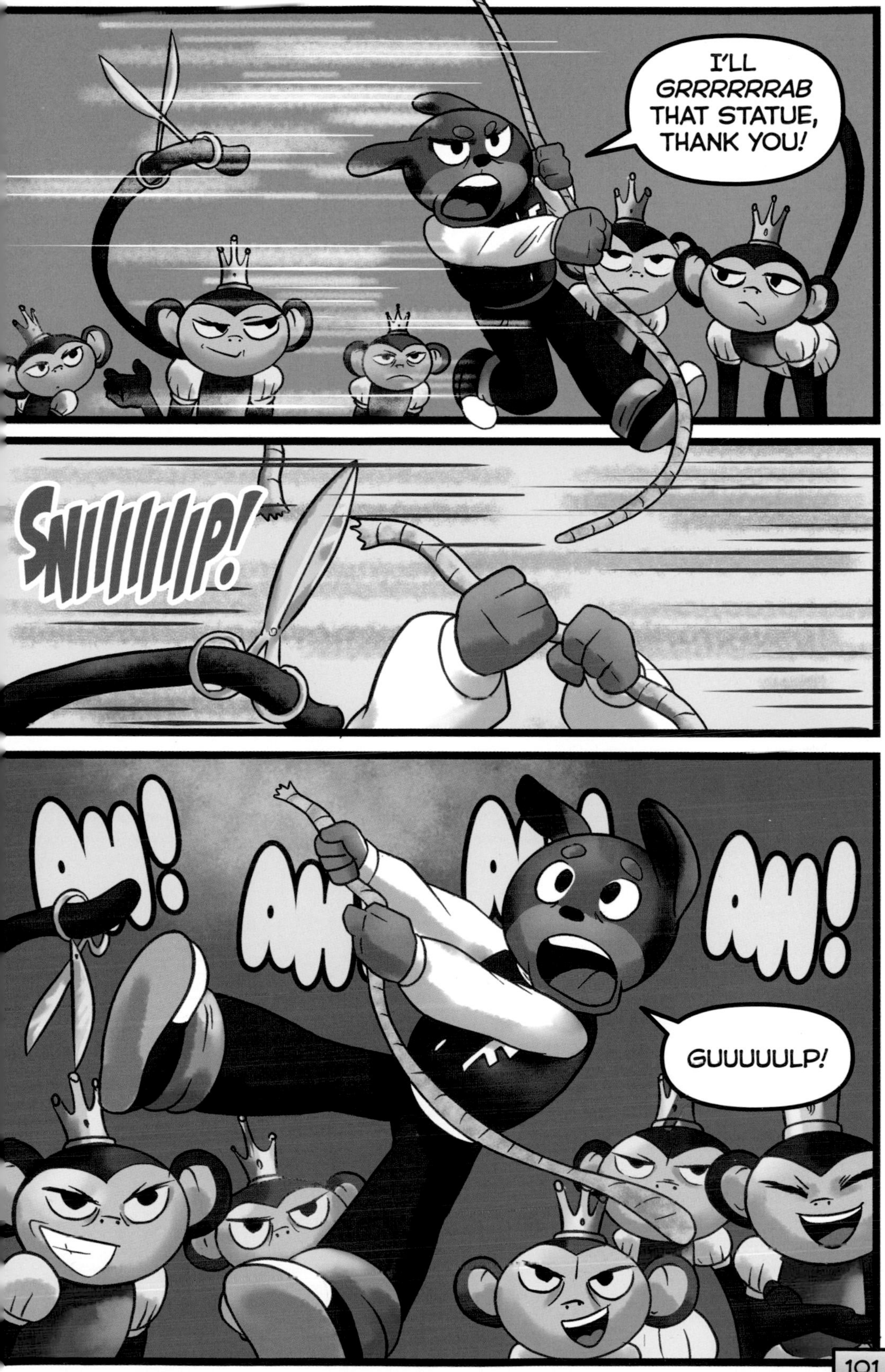
I'LL GRRRRRRAB THAT STATUE, THANK YOU!
SNIIIIIIIP!
AH!
GUUUUULP!
AH!

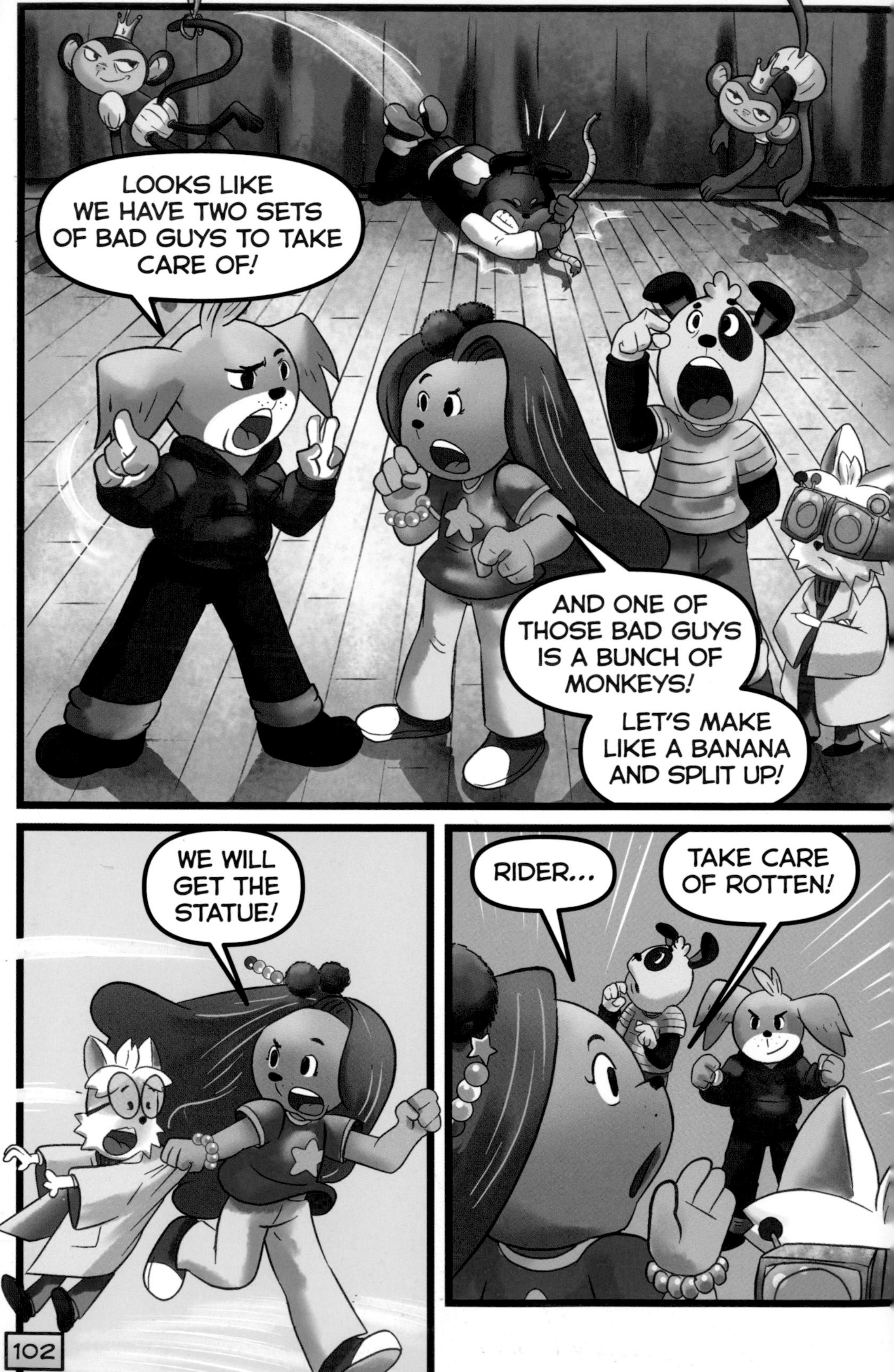
LOOKS LIKE WE HAVE TWO SETS OF BAD GUYS TO TAKE CARE OF!
AND ONE OF THOSE BAD GUYS IS A BUNCH OF MONKEYS!
LET'S MAKE LIKE A BANANA AND SPLIT UP!
WE WILL GET THE STATUE!
RIDER...
TAKE CARE OF ROTTEN!

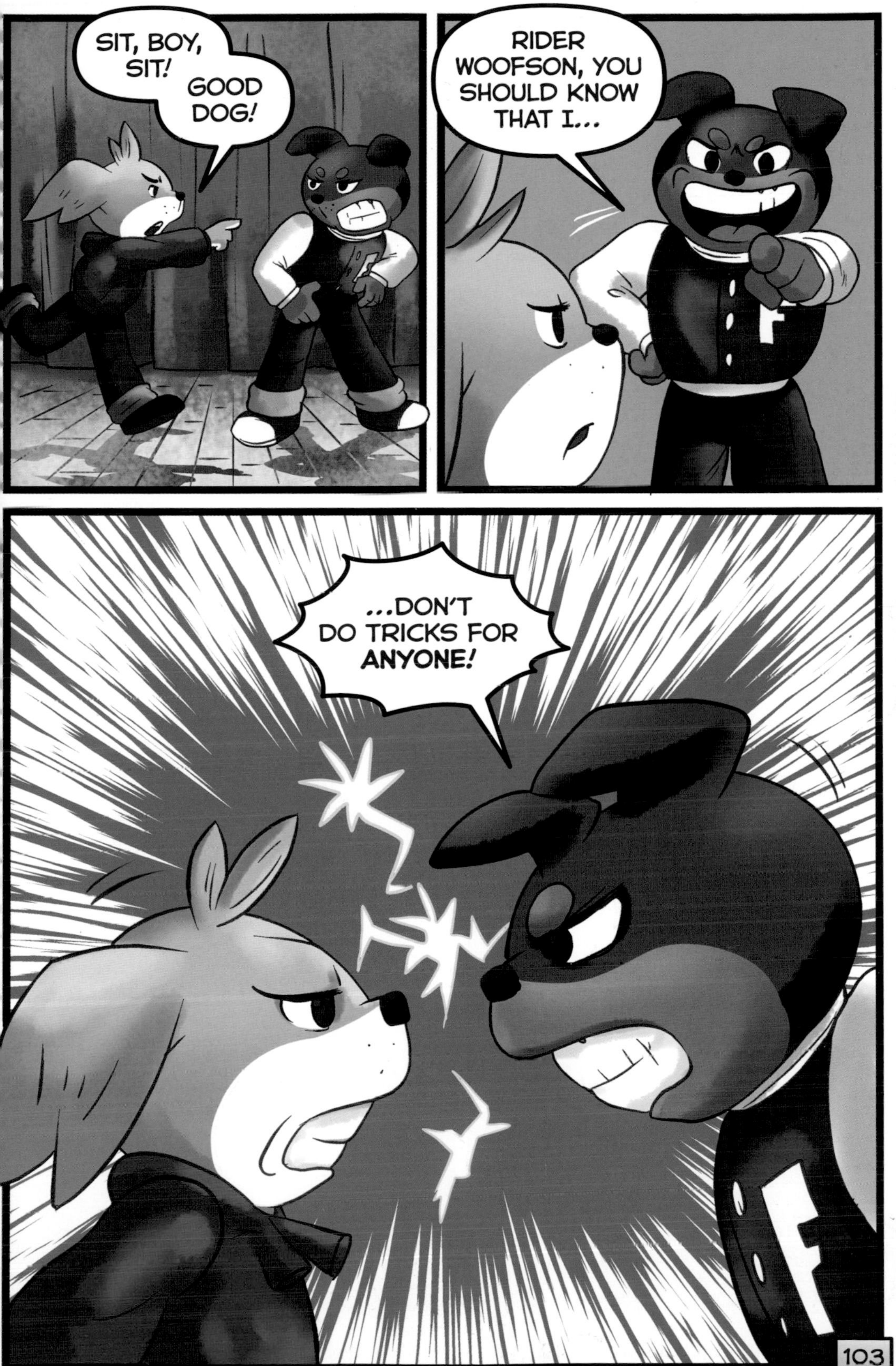
SIT, BOY, SIT!
GOOD DOG!
RIDER WOOFSON, YOU SHOULD KNOW THAT I...
...DON'T DO TRICKS FOR ANYONE!

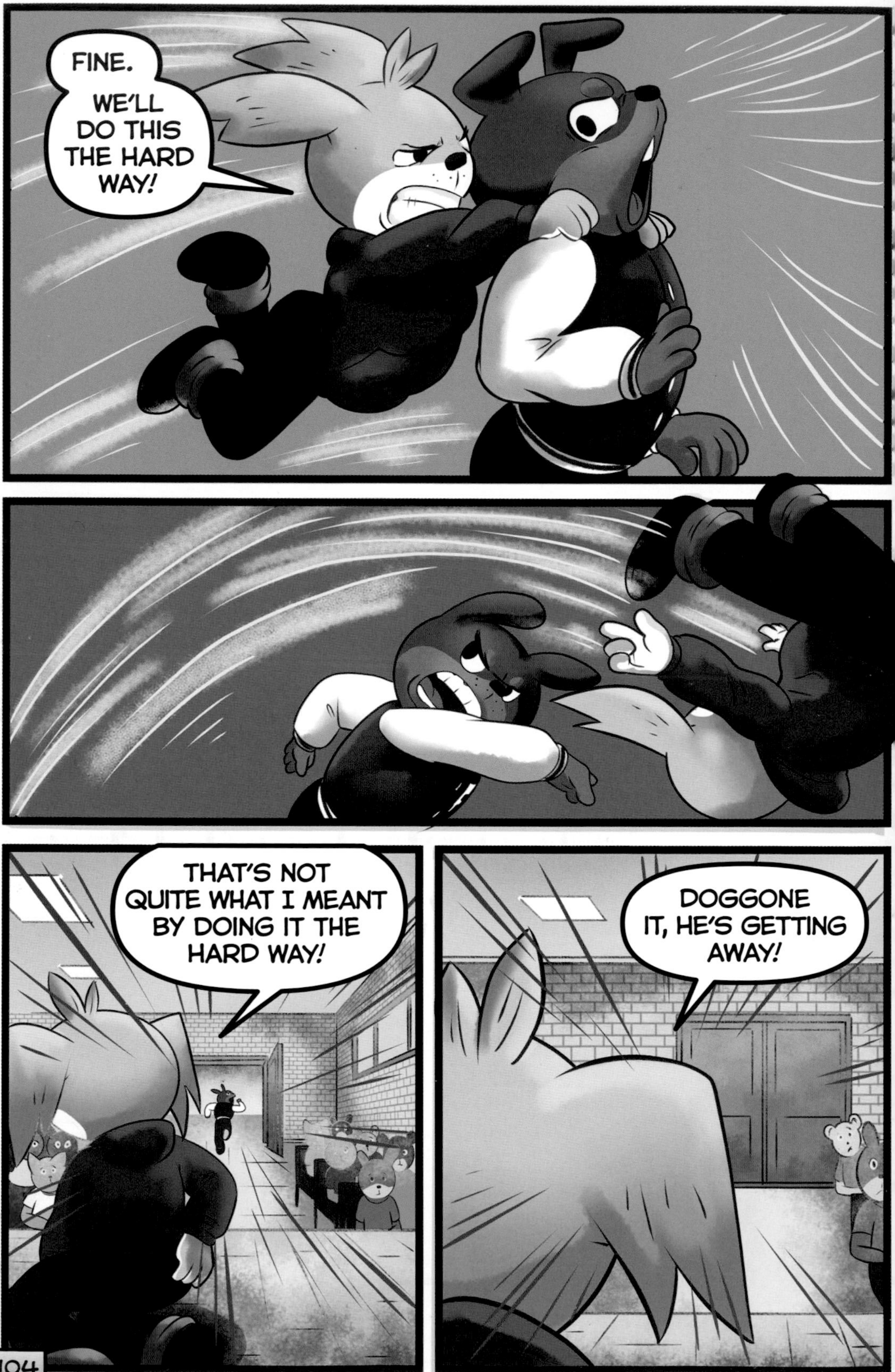
FINE.
WE'LL DO THIS THE HARD WAY!
THAT'S NOT QUITE WHAT I MEANT BY DOING IT THE HARD WAY!
DOGGONE IT, HE'S GETTING AWAY!

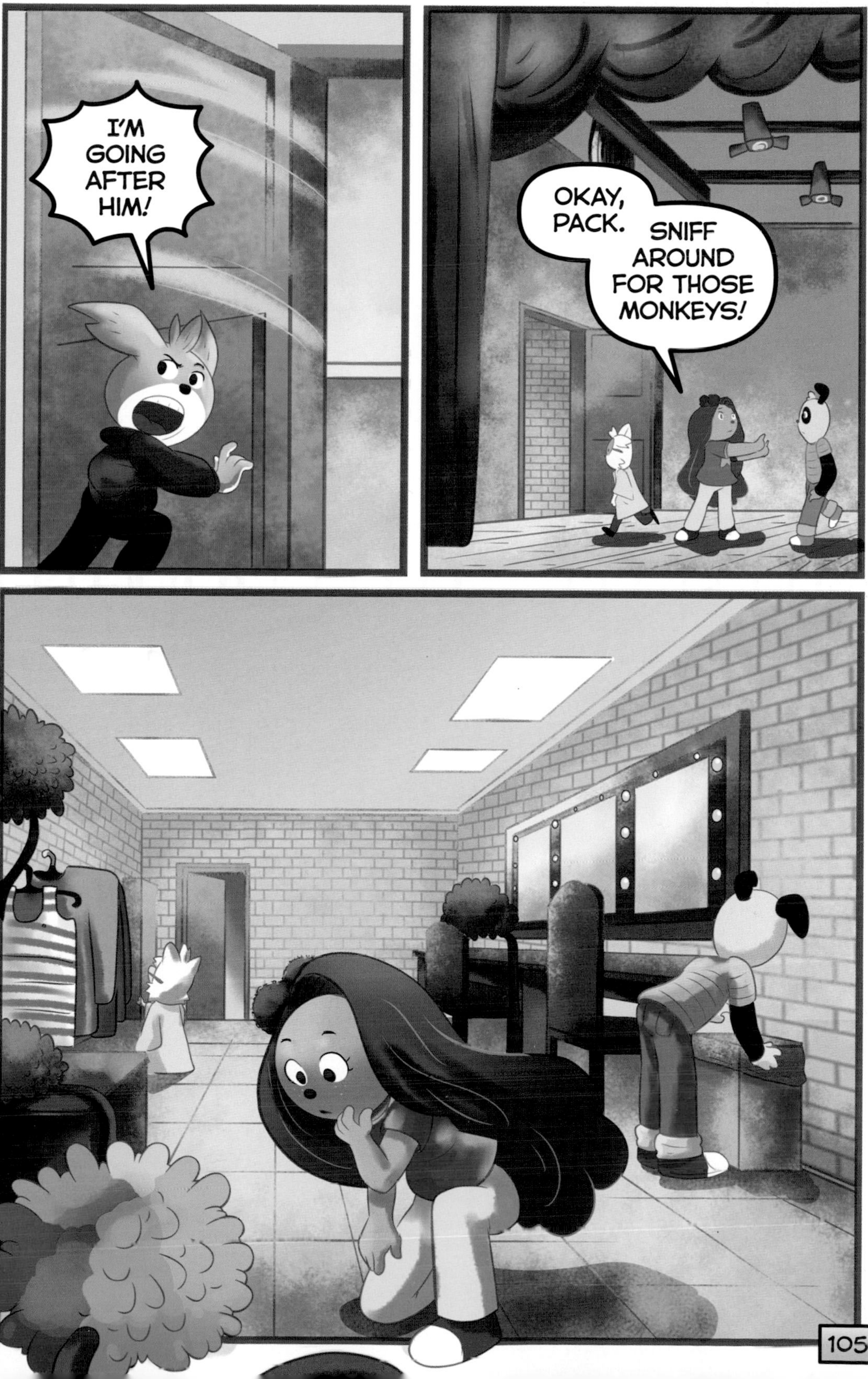
I'M GOING AFTER HIM!
OKAY, PACK.
SNIFF AROUND FOR THOSE MONKEYS!

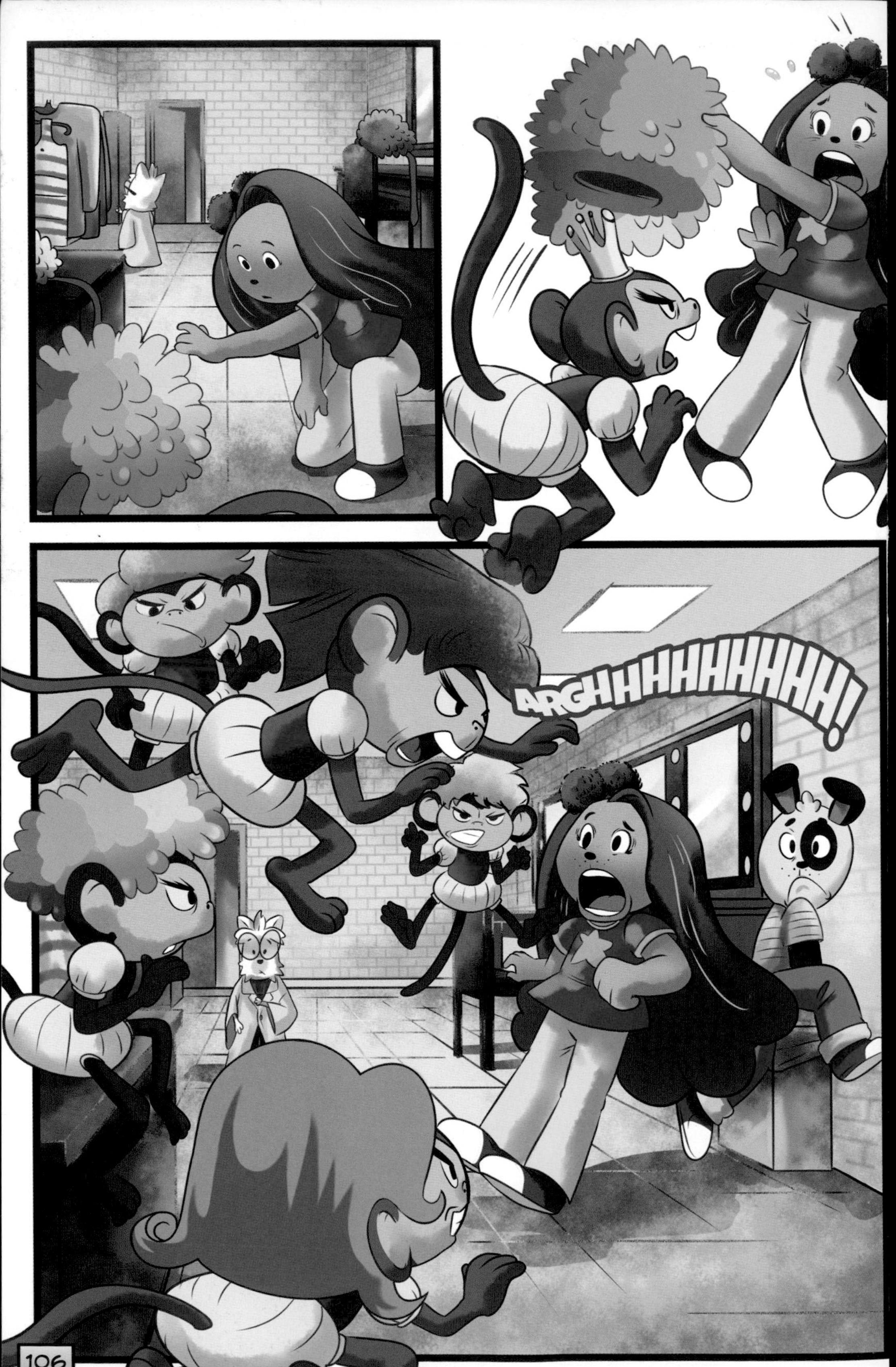
ARGHHHHHHHHH!

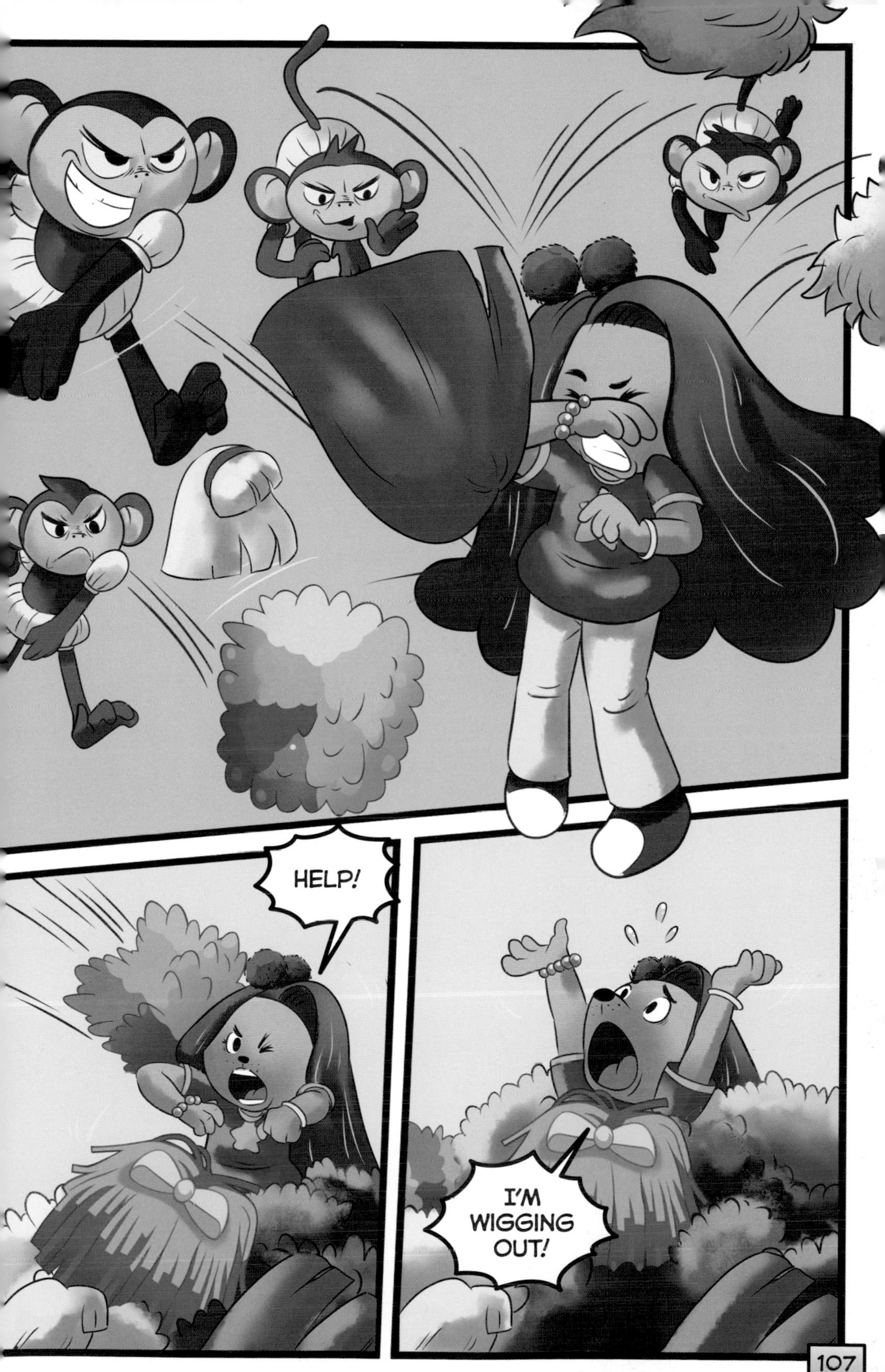
HELP!
I'M WIGGING OUT!

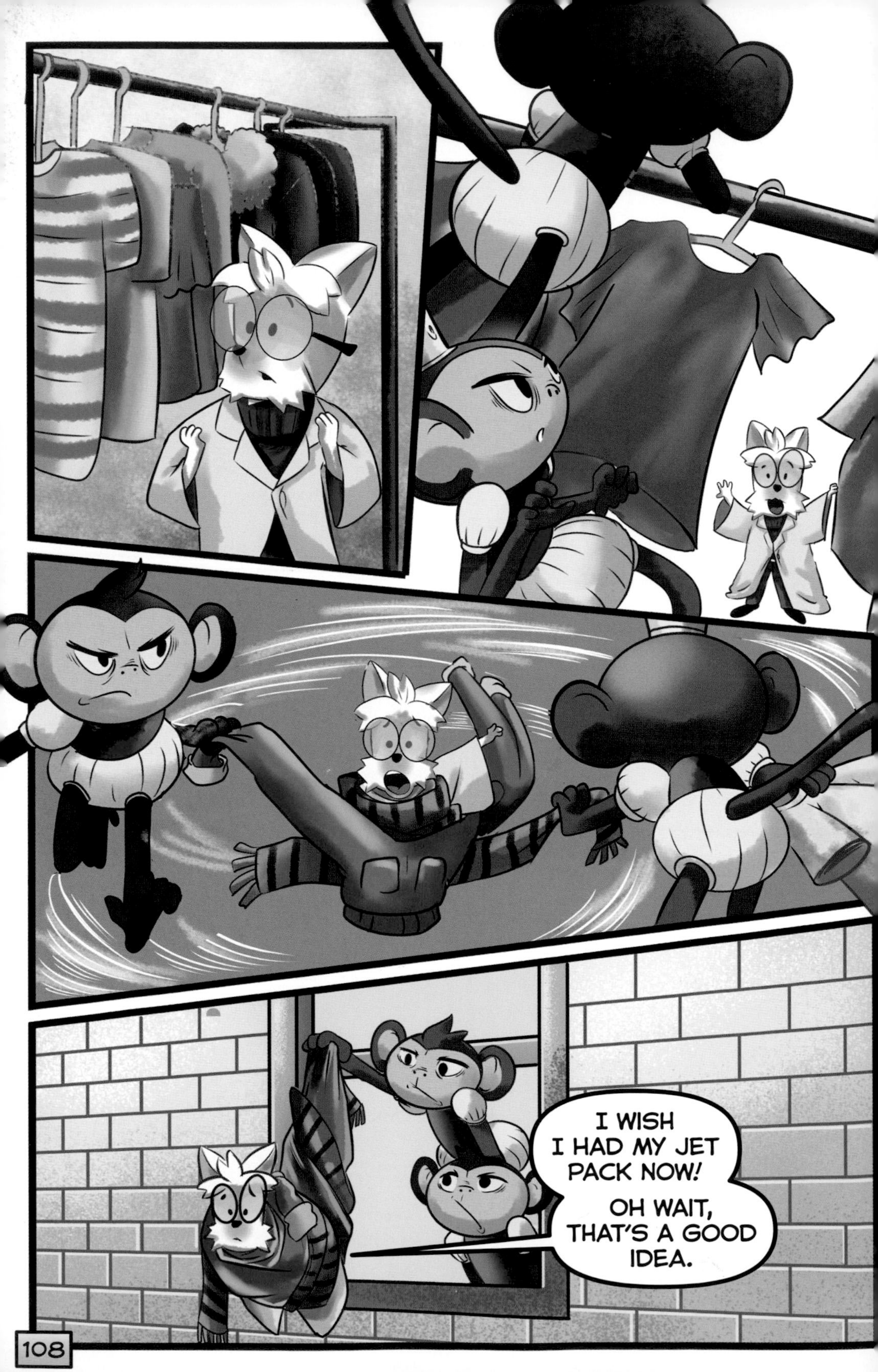
I WISH I HAD MY JET PACK NOW!
OH WAIT, THAT'S A GOOD IDEA.

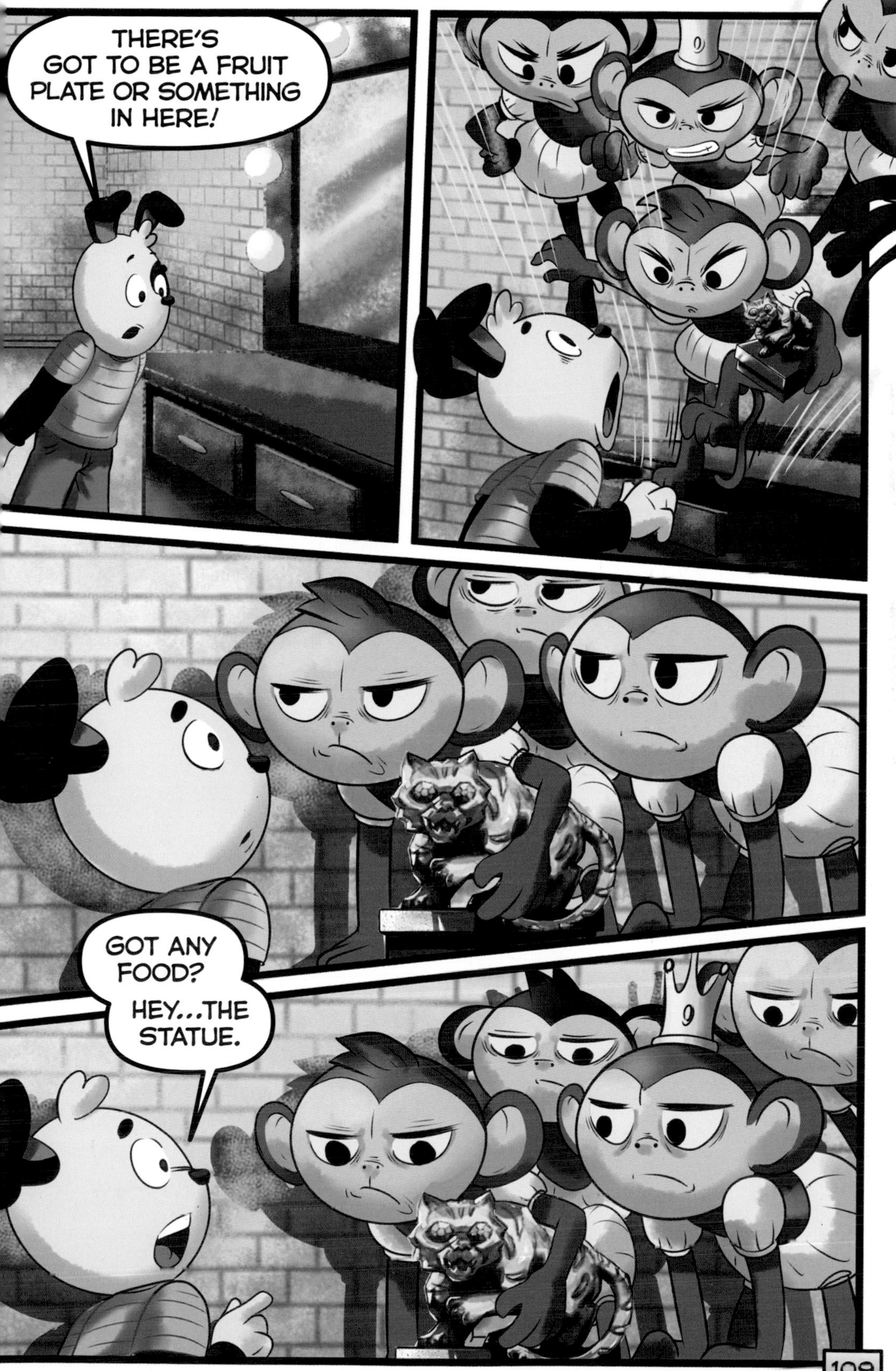
THERE'S GOT TO BE A FRUIT PLATE OR SOMETHING IN HERE!
GOT ANY FOOD?
HEY...THE STATUE.

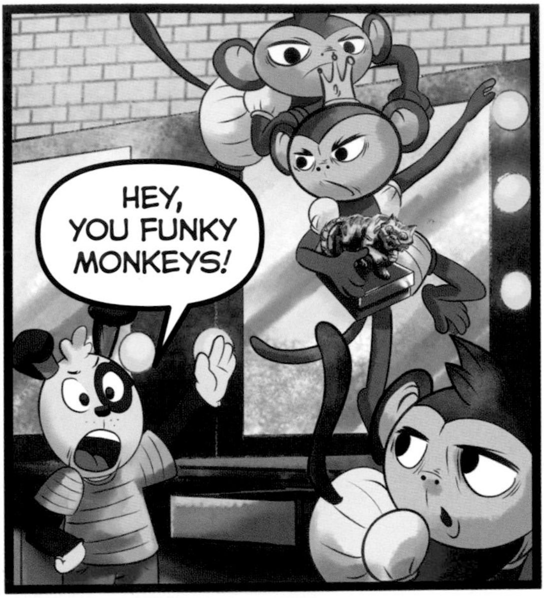
HEY, YOU FUNKY MONKEYS!
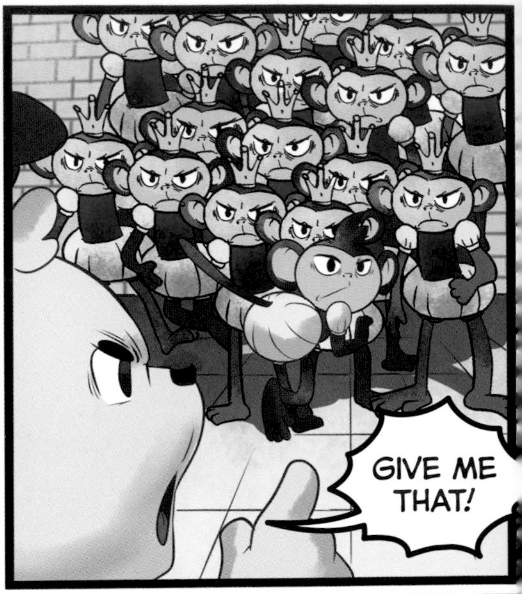
GIVE ME THAT!
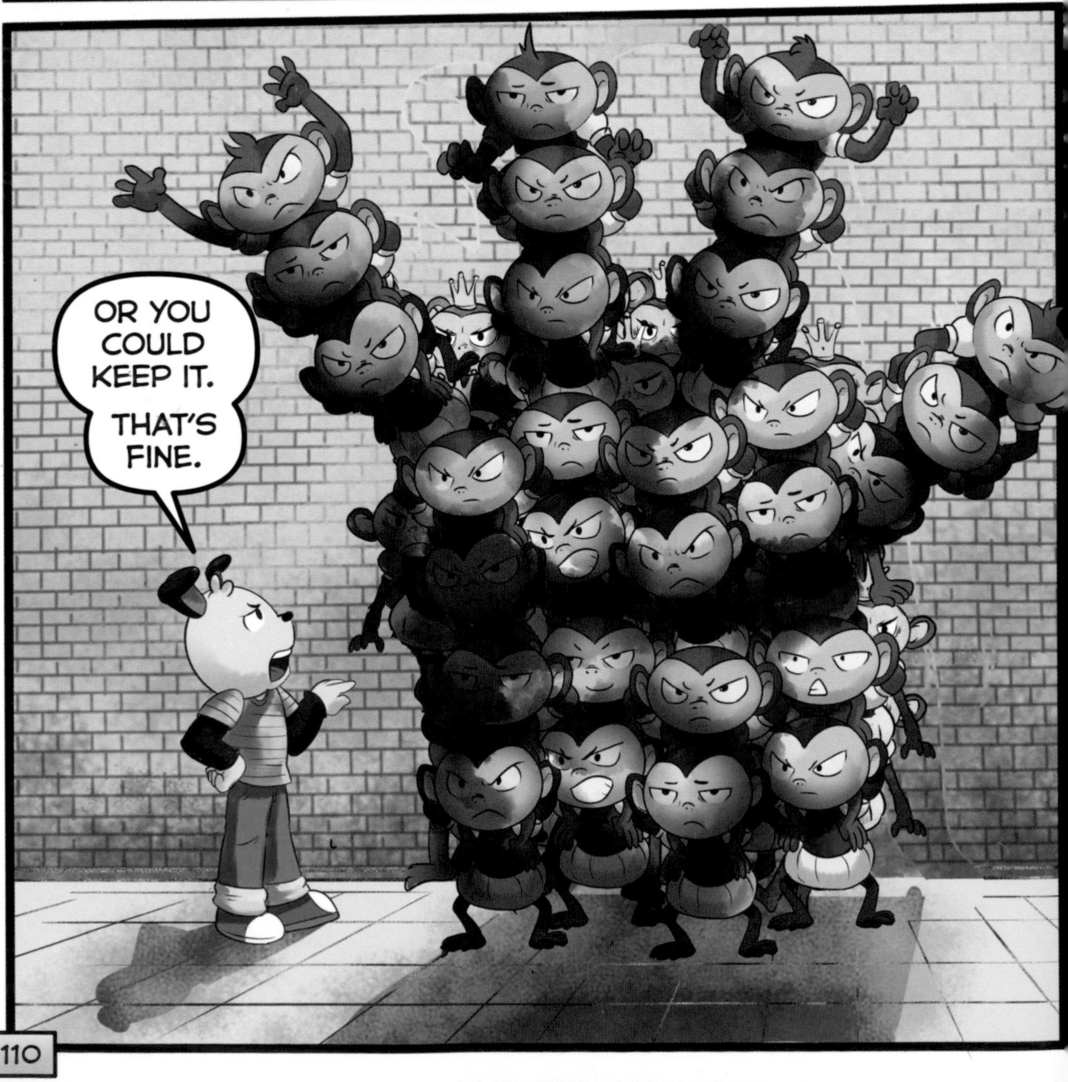
OR YOU COULD KEEP IT.
THAT'S FINE.

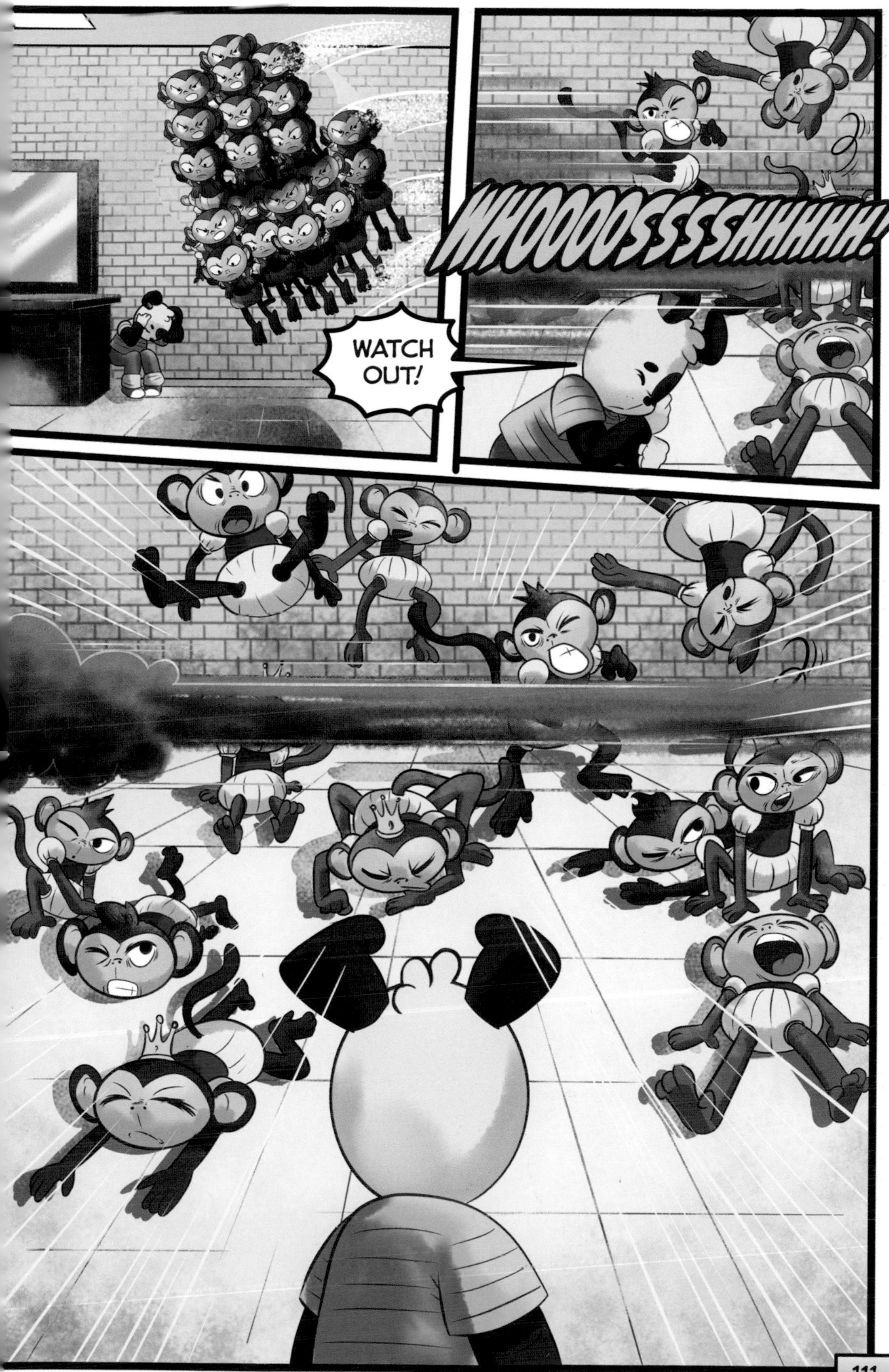
WATCH OUT!
WHOOOOOSSSSHHHHH!

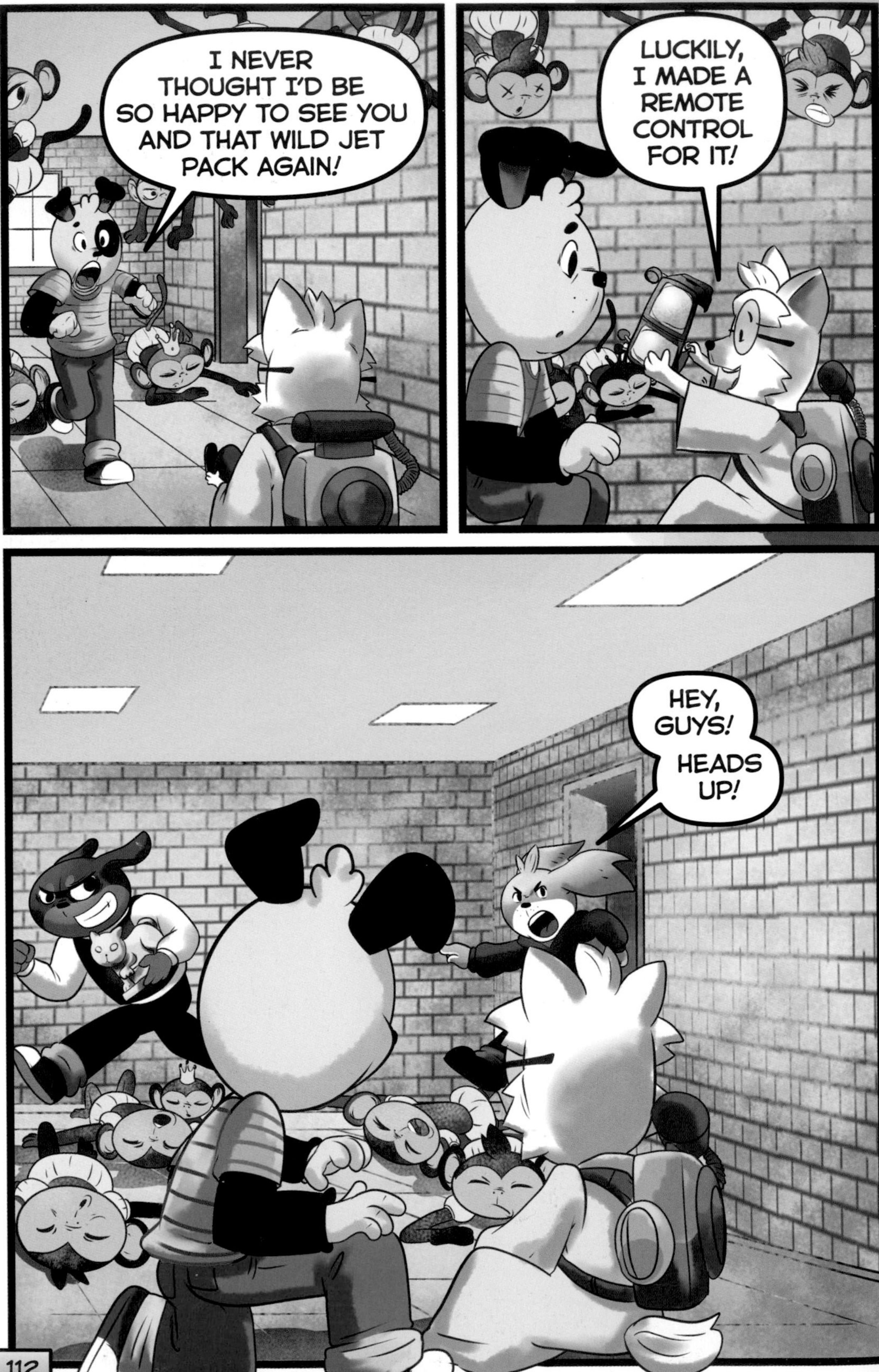
I NEVER THOUGHT I'D BE SO HAPPY TO SEE YOU AND THAT WILD JET PACK AGAIN!
LUCKILY, I MADE A REMOTE CONTROL FOR IT!
HEY, GUYS!
HEADS UP!

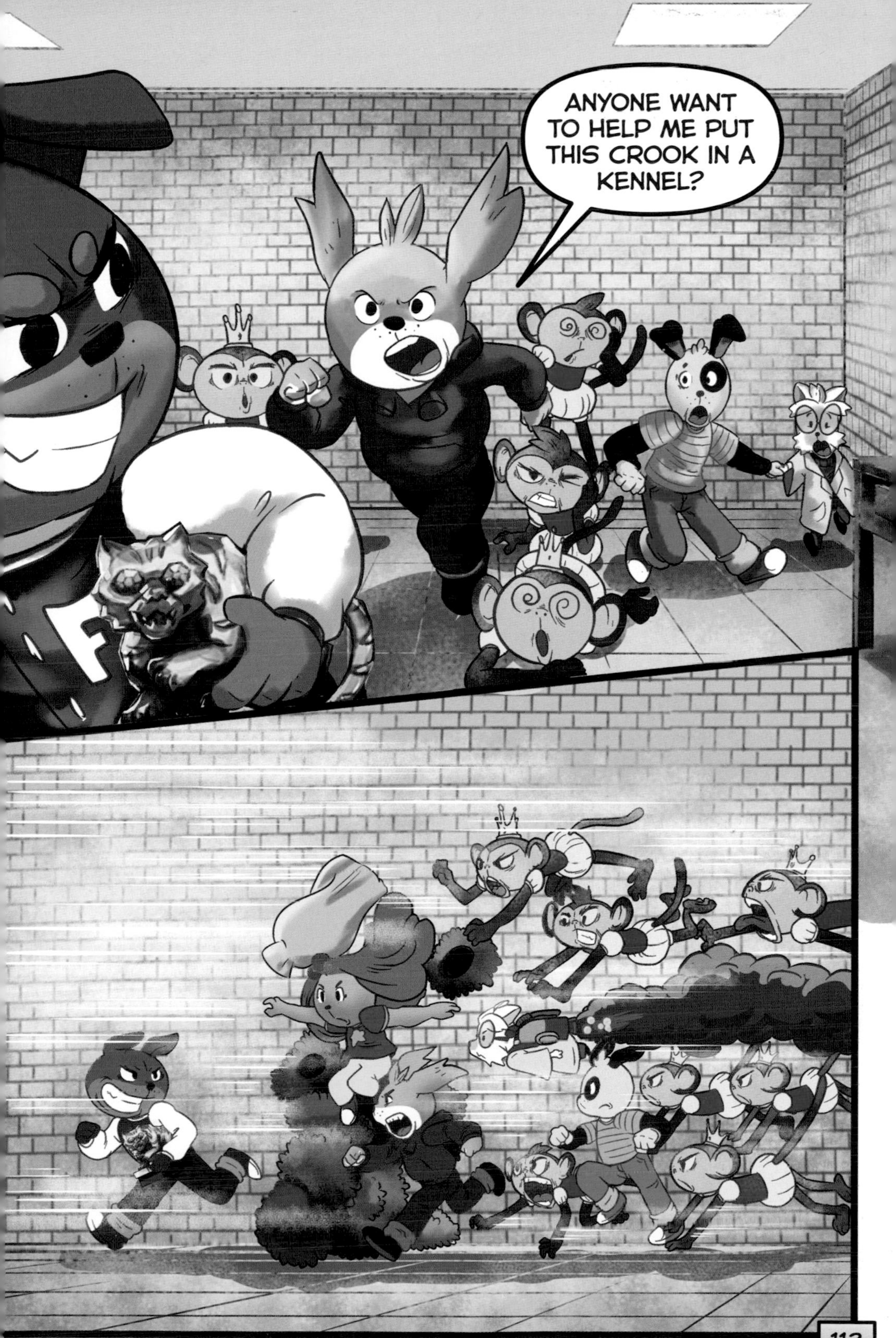
ANYONE WANT TO HELP ME PUT THIS CROOK IN A KENNEL?

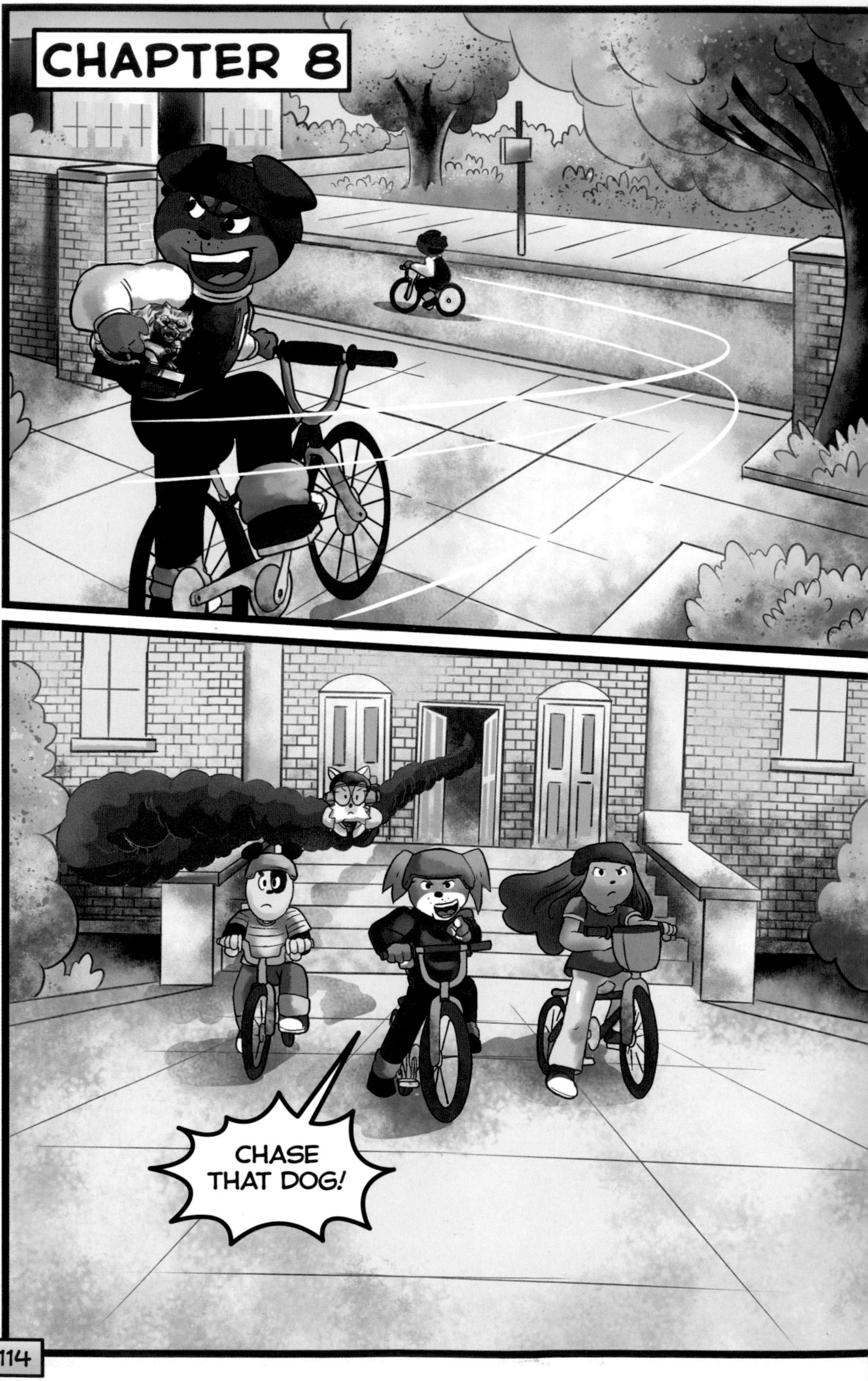
CHAPTER 8
CHASE THAT DOG!

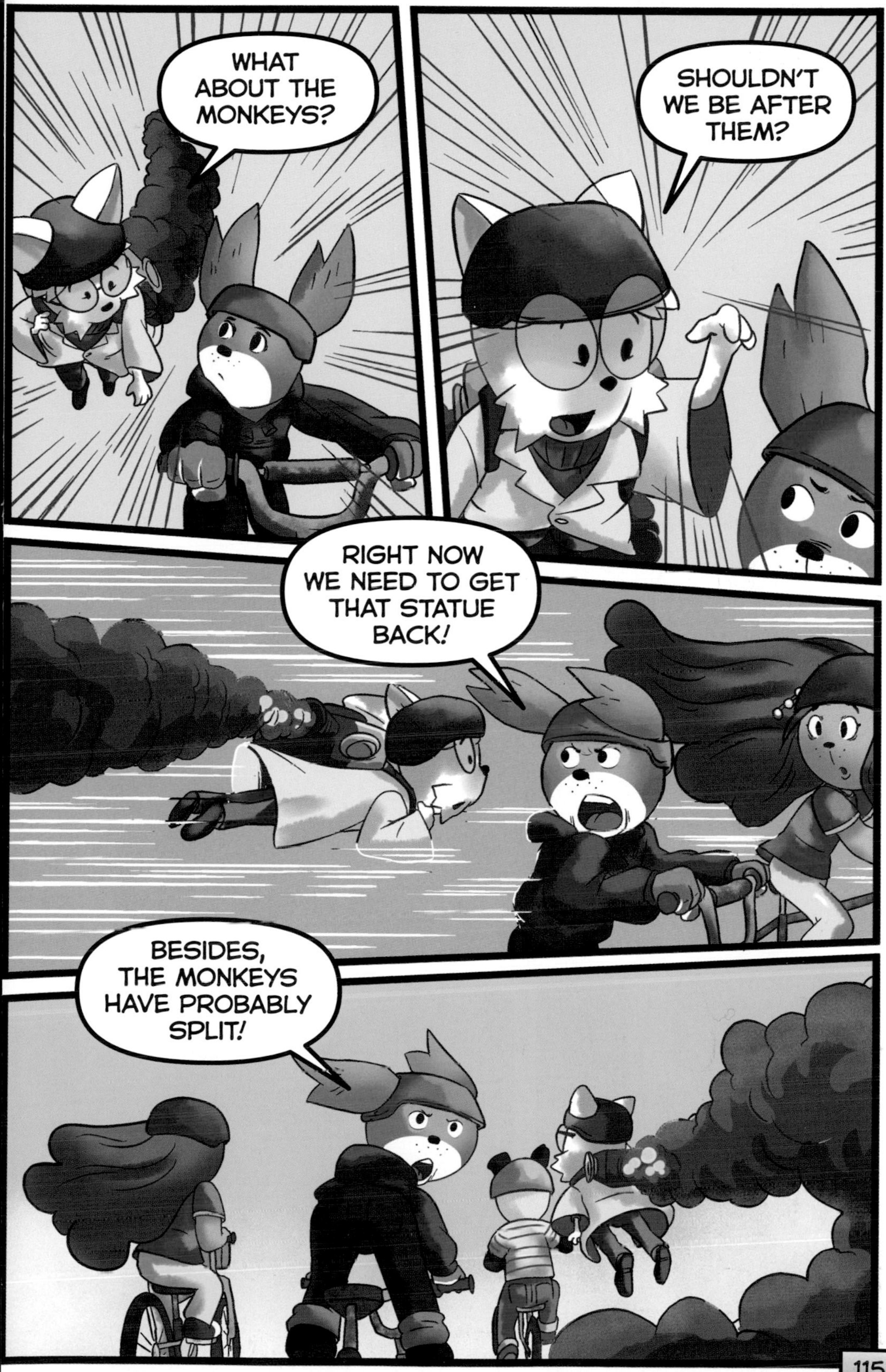
WHAT ABOUT THE MONKEYS?
SHOULDN'T WE BE AFTER THEM?
RIGHT NOW WE NEED TO GET THAT STATUE BACK!
BESIDES, THE MONKEYS HAVE PROBABLY SPLIT!

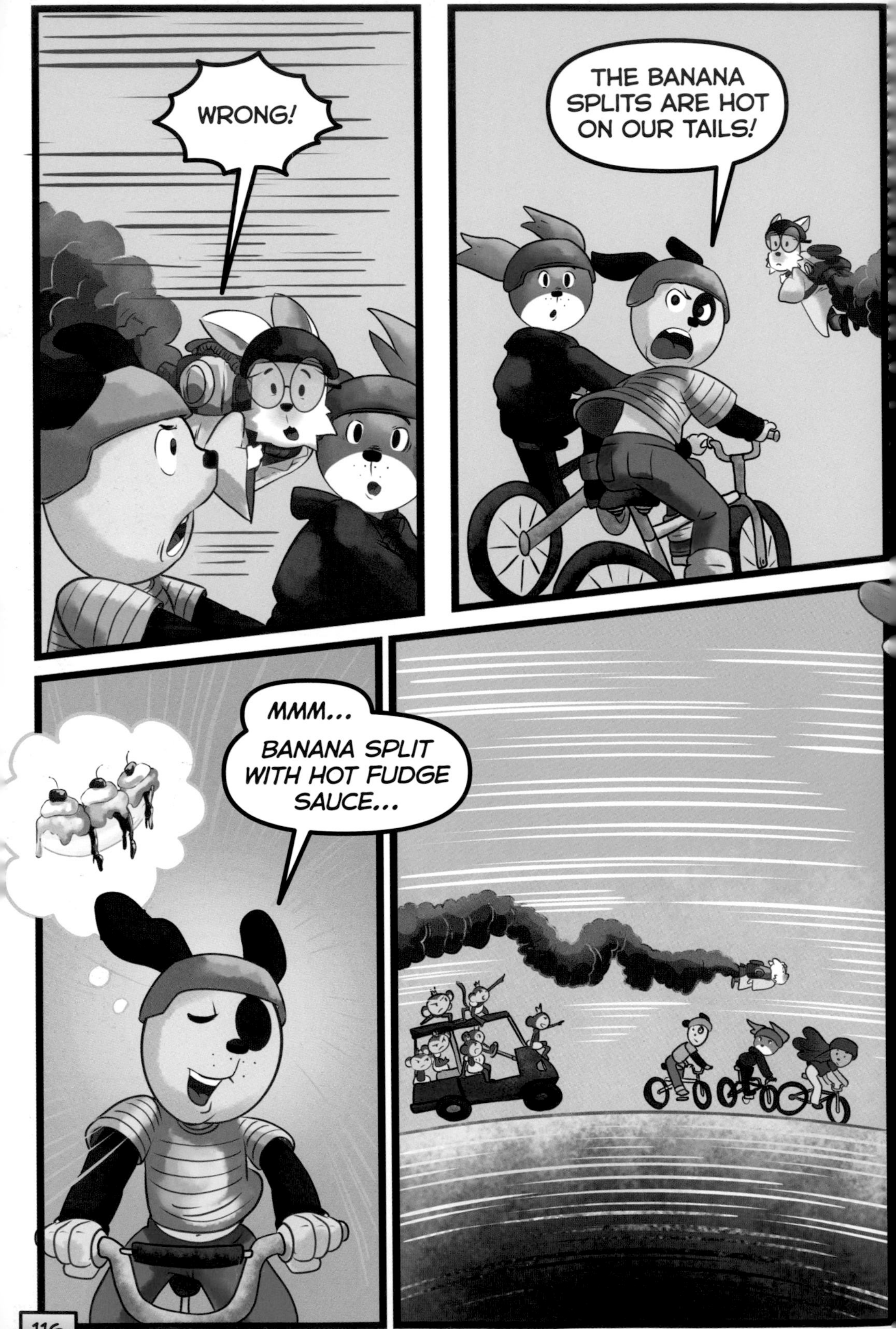
WRONG!
THE BANANA SPLITS ARE HOT ON OUR TAILS!
MMM... BANANA SPLIT WITH HOT FUDGE SAUCE...

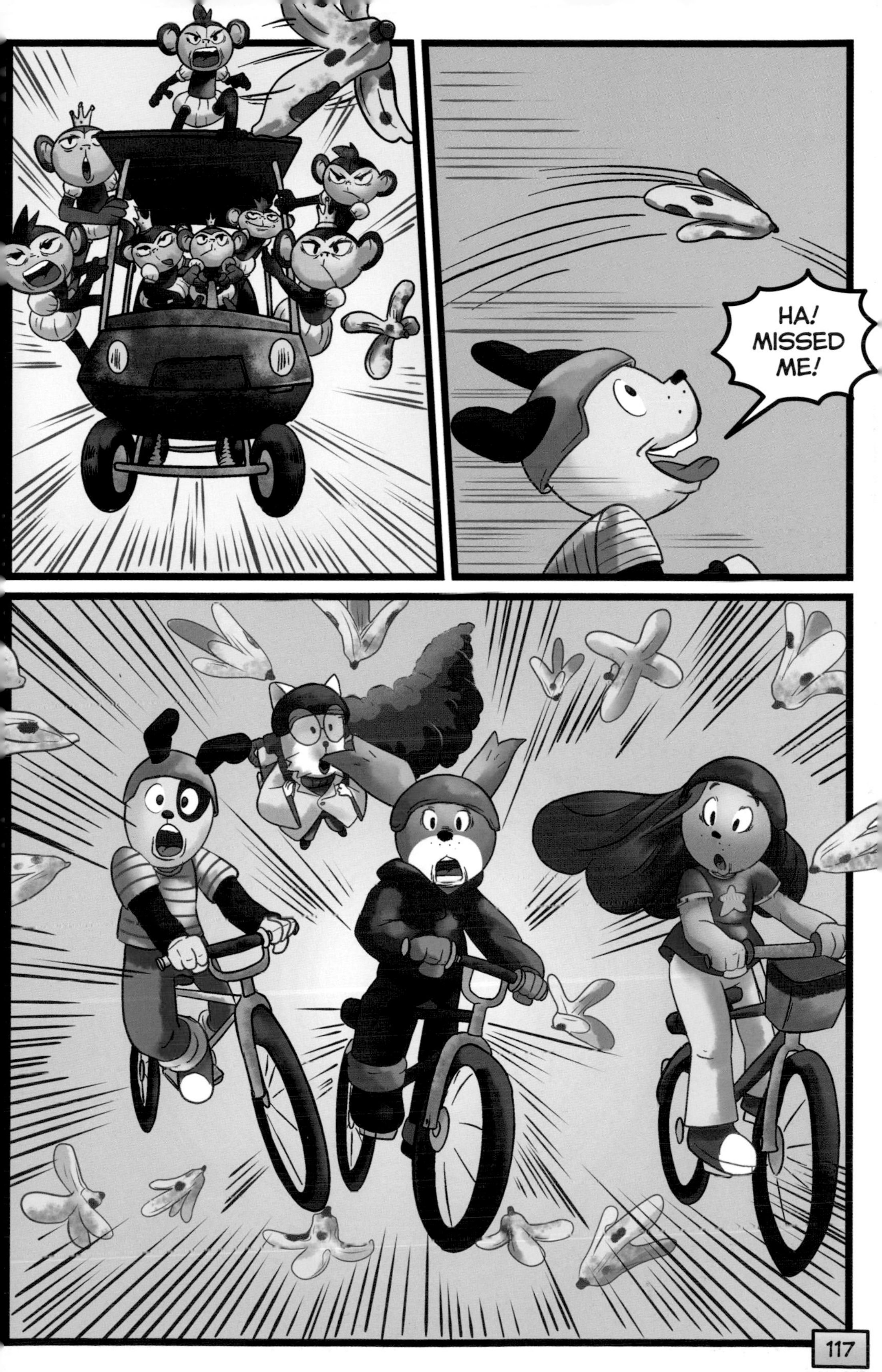
HA! MISSED ME!

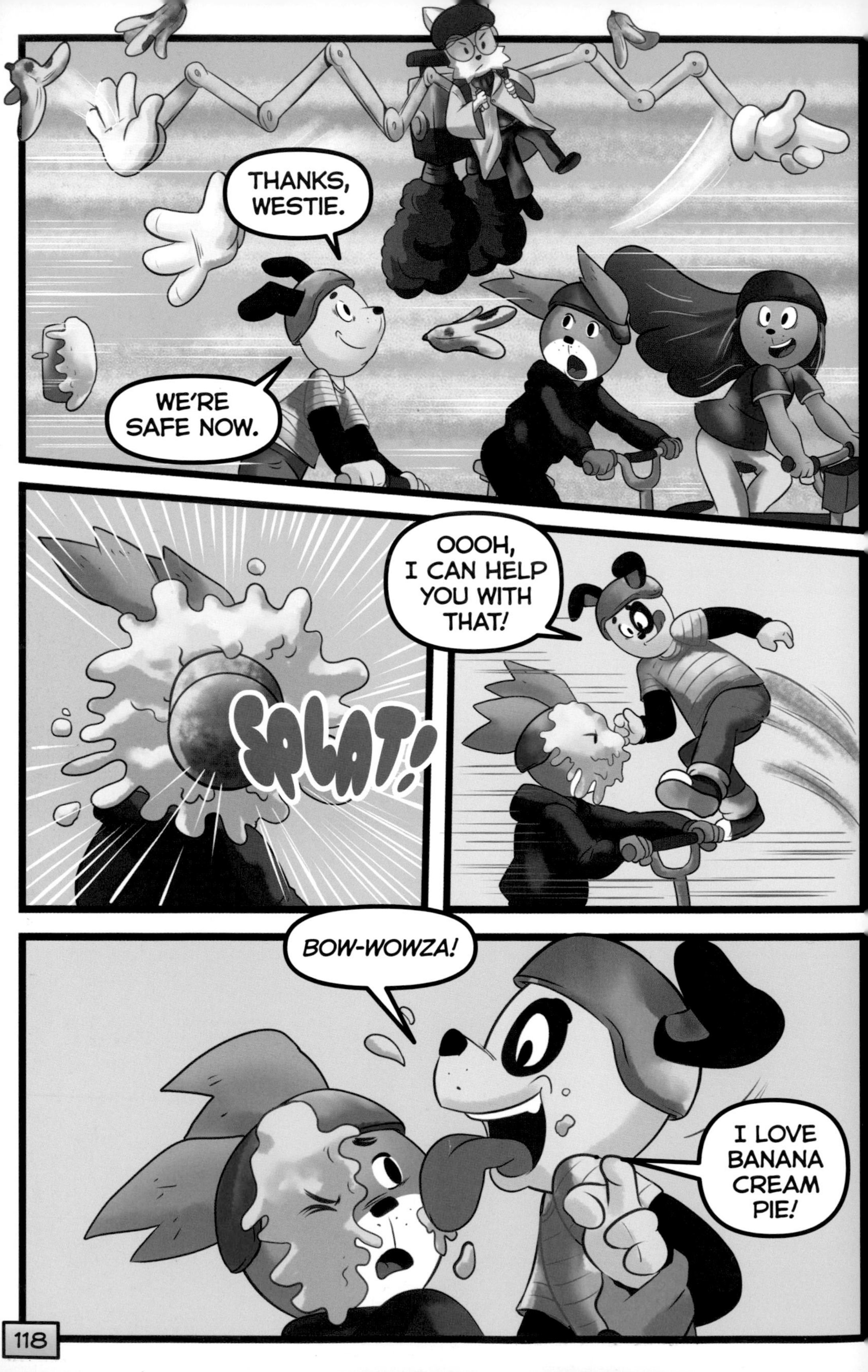
THANKS, WESTIE.
WE'RE SAFE NOW.
SPLAT!
OOOH, I CAN HELP YOU WITH THAT!
BOW-WOWZA!
I LOVE BANANA CREAM PIE!

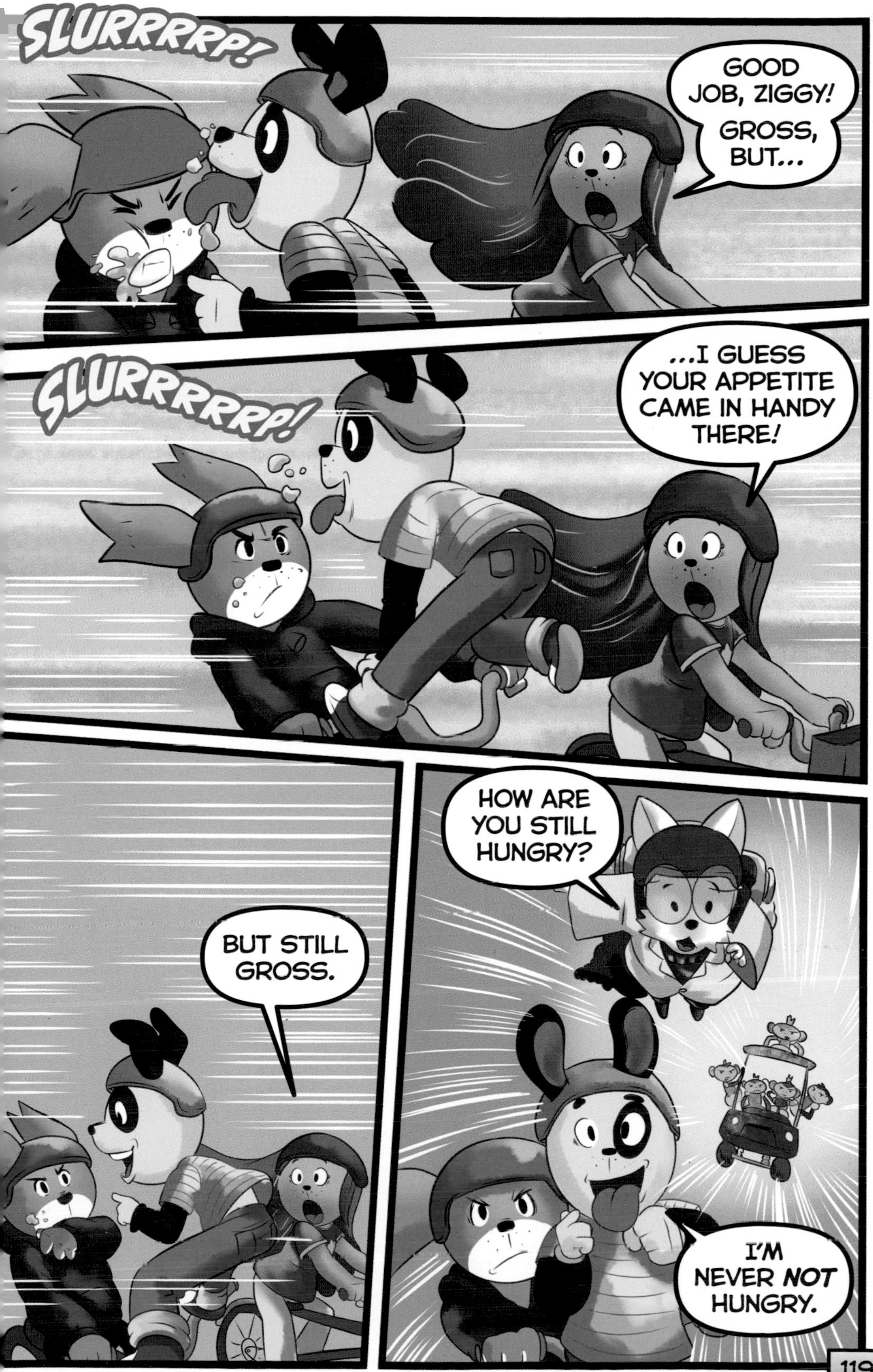
SLURRRRP!
GOOD JOB, ZIGGY!
GROSS, BUT...
SLURRRRRP!
...I GUESS YOUR APPETITE CAME IN HANDY THERE!
BUT STILL GROSS.
HOW ARE YOU STILL HUNGRY?
I'M NEVER *NOT* HUNGRY.

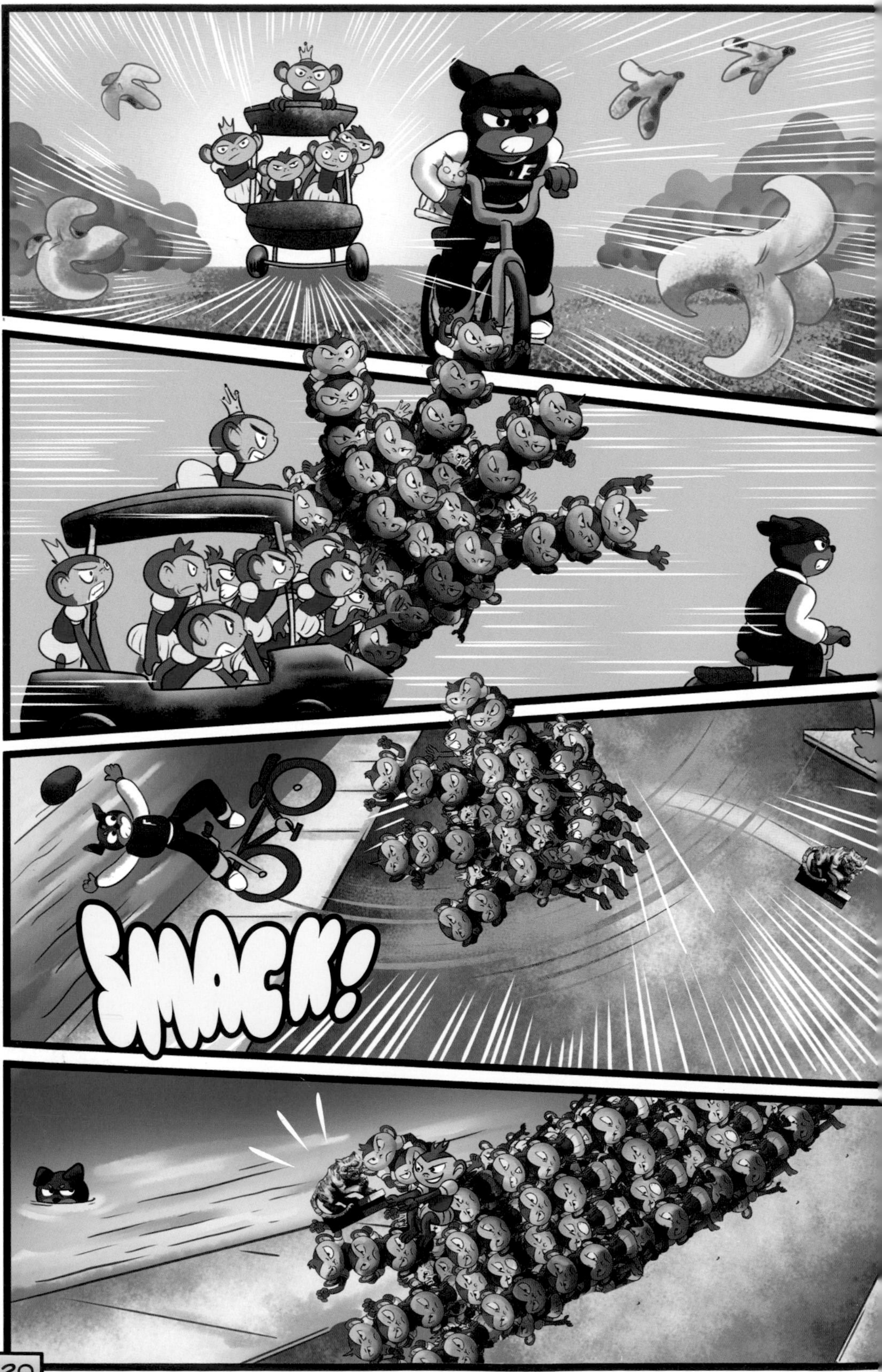
SMACK!

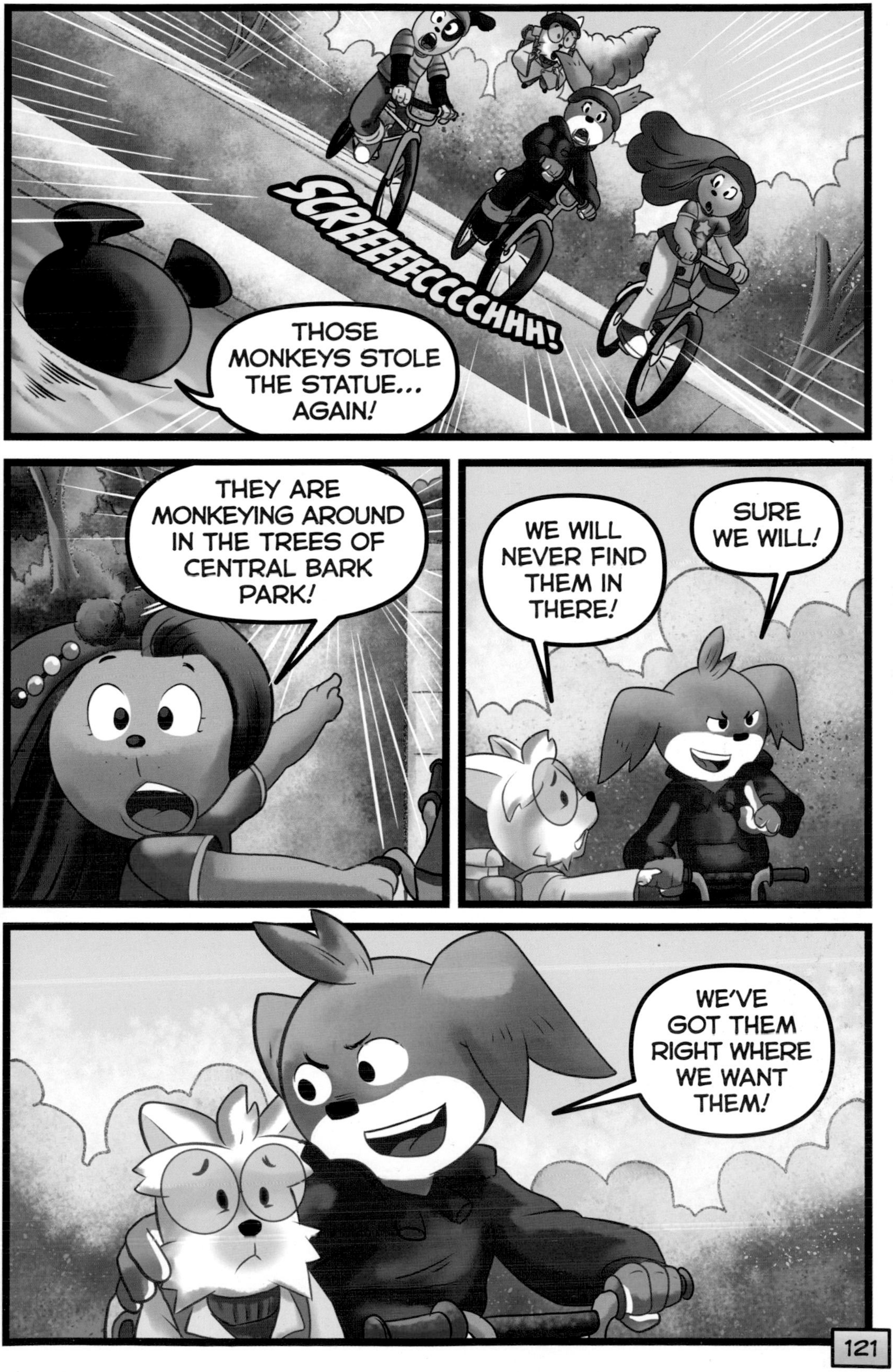
SCREEEEEECCCCHHH!
THOSE MONKEYS STOLE THE STATUE... AGAIN!
THEY ARE MONKEYING AROUND IN THE TREES OF CENTRAL BARK PARK!
WE WILL NEVER FIND THEM IN THERE!
SURE WE WILL!
WE'VE GOT THEM RIGHT WHERE WE WANT THEM!

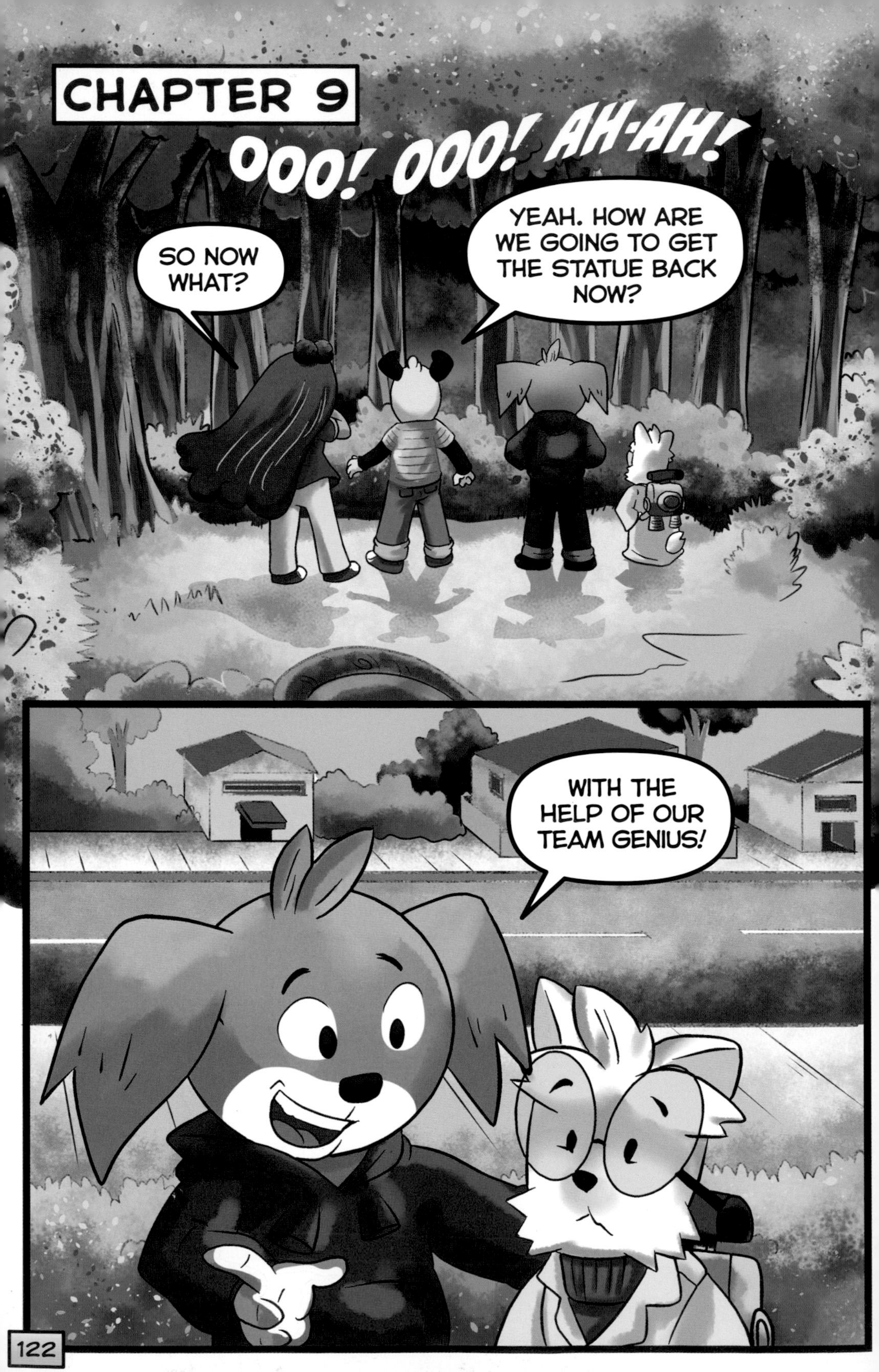
CHAPTER 9
OOO! OOO! AH-AH!
SO NOW WHAT?
YEAH. HOW ARE WE GOING TO GET THE STATUE BACK NOW?
WITH THE HELP OF OUR TEAM GENIUS!

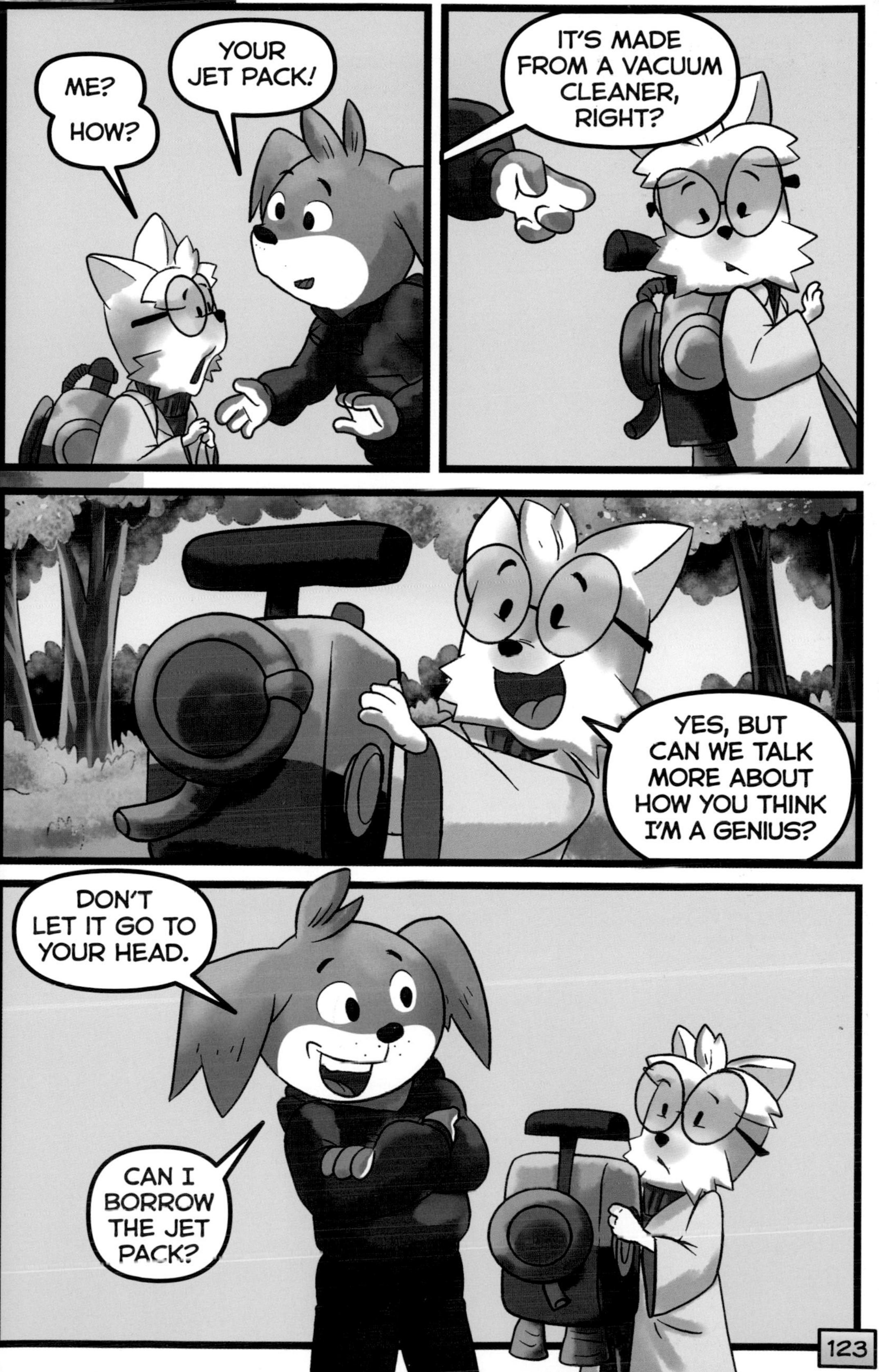
ME?
HOW?
YOUR JET PACK!
IT'S MADE FROM A VACUUM CLEANER, RIGHT?
YES, BUT CAN WE TALK MORE ABOUT HOW YOU THINK I'M A GENIUS?
DON'T LET IT GO TO YOUR HEAD.
CAN I BORROW THE JET PACK?

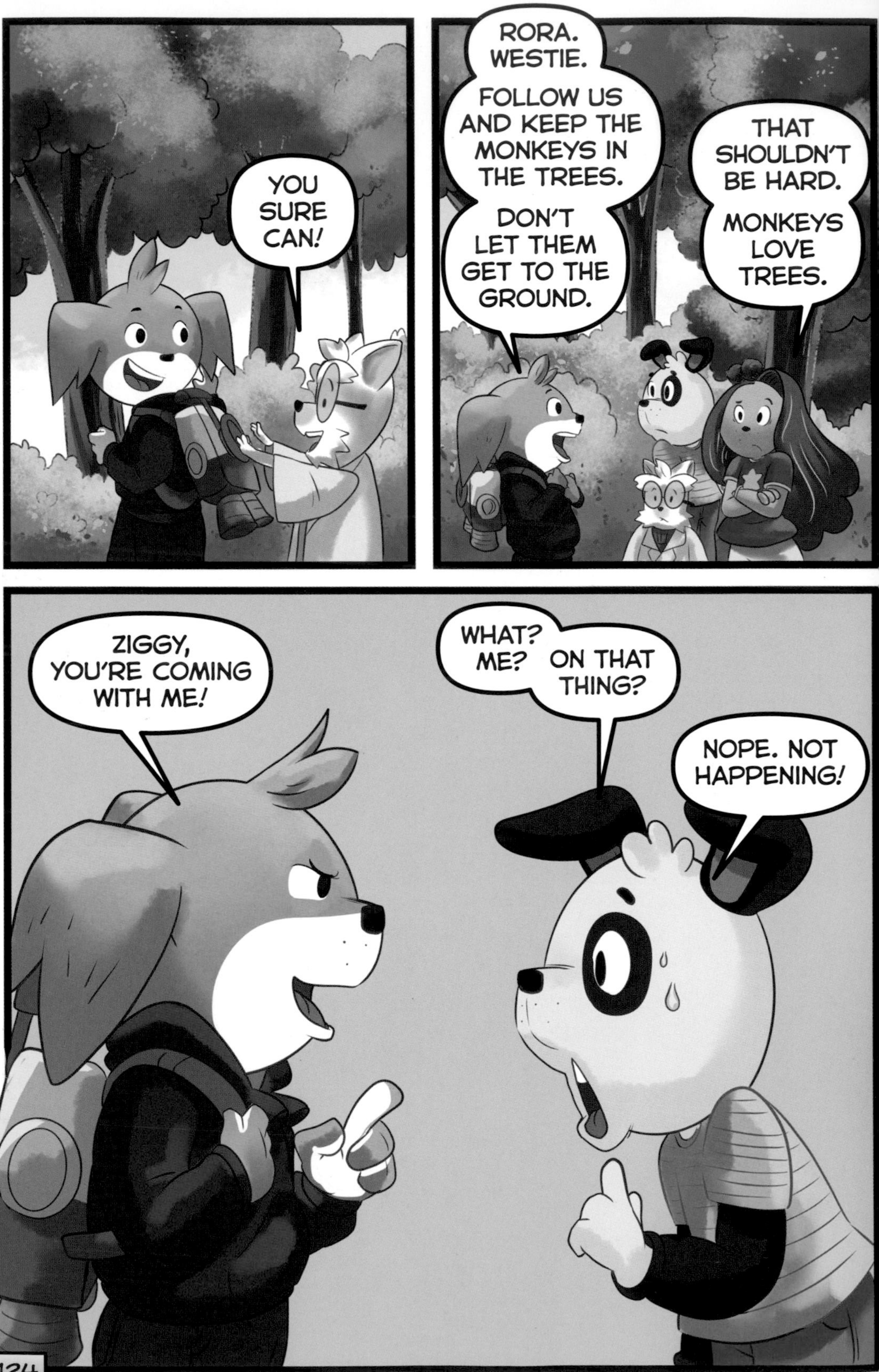
YOU SURE CAN!
RORA. WESTIE.
FOLLOW US AND KEEP THE MONKEYS IN THE TREES.
DON'T LET THEM GET TO THE GROUND.
THAT SHOULDN'T BE HARD.
MONKEYS LOVE TREES.
ZIGGY, YOU'RE COMING WITH ME!
WHAT? ME?
ON THAT THING?
NOPE. NOT HAPPENING!

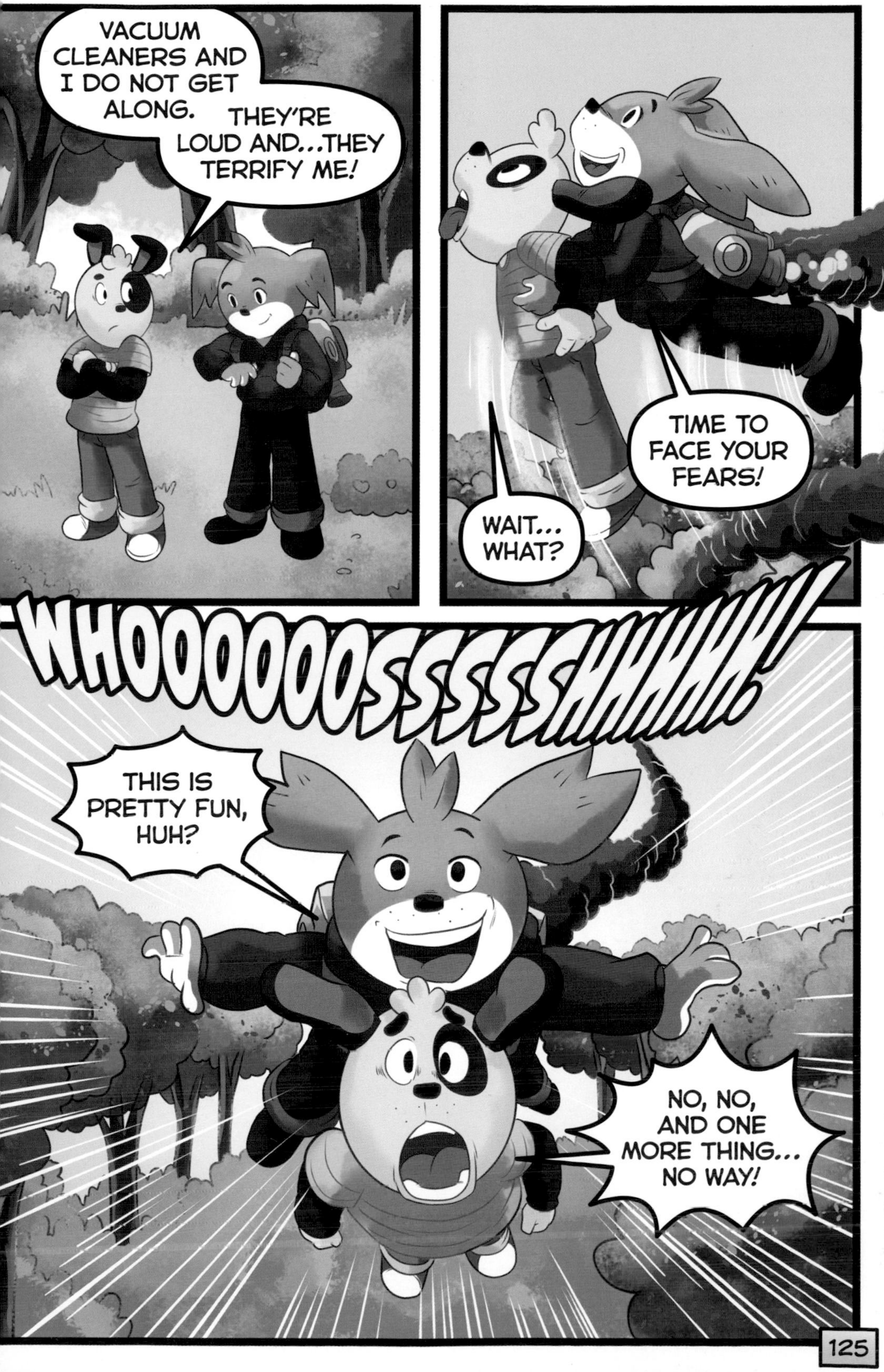
VACUUM CLEANERS AND I DO NOT GET ALONG.
THEY'RE LOUD AND...THEY TERRIFY ME!
TIME TO FACE YOUR FEARS!
WAIT... WHAT?
WHOOOOOOSSSSSHHHHH!
THIS IS PRETTY FUN, HUH?
NO, NO, AND ONE MORE THING... NO WAY!

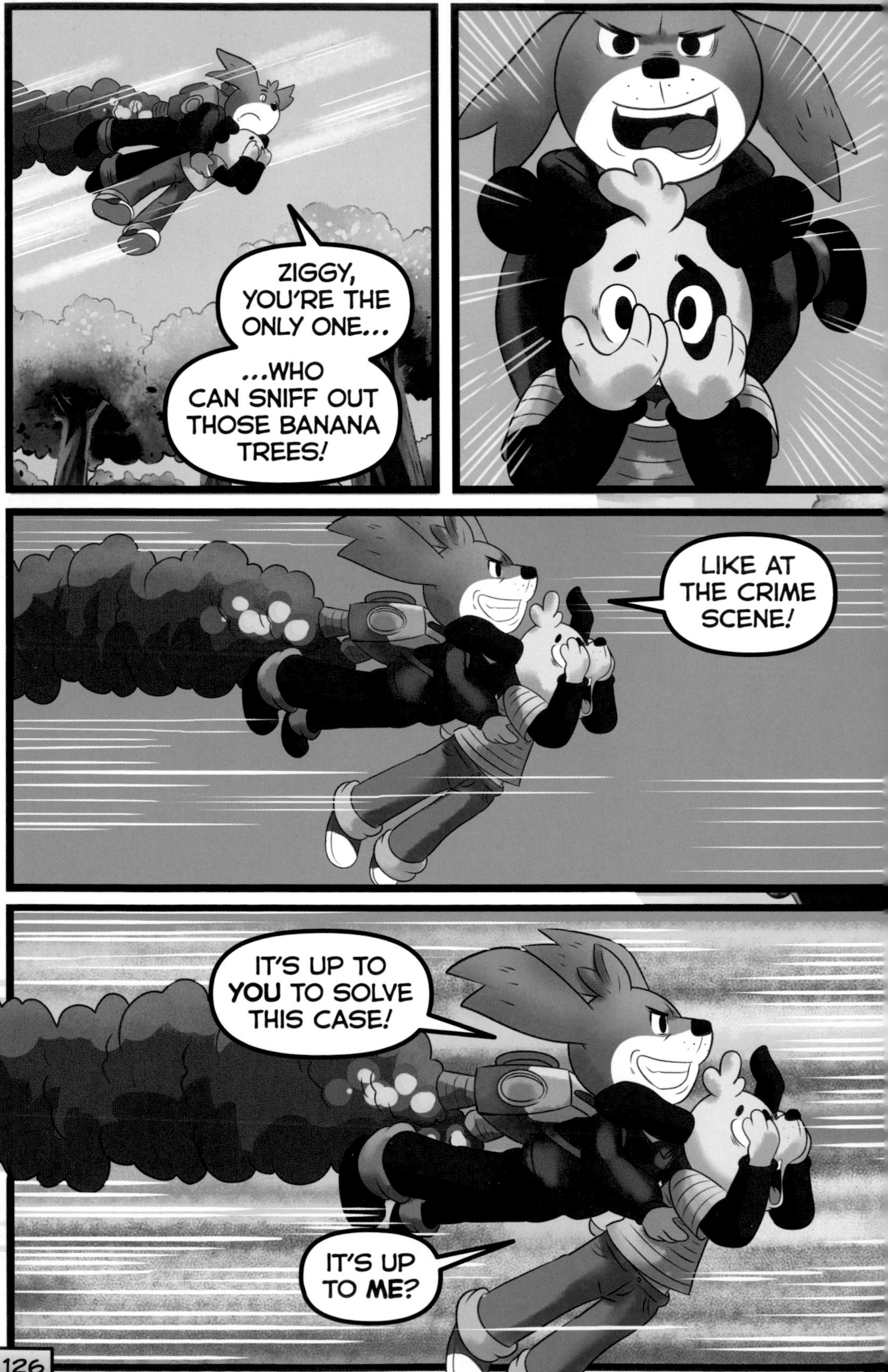
ZIGGY, YOU'RE THE ONLY ONE...
...WHO CAN SNIFF OUT THOSE BANANA TREES!
LIKE AT THE CRIME SCENE!
IT'S UP TO **YOU** TO SOLVE THIS CASE!
IT'S UP TO **ME**?

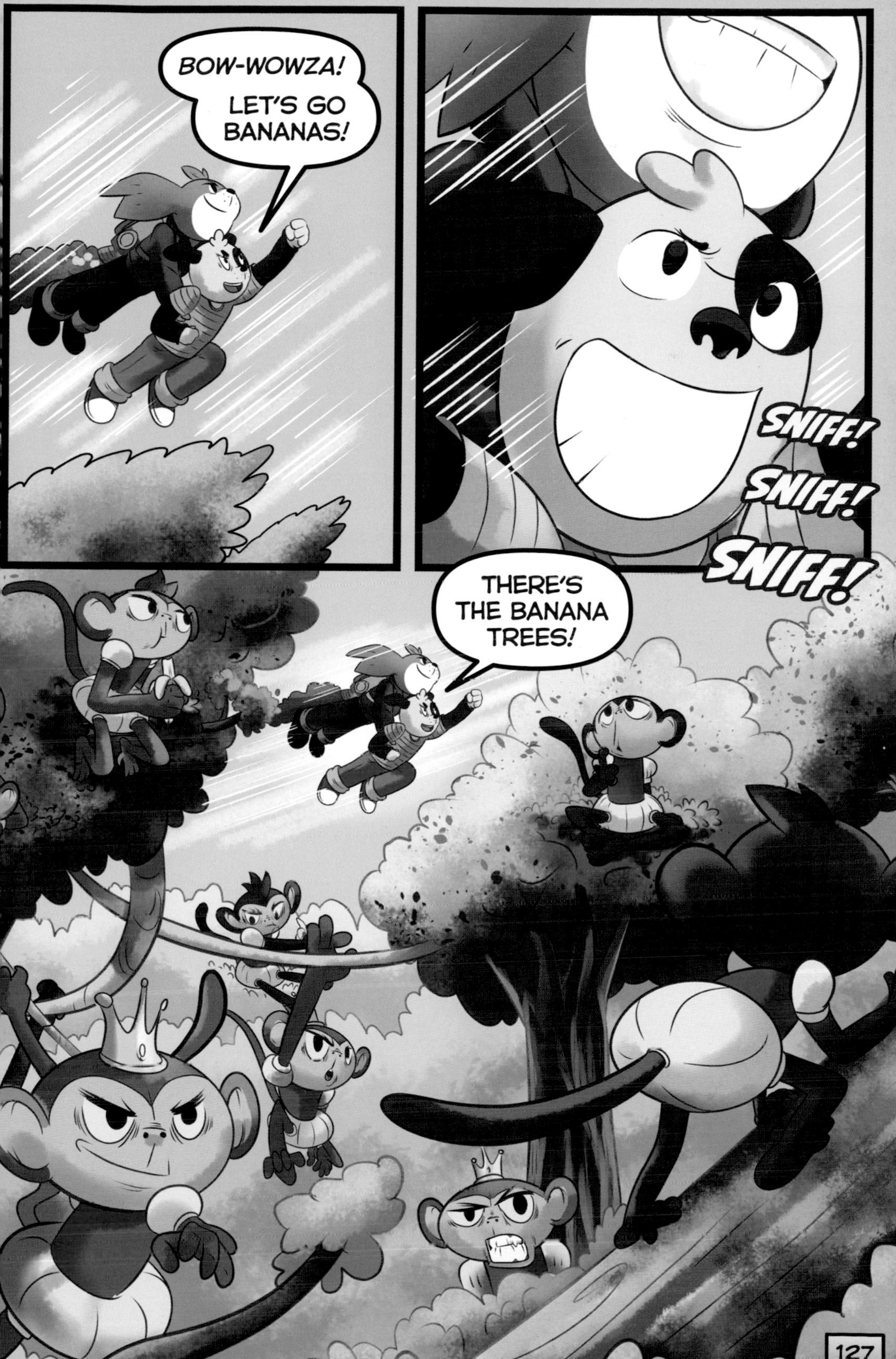
BOW-WOWZA!
LET'S GO BANANAS!
SNIFF!
SNIFF!
SNIFF!
THERE'S THE BANANA TREES!

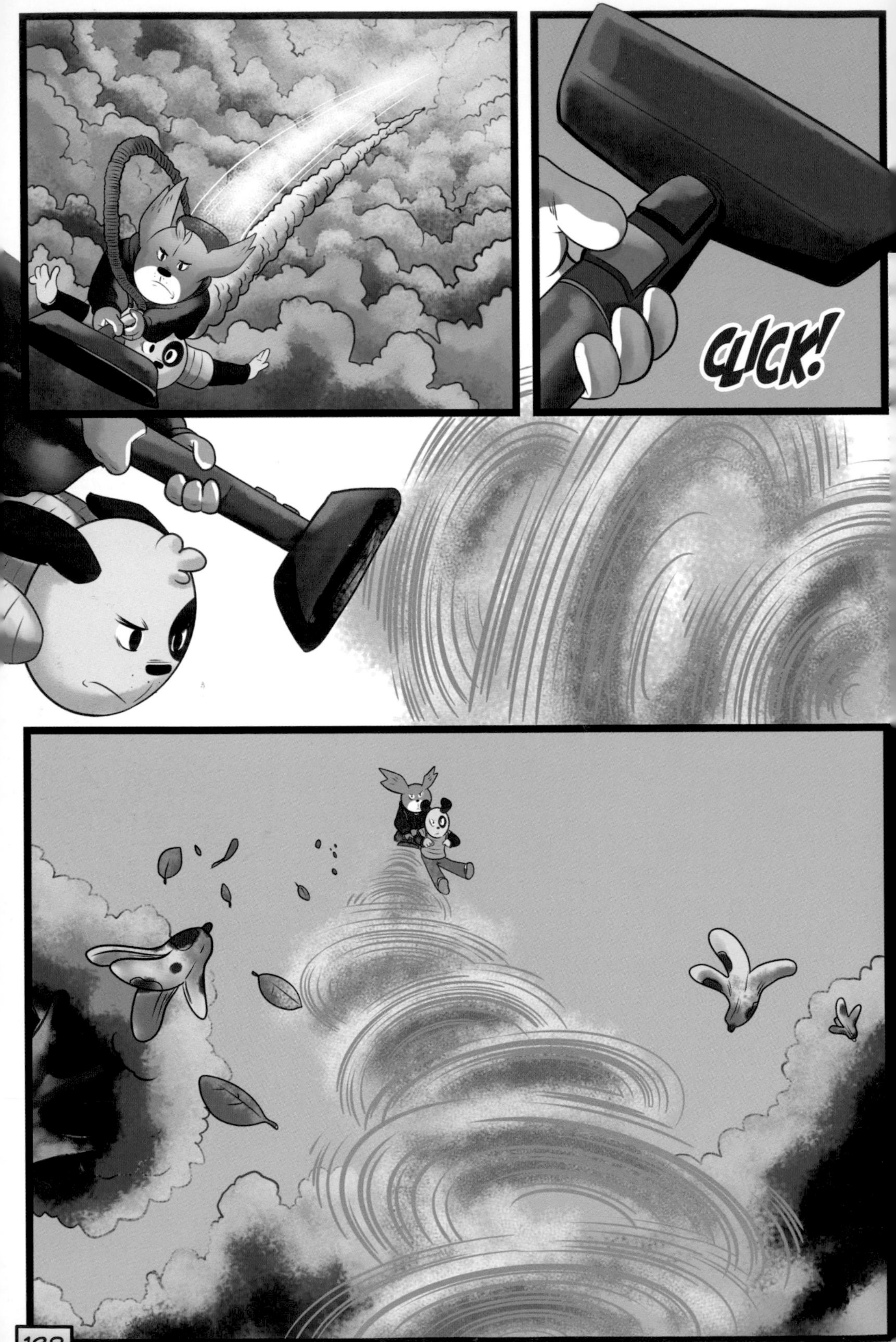
CLICK!

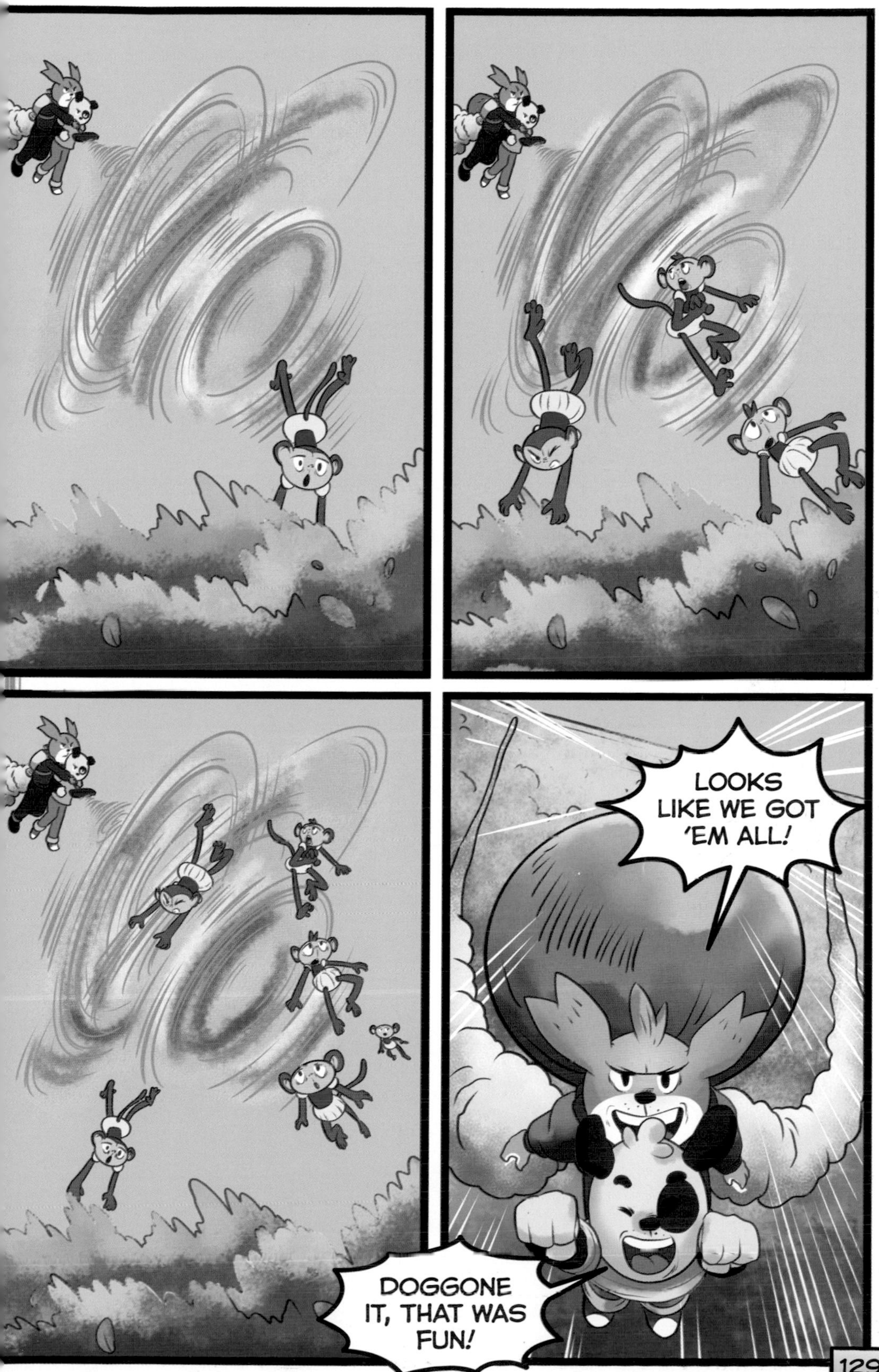
LOOKS LIKE WE GOT 'EM ALL!
DOGGONE IT, THAT WAS FUN!

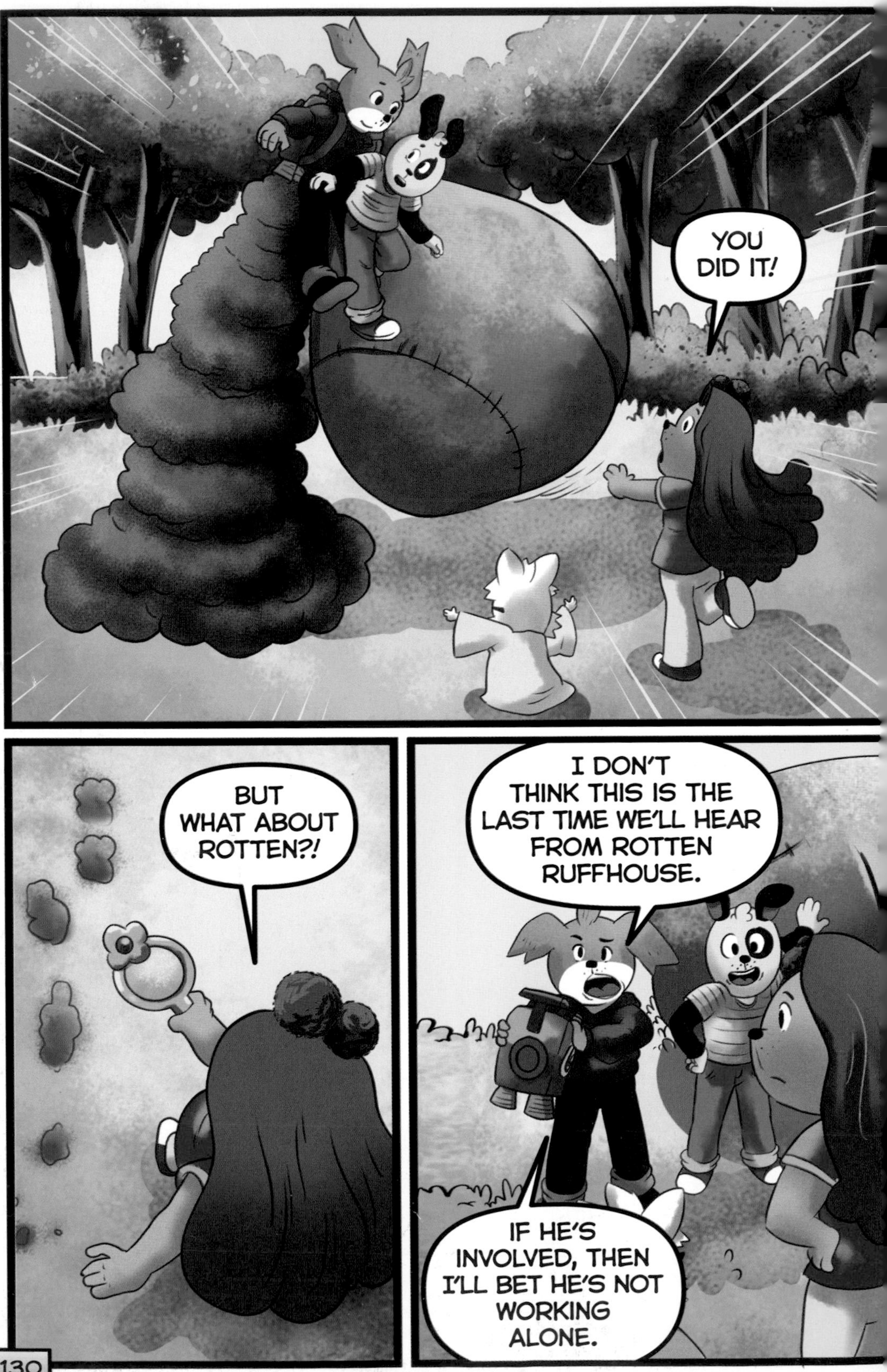
YOU DID IT!
BUT WHAT ABOUT ROTTEN?!
I DON'T THINK THIS IS THE LAST TIME WE'LL HEAR FROM ROTTEN RUFFHOUSE.
IF HE'S INVOLVED, THEN I'LL BET HE'S NOT WORKING ALONE.

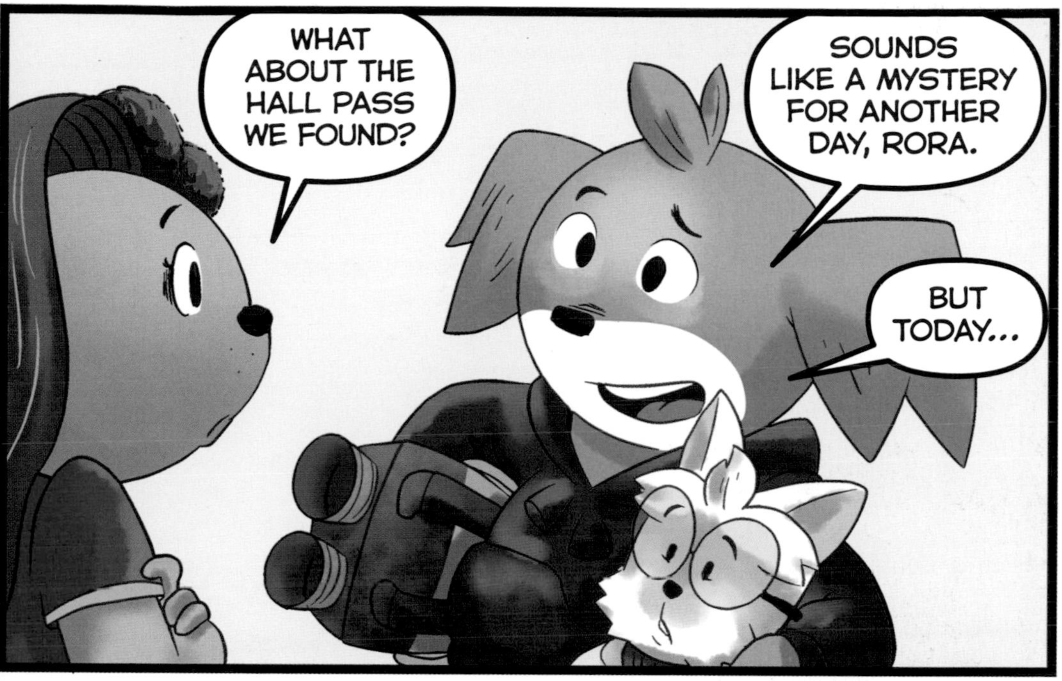
WHAT ABOUT THE HALL PASS WE FOUND?
SOUNDS LIKE A MYSTERY FOR ANOTHER DAY, RORA.
BUT TODAY...

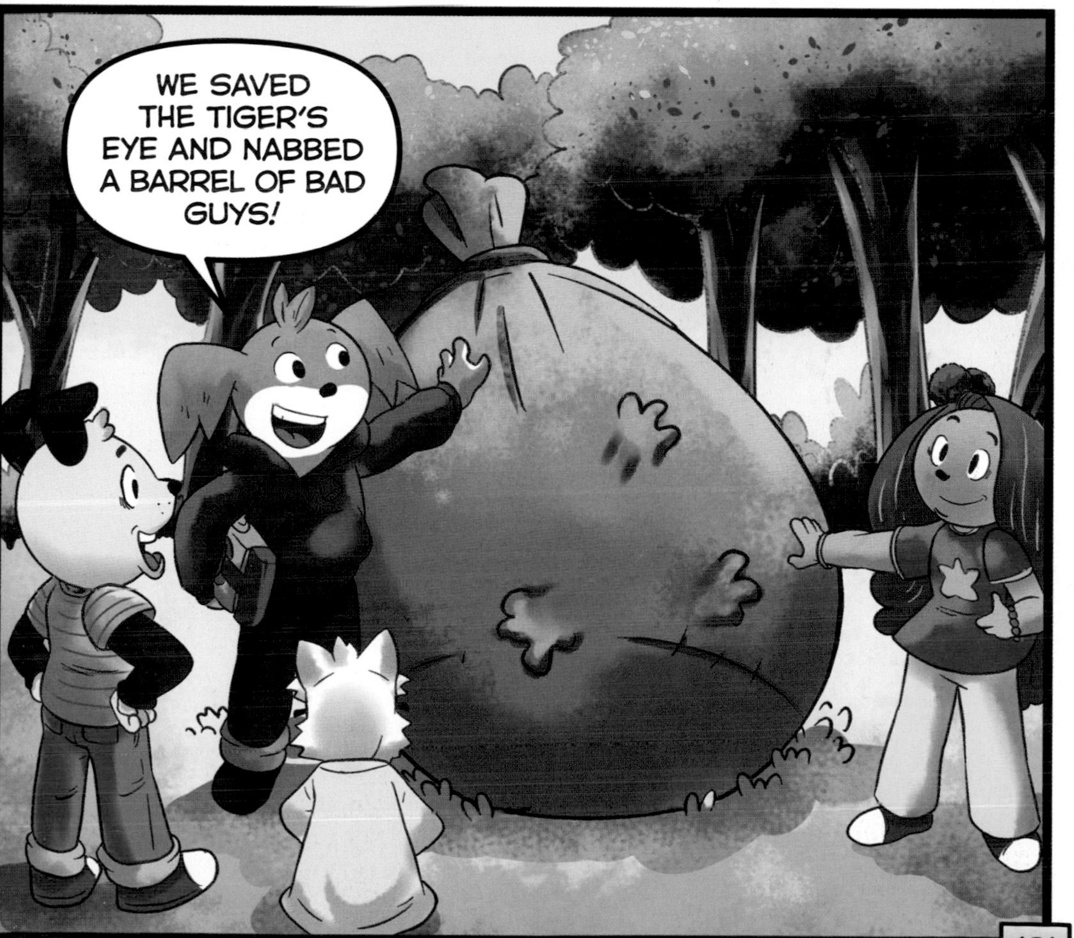
WE SAVED THE TIGER'S EYE AND NABBED A BARREL OF BAD GUYS!

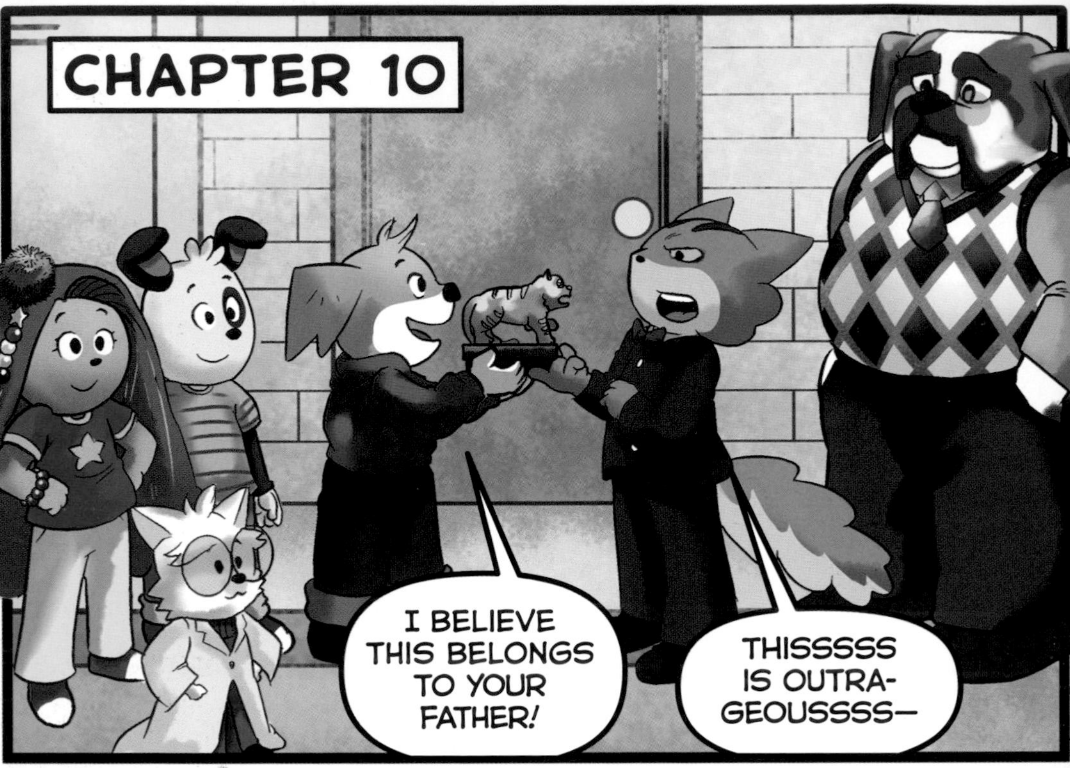
CHAPTER 10
I BELIEVE THIS BELONGS TO YOUR FATHER!
THISSSSS IS OUTRA-GEOUSSSS—

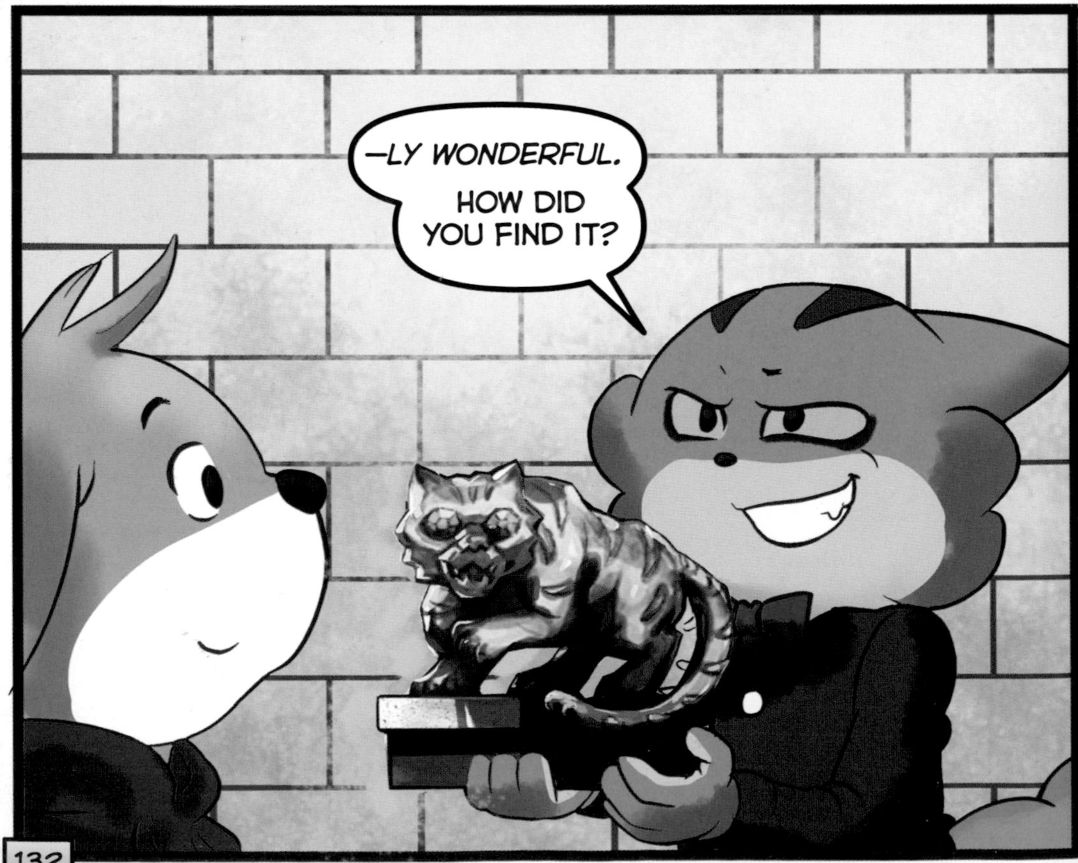
—LY WONDERFUL.
HOW DID YOU FIND IT?

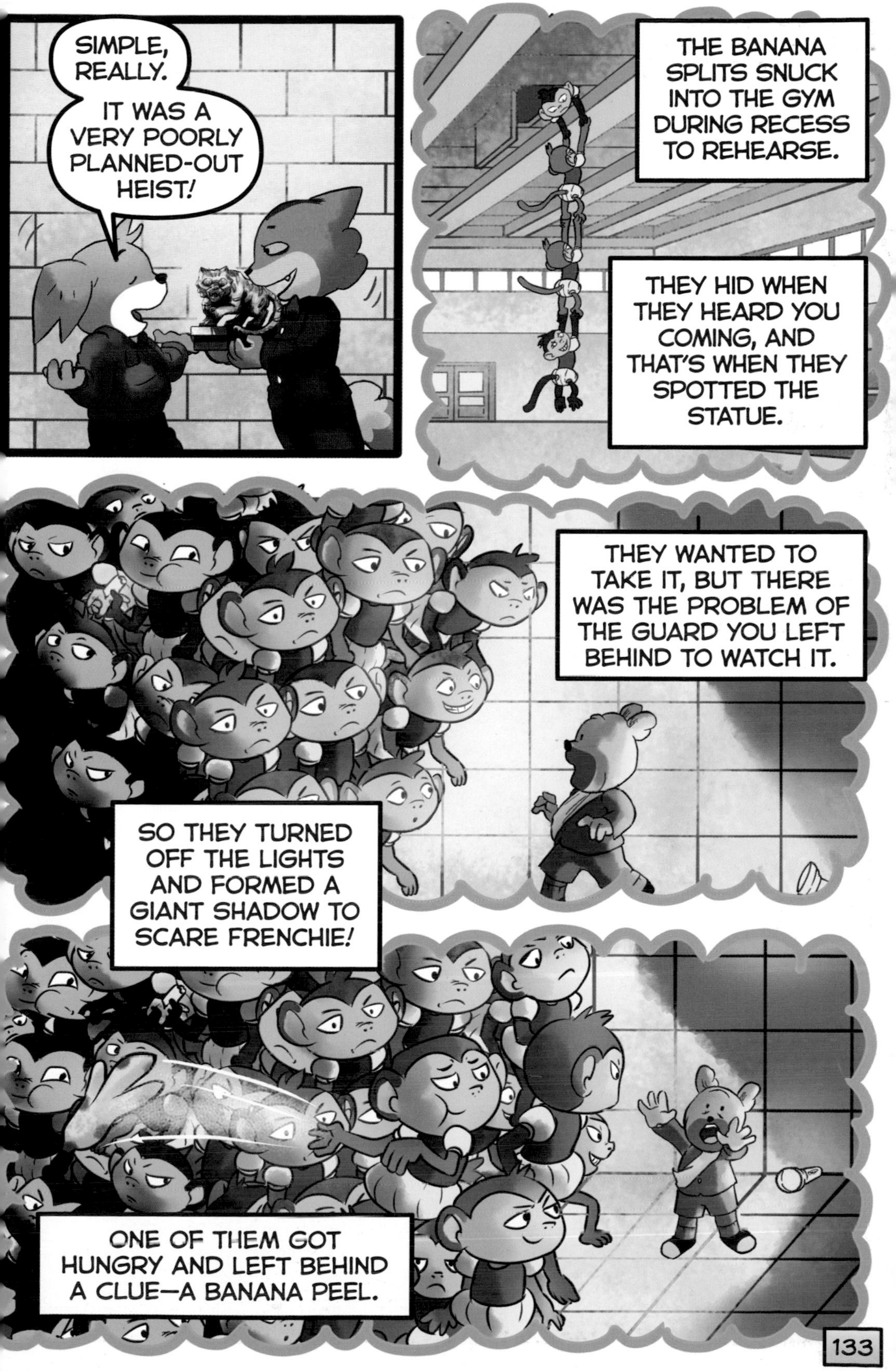
SIMPLE, REALLY.
IT WAS A VERY POORLY PLANNED-OUT HEIST!
THE BANANA SPLITS SNUCK INTO THE GYM DURING RECESS TO REHEARSE.
THEY HID WHEN THEY HEARD YOU COMING, AND THAT'S WHEN THEY SPOTTED THE STATUE.
THEY WANTED TO TAKE IT, BUT THERE WAS THE PROBLEM OF THE GUARD YOU LEFT BEHIND TO WATCH IT.
SO THEY TURNED OFF THE LIGHTS AND FORMED A GIANT SHADOW TO SCARE FRENCHIE!
ONE OF THEM GOT HUNGRY AND LEFT BEHIND A CLUE—A BANANA PEEL.

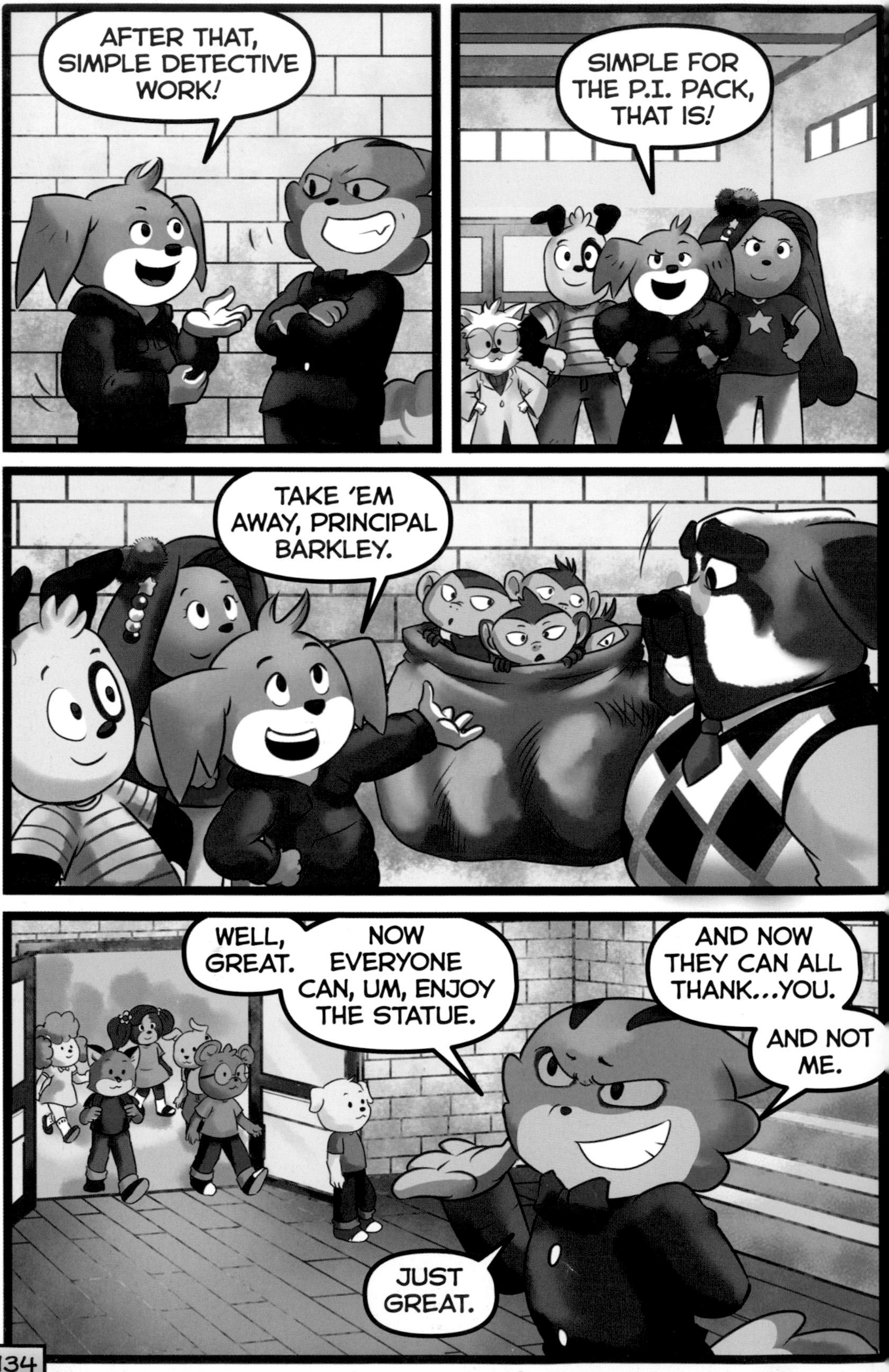
AFTER THAT, SIMPLE DETECTIVE WORK!
SIMPLE FOR THE P.I. PACK, THAT IS!
TAKE 'EM AWAY, PRINCIPAL BARKLEY.
WELL, GREAT.
NOW EVERYONE CAN, UM, ENJOY THE STATUE.
AND NOW THEY CAN ALL THANK...YOU.
AND NOT ME.
JUST GREAT.

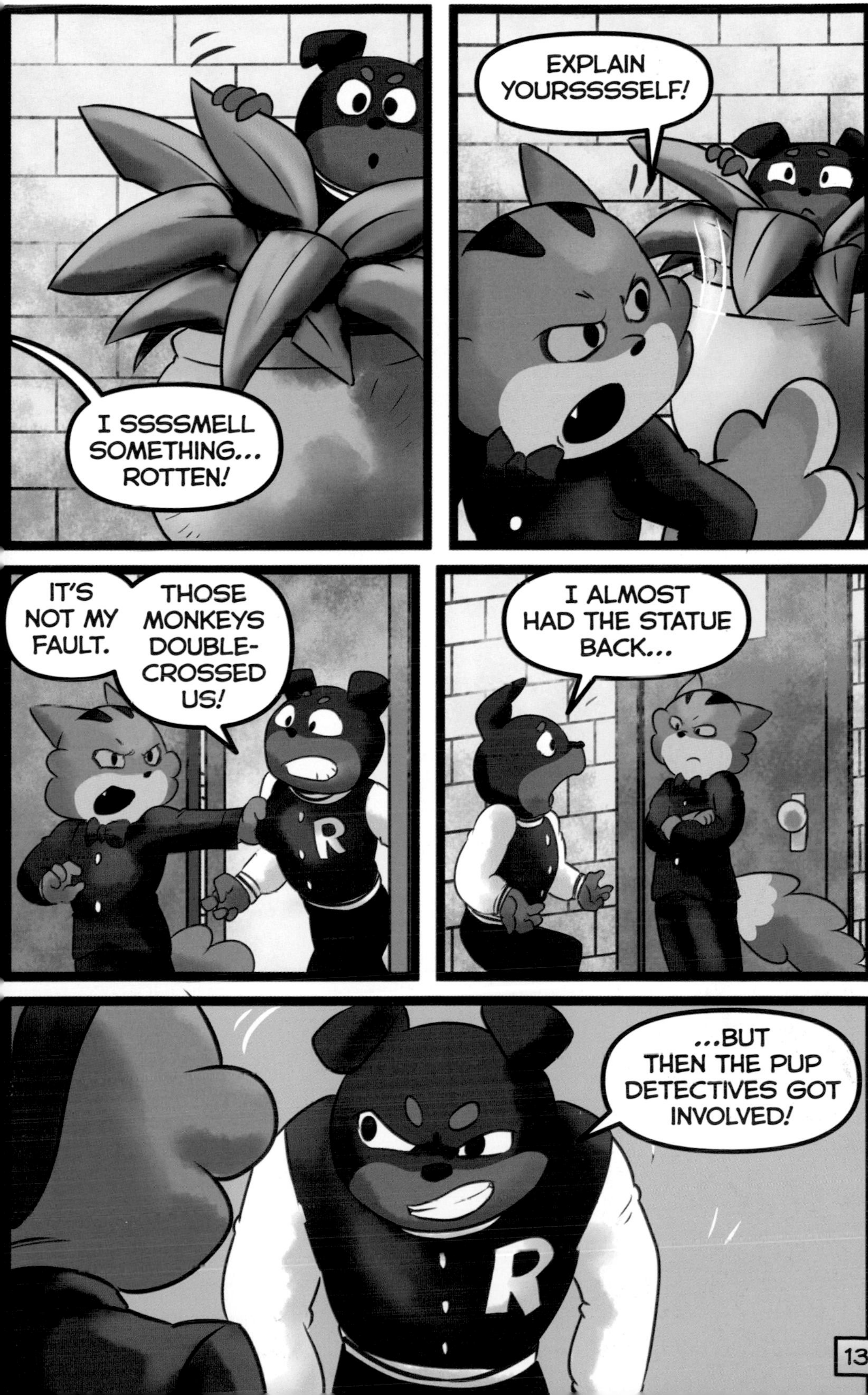
I SSSSMELL SOMETHING... ROTTEN!
EXPLAIN YOURSSSSSELF!
IT'S NOT MY FAULT.
THOSE MONKEYS DOUBLE-CROSSED US!
I ALMOST HAD THE STATUE BACK...
...BUT THEN THE PUP DETECTIVES GOT INVOLVED!

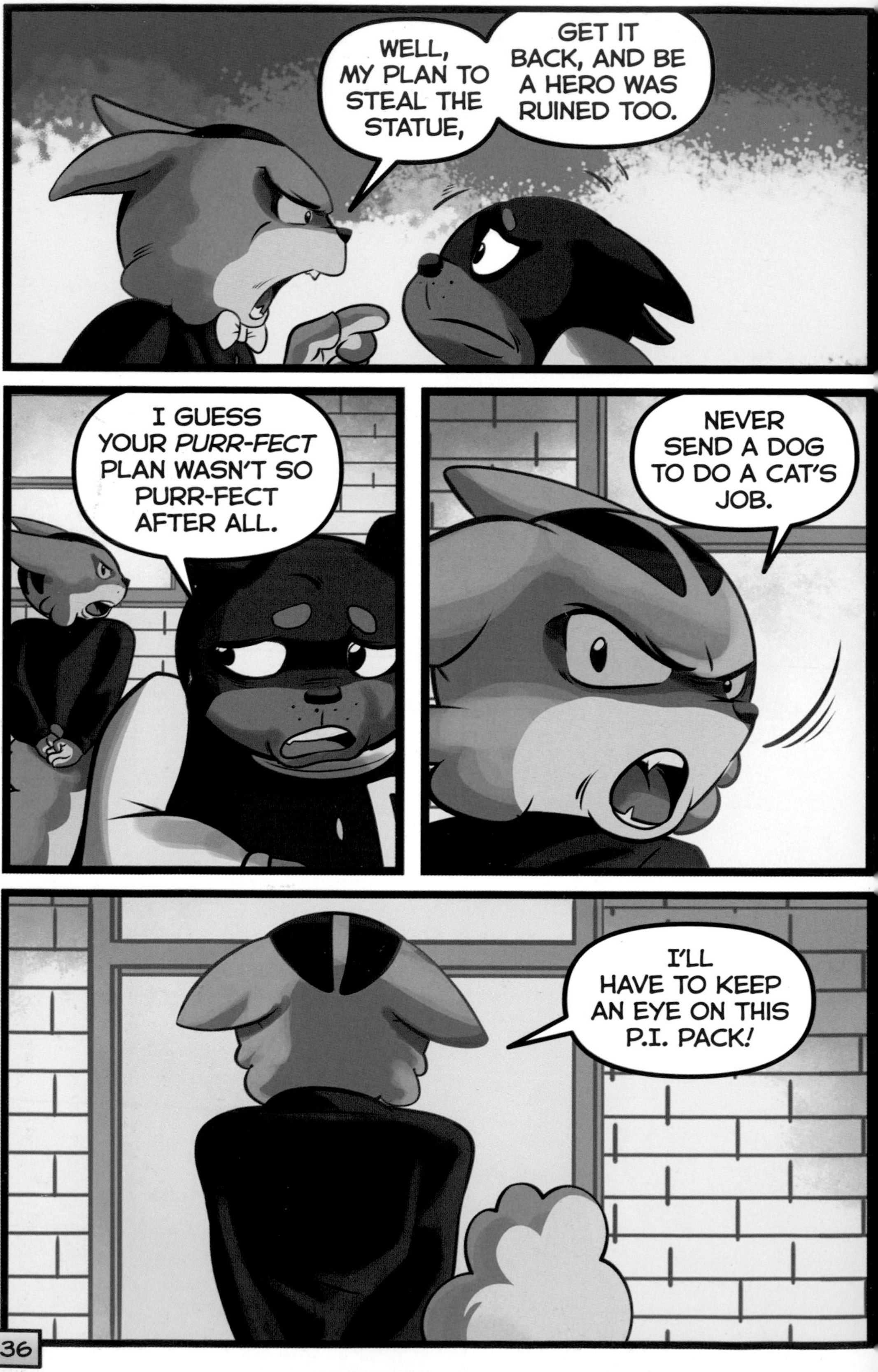

WELL, MY PLAN TO STEAL THE STATUE,
GET IT BACK, AND BE A HERO WAS RUINED TOO.
I GUESS YOUR *PURR-FECT* PLAN WASN'T SO PURR-FECT AFTER ALL.
NEVER SEND A DOG TO DO A CAT'S JOB.
I'LL HAVE TO KEEP AN EYE ON THIS P.I. PACK!

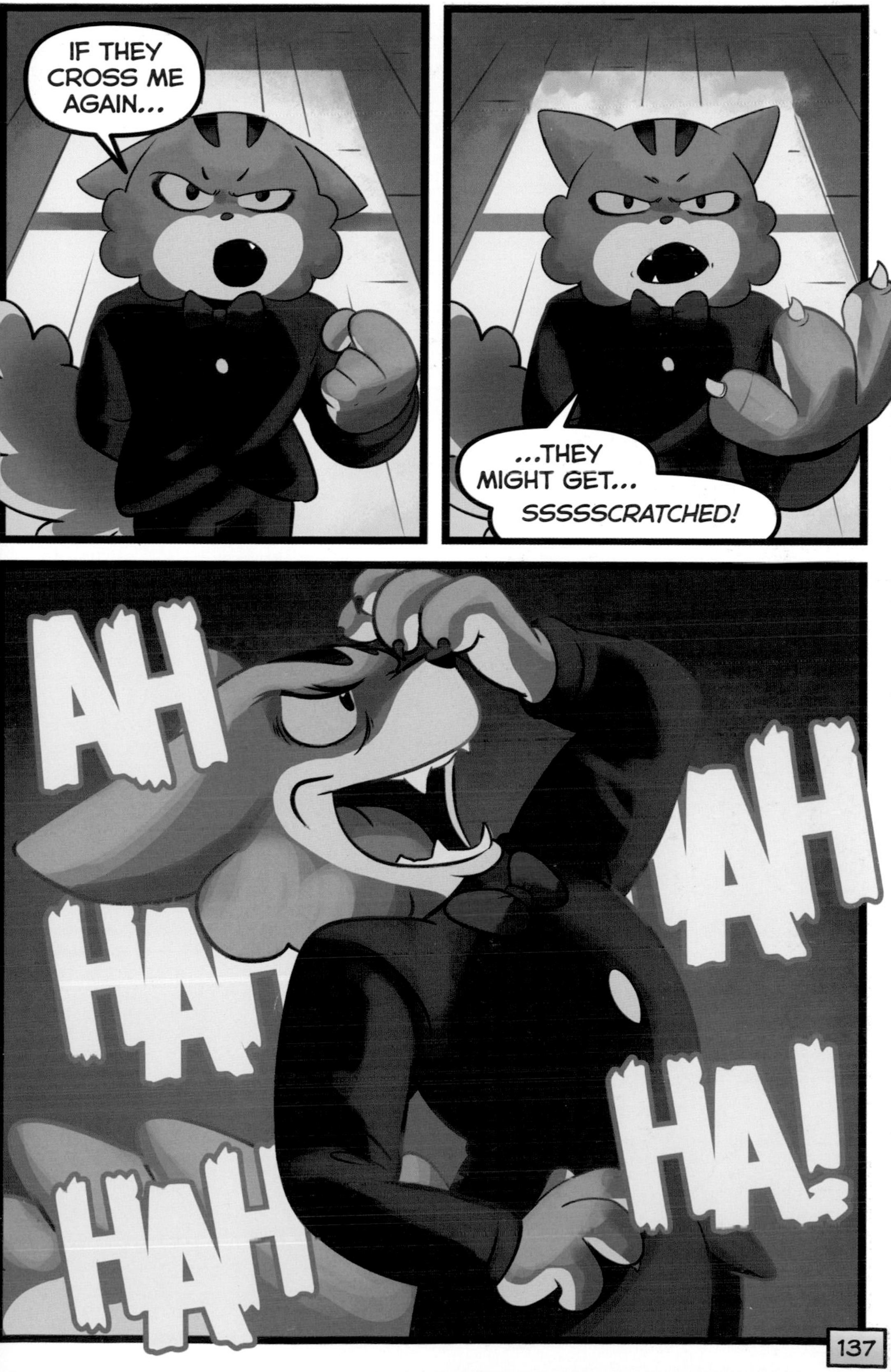
IF THEY CROSS ME AGAIN...
...THEY MIGHT GET... SSSSSCRATCHED!
AH HAH HAH HAH HA!

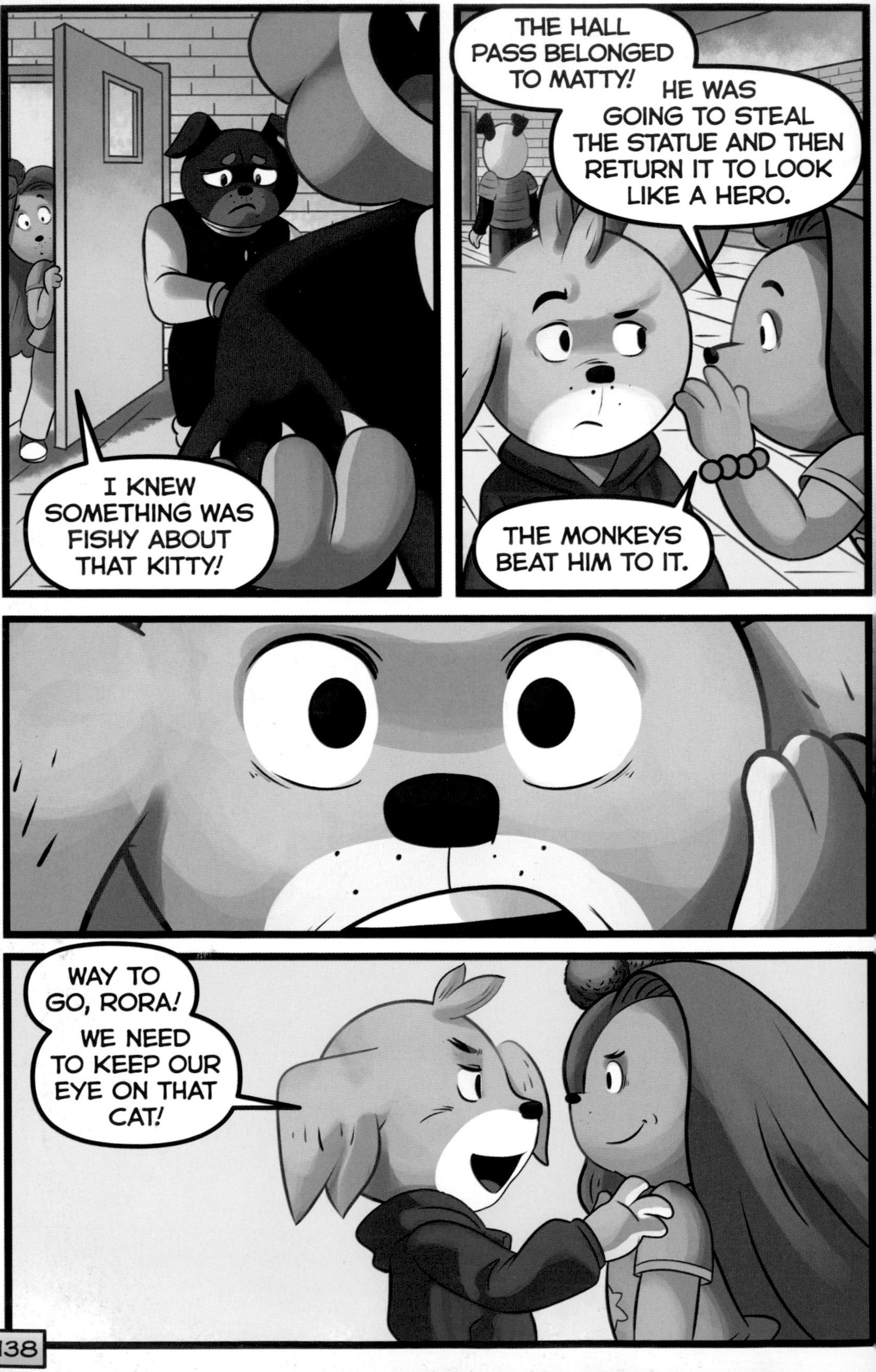
I KNEW SOMETHING WAS FISHY ABOUT THAT KITTY!
THE HALL PASS BELONGED TO MATTY!
HE WAS GOING TO STEAL THE STATUE AND THEN RETURN IT TO LOOK LIKE A HERO.
THE MONKEYS BEAT HIM TO IT.
WAY TO GO, RORA!
WE NEED TO KEEP OUR EYE ON THAT CAT!

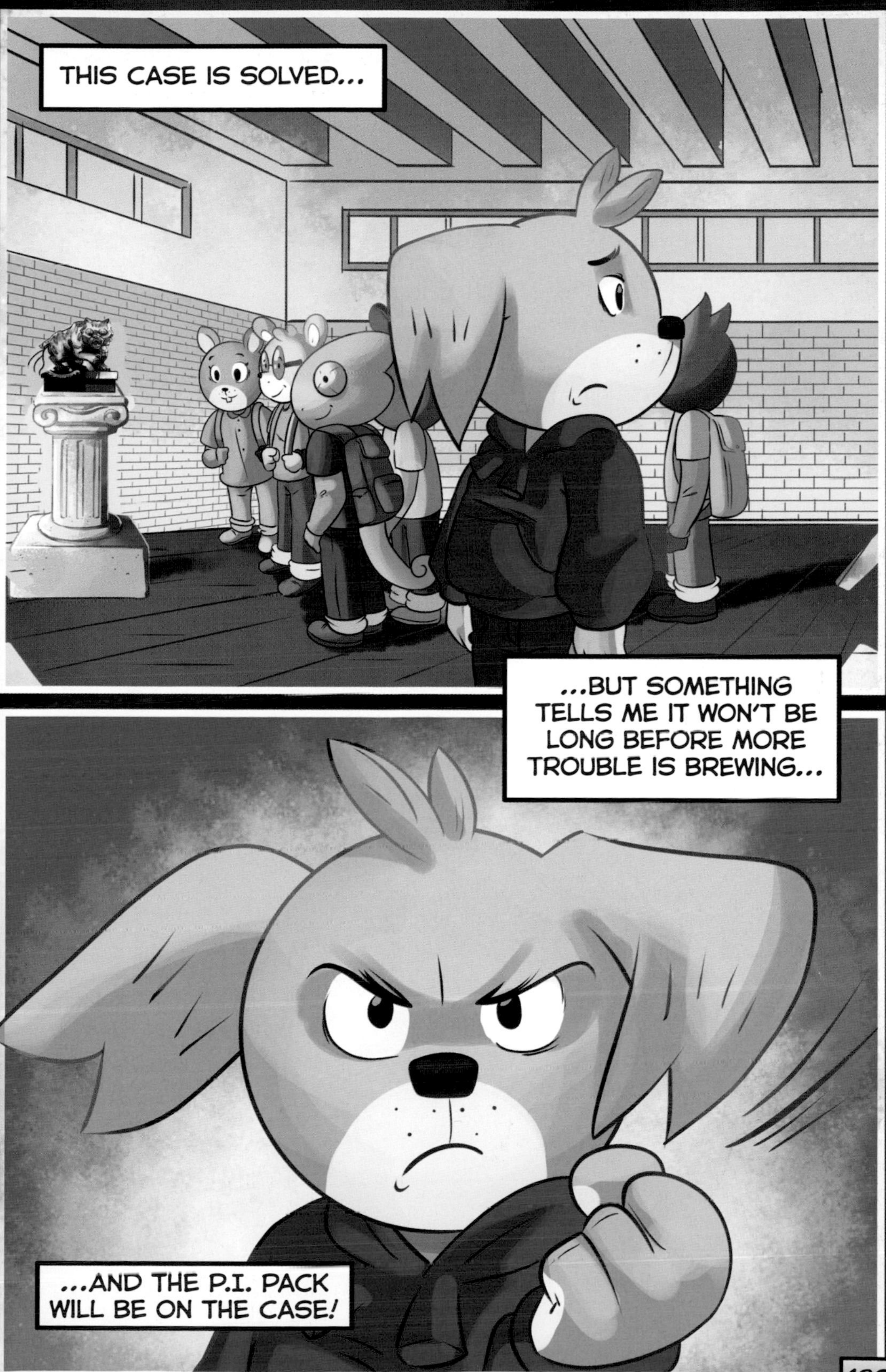
THIS CASE IS SOLVED...
...BUT SOMETHING TELLS ME IT WON'T BE LONG BEFORE MORE TROUBLE IS BREWING...
...AND THE P.I. PACK WILL BE ON THE CASE!

A NEW CASE AWAITS IN THE NEXT INSTALLMENT OF

Graphic Novel
PUP DETECTIVES
FEATURING...
THE SOCCER MYSTERY
MATTY MEOW
ROTTEN RUFFHOUSE
?
3

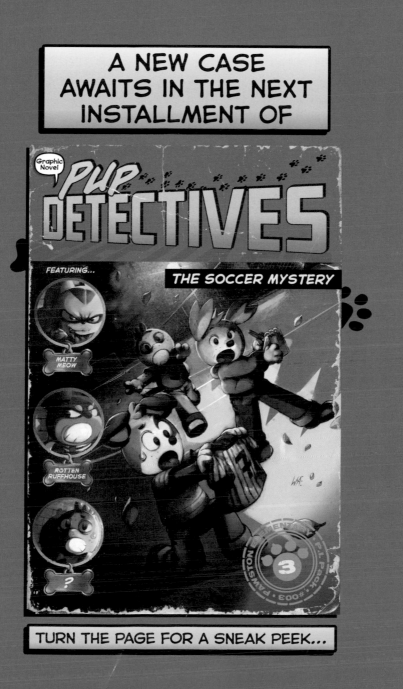

TURN THE PAGE FOR A SNEAK PEEK...

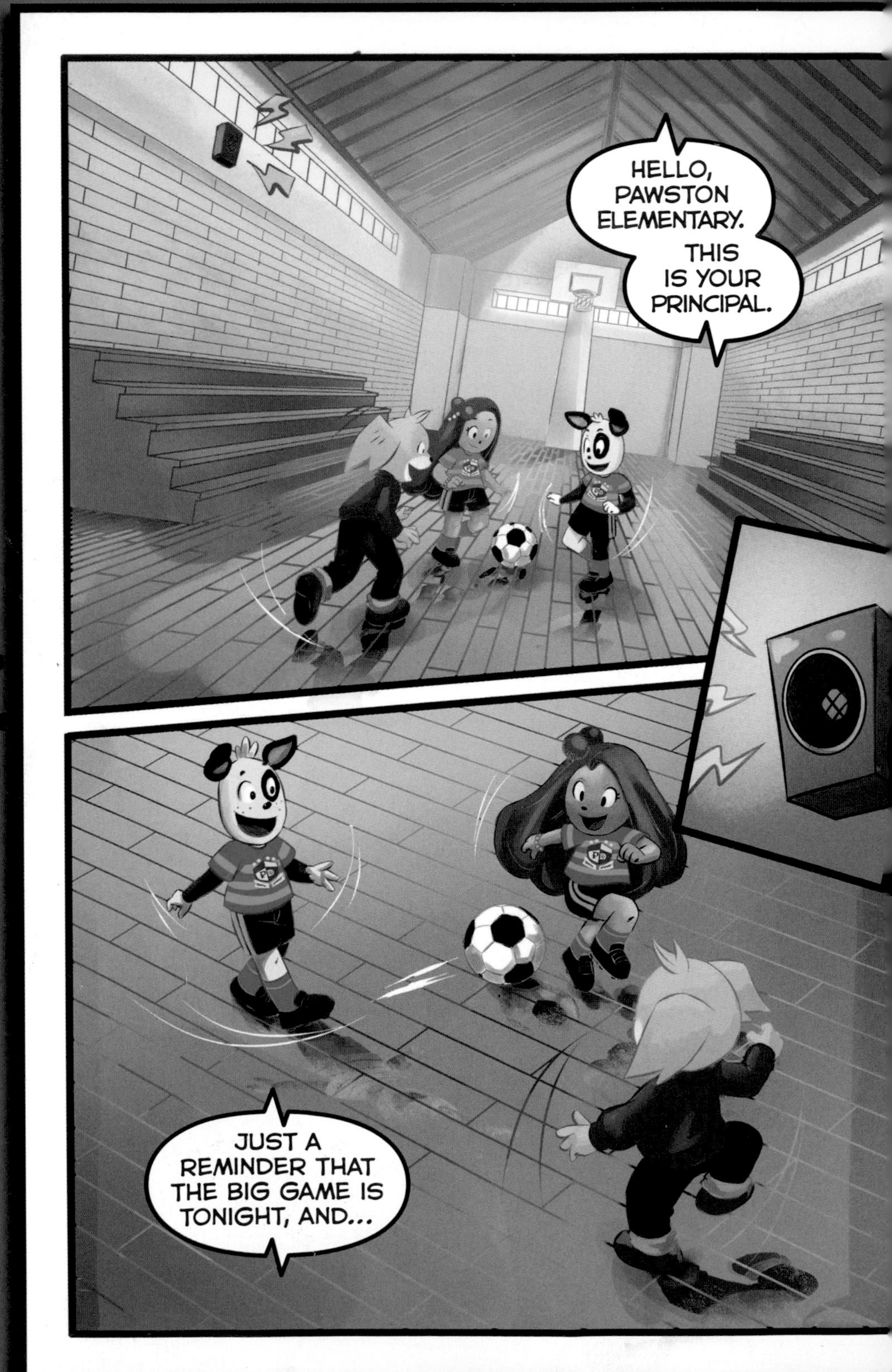
HELLO, PAWSTON ELEMENTARY.
THIS IS YOUR PRINCIPAL.
JUST A REMINDER THAT THE BIG GAME IS TONIGHT, AND...

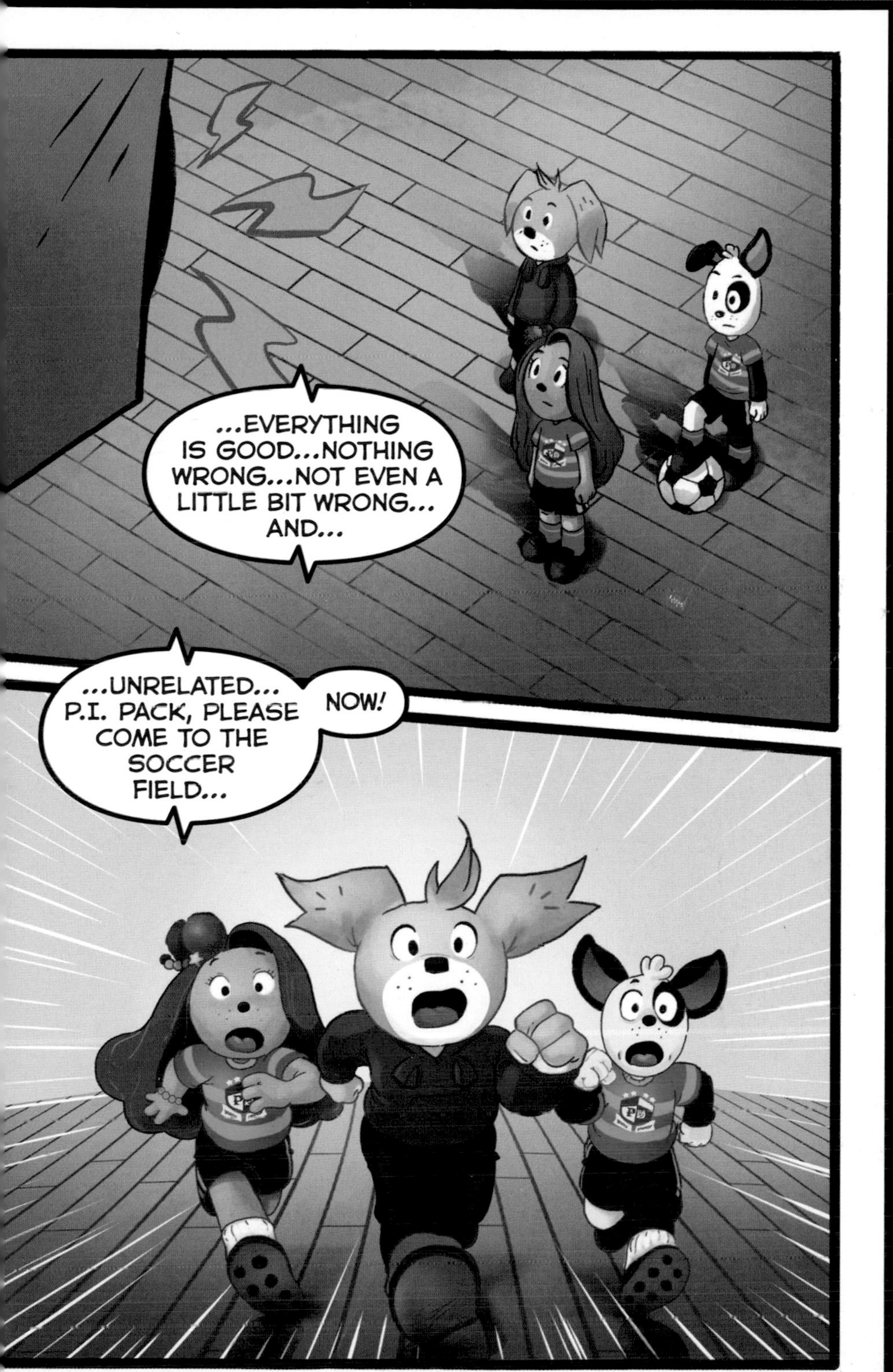
...EVERYTHING IS GOOD...NOTHING WRONG...NOT EVEN A LITTLE BIT WRONG... AND...
...UNRELATED... P.I. PACK, PLEASE COME TO THE SOCCER FIELD...
NOW!